AS YOU WISH

ALSO BY CHELSEA SEDOTI

The Hundred Lies of Lizzie Lovett

AS WICK YOU WISH

CHELSEA SEDOTI

sourcebooks
fire

Published by Sourcebooks Fire, an imprint of Sourcebooks, Inc.
P.O. Box 4410, Naperville, Illinois 60567-4410
(630) 961-3900
Fax: (630) 961-2168
www.sourcebooks.com

Library of Congress Cataloging-in-Publication Data

Names: Sedoti, Chelsea, author.
Title: As you wish / Chelsea Sedoti.
Description: Naperville, IL : Sourcebooks Fire, [2018] | Summary: In Madison,
    a small town in the Mojave Desert, everyone gets one wish that will come
    true on his or her eighteenth birthday, and Eldon takes his very seriously.
Identifiers: LCCN 2017008282 | (13 : alk. paper)
Subjects: | CYAC: Wishes--Fiction. | Magic--Fiction. | Friendship--Fiction. |
    Family life--Nevada--Fiction. | Nevada--Fiction.
Classification: LCC PZ7.1.S3385 As 2018 | DDC [Fic]--dc23 LC record avail-
able at https://lccn.loc.gov/2017008282

Printed and bound in the United States of America.
BVG 10 9 8 7 6 5 4 3 2 1

For my mom, who gave me
enough opportunities that
I never needed wishes.

CHAPTER 1

WELCOME TO MADISON

The trick is to be boring.

No one likes being bored, yeah? If a place is boring, you're not gonna stick around. You're not gonna ask any questions.

That's the way we like it.

It doesn't take much effort, because Madison looks totally ordinary. Just another dusty, desert town on Nevada State Route 375, the fastest way to get from nowhere to nothing. The kind of place you wanna leave as quick as you can.

The thing is, Madison isn't ordinary.

The couple in the car doesn't realize that. They're freaking clueless, and part of my job is keeping them that way. The other part is pumping gas.

After I get the nozzle into the tank and press the right buttons, I wander to the driver's side window and check them out.

The woman in the passenger seat won't be a problem. She has a blank look on her face. I see that expression all the time. Road trip daze. There's too much sameness in the desert, and after a while, it overwhelms you.

The driver, well, he's another story. He's studying a map, an actual paper map. Who even uses those anymore? Especially out here, in the middle of the Mojave, where there's only one road to get you wherever you're going. He's gazing at the map as if it's going to tell him the meaning of life and he already knows he won't like what he hears.

The guy rubbed me the wrong way from the start. When they first pulled up to the gas pump, he called me *son*. It's one of my pet peeves. I don't go around calling random dudes *dad*.

"Full service gas stations are rare these days," the guy says now, barely glancing up from the map.

Maybe he's trying to be nice, make casual conversation. If so, he failed. He's got this superior tone, like Madison is some back-woods town and I offered to cook up roadkill for dinner.

"We're old-fashioned around here," I reply with a smile. And it's a goddamn charming smile. I know it is. That's why I was hired in the first place.

The guy isn't charmed though. He keeps studying his map while I grin at nothing, feeling like the biggest jackass in the world.

I'd be straight with him if I could. Be like, "Dude, I know you'd rather pump your own gas, and believe me, I'd be happy to let you. But this is my *job*, so let's get through this without being dicks to each other." That's not how this works though.

Nope, Rule #1 of working at the gas station is *avoid honesty at all costs*. That's also Rule #2 and Rule #3.

So I pump the couple's gas, smile a lot, and try to make pleasant conversation. Hope my blond hair and blue eyes and straight teeth convince them I'm some harmless all-American kid, someone they can *trust*. The goal is to keep their attention on me so they don't look around and suspect that Madison is more than just a quiet, desert town.

For the record, my job sucks.

"This heat is a nightmare," the guy mutters.

I almost laugh. It's still spring, still hovering around ninety-five degrees. This guy doesn't have a clue about heat.

"You must not be from around here," I say, keeping my tone light, pleasant.

"No, thank God."

Original suspicion confirmed: this dude is a prick.

I clench my jaw. Then I glance at the gas pump behind me, as if that's gonna speed up the progress. The tank is probably only half-full. I bet the guy in the car would call it half-empty.

"Where you headed?" I ask.

He still doesn't look up from the map. His words are clipped. "My wife wants to see a UFO."

The woman turns from the window and frowns at her husband. I feel bad for her. I'm guessing he isn't exactly a joy to live with.

"You're going to Rachel," I say. "Keep on this road, and you won't miss it."

The guy still doesn't put away his map.

Unless these two decide to do a little off-roading in their compact sedan, they aren't going to get lost. The map is about as pointless as a parka out here. I'm not exaggerating.

The woman looks past her husband and smiles at me. "I read about a restaurant in Rachel. Where all the UFO hunters go?"

"Yep. The Little A'Le'Inn."

"Cute," the man says dryly.

The woman ignores him. "They say you can see strange things there at night."

"This is a strange part of the country," I tell her, and it's not a lie.

"What about you? Have you seen anything?" She leans over her husband, over the map, to see me better.

"I could tell you..." I say. "But don't be surprised if guys in black SUVs pull you over for a little debriefing."

"Really?" she asks, her eyes shining.

I wink at her. She smiles again. Maybe blushes a little, even though she's old enough to be my mom.

Most of the traffic through Madison comes from people like this. They stop here on the way to Area 51. Apparently, they're under the impression the government has UFOs parked off the highway or something. Sometimes, I see the same people on their return trip, all sad because they found out Rachel is just a big tourist trap.

Newsflash: there's nothing to see at Area 51. Unless you're looking for cheap alien merchandise and a bunch of conspiracy theorists. I've lived in Madison my whole life, and guess how many times I've seen a mystery object in the sky? Zero. We've got plenty of secrets around here, but they don't have anything to do with extraterrestrials.

"I have a friend who got into Area 51 once," I tell the woman.

Her husband sighs. The woman leans even farther over him. She's practically in his lap. "What happened?"

I look around for a second, as if I'm worried someone might overhear us, then duck down to the level of the window and lower my voice. "He came back with all these stories. I won't even repeat them. There are *things* out there in the desert though. Things no one wants us to know about."

The woman's eyes widen. She loves it. "You can't tell us *anything?*"

"Look," I say, furtively glancing around again. "My friend ended up leaving town in the middle of the night. Left a note saying he was moving to Vegas, had an aunt living there or something. We haven't seen him since. I'm not saying anything bad happened to him. But none of us ever heard him mention an aunt before."

Because there isn't an aunt in Vegas. There isn't a friend either. I can tell from the guy's sour expression he knows my story's bullshit. The woman probably does too, but she's having fun playing along. She settles back in her seat, satisfied. Her husband finally folds the map.

I look at the gas pump again, wish it would hurry, wish the couple hadn't pulled in needing a full tank. Wish Moses Casey, my boss, would stop being so stingy and update the equipment so it isn't so freaking slow.

Seconds tick by. A gust of wind rattles the gas pump, blows sand into my eyes. The man taps his fingers on the steering wheel and gazes out the window, examining the sun-bleached buildings that line Madison's main street.

I wonder if anyone else in Madison is hiring. This gas station routine is getting real old.

"Tell me, son," the guy says suddenly. "Where do you pray around here?"

I hesitate. What's this dude talking about?

"Pray?"

"Yes, pray. Worship. Whatever. Where are your churches?"

"Are you missionaries?" I mean it as a joke, but it doesn't come out that way. It sounds like I'm stalling, which I am.

"I've just never seen a town without a church," says the guy.

My mouth feels full of dust. I swallow hard. I have absolutely no good answer to his question. But I pull myself together, flash a smile, act like I'm totally chill. The more confident you act, the less likely anyone is to suspect you're lying through your teeth.

"Maybe you should get your eyes checked. You drove right by one."

"No, we didn't."

"I think I know this town better than you."

The man frowns. He stares at me. I stare back. A lifetime passes. I fight the urge to wipe my sweaty palms on my jeans.

Then I hear the sweetest sound in the world: the click of the gas pump. The tank is full. I quickly complete the transaction, saying all the right things, telling the couple I hope they have a good trip, hope they spot a UFO.

"Just stay out of Area 51," I say, winking at the woman again. She laughs.

I watch their car retreat from Madison, flying past Joshua trees and kicking up dust. And the whole time I'm thinking, *Stupid, stupid, stupid.*

What if they come back through town? What if they look for the church?

I know *exactly* what'll happen if they look for the church. They won't find it. Because it doesn't exist. They'll wonder why I'd lie about something like that. They'll ask questions.

I should have told them the town is too small for a church, that we run services out of someone's home or something. I mean, pretty much anything would've been better than claiming we have an invisible church on Main Street. *You can't miss it. It's over there between Santa's workshop and the unicorn corral.*

The guy caught me off guard, with his *son* and his map. I've worked at the gas station since I was fifteen, and I've answered all sorts of strange questions, stuff like, *How do you keep cool around here?* (Air-conditioning.) And, *Is the alien jerky really made of aliens?* (No.) And, *Is this one of those small towns where everyone's married to their sister?* (Why would someone even ask that?) But no one's ever asked about churches.

Who drives around the desert looking for churches anyway?

I tuck the two-dollar tip into my pocket and lean against the gas pump, casual, though I feel pretty edgy. I watch the road, wait for the next car, though I doubt there'll be one. Not two in one shift.

Where do you pray? Of all the things to ask.

I briefly wonder what would've happened if I told the truth. If I'd laughed and said, "This is Madison. What the hell do we need churches for?"

Because no matter how it appears, Madison *isn't* like other towns. Not at all.

I'm not talking about aliens or anything ridiculous like that. No, the unusual thing about Madison, what we work hard to make sure no outsiders find out, is that everyone here gets to make a wish.

Mine is in twenty-six days.

CHAPTER 2

COUNTDOWN: 25 DAYS

should be freaking ecstatic. That's how it's supposed to go, at least. The closer it gets to your wish day, the more hyped you're supposed to get. Everyone goes on and on about what an honor it is, how lucky we are to live in a place where wishes come true.

And everyone wants to know what you're gonna wish for. Like, the whole town gets on your case about it. They're all, *Make it good. You only have one shot.* As if somehow, that detail may have slipped your mind.

Which is why I'm on the fence about going to the hot springs. It's Saturday, so half the school will be there. And instead of having a few beers and chilling, I'll have to deal with everyone being up my ass asking what I'm going to wish for.

The weird thing is, a year ago, I would have thrived on the attention.

In the end, I decide to go to the hot springs anyway. Of

course I do. How else are you gonna pass time in Madison on a Saturday night?

I'm about to open the front door when my mom calls my name from the kitchen.

"What?" I shout back, hand still on the knob, ready to bolt.

"Come here, please."

I sigh.

Ma's at the kitchen table, cutting coupons. It's become her favorite hobby, though far as I can tell, it has yet to save us money.

I lean against the doorframe, trying to make it clear I'm not committing to a lengthy conversation. Maybe she'll get the hint, see I'm on my way out.

"Sit down for a minute," she says.

Or maybe not.

Something about couponing gets Ma all amped up to lecture me. I'm definitely not in the mood. But if I blow her off, she'll launch into the I-gave-birth-to-you crap, and I'm even less in the mood for that. I slide into the chair across from her.

"Eldon," she says, "I think we should talk about your wish."

"Right now?"

Thing is, we *have* talked about it. We've talked about it on every birthday I've ever had. After I turned seventeen, we talked about it once a week. Though I guess it's more accurate to say *she's* talked about it.

"Yes, right now," she says, pointedly looking at the wall calendar. "The clock is ticking, kiddo."

Gee, thanks. As if somehow I've missed that my birthday is coming up.

"I know, Ma," I say, trying my hardest to be patient.

"If you know, why haven't you decided on a wish? You need to think about the future, Eldon."

"I *have* thought about it."

She puts down her scissors and looks at me. "And?"

"And I'm still thinking."

The frown lines on her face deepen. She pulls a cigarette from the pack sitting next to her and lights it, not caring about the bits of ash raining down on her coupons. Not caring that she's probably giving me lung cancer.

"Just remember, kiddo, we're not in a good place." She gestures around the room with the cigarette. Scarred linoleum countertops, stacks of unpaid medical bills, appliances that haven't been updated since the house was built thirty years ago. As if I need a reminder about our financial situation. As if I don't live here too, don't see how much we lack.

"I know how it is," she goes on. "You kids want to wish for something frivolous. But you're not a little boy anymore. You have to do what's right, Eldon."

What about you? I want to ask. *What about what* you *wished for?* Instead, I say, "Yeah, Ma. I get it."

She takes a long drag on her cigarette. "Fine. Go then. I know you want to."

I don't need to be told twice. When I leave the table, she has her scissors in hand again, cutting out a coupon for dog food.

We don't even own a dog.

* * *

I step into the warm, windy night, ready to make my escape to the hot springs. But I hesitate in the middle of the yard. The light is on in our detached garage, and after a moment, I drift over to it.

Sure enough, my dad is inside. He's standing at his wood-working bench, hand-planing a two-by-four. It's a good day for him. He doesn't need his crutches.

He glances over at me and smiles. "You look like you just had a conversation with your mother."

"Guess what the topic was?"

"I'd put my money on wishing."

"Ding, ding, ding."

I fall onto the couch and turn on the TV, a tiny set with bad reception that my dad picked up at the pawn shop last month. Ma flipped when he brought it home. Asked which of us should go hungry thanks to his impulse purchase. I'm surprised she let him keep it.

My gaze flicks back and forth between the TV and my dad. Watching him work always makes me less tense—or maybe it's being in the garage. I mean, it isn't exactly paradise out here. The garage is so cluttered that it couldn't fit a car even if Dad didn't use it as a workspace. It's dusty and turns into an incinerator during the summer, and I'm pretty sure black widow spiders have taken up residence in the corners. Still, I love the garage for the same reason my dad does: it's a place to drop the charade.

"I'm getting pretty sick of everyone asking about my wish," I say.

"It's a big moment for you," Dad replies without looking up from his workbench.

"For me or for Ma?"

He hesitates. He won't say anything bad about her, I know. He sets down his planer and walks over to the couch, sits next to me. "Listen, buddy, your mom only wants what's best for you."

Bullshit. It's not me she's thinking about. My mom has two children, and one of them has always come first. Spoiler: it's not me.

There's no point bringing that up with my dad though. Instead, I say, "Whatever I wish for should be *my* decision."

"You're right. It absolutely should be." I guess I look surprised, because he says, "What? You thought I was going to tell you that you have to wish for money?"

"Well…yeah."

"Eldon, wish for whatever you want."

I feel such a surge of love for my dad that if my wish was right now, I'd wish for his happiness, forever. It's nice to know someone thinks of you as a person, not an opportunity.

I pause, trying to phrase my response in a way that doesn't sting. "If I wish for money, that still doesn't guarantee—"

"I know, buddy," my dad says. "I know."

Even though I hadn't finished my thought, I'm hit with a tidal wave of sadness. You'd think I'd be used to this agony by now, but it always catches me off guard. Anyone who says grief fades over time is a fucking liar. It never goes away. It just gets better at hiding. You never know when it's going to spring out of the shadows and sucker punch you in the gut.

Grief is a real asshole.

The mood in the garage has shifted. My little sister's presence— her *lack* of presence—fills the small space. I glance at my dad. My heart isn't the only one being run through a meat grinder. I wish I'd kept my mouth shut.

We sit in silence, both pretending to watch TV. Some news show out of Vegas is playing. Madison isn't big enough to have its own station. It isn't big enough to have news to report.

"If you could go back," I ask finally, trying to rewind the conversation to a safe topic again, "would you wish for something different?"

"Of course I would," my dad says without hesitation.

I look at him. Wait for more. He gets up and limps to the mini fridge, grabs two beers. He hands me one and takes a long swig of his own before continuing.

"When you're eighteen, all you think of is the moment. I wished to be the best football player in the school, and it didn't occur to me that I'd graduate in five months, and what then?"

Nothing, I know. Even if graduation hadn't ended his football career, his injury would have.

"Don't get me wrong, I love coaching. I love watching you play. But I wish I knew then what I do now."

"I get the feeling most wishes are worthless," I say.

"Not your mother's."

I'm not even going to go there with him.

"Anyway," my dad says abruptly, moving back to his workbench. "You've got a month left to decide. You'll figure it out."

"I'm glad one of us is confident about that."

My dad turns over the two-by-four and starts planing the other side. I watch the news. Lake Mead is drying up, a new casino is being built, another pedestrian got hit by a car. Vegas news is the same every day. They could probably run the same exact show, and no one would notice.

"What are you making?" I ask after a while.

He gestures to an ancient sink sitting on the ground in the corner. "Finally getting that installed out here. I'm prepping wood for the base."

The sink came from the junkyard. It's scratched and chipped and has corroded copper pipes still attached to it. Who knows if it'll even hold water. My dad has never been able to resist bringing home random junk and turning it into a project.

I'm about to ask why he needs a sink in the garage when the door swings open and Ma steps into our safe space.

"Harmon—" she begins but stops when she sees me.

She looks disappointed, which gives me an instant guilt attack. I'd bet money she's wondering why I was so anxious to get away from her and why that doesn't apply to my dad. Dad's just easier to be around, but something tells me that wouldn't exactly lift Ma's spirits.

She redirects her gaze to my dad. "Harmon, I got a call from the bar."

My dad sighs and looks annoyed. I don't blame him. There's only one reason a bar would be calling our house. My uncle Jasper needs to be escorted home. Again.

"The bar in Alamo," Ma continues.

My dad's eyebrows shoot up. "Alamo? What in God's name is he doing there?"

I'm surprised Alamo even *has* a bar. It's a town half an hour south of us, smaller than Madison and nearly as depressing.

"I have no idea why Jasper does anything he does," my mom says. "Can you get him?"

"Luella…" my dad begins but trails off. We all know he's going to do it. He'll do anything Ma asks.

"If they kick him out, he might wander into the desert and—"

"OK, honey. Don't worry. I'll take care of it."

My mom nods and leaves. She doesn't bother saying thank you.

"Well," my dad says to me. "Looks like my night just got busier."

"You should leave him there," I say. "He's never gonna learn if you keep enabling him."

"Enabling him?" My dad looks amused.

"Mr. Wakefield taught us about it last year. It was part of that whole antidrug kick he was on."

"Ah, I see. Well, Eldon, you're probably right. But it's your mom's choice, not mine."

Everything in our house is her choice.

My dad puts away his tools, pats his pocket for his keys. "Want me to leave this on for you?" he asks, gesturing at the TV.

I consider staying and watching the rest of the news. I consider going to the party at the hot springs. "Actually, I'll go with you."

"I'm sure you have better things to do on a Saturday night. I remember what it's like to be young, you know."

He's right. Rescuing my alcoholic uncle isn't my idea of a thrilling time. But I hate the thought of my dad driving alone from one crap town to another. I hate that he has no control over his own life and never will. I hate that I can't change anything for him, that the best I can offer is riding shotgun while he's my mom's errand boy.

"Nah," I say. "There's not much going on tonight."

"I won't turn down your company then."

A few minutes later, we pass Madison's town limit. The desert around us is so dark it's like driving through a void. A jackrabbit darts in front of the minivan, and my dad swerves, barely missing it.

I glance at the clock, then turn on the radio and dial to an AM station in time to hear, *"Live from the loneliest corner of the Mojave, you're listening to Basin and Range Radio, where we keep an eye on the night sky. This is your host, Robert Nash."*

My dad laughs. "I don't know why you listen to this."

I shrug. It's not like I buy into Robert Nash's bullshit, but he's been a staple in my life since I was a kid. Ebba and I used to listen to his show together, late at night, when our parents thought we were sleeping. She'd sneak into my room, and we'd huddle under the covers, following Robert Nash's attempts to unveil conspiracies. Ebba believed in aliens. She believed in everything.

"...talking with a Las Vegas man who's certain he's uncovered the extraterrestrial agenda. Who are these strange beings? Why did they contact him, not once, but on three separate occasions? And, most importantly, when will they be back? Tonight, on Basin and Range Radio, you'll get the answers..."

I push my sister out of my mind. I listen to Robert Nash interview a dude who insists aliens are speaking to him through the hum of his air-conditioning unit.

I try to pretend my dad and I are on a road trip, heading somewhere more exciting than Alamo. I try to pretend that Madison doesn't exist. That *wishing* doesn't exist.

I'm not good at pretending.

When it comes to wishing, maybe Ma is right. I should wish for money and be done with it, yeah? No more agonizing. No more worrying about making the wrong choice. No more feeling like I have one shot, and if I screw it up, my life will be over. Just ask for cash. Live comfortably. No regrets.

That's the problem, of course. At least, part of the problem. In Madison, regrets are as commonplace as wishes. And there's no such thing as do-overs.

CHAPTER 3

COUNTDOWN:
24 DAYS

Madison has a problem with wind. The problem is that it never stops.

You'd think the mountain ranges would block the wind, but instead, they trap it in our valley. The wind rattles windows; it pushes cars into lanes of oncoming traffic. Sometimes, on nights the gusts are especially strong, I swear coyotes howl back at it, as if the wind is a missing member of their pack.

Worst of all, the wind covers everything in dirt.

Once, in history class, we studied the Dust Bowl. Our teacher showed us these pictures of people stuffing wet blankets in the cracks under their doors, of sand piling up against the sides of their houses. And I was like, "Well, that's pretty much a regular day in Madison."

Even though Merrill's house is next door, I get a mouthful of dirt as I run across the yard. The sand is gritty against my teeth. My eyes sting.

Still, there's no need for a surgical mask.

"Overkill, Merrill," I say when he opens the door.

His voice comes back muffled. "Dude. I'm very sensitive to allergens. You *know* this."

Truthfully, the wind *is* unusually strong for May. Generally, it's not until midsummer, when temperatures peak, that the wind gets super intense. Some days are so bad that the town shuts down, the way other places—*normal* places—have snow days. I try to comment on that while Merrill and I let ourselves into the ancient Ford Mustang sitting in his driveway, but a gust steals my words.

The original owner of the car was Merrill's grandfather, who wished it into existence. He'd probably rise from the grave for vengeance if he knew how it's been treated since he died. Though the Mustang technically belongs to Merrill's dad now, we use it whenever we want, because Benny Delacruz is seldom in a condition to drive, even on days he has work—which are getting to be rare.

When we're shut in the safety of the car, Merrill rips off his mask. "Fuck this town."

"The mask is really overkill," I say again.

"Fuck you too. Do you know how many pounds of dirt I've swallowed in my lifetime?"

"All I'm saying is maybe this is why girls don't like you."

"Who says girls don't like me?" Merrill asks, adjusting his thick glasses, smoothing down his wild hair. "Besides, I don't exactly see them lining up for you these days."

"Yeah, well…" I can't think of how to finish. Because, you know, he's right.

Merrill glances at me. "Oh, come on." He rolls his eyes.

"What?"

"It was a joke."

"I know." But I can't keep the edge out of my voice.

He looks at me for a long moment. "What, you want us to cry together? Have an early-morning pity party?"

"Just drop it," I snap.

Another drawn-out, awkward silence. When Merrill speaks again, his voice is softer. "Are you seriously still bummed, Eldo?"

I can't believe he has to ask.

Well, Merrill, I consider saying, *the girl I was totally in love with ditched me when I needed her most. Now I'm miserable and alone while she's hooking up with one of my football buddies. Why would I be bummed? Nope, I'm freaking awesome.*

"No," I say. "Let's go. We're gonna be late."

"So? The first class is only an overview."

I can usually cope with Merrill's cavalier attitude toward what he calls *the establishment*. Or maybe over our lifetime of friendship, I've gotten used to it. But today's different. "Can you just drive? Please?"

Merrill shrugs and turns the key in the ignition. The car sputters to life after only two tries, which proves miracles *can* happen. Then we're on the road, dust raining on the windshield and seeping in through the cracks.

Merrill doesn't bring up Juniper again. I'm grateful.

* * *

There are three upcoming wishes on the calendar. Penelope Rowe, me, and Archie Kildare, in that order.

I find this out within seconds of stepping inside a meeting room at the community center. It's the same place I took driver's ed classes. The same place half the town attends weekly AA meetings. An ancient blackboard at the front of the room has *Congratulations, Wishers!!!* scrawled on it.

"When's your birthday?" Archie demands before I'm fully through the door.

He gets right up in my face. I don't like his proximity. Or his tone. Really, I just don't like Archie.

I level my gaze at him and wait for him to step aside. For a moment, I don't think he's going to, which would mean my social standing at Madison High School has slipped more than I realized. After a slight hesitation, Archie backs away. I'm relieved. I have about four inches on him, but he's built like a bodybuilder. He could destroy me.

"May twenty-seventh," I say.

"What about you?" he asks, turning to Merrill.

"Don't get your panties in a bunch. I already had my wish."

Archie nods, pleased. "I'm June first. She's May fifteenth."

"He's worried someone shares his wish day," says Penelope

from across the room. She's sitting in the front row. For some inex-plicable reason, she's wearing her cheerleading uniform. It's Sunday.

"Why does it matter?" I ask.

"Bro, are you retarded?" asks Archie.

Penelope looks aghast. "Please don't use that word."

Merrill slides into a desk at the back of the room and kicks up his feet. "Archibald here probably believes the old multiple-wish superstition."

Archie crosses his arms. "It's not a superstition. And my name is Archie."

"What's the superstition?" I ask, sitting next to Merrill.

"It's *not* a superstition," Archie insists. "It's happened. If you have the same wish day as someone else, you'll only get part of your wish."

"It's a superstition," Merrill confides to me.

I shrug. "Never heard of it."

"That's because no one actually believes it." Merrill gives Archie a pointed look. "No one intelligent anyway."

Merrill is playing with fire, and he knows it. He lives for this. It's like a game—seeing how far he can push someone before they snap. Of course, I'm the one who'll have to listen to him whine when he's walking around with a black eye and his arm in a sling.

"Maybe we should wait for our instructor before we talk about this," Penelope suggests.

"It's *happened*," says Archie. "In the fifties or something. Three kids had the same birthday. And they made their wishes at the same time, and the wishes came only part true. OK? It's *happened*."

Merrill begins a slow clap. "Let's hear it for the town historian."

"Listen, faggot," Archie says, advancing on Merrill's desk.

At the front of the room, Penelope's eyes widen in horror. "Please don't use *that* word either."

"Believe what you want," Archie continues without sparing a glance at Penelope. "But I'm not gonna lose my wish because some asshole has my birthday."

I can't help but wonder what Archie would have done if someone *had* shared his wish day.

"No, *you* listen," Merrill says. He swings his legs from the desk and leans forward. "If you believe getting a less powerful wish is the biggest problem with this whole setup, then you're even more clueless than I thought. These wishes are poisonous, and we're *allowing* ourselves to be poisoned. We're like the Jonestown settlers drinking cyanide Kool-Aid. If you get less than you wish for, you should get down on your knees and thank God, because maybe you'll die a little slower than the rest of us."

I sigh deeply. It always comes to this. "Look, guys, it doesn't matter. None of us share a birthday."

"That's not the point, Eldon," Merrill says. His face is bright red. When Merrill starts one of his rants, he forgets to breathe.

"Forget it, man," Archie says, eyeing Merrill like he's a rabid animal. He moves to sit down.

"No. I won't forget it. The powers that be want us to naively accept everything they tell us about wishing and I, for one—"

"Merrill Delacruz," says a voice from the doorway. "I don't have you on the wish schedule."

And just like that, I say goodbye to any hope of having a decent day. Of all the wish instructors we could've ended up with, we got Mr. Wakefield.

"In fact, if I remember correctly, you made your wish last November."

Merrill sighs and comes down off the high from his rant. "I'm here for moral support."

"I'm sure Mr. Wilkes can manage without you," Mr. Wakefield says, walking to the front of the room.

"He can't, actually," Merrill grins, his anger already forgotten. "I mean, the kid is a disaster. Who knows what he might do or say if I'm not around? In fact, if I leave, it'll dramatically reduce his ability to absorb information. Do you really want to be responsible for Eldon's lack of education?"

I don't bother stifling my laugh. Penelope, who's turned around to look at us, rolls her eyes.

"Mr. Delacruz, is it possible you're suffering from transference? Perhaps you worry about your own ability to function outside of your friendship from Mr. Wilkes."

Mr. Wakefield is a trip. At some point, he missed a very important memo, the one informing him he's our principal, not a therapist. The dude has some intense fixation with psychology—specifically, with Sigmund Freud. I think he even tries to look like him.

"You know what, sir?" Merrill says. "I think you're right. I *am* having some issues. Certainly, there's no better cure than staying here, where I can benefit from your expert guidance."

Mr. Wakefield considers for a moment, stroking his pointy beard. "Fine. You may stay. But don't be a distraction."

"I wouldn't dream of it."

*   *   *

Outside, the wind howls, and inside, Mr. Wakefield discusses the mechanics of wishing.

"But, Mr. Wakefield, *why* are there wishes?" Merrill asks earnestly, as if he really wants the answer. He doesn't. He's being difficult for his own amusement—and mine, I suppose.

In the front row, Penelope sighs.

No one—certainly not Mr. Wakefield—knows why there are wishes. No one knows how wishing works or when exactly it started. All that matters is that it *does* work. It *did* start. Everything else, well, maybe you don't want to question it too much. Maybe some mysteries are better left unsolved.

"You stand on the brink of the most pivotal moment of your young lives," Mr. Wakefield says, ignoring Merrill. "A

moment that will be cemented in your consciousness. So powerful that it will touch the deepest part of you and leave you
forever altered."

He paces back and forth in that weird way of his, on the
balls of his feet. Maybe he's trying to make himself seem bigger.
I could probably pick up Mr. Wakefield with one hand. I have
a vision of doing that, picking him up by his collared shirt and
throwing him out of the room. Class has barely started, and his
psychobabble is already hard to deal with. Anyone would have
been a better instructor than him.

"I recommend that all my wishers keep a journal to track this
very emotional journey."

I mean *anyone*.

Mr. Wakefield claps his hands as if a brilliant idea occurred
to him. "Why don't we spend some time exploring our feelings
about our wishes? Who would like to begin?"

"I will," says Penelope.

Surprise, surprise.

"I'm both excited and nervous. I've had my wish picked out
for more than a year. I repeat it to myself every night before bed
to get the wording perfect. You have to be very careful about your
wording. This might be my best chance to make the world a better
place, and I plan to take advantage of it." Penelope smiles like a
contestant in a beauty pageant. I'm sure she's barely suppressing the
urge to wave and blow kisses at us.

"I think I threw up in my mouth," Merrill whispers to me.

"Lovely, Miss Rowe, simply lovely," Mr. Wakefield says, beaming. "What about you, Mr. Kildare?"

"It's Archie."

"Yes, yes, it is. And how do you feel about your approaching wish?"

"How do you think I feel? I feel fucking *awesome*."

Mr. Wakefield sniffs. "As much as I appreciate your enthusiasm, I ask that my wishers find civil ways to express themselves. Let's leave the vulgarities for peer time, yes? Mr. Wilkes, what say you?"

"About vulgarities?"

Merrill laughs.

"About your *wish*, Mr. Wilkes."

All eyes are on me. I'm used to that. The part where I have no idea what to say or do? Totally unfamiliar. "Uh. I don't know. I feel fine."

"You must have more to say than that. Are you excited?"

I don't respond.

Mr. Wakefield nods sympathetically. "Wishing can be overwhelming. One can experience many emotions building up to the big event. It's hard to know where to direct those feelings. Tell me, have you ever found yourself crying after an important football game?"

Jesus.

"It's not *that*," I say. "I just haven't decided what to wish for."

"I'll take your wish off your hands if you can't think of a way to use it," Archie offers.

"Thanks, but no thanks."

"Perhaps you should make a list of everything you consider important," Mr. Wakefield suggests. "Sometimes, taking inventory of our past and present allows us to better forge a path into the future."

"Yeah. I'll get right on that," I say.

Merrill laughs again.

I'm struck by how simple everyone makes wishing sound. Like it's no big thing. Sure, it has the power to change your entire life. It has the power to *ruin* your life. But whatever. Pick a wish and move on. And if you end up with a lifetime of regret, well, you learn to deal with it.

"We'll return to our emotional responses in a bit," says Mr. Wakefield. "Let's switch gears for a moment and discuss what you can expect on your special day."

He passes printouts around the room. It's a map of the cave system where wishes have been made since Madison was founded about a century ago. Mr. Wakefield leads us through the route we'll take, what we'll see, what we'll hear. He tells us how it'll work, from the moment we meet Mayor Fontaine in the parking lot until we say our wishes out loud.

That's the simple part, the part that comes with easy-to-follow instructions. It's what happens before and after that fills me with uncertainty. The part where I have to decide on a wish—and live with the consequences.

CHAPTER 4

COUNTDOWN: 23 DAYS

I'm not one of those people who thinks wishing for a ton of money will, like, fix my whole life. Obviously. Except it would be nice to have a car. On the rare days when Merrill can't get the Mustang, we have to walk to school. That sucks any time of year, but especially when it starts getting hot.

Both of us are sweating before we've left our neighborhood.

"That's what I've been saying," says Merrill, though I'm pretty sure I didn't actually agree with anything. "The whole idea of wishing is screwed up."

"That didn't stop you from making your wish," I point out.

We walk past cheap tract homes built on dirt lots, then some dirt lots without any homes. Someone got real optimistic when they built our neighborhood back in the eighties. They laid out a grid of streets, got them paved, poured sidewalks. But only a handful of houses were built before money ran out. Who did the contractor think was going to move in anyway? It's not like new families are relocating to Madison all the time. Or ever. We do everything we can to discourage that.

There are few houses near mine, on the corner of Gypsum Road. Past that, there are empty foundations. And way in the back, at the foot of the mountains, is a row of homes where construction was started, but stalled, skeleton houses with wooden bones and nothing else. I live in a ghost neighborhood.

My sister used to make up stories about interesting people moving to Madison and restarting construction on the houses. I teased her about how ridiculous that was. I'd give anything to reverse the clock and hear one of those stories again. My eyes sting at the thought. I blink rapidly and hope that if Merrill notices, he assumes it's from dust blowing into my eyes.

"Maybe you shouldn't wish," Merrill goes on as we turn left and make our way toward the center of town.

I stop walking, happy to think of something other than Ebba. "What?"

"Don't wish. If it's that agonizing to you, don't do it."

"My mom would kill me."

"Your mom made her wish. You can do whatever you want with yours."

That's not exactly true. It's an unspoken rule that parents are allowed—*expected*, almost—to put pressure on their kids. It's an opportunity to make up for their own regrettable wishes. It's why my mom always bitches about the Tuttles and their seven kids. She thinks it's unfair they have so many chances to get great wishes when all she has is me.

And that takes my thoughts right back to my sister. My mom *should* have two shots at wishing. A few years from now, Ebba should be preparing to make her own wish. But all that's gone now. It only took a split second for that future to be ripped away. Ebba can't even speak anymore, let alone wish.

"Eldon?" Merrill asks.

I pull myself back to the present. I try to push my sister from my mind. Though if the past few months have taught me anything, it's only a matter of time before my thoughts will return to her.

"I guess you're right," I say to Merrill. "I *could* refuse to wish."

"Sure you could. Wishing is a privilege, not a death sentence. No one's forcing you. At least, that's what they want you to believe. Which if you want to know my opinion—"

"It's too early for conspiracy theories, Merrill. Besides, it's been done before."

"Once," says Merrill. "Only once, in the entire history of this town."

"Once is enough to prove it's possible."

We start walking again, fighting the wind, heads ducked to avoid the bright morning sun. We turn onto Main Street. A car is parked haphazardly with one of its front wheels on the sidewalk in front of the drug store. Inside, a man dozes with his face pressed against the window. At least, I hope he's dozing.

"Isn't that your uncle?" Merrill asks.

I sigh and knock on the window. My uncle Jasper startles awake.

"You can't sleep here," I say when he's rolled down the window and mumbled a bleary hello.

He looks around, disoriented. His eyes are bloodshot, and he's got mad-scientist hair.

"I was resting my eyes," Uncle Jasper says. He grins at me sleepily, not the least bit ashamed at being caught passed out on the side of the road. "I had the most wonderful dream."

"Resting your eyes, huh?" Merrill asks.

"I was wearing magic shoes," Jasper confides.

I already have my phone in hand. "I'm texting my dad. He'll come get you."

A belligerent look crosses my uncle's face. "Don't do that. I can drive."

I reach into the car, wincing at the smell of alcohol and sweat, and pull the keys from the ignition. "Too late."

Though maybe it would've been better to not alert my dad. Let Sheriff Crawford or the mayor find Uncle Jasper. A few nights in jail might be good for him.

I pocket Jasper's keys—I'll give them to my dad and let him deal with it—and head toward school again.

Merrill falls into step behind me. "Tell me more about the magic shoes later!" he shouts back at Jasper.

"Don't encourage him," I say.

"What, you think he's actually going to remember any of this?"

I shrug. Merrill wouldn't be making jokes if his dad was the one passed out in the car. Of course, Benny Delacruz isn't the same kind of drunk as my uncle. Jasper is irresponsible and reckless, but I've never been terrified of him.

Madison High School comes into view, a small dingy building with beige stucco and a faded Spanish tile roof. Kids stand around outside, enjoying their few last moments of freedom.

Merrill stops me before we join the crowd. "Hey, Eldo, I didn't mean that thing I said."

"About my uncle?"

"About giving up your wish. You're never going to get another opportunity like this. You don't want to look back and regret not taking it."

"Would that be worse than regretting my wish?" I ask.

"Why are you so sure you're going to regret it?"

"Because practically everyone does."

"Not me," says Merrill.

"No?" I raise my eyebrows. "Then why are you still wearing those glasses?"

For once, Merrill doesn't have a quick response.

"Look," he says. "I'm just saying, you need to think about it. Don't give up your wish on a whim."

"I won't."

But I don't actually have a clue what I'll do, and Merrill knows that as well as I do. We stop talking about it though. We go to school.

* * *

There are lots of things that suck about going to a small school. One is that it's impossible to avoid anyone. I run into Juniper Clarke before second period.

Juniper was always pretty, but her wish made her so gorgeous, it's almost hard to look at her. It's like staring into the sun or opening your eyes underwater. You know it's probably going to hurt, but you can't *not* look. Even the threat of pain or permanent damage can't stop you from looking.

Except it doesn't change the fact that I hate her.

"Eldon," she says.

"Junie," I say back.

She smiles at me. Her lips are full, and her dark skin makes her teeth look dazzlingly white. Her mouth is perfect. And her eyes. They're almost gold. No one else has eyes like that.

She looks at me like she's waiting.

Like maybe she wants me to say I'm still in love with her, then she'll tell me everything that's happened over the last few months was a horrible mistake, and she wants to get back together. Not that I would.

It's also possible she wants me to move so she can get to her locker.

I don't move.

"How's it going?" I ask.

Juniper shrugs. "It's going."

"How's what's–his–name?"

"Eldon. You know his name."

Of course I know his name. I've played football with that ass-hole since I was nine.

"Well, I hope everything's good," I say.

"Thanks. You too."

I step aside so she can open her locker. I don't leave.

Juniper exchanges her books. She adjusts her hair in the mirror hanging inside in door. Her hair is long and curly. She's never straightened it. The same way she's never worn a ton of makeup or bought clothes because some magazine says they're in style. Juniper does her own thing.

"Was there something else?" she finally asks.

"Not really."

But I still don't leave.

I know Juniper won't always be the most beautiful girl in Madison. Pretty soon, another girl will have her wish day, and she'll take Junie's place. Maybe in a few weeks, it'll be Penelope. But Juniper will still be special.

Because it's not just her looks, yeah? It's the way being around her feels *right*. Like how her laugh can wipe away all the bad stuff going on. And how you never get bored when you're hanging out with her, even if you're doing boring things. And how nice she is, to everyone, even the people no one is nice to.

At least, she *used* to be nice.

"Eldon," she says.

"Yeah?"

"You need to stop doing this."

"Doing what?"

She sighs. "Hanging around. Waiting."

"I wasn't waiting."

Juniper closes her locker and looks at me for a long moment. "OK."

"You think I'm lying? Jesus, Junie, it's a small school. Do you think everyone you run into is stalking you?"

"I'll see you later, Eldon. OK?" She sounds sad.

"Yeah. Fine."

I watch her walk down the hall and feel like an enormous jerk.

"Congratulations," says a voice behind me. "That wins the award for most awkward interaction of the day."

I turn to find Norie Havermayer in front of her own open locker. She has this look on her face like she feels bad for me. A year ago, if someone told me *Norie Havermayer* would feel sympathy for *me*, I would have laughed. Norie is nobody. She couldn't even wish her way into Juniper's league.

"You're trying way too hard," Norie says, as if I'd asked her opinion.

"I wasn't *trying* anything."

Norie smiles, and there it is again. Sympathy. "Sure you weren't."

"What do you care?" I snap.

"You've been having this weekly drama next to my locker for…what? Three months? It's hard to ignore."

She smiles again. And I have a sudden, disturbing thought: it's not sympathy on her face. Norie is *amused*.

So it's come to that. Norie Havermayer is mocking me.

"Your wish day is coming up, isn't it?" she says. "You can always wish to get Juniper back."

I'm so dumbfounded that I don't know how to respond.

"Something to think about anyway," Norie says with a shrug. She closes her locker and heads toward her next class.

I have the urge to sprint after her and explain myself. To wipe that smile, really more of a smirk, off her face. I want to ask her who the hell she thinks she is, talking to me that way.

I fight the impulse, take a deep breath, and count to ten. Getting in Norie's face would only land me back in Mr. Wakefield's office. Another meeting with the principal and my parents, everyone discussing how I need to think before I act.

By the time I finish counting, my anger has subsided. I'm not going to flip out, but I still want to tell Norie I'd never wish for Juniper to love me. I know the consequences of a wish like that all too well.

* * *

Every Monday is the same. My mom makes broccoli and rice

casserole. And every Monday, my dad says, "I really think of this as a side dish."

Every Monday, my mom replies, "When you start making more money, we can have meat every night."

The casserole's more about prep time than money though. My mom only blames money to be a bitch. Monday is the day she stays late at the doctor's office, catching up on paperwork from the weekend, getting ready for the coming week. There are too many phone calls to answer and patients to sign in. My mom regularly reminds us how little free time there is in the life of a receptionist.

"Where were you last night?" she asks me after she and Dad get through the requisite conversation.

"Hanging out with Merrill."

"I thought you might come home and tell us how wish class went."

Clearly, she thought wrong.

"It was fine," I say.

"You know, kiddo, most people are excited about their wish. They're grateful for this opportunity."

"Well, most people know what to wish for."

My mom frowns deeply, and it makes her look about twenty years older than she is. "We've discussed this."

"Believe me, I know."

"Eldon, we need the money."

"Leave him alone, Luella," says my dad. "You can't pressure the boy."

That is absolutely the wrong thing to say.

"Don't talk to me about pressure, Harmon Wilkes. I've seen what you do to him on the football field."

"That's different. You have to push kids on the field. That's what a coach *does*."

I eat the casserole and keep my eyes focused on the empty chair across the table from me. I hate that empty chair. It makes every dinner tense and miserable. I don't know why we even bother sitting down to eat as a family anymore. Our family is broken.

"Don't use that as an excuse," my mom says. "And don't tell me what I can or can't talk about with my son. He's a member of this family, and that means looking out for the rest of us."

My dad opens his mouth to speak but closes it again. He swallows heavily, as if something is caught in his throat. Something *is* caught—his words.

"You...you're..."

"Yes?" asks my mom.

My dad tries to clear his throat.

"Come on, spit it out," she says, taunting him.

He struggles for another moment then blurts out, "Whatever you think is best."

"Yes," my mom says, so bitterly that it turns the food in my mouth to ash. "Yes, that's what I thought."

"Maybe we could talk about something besides wishing?"
I suggest.

No one replies.

It isn't that surprising. What else is there to talk about?

✹ ✹ ✹

One of the problems with cheaply built houses is that the walls are
so thin, they're as effective as cardboard. It's impossible to keep
secrets here.

It's late, and the murmur of my parents' voices seeps into my
room. My mom is arguing. My dad is trying to.

It makes me sad for both of them.

I turn on the radio, hoping to drown out their voices.

"*...had just turned onto the Extraterrestrial Highway,*" says a man.

"*Mmm-hmm, and about what time was this?*" Robert Nash asks.

"*Oh, probably about two in the morning. There weren't any other
cars on the road. Suddenly, ahead of me, a light appeared in the sky. As I
drove toward it, it seemed to descend and get brighter...*"

The radio isn't enough distraction. I can still hear my parents
loud and clear. My mom starts to cry.

I think about climbing out my window, wandering through
the empty neighborhood to get some space. But the threat of the
wind is too much. Sand is being flung against the side of the house,
and if I go outside, I'd probably end up lost and buried. The last
thing I'm going to do is leave my parents with no children.

The man on the radio finishes telling his story, and Robert Nash says how very interesting it is, asks his audience to call in with their thoughts. I consider calling in. Saying, "Yeah, the story was cool and all but not as dramatic as my parents fighting or my thirteen-year-old sister slowly dying in a nursing home and, oh yeah, my wish day is coming up. You thought *aliens* were mysterious? Let me tell you about *Madison*."

I close my eyes and count to ten. Robert Nash says, "*Next up on Basin and Range Radio: Joshua trees—indigenous to the Mojave Desert or brought here by alien farmers? That, and more, when our programming returns.*"

I switch off the radio and quell the urge to throw it against the wall. It's not Robert Nash's fault that he can't distract me tonight. Plus, if I put another hole in the wall, my mom will kill me. I've put my fist through the drywall so many times that I've run out of posters to hide the evidence.

Tension builds inside me, and I have to do something, or I'll totally lose it. Mr. Wakefield would jump at the chance to analyze me right now. He'd probably say some crap about misplaced anger. He's used that bit on me before.

Thinking of Mr. Wakefield reminds me of wish class and his suggestion to make a list of everything that's important to me. It's not a terrible idea. Not that I'd admit that to Mr. Wakefield. The last thing I want to do is encourage him. My evening is already on a downward spiral; I might as well use the time to figure out my wish.

I grab a notebook and pen from my backpack, open to a clean sheet of paper. *Things I Care About.*

Number one, Ebba. That's a no-brainer.

Number two, my parents. Another easy one. I love them, even if I sometimes hate them.

But what does that mean, exactly? That I should wish for whatever my parents ask me to? Does it mean my wish should be to save Ebba?

I'm not even sure I *can* save Ebba. In fact, I'm pretty sure I can't. There are too many logistical difficulties. Too many ways it would go against the rules of wishing.

Number three.

I pause. What else do I care about?

A few months ago, I would have written Juniper's name. A few months ago, I was convinced we'd be together for the rest of high school, maybe even the rest of our lives.

I care about Merrill. He's been my best friend since we were kids, and I'd be lost without him. But our friendship's not really something to wish on. And my other friends, well, they aren't real friends. They're people I hang out with at school or go to parties with.

Football isn't going on the list either. It would break my dad's heart if I said it out loud, but football doesn't mean as much to me as it does to him.

I look at the mostly blank page. Why can't I come up with things I care about? What's wrong with me?

I throw down the notebook. Sorry, Mr. Wakefield, but your experiment is a failure.

I lie in bed, take a deep breath, and start counting again. I go past ten and get all the way to a hundred before the house goes quiet, my parent's argument finally over. I get up and slip down the dark hallway, heading for the garage. I can watch TV out there. Steal one of my dad's beers. Numb myself.

I don't get that far. My mom is sitting at the kitchen table, cigarette in one hand, scissors in another, coupons spread out in front of her.

"You're awake," she says, looking at me.

"Couldn't sleep."

"Me either."

I drift over to the table and sit down.

"Anything good?" I ask, nodding at the coupons.

"It's never enough," she replies. "It doesn't matter how much money we save if we don't change what we're bringing in."

"Then why bother?" I'm not trying to be a jerk. I really want to know.

Ma takes a long drag of her cigarette, watches the smoke twist and turn in the air. "Because I can't just sit here. I need to do something."

"Yeah," I say softly. "I get that."

Her gaze meets mine, and all the sadness I see is a knife in my heart.

"Oh, Eldon," Ma sighs. "I want your life to be better than this. I wish I would have known when I was your age."

"Known what?"

"How different it could be."

We sit in silence, the dim fluorescent light crackling above us. For a minute, it's as if I see my mom through a filter. The lines on her face smooth out, the gray streaks fade from her hair, and the sadness leaves her eyes. I see her the way she must have been when she was my age.

"Tell me about your wish," I say.

She laughs dryly. "You know my wish."

"I know the result. Tell me what happened before that."

She takes another drag on her cigarette and blows smoke toward the ceiling, adding to the stains of a million other cigarettes smoked sadly in the middle of the night.

Then she starts talking.

CHAPTER 5

THE WISH HISTORY: LUELLA WILKES

Imagine this:

You've got a history book in front of you. The whole, screwed-up history of a town in the middle of the Mojave Desert. A town called Madison.

Open the book.

Flip through the pages.

Now stop.

See where you've landed.

It's 1992, and a girl named Luella is about to make her wish.

She's seventeen years old, and she'll be a Wilkes soon enough. But for now, she's still Luella Maylocke.

And Luella Maylocke is deeply in love.

Check her out, hovering outside Harmon Wilkes's Spanish classroom. See how, when the bell rings and kids file out, Luella looks away. She's all chill, like she wasn't waiting to see him, like she happened to be passing by.

What does Harmon do? He frowns when he notices her, because she's not fooling anyone.

This little dance they're doing—Luella pretending not to look for Harmon, Harmon pretending not to see her waiting, Luella pretending she doesn't care that his gaze skips over her—it's getting to be a daily routine.

Turn to the next page in the history book.

There's Luella doodling Harmon's name in her diary.

Next page.

She cheers from the sidelines while Harmon scores yet another game-winning touchdown.

Next page.

Now Luella dials Harmon's number but hangs up the phone when he answers. She promises herself that next time, she'll speak. She'll find the words to express what she feels. Or at the very least say hello.

Page after page after page, it's all the same.

You could fill an entire book with how much Luella Maylocke loves Harmon Wilkes.

You could fill another book with how much he doesn't love her back.

Luella's starting to wonder where she went wrong. She thinks maybe she's not pretty enough. Not interesting enough. Not popular enough. Not for a guy like Harmon Wilkes, the star of Madison High School.

Unlike Luella, we have the benefit of perspective. And although our history book doesn't tell us exactly what Harmon's thinking—not in this chapter anyway—we've got a pretty good guess.

It's hard to love a person who reeks of desperation.

Imagine:

Someone hanging on your every word.

Someone mindlessly agreeing with everything you say.

Someone making their life about you, and only you, all the time.

Luella thinks she's better for Harmon than the other girls he dates. She'd put him first, see his needs get met, devote herself fully to him. She'd do all that because she loves him so, so much.

Newsflash, Luella: not everyone wants to be worshipped.

Someone should tell her that. Oh wait. Someone tried to.

See Jasper, hovering awkwardly in her bedroom doorway. Luella glances up at her brother from the newspaper article she's reading about last week's football game.

About Harmon Wilkes.

The superstar.

"What, Jasper?" she snaps at her younger brother. She quickly turns the newspaper over so Jasper can't see the photo of Harmon she's been gazing at.

"Are you going to the hot springs tonight?"

"I don't know," Luella says. "Who's going to be there?"

Jasper shrugs. "Everyone."

Luella doesn't care about everyone. *She cares about Harmon. She tries to keep her tone casual, her expression neutral. "Do you think Harmon will show up?"*

Jasper rolls his eyes. "If he does, he'll have Harriet with him."

Harriet.

His girlfriend.

Yeah, that's a detail Luella's happy to push to the back of her mind. This dude she's obsessed with? He's not even single.

Luella struggles to stay composed, to not show how the mere mention of Harriet makes her want to scream.

"Lu," *Jasper says.* "Maybe you should give it a rest."

"Give *what a rest?*"

"He's never going to like you like that," *Jasper blurts out.*

Look closely at Luella.

Do you see the way she flinches? Do you see the way she bites her lip to stop it from trembling? Do you see the shock of hearing out loud something she already almost certainly knows?

"People are laughing at you," *Jasper says.* "They're saying you're—"

"Get out!" *Luella screams. Without thinking, she wads up the newspaper sitting next to her, crumples Harmon's perfect, smiling face, and throws it at her brother.* "You don't know anything about it!"

Jasper holds up his hands, takes a step back.

"I'm just trying to help," *he says.*

"I don't need your help."

"Fine, forget it." *Jasper pauses.* "But can you give me a ride to the hot springs?"

Flip through a few more pages in this history book.

Skip past the part where Luella's crying in her room.

Skip past the part when she tries to start a conversation with Harmon and gets blown off.

Skip past day after day of Luella watching Harmon like he's her favorite TV show.

Stop on the night before Luella's wish.

And pay attention.

Luella's mother sits her down at the dining room table.

"Honey," she says, "tomorrow's a really big day."

Watch the way Luella rolls her eyes. No kidding, *she thinks.*

"I want to talk to you about your wish."

"OK."

Luella's mother hesitates. "Sometimes...sometimes we think there's something we really want. But the only reason we want it so badly is because we don't know what else is out there."

"OK," Luella says again.

"What I mean is...well, I haven't asked what you plan to wish for. Because I know you're a smart young woman, and you'll do the right thing."

Luella and her mother stare at each other for a long moment.

"You know, honey, beauty and popularity will fade. But money can open doors for you, for this family, forever. You know that, right?"

"Why don't you tell Jasper to wish for money?" Luella asks. Why should it be *her job to make her family rich?*

But they both know Jasper can't be counted on. For anything. It's impossible to anticipate what he'll wish for when his own eighteenth birthday comes around.

"There are rumors, Luella."

"Don't worry about me, Ma," Luella says. "I know what I'm doing."

A relieved smile spreads across Mrs. Maylocke's face. "That's my girl "

Now we've arrived at the pivotal moment—Luella Maylocke's wish day.

Even without reading ahead, you've probably figured out she has no intention of wishing for money. Luella doesn't wish to be beautiful either. Give it enough time, and someone more beautiful always comes along, yeah? She doesn't wish to be the most popular or most intelligent or most athletic. There'll always be someone who's more than her.

No, Luella wishes for exactly what everyone expected and feared. In the cold silence of the cave she says, "I wish for Harmon Wilkes to be in love with me, and only me, forever."

Let's watch how that plays out.

The next day at school, Harmon approaches Luella at her locker. Look at how the other students smirk and nudge each other. See how they laugh when Harmon asks Luella on a date.

Two years later, when Harmon asks Luella to marry him, no one's surprised.

This is Madison, after all. This isn't the first love affair to begin with a wish.

And because this is Madison, the fairy tale doesn't end with happily ever after.

When do Luella's feelings for Harmon fade? Flip through the pages, and see if you can pinpoint the exact moment.

Was it when his football injury ended his career?

Was it when they moved into their tiny, sad house, and Luella realized it was the best she'd ever have?

Or maybe it's less easy to define.

Maybe it's the way Harmon is always around, gazing at her adoringly with his puppy-dog eyes, hanging on her every word. Maybe it's his infatuation, the way Luella is the only person who gives his life meaning.

Maybe Luella doesn't want to be worshipped.

Skim through the pages one more time. Pass year after bleak year.

See Luella today, sitting at the table in her worn-down kitchen, cutting coupons like it's all she has to live for.

Look closely at her eyes.

Do you see the resignation in them?

She knows there's no reversing her wish. She could divorce Harmon and move out of Madison. She could go to the other side of the world. But no matter what she says or does or how far away she moves, Harmon Wilkes will never stop loving her.

This is Luella's punishment for being young and impulsive and in love. And Harmon Wilkes? He's being punished for no reason at all.

CHAPTER 6

COUNTDOWN: 21 DAYS

F ootball isn't some great passion of mine, not the way it is for my dad. But I enjoy it the way I enjoy anything I excel at. Even when the game bores me, it feels good to go out on the field and be the best.

Except I'm not the best anymore.

And yeah, that kinda pisses me off.

I'm at practice, making one mistake after another, trying not to lose my cool. The other guys on the team shoot me sympathetic looks, and I start to wonder why I'm even here.

We played our last official game in December, but in Madison, the football season never really ends. There's a short break in winter, then practice starts again in spring. It's pointless for the seniors, because it's not like we have anything to practice *for*. Which is why the end-of-the-year game was created. The school wanted to give senior players one last hurrah, an excuse to hang on to our glory days a little longer.

So every year, on the weekend before graduation, Madison

and Tonopah face off in a game we call the Clash. The Tonopah Muckers are our biggest rivals. They also have the second worst mascot in Nevada. Muckers is a mining term, which is relevant to our area, but it guarantees that just about everyone refers to the team as the Tonopah Mucker Fuckers.

Still, I'd rather be a Mucker Fucker than a Madison Drosophila. When the high school was built, we were the Madison Rattlers. But in the seventies, some science nerd who'd been bullied by football players wished for the team to be renamed. Our mascot is a fruit fly, a *Drosophila*, wearing a football helmet. Not only do we win the award for worst mascot in Nevada, we probably have the worst mascot in the world.

Needless to say, I'm ready to leave my days as a Drosophila behind me, but I can't skip out on the last game. My dad would never forgive me.

Today's a bad day for him. He limps around on his crutches, which always makes him more of a dick. I think he's afraid the guys will see him as weak, so he gets extra aggressive to make up for it.

"Jesus Christ, Boyd!" he screams. "What are you waiting for? *Move!*"

And to Alvarez, "Quit acting like you've never held a football before!"

I'd take pleasure in his insults, except his eye might turn on me next. I get no special treatment for being his son. Sometimes, it's like he's two people. There's Dad at home, and then there's Coach on the field.

Under my dad's pissed off glare, I run a five-yard curl, turning just as Clem Johnson throws the ball my way. The football spirals through the air, a perfect pass. The defense has left me wide open. It's an easy play, one I should be able to handle in my sleep. But the ball bounces out of my hands and falls to the ground.

I swear under my breath, and my dad blows his whistle with enough force that his head might straight-up explode.

I'm not used to sucking so much. I've played football since elementary school, and I wasn't good by Madison standards. I was *good*.

"I think some of my wish rubbed off on you," my dad told me once.

I don't think it works like that. Wishes can't rub off. But honestly, I'd never thought about it one way or another. There hadn't been any reason to. Being good at football was just another item on the list of Crap I Took for Granted. I'd always been good at football. I'd always been good looking. I'd always been popular.

Until we hit senior year, and the wishing started.

First was Calvin Boyd. His birthday is in August. We were hardly back in school when I noticed practices weren't going well. Something was off. That feeling grew and grew until the team dynamics weren't just off, they were desperately wrong. But I couldn't put my finger on why. Then, during the first game of the season, I figured out what it was: everyone was watching Cal instead of me.

It was dominos after that. Another kid's wish day arrived, and he wished to be the best player on the team. Then a kid who wasn't even on the team wished to be the best. As birthdays passed, everyone who'd wished previously or hadn't wished yet was pushed lower down the ladder. And now, here I am, at the freaking bottom.

Maybe it wouldn't be a big deal if it was only football, yeah? But it's not. By halfway through the year, the halls of Madison High School were filled with kids who looked as if they'd stepped off movie sets. I was lost in a mob of attractive, smart, talented kids.

What I'm saying is, these days, I'm nothing special.

And that messes with you, you know? Makes you think maybe you weren't that special to begin with. Makes you wonder what you're *actually* good at.

These days, I walk around with a big question mark over my head.

It doesn't help that, when I was at my lowest, feeling the most lost, Juniper Clarke dumped me for someone better. Someone like the person I used to be, Eldon 2.0.

"Poor Eldon," Merrill joked, once it became obvious what was happening. "You'll have to learn to be *average*."

"Not funny."

"Believe me. I don't like it any more than you do. I had

this whole popular-by-association thing going for me. You think I can stand on my own? No way. You're not the only one impacted, buddy."

But it was bullshit, and we both knew it. Merrill is plenty popular on his own. His popularity isn't based on looks or athletic ability. People simply *like* him. For all my years being the center of attention, I'm not sure I was ever really *liked*.

The thing is, I can change my current situation. On my wish day, I can turn back the clock, make myself into the person I was before. I just don't know if I want to.

My dad blows his whistle again and motions everyone to the sidelines. We jog over and take a knee.

"Who taught you how to play?" he demands, still shouting like we're across the field.

No one speaks or meets his gaze.

"I asked a question!"

"You taught us to play, sir," Otto Alvarez mumbles.

"I sure as hell didn't teach you to play like *that*," my dad says. "Keep this up, and the Mucker Fuckers are going to annihilate us in the first quarter."

"We're having an off day," Otto says.

"You're not allowed to have *off days!*" my dad snaps.

Full disclosure: the outcome of the Drosophila-Mucker Clash doesn't matter. The game is supposed to be friendly. The score isn't recorded as part of our season. All the winning team gets is an old football that's been spray-painted gold. It's so ancient that half the paint has chipped off, but people around here act like it's the freaking Holy Grail.

"Listen," my dad says, "I'm done watching you skip around the field like you're at a dance recital. Get out there and play football."

"Sir," Calvin Boyd says with so much authority that the whole team looks at him. "With all due respect, it'll be easier to plan for the Clash if we went over the depth chart."

The field goes silent. Even the wind has stopped. The hostility fades from my dad's eyes and turns into something worse—sadness.

We've all been anticipating this moment for months. The big question: is my dad gonna keep me at the top because, you know, I'm his son? Or will he do what's best for the team?

My dad clears his throat, hesitates, then shoots an apologetic glance at me.

"Cal will be the primary wideout," he says.

I want nothing more than to punch the smug look off Calvin's face.

Football isn't everything to me. I won't cry the day I walk off the field for good. But I've *always* been the best wide receiver. Even when I was the only freshman on the JV team.

I avoid looking at my dad as we get back to practice. It's not so much that I'm angry at him. I just can't bear his disappointment.

✶ ✶ ✶

Merrill's waiting for me outside the locker room. He's watching a video on his phone, and based on the engine roar coming from the speakers, I'm guessing it's some footage of a fighter plane.

"Hey," he says when he notices me. "Need a ride to work?"

I don't *need* a ride, because almost everything in Madison is within walking distance. But Merrill's probably bored, and I'm not real anxious to be left alone with my thoughts. So I nod, and we start down the hall together.

"How was today's thrilling display of brute force and athletic prowess?" Merrill asks.

"Practice sucked."

"That's the spirit," he laughs.

We're nearing the end of the hall, almost out of the school, when a classroom door in front of us swings open. It's the room where all the AP classes take place. I've never once been inside of it.

Fletcher Hale steps into the hallway. When he sees us he halts, a deer caught in the headlights.

I stop walking too.

Fletcher's face goes pale, as if he thinks I'm gonna start something. Which, who knows? Maybe I am. My heart is already beating faster, anger burning through my body. Fletcher doesn't look like the kind of guy you'd want to destroy. He's a scrawny kid with a bad haircut and his shirt tucked neatly into his jeans. He looks like any other harmless nerd. That doesn't change the fact that he's a monster.

It's not that we haven't seen each other lately. We have two classes together. But the last time we were alone like this, without adult supervision, I was kicking his ass. And I haven't quite gotten past the urge to do it again.

"Uh, hi," Fletcher says tentatively, drawing his calculus book close to his chest like a shield.

A wave of heat washes over me. How dare this dude even *speak* to me? How dare he act like I'm just another student? My hands clench, and I spiral back in time, remembering how good it felt to smash my fist into his face.

"Eldon?" Merrill says casually, like everything's totally chill. "You're going to be late for work."

I take a breath. Try to steady myself. I can't do anything to Fletcher. I can't get suspended again. Mr. Wakefield made it very, very clear that I can't get suspended again.

Fletcher sees his opportunity and makes a break for it.

"See you around," he says, moving past me.

I turn and watch him go.

"Eldon," Merrill says again, this time with a more serious tone.

"OK," I say, shaking myself. "OK, let's go."

We walk out of Madison High School and into the dry, desert afternoon.

"He's not worth it," Merrill says as we make our way across the parking lot to the Mustang.

That pulls me up short. I turn to Merrill. "Not *worth* it? What the hell do you know about it?"

Merrill's still using that calm, reasonable voice, and it's starting to annoy me. "Beating up Fletcher won't change what happened."

"Easy for you to say," I snap, my voice rising. "It's not your sister—"

"I've lost people too, Eldon. I know how hard it is."

That's different. It's *completely* different. Merrill's mom was sick. No one was at fault for her death. But what happened to Ebba? Well, there *is* someone to blame. Fletcher Hale caused the accident. If weren't for him, my sister would still be here.

I close my eyes and remind myself that Merrill's not the one I'm upset with. According to Mr. Wakefield, I need to stop taking out my anger on people who don't deserve it. It's an "unhealthy coping mechanism."

"You want to call in to work?" Merrill asks. "We could go somewhere and talk."

I don't want to talk. The last thing in the world I want to do is *talk*.

"No," I say simply.

I climb into the Mustang, and Merrill follows. I turn up the radio loud, too loud to have a conversation. Unfortunately, nothing is loud enough to drown out my thoughts.

✻ ✻ ✻

I'm pretty sure I won't be employed at the gas station for much longer.

I was hired for a specific reason. I was the poster boy for our town. The idea is people stop at the gas station and I distract them with my charm. I don't convince them nothing is amiss in Madison. Rather, I keep them so fixated on me that they don't realize anything's weird in the first place. You can't see something you're not looking for.

Ever since the gas station was built, some Madison kid has worked this same con.

It's not too challenging, because Madison isn't exactly a hotspot of activity. There's nothing interesting in town like you'd find if you kept going north on the Extraterrestrial Highway toward Rachel. We don't have kitschy tourist shops or roadside attractions. Madison has a movie theater with two screens and a bowling alley with two lanes. One bank, one diner, and three bars. We have a park that's abandoned all summer, thanks to the heat. There's absolutely no reason to linger. Tourists fill their gas tanks and get back on the road before they die of boredom.

That's pretty much the Madison motto. *Everything's boring here.*

The reason I think I'm going to get fired isn't only because other people are better suited for the job now. It's because I stopped caring.

A hippie guy pulls into the gas station in a painted van, and I *should* ask where he's headed. But I'm not in the mood to hear about Burning Man or whatever, and I'm too fatigued from football practice and my run-in with Fletcher to pretend everything in Madison is on the up-and-up.

"Hey, man," the guy says, leaning out the window. "Is this, like, the alien place?"

"Nope," I say, keeping my gaze on the gas pump.

"Cool," he replies but doesn't settle back in his seat. He watches me, and I pretend not to notice. "You like living in the desert?"

I shrug. "Dunno. I've never lived anywhere else."

"Right on."

The guy seems to be done talking. I *hope* he's done talking. But then he says, "The desert's spiritual, huh?"

"Not this desert." The gas pump clicks, and I pull the nozzle from the van. I look the hippie guy straight on. "Dude, you can't even imagine how screwed up this place is."

The guys squints at me, as if he's trying to figure me out.

I tell him how much he owes and try not to have a meltdown when he pays in loose change. As he counts out pennies, I glance at the other gas pump, where Merrill's sitting on the hood of the Mustang. He frowns at me.

"Man, I'm short on a tip," the hippie says.

"Don't worry about it," I reply. I wonder where exactly he's going that doesn't require funds.

"Wait." He reaches over and rifles through junk on the passenger seat. "Have this." He hands me a fortune cookie.

It takes all the willpower I have left to keep a straight face. "Thanks." I slap the side of the van. "Have a safe trip."

The hippie pulls out of the parking lot and leaves Madison for greater adventures. I wander over to Merrill, unwrapping the fortune cookie as I go.

"Eldo," Merrill says, "was that self-sabotage? Do you need to have a sit down with Mr. Wakefield?"

Merrill's tone is flippant, but there's no mistaking the concern on his face.

I shrug.

"I mean, the goal here is to *not* tell tourists this town is screwed up."

"It just came out," I say. "I wasn't thinking."

"Which is why they'd never hire me for this job."

"*One* of the reasons anyway," I joke.

"Hey," Merrill says, as if he suddenly got a brilliant idea. "Maybe you can wish to not be an asshole anymore."

"Maybe," I agree, not having the energy to come up with a clever response. I crack open the fortune cookie. I get it in my mind that the slip of paper inside will say something prophetic— something about wishing. Something to make sense of my life.

I'm wrong. I laugh, and Merrill raises his eyebrows.

I read, "The fortune you seek is in another cookie."

Merrill grins. "Want me to chase down Jerry Garcia and ask for another?"

Before I can reply, another car pulls into the parking lot.

I groan.

"Chill, it's just that Eleanor chick," Merrill says.

I look closer. He's right. The car stops at the gas pump, and Norie Havermayer gets out.

"I can pump my own gas," she tells me.

I shrug and boost myself onto the hood of the Mustang.

"So," Norie says to me after swiping her card and starting the pump. "Are you going to do it?"

"Do what?" asks Merrill.

"Eldon was contemplating wishing for Juniper Clarke's affection." Norie has that obnoxious smile on her face again. It instantly fills me with rage.

Merrill turns to me in surprise. "Really?"

I scowl. "*No*, not really."

"Tell me, Eldon," Merrill says, clearly enjoying the moment, "what would have given Eleanor that impression?"

"I believe she prefers to be called Norie," I say.

"I also prefer not to be talked about like I'm not here," Norie adds.

"And *I* prefer you guys not change the subject." Merrill looks from me to Norie then back to me. "What's the deal with Juniper?"

He's going to harass me until I spill. I sigh. "I made a fool out of myself in front of her."

"Again?"

I don't respond.

"Eldo, we discussed this. If you keep following Juniper around, you're gonna look like a creep."

"Too late," I say, trying to match Merrill's joking tone but failing miserably.

The sun beats down, and I'm aching from the hits I took at practice. I don't mind Merrill making jokes at my expense, but Norie hardly knows me. She definitely doesn't know anything about me and Juniper. I want to be left alone.

"I'm not wishing for Juniper to love me, OK? Can we drop the subject?"

"What *are* you wishing for?" Norie asks.

I sigh. For the millionth time, I wish our gas pump didn't take a lifetime to fill a tank.

"That's Eldon's least favorite question these days," Merrill says. "Meaning he has no clue."

Norie tilts her head and looks at me as if I'm a scientific anomaly. "Really?"

"I'm not one of those people who's had it planned since I was a kid," I say.

I'd *thought* about it, obviously. How could I not? When I was five, I told people I was going to wish for my action figures to come to life. When I was eight, I was going to wish for a bike for my sister. She was stuck with my hand-me-down, and I knew she wanted a pink bike with streamers and a basket. When I was thirteen, most of my wish daydreams revolved around sex. A year ago, I assumed I'd wish for money and didn't give it much thought beyond that.

But contemplating wishes is a lot different from planning one wish. It's different from having a wish you're sure is *the wish*. I grew up changing my mind about wishes as often as I changed my socks.

"Maybe it's good you're not sure yet," Norie says. "This way, you'll know you're making the right choice, not wishing for the first thing that popped into your head."

This is not the response I expected. "Thank you, Norie." I give Merrill a pointed look.

"So, Miss Careful Thought and Planning," Merrill says, ignoring me completely. "What did *you* wish for?"

Norie hesitates. She looks down at her hand, twirls the ring on her finger. "I'd rather not say."

Another unexpected response. Most people are eager to talk about their wishes.

"That's highly unusual," Merrill says.

"Everything about wishing is highly unusual," Norie replies. The gas pump finishes, and Norie removes the nozzle from her car. "See you guys later. Good luck finding a wish, Eldon."

"She's an odd one," Merrill says when Norie's gone. "You know, the other day, I overheard her talking to Otto Alvarez."

"So?"

"She was telling him about Jesus."

That gets my attention. "What was she saying?"

"I wasn't exactly going to stop and join the conversation, Eldo."

I'd heard rumors about Norie and religion, but I figured it was gossip. As far as I know, no one in Madison has ever been religious.

"Weird, right?" Merrill asks.

I pop the remainder of my fortune cookie into my mouth and chew before answering. "Yeah, weird. But also intriguing."

Merrill takes off his glasses and looks at me dramatically. "Can it be? Has Eleanor Havermayer taken your mind off Juniper?"

"The Jesus thing is intriguing, not *her*."

Merrill shrugs and puts his glasses back on.

"I wonder what she wished for," I ponder. "Certainly not looks."

"You're an asshole," Merrill says, but he laughs a little anyway.

To be fair, Norie's not unattractive. In any other town, she might even be considered pretty. But in Madison, with tons of girls wishing to look like supermodels, Norie doesn't have a chance. She's never going to be beautiful like Juniper.

"How many other people you think keep quiet about their wishes?" Merrill asks.

I'm wondering the same thing. The residents of Madison are so focused on keeping secrets from outsiders, I never stopped to consider what we've been keeping from each other.

CHAPTER 7

COUNTDOWN: 20 DAYS

In English lit, Mrs. Franklin drones on and on. This is my least favorite class, not because of the subject but because Mrs. Franklin makes me extremely uncomfortable.

There's no question what she wished for when she turned eighteen. It's right there on display. Or maybe I should say *they* are. Mrs. Franklin has the biggest tits I've ever seen in my life. You can't take your eyes off them, and I don't mean that in a good way.

People say Mrs. Franklin was flat as a board before her wish. She definitely went too far in the opposite direction. Like, even when she was young, her boobs were probably more creepy than hot, and now Mrs. Franklin is ancient. There's a steady stream of jokes about her around Madison High School. I don't know what the hell she's thinking, working around teenagers.

Mrs. Franklin is talking about the significance of the last line in *The Great Gatsby* while I, and every other kid in class, look out the window or at the ceiling or at our books. Anywhere but at her.

You can't even talk to her without your eyes straying to her chest, and then you feel like an asshole.

When the PA system squawks, everyone sits up a little. The voice of the school secretary, Miss Treadway, comes through the speakers.

"Eldon Wilkes, please report to the principal's office."

I groan loudly, make a big production out of it. Everyone laughs, because they feel my pain. Getting sent to Mr. Wakefield's office rarely means you're in trouble. More likely, he's decided it's time for a mental health checkup. Hearing your name called over the PA means an impromptu therapy session is in your immediate future.

I leave English and slowly make my way through the empty halls. Maybe I should make a break for it. Walk out of school. Right out of Madison, even. I could be like the travelers who tear out of town, speeding toward the horizon. And after that, after Madison, what then? *Anything.*

Instead, I continue to Mr. Wakefield's office.

When I pass the trophy case, my eyes linger on the beat-up gold football inside. Last year's victory in the Clash was one of my best nights on the field. Afterward, Juniper wrapped her arms around me and whispered, "You're amazing." I didn't even say thank you, because, you know, I agreed with her. My family wanted me to have a celebratory dinner with them. Ebba bounced up and down, talked about getting ice cream. I ditched them for a party at the hot springs instead. Got so drunk, I puked in Juniper's car when she drove me home. She had to wake up my dad to help get me to bed.

The memory makes me cringe. I can be a hero and a villain all in one night.

I hurry the rest of the way to Mr. Wakefield's office and knock on his closed door.

"Enter!"

He's standing in front of the window, poised, one finger pressed against his lips like he's in great contemplation. An actor, frozen before the curtain rises. Also like an actor, I'm sure he's rehearsed this moment and is waiting for his cue.

"You wanted to see me?"

"Young Mr. Wilkes. Come here."

I sigh and make my way to the window.

"What do you see when you look out there?" Mr. Wakefield asks, still in his deep thinker pose.

"The parking lot?"

"And?"

"And...the outside. Cars and buildings and stuff."

Cars that don't rust—they can't in such dry air. Worn-down buildings the desert has sanded smooth, stucco siding cracked from blistering heat. And there's the earth itself, of course. The dirt, the cacti. I know there are places with green trees and blue water and yellow sunshine peeking through clouds. But I've never seen anywhere like that.

"What you see," says Mr. Wakefield, "is a world of endless possibility."

"Oh."

Mr. Wakefield finally turns from the window and motions to a chair. "Let's chat."

I sit and say goodbye to my hope that it'll be a quick meeting.

"Mr. Wilkes, I feel that you are in crisis."

I laugh.

He doesn't.

"Because of my wish, you mean?" I ask, struggling to keep a neutral face.

"Yes. What else is there?"

A world of endless possibility, I think.

"Your lack of enthusiasm distresses me. I wonder if there isn't something deeper going on." He strokes his beard while he talks. It's one of those too-perfect beards. You can tell he spends hours trimming it into the right shape.

"Um, I don't think so," I say.

"Have you thought of a wish yet?"

"Not exactly."

"Perhaps you're unconsciously limiting yourself."

I don't say anything. My gaze lands on the framed portrait of Sigmund Freud that sits on Mr. Wakefield's desk, in the spot where other people would have a picture of their family. Dude is so freaking weird.

"It makes sense," he continues. "You're young. You've only touched the surface of knowing. How can you possibly tap into the infinite?"

"I sort of think it's the other way around," I say. "It's *the infinite* that's the problem."

Mr. Wakefield frowns. "Go on."

I think for a moment. "Well, say you only have two choices. You can like red or you can like blue. It's easy to look at those two colors and decide that, between them, you like red. But when you consider all the colors in the world, then what? You could narrow it down to liking red, but what *shade* of red? Some of them are practically the same. And some are way different. But they're all red, so you like them all, because who ever said a person can like just one color and that's *it*? But you're asking me to pick one color and like it for the rest of my life."

My voice gets louder as I talk. It makes me feel like Merrill with his rants. Even more so when I see the look of surprise and concern on Mr. Wakefield's face.

"And," I go on, "every time you talk to someone who's already picked their color, some adult who's had their whole life to think about their decision, you know what they say? They regret what they chose. So now they're stuck their whole life with orange, but they've realized orange was a shit color to start with."

"Well, that's very…" Mr. Wakefield trails off.

I wait.

"You've been having a tough year, haven't you, Eldon?"

Oh, spectacular. He's ready to psychoanalyze me.

"I guess?"

"It's no secret that wishing has caused you some problems. It makes sense that you'd resent it."

"What, because of football? Because I'm not as popular now? I don't care about that."

"Of course you care. Your entire identity is wrapped up in your social standing. You must feel very lost. But that wasn't what I was referring to. I was talking about your sister."

I look away from him.

"You can share your feelings with me. Nothing you say here will leave this room."

"I'm fine," I say through clenched teeth.

"All right. Just remember, you're not alone. We've all lost loved ones."

I want to scream at him, flip his desk over, punch him in his bearded face. I'm sick of people saying I *lost* Ebba. I didn't *lose* her. I know exactly where she is. I know where she is, and I can't fix what happened, and that almost feels worse than losing her outright.

My mind flashes to my sister in the nursing home in Las Vegas. After the accident, the doctors put Ebba's body back together, and we thought that meant she was going to be OK. We had all the hope in the world. Until a doctor sat my family down and had a chat about brain injuries. Told us how our brain sends signals to our legs to walk, our mouths to chew, our lungs to pull in air. And Ebba's brain, well, it forgot how to do those things. It forgot, and it will never, ever remember.

It turns out, there's more than one way to be dead.

I take a deep breath. Count to ten. This counting-to-ten strategy was recommended a few months ago while my dad and I sat in this very office. It was after Fletcher fucking Hale, the fight, and my suspension.

"Eldon…" Mr. Wakefield says cautiously. "Perhaps you'd like to hear about my wish? Get a different perspective?"

No, I don't want to hear about his wish. I want him to shut up and leave me alone. But I shrug.

"When I was a young man," he says, gearing up, "I dreamed of being traveled. Educated. I had this idealistic existence in my head, a sort of East Coast prep school life. Which was why I wished to travel to Europe."

I'm not sure what Europe has to do with the East Coast, but I'm not going to argue. I take a deep breath and keep counting silently.

"I ended up in Vienna. Which is in Austria, you know."

Said like he's sure I *don't* know.

Which I didn't.

"I wanted to go to the zoo there. I'd read a novel about it, a very idealistic novel…but anyway, that's not the point. I had some time to kill one afternoon, and I chanced upon a tour of Sigmund Freud's neighborhood."

Jesus. It's like his superhero origin story.

Mr. Wakefield goes on and on about the tour and everything he learned about Freud's life and work and how it changed his life. An epiphany. I wait until he's done to ask the obvious question.

"If you loved Vienna so much, why'd you come back to Madison?"

Of all places.

"This is my *home*, Mr. Wilkes. This is where I knew I could do the most good."

"Then why didn't you get a psychology degree and become a therapist?"

Mr. Wakefield falters. "The point is, my wish changed my life for the better."

Yeah, or gave him a glimpse of a world, a life, that'll never be his, and left him in a constant state of wanting.

"OK, cool," I say abruptly. "Thanks for the perspective."

"You're welcome." He looks satisfied. He probably *waits* for the chance to tell that story.

I glance at the clock near the door. English is over, and I'm supposed to be in government.

"I should get to class."

"Yes, I suppose. But think about what I said. Wishing is an amazing opportunity."

"Yeah, I get it."

"Maybe you could talk to other wishers?" Mr. Wakefield suggests, guiding me to the door. He's hesitant at first, feeling out the idea as he speaks. But as he continues, his voice gains confidence. "Yes, that's it! It will be your project. The Wish Project. You can interview people and ask them about their wishes, learn about the full spectrum of experiences before deciding on your own. Make a truly informed decision."

I'm skeptical. I already know most people's wishes.

Don't I?

I know the wishes of the people I'm close to. I know the most famous wishes. Beyond that, I'm not so sure. It's a small town, but there are still a lot of people in Madison—relatively speaking—and every one older than eighteen has made a wish.

Mr. Wakefield is ridiculous, but this idea is kinda interesting.

"I'll think about it," I say. That's the best Mr. Wakefield is going to get. He seems to know that and beams at me.

"Wonderful!"

He's so thrilled that it makes me wonder if anyone has taken his suggestions seriously before. Of course, his usual recommendations involve dream analysis, and no one wants to tell the principal their dreams.

"This could really benefit you, Mr. Wilkes. I can give you some resources to guide you along the way. You might want to start at the museum. In fact, I'll call and tell them about your project. They might be interested in getting a copy of your final—"

"Thanks for your help, Mr. Wakefield," I say, moving toward the door.

"Don't you want to discuss your approach?"

"I'll let you know how it turns out."

I leave the office and hurry toward government class before Mr. Wakefield decides we should partner up on this wish project. No one in town would have a heart-to-heart about their wish with him hovering nearby.

How has Mr. Wakefield not realized that most people don't want to be analyzed? Most people want the secret part of themselves to *stay* secret. After all, what's the point of analyzing a part of yourself that can't be changed?

CHAPTER 8

COUNTDOWN: 19 DAYS

It's a regular Friday night. Merrill and I are chilling at one of the skeleton houses in our neighborhood before going to the hot springs.

There's a house we like best, the last one in the row. We've been coming here for an eternity. Despite the age of the half-built house, the wood frame is still sturdy enough to support us. We climb to the top, underneath what would have been the pitched roof. The Mustang is parked in the driveway, as if this is a real home, as if we live here.

"Seems like this wish project will be a lot of work," Merrill says.

"It's just talking to people."

"Exactly. That's a lot of work."

I shrug. My feet swing back and forth in the air over a living room where no one will do any living.

"Look, Eldo. Be straight with me. Why are you having so much trouble with this?"

I hesitate before replying. I'm not entirely sure of the answer myself. "It's a big deal. I don't want to get it wrong."

"Since when do you care about that?"

"Probably since I started getting everything wrong."

Merrill rolls his eyes. "You're such a tragic figure. A girl dumped you for someone else. You're not the star of the football team anymore. How *do* you survive?"

"It's more than that, asshole."

"Yeah? Enlighten me."

But I don't know how to explain it without sounding pathetic. For the past few months, it feels like I've been lost in a fog. Nothing in my life feels real anymore. It feels like *I'm* not real anymore.

I feel like a phantom. Does a phantom have desires? If not, how can a phantom wish?

I can't tell Merrill that I worry I won't figure myself out, and if I don't make the right wish, then I'll be lost in that fog forever. What if my wish is my last chance to make sense of life, of who I am? If I don't meet the deadline, I can pretty much give up on ever being a real person again.

"So how would all this work?" Merrill asks when he realizes I'm not going to answer.

"It's not some epic homework assignment, Merrill. I'll talk to people about their wishes."

"And then what?"

"I'll figure out which wishes worked. Which wishes have the

best results." The more I talk, the more I sound infected by Mr. Wakefield's optimism. I sigh. "Look, the idea is probably crap. But it's all I've got."

In the distance, a coyote howls. The sun sinks behind the mountains, and the sky becomes tie-dyed shades of pink and orange. I've heard that desert sunsets are the most breathtaking in the world. I don't know if that's true. I've never seen any others.

Finally, Merrill says, "All right then. Let's do this."

"You'll help?" I ask, surprised.

"What else have I got going on? Take a look around you, Eldo. Madison ain't exactly hoppin'."

"OK then." I try to sound nonchalant. I'm not going to hug Merrill and gush about the warm and fuzzy feelings I'm having. But damn, it's good to remember he has my back.

"Why don't we start with your wish?" I say.

Merrill laughs. "If you don't know my wish, we've got a serious problem. You taking too many hits to the head in practice?"

Yeah, I know Merrill's wish. After all, he's talked about wishing for perfect eyesight since we were kids. But I'm a little unclear on the details. On how he *feels* about his decision. Not because he hasn't told me. I suspect he *has*. It's just, well, these past few months, I've been kinda caught up in my own stuff.

I don't know how to admit that though, how to admit I'm a freaking terrible friend. So instead, I push away my guilt, lean back against a splintery wooden beam, and ask, "How'd you know you were making the right choice?"

Merrill thinks for a moment. He takes off his glasses and cleans them on his shirt before speaking. "It's not like I didn't question it. I had people left and right telling me I was a dumbass. Saying crap like, 'Wish for money, and you can *pay* to have your eyes fixed.' Only surgery can go wrong, you know? What if I ended up blind?"

If he ended up blind, he'd have to kiss his dream of being a pilot goodbye. Same reason he had to fix his eyes in the first place. You can't fly with terrible vision. I know this, because Merrill's dad took cruel pleasure in pointing that out when we were ten.

"I get your internal struggle," Merrill goes on. "I'm just saying I never had one. From the start, I knew what I wanted. Even when my dad started freaking out, telling me I had to pull us out of our current economic situation. Which, as you know, is *no bueno*. It was pretty messed up. Dad didn't get on Royce's case. Just 'cause I was born second, it's my job to save the family? Meanwhile, my big brother is in his room with enough weed to supply Woodstock. He's eating through half our grocery budget, and my dad's booze takes the other half. Yet *I'm* the one who gets lectured?"

If Merrill wants to call it *getting lectured*, I won't correct him. But the walls of his house are as thin as mine, and I've heard shouts and crashes. There's a reason we don't hang out at either of our homes. There's too much rage in Merrill's house and too much sorrow in mine. Either way, it's suffocating.

When we were kids, I practically lived at Merrill's. That was before cancer killed his mom, before his dad got bitter and angry and perpetually drunk. Back then, Merrill's house felt like a *good* place. And Merrill's mom, she was an angel.

Although, that wasn't always true. Once upon a time, Merrill's mom did something awful, so awful that her wish was for the entire town to forget it. The wish worked so well that afterward, even *she* couldn't remember what she'd done. And it haunted her. Probably, what we can imagine is way worse than anything we've actually done. Merrill's mom spent the rest of her life atoning for her mystery sin by trying to be the best possible version of herself. She was one of those people who was so kind that simply being with her made you happy.

If she hadn't died, who knows how different Merrill's life would be?

But I'm doing it again, tuning Merrill out. He's getting heated. His words are coming faster, and he's forgetting to breathe.

"—my dad though. *Everyone* told me to wish for money. And yeah, there was a moment. OK, a *few* moments, when I started to think maybe they were right. Maybe money *was* the solution to all my problems. Maybe being rich was better than flying. But it was *my* wish, the only one I'd ever get. I didn't want cash. I wanted the fucking *sky*."

I wait quietly for Merrill to recover from his rant. When his face returns to its normal color, I ask, "So what happened on your wish day? What specifically happened?"

"Same thing that happens for everyone. The mayor was there, being his usual creepy self. I swear, that dude was a serial killer in a past life. Hell, maybe he's a serial killer in *this* life."

I laugh but have a flash of dread too. I'm definitely not looking forward to dealing with Mayor Fontaine. I'm not saying he's a serial killer, yeah? But the guy makes me ridiculously uncomfortable.

"The mayor had his goons with him," Merrill says. "What's up with *that*, Eldo? Why does he need soldiers? They kept their eyes on me the entire way to the cave. What were they expecting me to *do*?"

"But they left you alone after you were inside, right?"

Merrill nods. "Yeah. Once I was in, I followed the map—all that stuff Mr. Wakefield went over with you. I found the right cavern and made my wish. And that was it."

The most important moment in a Madison kid's life, and it boils down to a few minutes inside a cave. It's that simple to transform from a regular person into someone who's had their wildest dreams come true.

"Did your eyesight change immediately?" I ask, wondering how, months later, I'm only *now* thinking to question this.

Merrill looks away from me, gazes at the fading sunset. "I guess so. It was kinda hard to tell, since the cave is pitch-black, and

I only had a freaking candle to see by. And what's the deal with that, by the way? Hasn't this town ever heard of flashlig—"

"But it worked," I interrupt.

"Yeah, of course it worked."

"And you're happy?"

Merrill shrugs and flashes a wide grin at me. "As happy as anyone can be in this town."

"But you keep wearing those glasses."

Merrill sighs. "We've talked about this. I feel uncomfortable without them."

"I still don't get it."

Merrill takes off his glasses again and looks at them for a long moment. "My aunt told me this story once. She was fat, you know? And her wish was to be skinny. She said it wasn't right, having it happen so fast. It would've been different if she exercised and lost weight the way other people do. But when she wished, it happened all at once. She said she felt like an imposter, like she was wearing someone else's skin. I get it. After a lifetime of wearing glasses, my face feels naked without them." Merrill puts his glasses back on and smiles wryly. "So I got fake lenses put in. Best of both worlds, right?"

For years, Merrill complained about his glasses. How had wishing turned something he hated into something he *wanted*? "Sounds to me like your wish isn't so cut-and-dried after all."

"Nothing is, Eldo."

The sky is mostly dark now. Stars replace the sunset. Out in the desert, creatures creep out of their daytime hiding places. In the hills, the wish cave is dormant, waiting for the next birthday. Waiting to change someone's life.

"Eldo?" Merrill asks.

I look at him.

"Are we going to the hot springs or not?"

"Yeah," I say. "Let's go."

I swing my feet up and walk across the beams to the unfinished staircase. Wishing can wait until tomorrow. Tonight, there's a party.

✶ ✶ ✶

Teenagers in Madison are always getting lectured about safety. Reminded not to let the boredom of living here make us reckless. Clearly, we don't heed those warnings, because partying at the hot springs is definitely a hazard.

Still, no adults try to stop it. Sheriff Crawford never busts us. Even Mayor Fontaine is willing to overlook our parties, which is much more surprising. I guess it's because they were teenagers in Madison once. *They* went to the hot springs to party too. A couple of kids I know have found their parents' names in old graffiti. So-and-so loves so-and-so forever. Mostly, it turned out to not be true.

In one of the caves near the springs, way in the back, there's some Eldon + Juniper with a heart around it bullshit. She drew it right after we started dating. I don't go in that cave anymore.

The most dangerous part about the springs isn't *getting* there—it's coming back. At least on the way there, you're probably sober.

Going in, the hot springs are a half-hour walk from the road, mostly through a narrow canyon. Coming back, who knows how long it might take. I swear, Merrill and I were out there for hours once, thinking we'd gotten lost. It was winter, and he was drunk and blubbering about hypothermia.

It's not an easy hike either. The first half is level, then there's a lot of rock scrambling. You have to be careful, because even with flashlights, it's hard to see. There are dark patches between the rocks, invitations to twist an ankle. At least we don't have to stress about rattlesnakes. Someone wished the snakes out of Madison a long time ago.

This one part of the hike, the hardest part to do drunk, is so steep, you have to use a rope to get up or down. The kids who go rock climbing instead of playing football after school say it's nothing. They don't touch the rope. Show-offs.

The danger is totally worth it though, because the hike ends in paradise.

The spring isn't one big pool. There are probably fifteen of them, going way back into the canyon. Think clear blue water with vegetation growing around the sides. The water is as warm as a hot tub, and as long as you don't duck your head under—brain-eating parasites, yeah?—you'll be fine.

Surrounding the springs are boulders to sit on, ledges to start campfires, tons of little caves. It's the only place in Madison where teenagers can be alone.

Merrill and I show up late, so we don't get stuck with cooler duty. The only thing worse than making the hike at night is making it with a cooler full of beer. Let the rock-climbing show-offs deal with that.

The party's packed, and everyone's already drunk or stoned. There's a fire blazing even though it's a million degrees outside. Thankfully, someone remembered a radio. It sucks when the only background noise is howls and buzzing insects.

Merrill and I make the rounds, checking out who's here. Pretty much everyone. Where else would they be?

"Eldon, *hi!*"

Someone throws their arm around my neck. I pull away. Penelope Rowe. She reeks of some fruity-sweet drink. When she wobbles, I grab onto her *Save the Earth* T-shirt to keep her from toppling over.

"I'm *so* glad you came," she says.

"Oh yeah?"

"Yeah, there was something I wanted to ask you," she gushes. "About the bake sale?"

"I have no idea what you're talking about."

Penelope giggles. "Me either."

I always like Penelope a lot better when she's drunk. She's exhausting when she's sober. Not that I spend a ton of time around her anymore. My idea of entertainment isn't hanging out with my ex-girlfriend's best friend.

"Come get a drink," Penelope says, grabbing my hand and pulling me toward a cooler.

I look at Merrill and raise my eyebrows.

It's the old code. Me saying, *I could so hook up with this girl tonight if I want to.*

Merrill winces and shakes his head. *Dude, you would so regret it in the morning.*

"We'll be there in a minute," I tell Penelope, pulling my hand back.

"OK. Find me!"

"Way too drunk," Merrill says when she's gone. "Besides, she'd probably try to sign you up for a social action committee *postcoitus.*"

We walk around the party, drink cheap beer, stop to talk to people. When someone asks about my wish, I keep walking. We check out the sophomore girls sitting in one of the pools in their underwear. It happens every party. Some girls show up and realize they "forgot" their bathing suits, say it isn't a big deal, because their underwear covers just as much. Pretend they don't know how see-though it is, that all the guys are watching them.

A while back, these girls would've been all over me the second

I got here. It used to be that when I came to these parties, I was treated like a god. I'm not saying I necessarily *deserved* that attention, but yeah, I kinda miss it.

"Well," says Merrill, watching the girls, "looks like I know where I'll be hanging out."

"We just got here," I say, which translates into, *please don't ditch me. I don't want to be alone right now.*

Merrill shrugs.

We wander more. Flirt with some girls. Joke with some football players. I'm feeling good and well on my way to drunk when I see Juniper.

She's sitting on the edge of one of the pools. Her pants legs are rolled up, and her feet are in the water. The moonlight makes her skin shimmer. She laughs, and the sound cuts across the party and gets into my head, reminds me of how good it felt when she laughed at one of *my* jokes. Then she leans on Calvin Boyd, who's sitting next to her, and the vision of her like a goddamn water nymph collapses.

"Shit," I say, still watching her. Watching *them.*

"Easy there," says Merrill.

"I can't believe she showed up with him."

"They're dating, Eldo. What do you expect?"

I know what I *didn't* expect. I didn't expect her to look so happy.

"Come on," Merrill says. "Let's not stalk any ex-girlfriends tonight."

I let him lead me back to the cooler.

But I can't erase the image from my mind. Seeing Calvin with Juniper is like watching an imposter take over my life. *I* was the one who should have been by Juniper's side making her laugh, gazing into her eyes, feeling her body next to mine.

"Well, Merrill," I say. "I think I'll be getting very drunk tonight."

* * *

And I do.

I lose track of time. I lose track of Merrill too. Last I see him, he's with the sophomores in their hot spring. He's cracking jokes, but I can tell he's gearing up for a rant. Probably one of his ridiculous conspiracy theories. Like every city having their own wish cave and each thinking they're the only ones while we all try to hide it from one another.

I consider sticking around to point out his hypocrisy—something I only do when I'm buzzed. Despite all his conspiracy theories, he sure as hell didn't reject his own wish. I know saying so will only lead to a fight, so instead, I wander deeper into the party.

I look away when I see Fletcher Hale chatting with a freshman girl I don't really know. It infuriates me that he'd even show up at a party. You'd think having someone's death on your hands would make you uninterested in normal high school activities. But I push Fletcher from my thoughts. I'm not gonna fight with anyone tonight. Not even him.

I wander and I drink, and eventually, everything blurs, softens, and I start to feel numb.

I don't remember getting in the hot springs, but I must have, because my shorts are wet. I have no idea where my shirt is. I have a fuzzy memory of talking with some nerdy kids from debate club. I think we took a selfie together.

For some reason, I think of Norie Havermayer. I get it in my head that I need to call her, ask her why she isn't at the party. I pull out my phone and scroll through my contacts, then remember I don't have her number.

I land on my sister's name instead. I press the call button.

It goes straight to voice mail. *"Hey, it's Ebba! Say something fascinating, and I'll call you back!"*

There's a beep. I don't speak, just breathe into the phone like some horror movie killer.

Despite our financial issues, my parent's will probably pay to keep Ebba's phone on for another year. Another decade. As long as they're alive, I'll be able to call my sister. Hear her voice and make believe that she'll listen to my message and call me back.

For weeks after the accident, I'd pick up my phone and start texting Ebba. It was such a part of my routine that it took a while for my brain to remember there was no one on the other end.

I hang up the phone.

"Hey," I shout to a freshman kid walking by. "Do you have Norie's number?"

He looks at me like I'm speaking another language.

I put my phone in my pocket, push both Ebba and Norie from my mind, and wander the party again.

I end up in a weird conversation with Dessie Greerson. For some reason, I keep calling her Jessie, and she keeps laughing like it's hilarious. I don't have a clue what I'm doing.

"So, Eldon Wilkes," she says. "Someone has a birthday coming up."

I laugh. "Yep, that's a thing."

"And what are you going to wish for on your super special day?" She thinks she's being seductive, which makes me laugh harder.

"Who the hell knows? World peace, maybe."

She raises an eyebrow. "Naughty boy. That's against the rules."

I grin at her, the slow, lazy smile that's worked on pretty much every girl I've ever talked to.

"What're you gonna do about it?" I ask.

She tries to match my suggestive stance. "You wanna go somewhere quiet?"

I consider telling Dessie that nowhere is quiet enough to block out my thoughts.

"There's a cave in the back," I suggest.

I don't know if Juniper sees us walk past. I make a point to not look at her. I don't look at the graffiti on the cave wall either. Eldon + Juniper in a big, sloppy heart. Because we're ancient history, and I don't care anymore. From here on out, I'm all about the future.

"So, Jessie," I say, and she giggles. "What are we gonna do now that we're all alone?"

I can tell from her expression that she has a few ideas.

CHAPTER 9

COUNTDOWN: 18 DAYS

When I wake up Saturday morning, the room is shaking. At first, I think I'm still drunk, then I realize it's an earthquake. Madison's earthquakes aren't serious. But when you feel the way I do, they can still make you puke.

I curl up in the fetal position and wait for the shaking to stop.

Hours later, long after the earthquake ended, I still haven't gotten out of bed or recovered from the party. Merrill texts in the late afternoon to ask if I'm down for another round at the hot springs.

Yeah, right. I have an uncomfortable suspicion that I embarrassed myself the night before. Especially considering the text I get from Dessie Greerson starting, About last night... I don't read the rest of the message. In fact, I don't read any messages for the rest of the day.

Instead, I occupy myself by playing mind-numbing games on my phone and listening to the silence coming from Ebba's room.

My parents never told me to stay out of her room. It was one of those things we all simply knew to do. We keep the door shut and pretend it exists in another dimension. You can feel it there next to you, but you can't see it. Definitely can't access it.

When Ebba still lived with us, she was *loud*. Always talking on the phone in her high-pitched, breathy voice about boys and school and who hated who and everything else in the world. Her voice flew around the house like a tornado.

Compared to her, I don't have a voice at all. I'm like my mom, keeping my words locked up tight. Better to stay quiet, because if you don't, the words might never stop coming. And when you're spouting off everything on your mind, it's hard to pretend you're doing fantastic.

The silence is interrupted by a knock on my door.

"Yeah?"

"Hungry?" my dad asks, poking his head into the room. He's using his crutches.

"Yeah, sure. I'll be right there."

"All right." But he continues to hover in the doorway. "Eldon...are you doing OK, bud?"

"I'm hungover."

He frowns but doesn't lecture me. He knows how it is in Madison.

"I mean lately. You haven't been yourself."

I want to bury my head under the pillow until he goes away. Instead, I say, "Well, it's sort of a shitty time."

"Because of football?"

I almost laugh out loud. Of all things, *football*.

"I know it's rough," my dad continues. "You never really had to work at it before."

There's nothing I can say without destroying his vision for my future, so I mutter, "It's fine, Dad. Really. I'll get through it."

"I know your breakup didn't help."

Oh God. We should have stayed on football.

"It's not a big deal."

I get up, signaling an end to the conversation, but my dad doesn't take the hint. "I want you to know if you ever want to talk about anything, anything at all, I'm here. And if you want to do some extra training in the evenings, I'll help you with that too."

"Thanks. I appreciate it."

And I do. I wish he *could* help me. I wish it were that simple.

My dad smiles. "Anything for my boy."

We walk to the kitchen together, my dad limping along and me holding back, letting him keep up.

* * *

Later, when I'm in my room again, I try to chase away the silence with Basin and Range Radio. I tune in to hear, "...*your host, Robert Nash. Tonight we're taking a break from sky watching to talk to a woman who's had a close encounter with the infamous Blue Diamond Sand Yeti...*"

I snort. Robert Nash must be hard up for material.

The woman begins her spiel about the yeti, and I turn on my side and face the wall. When we were little, Ebba and I talked about cutting a secret tunnel between our rooms. We built forts out of pillows and blankets and denied our parents entry. When we didn't have money for board games, Ebba and I made our own. I taught her how to play poker; she taught me how to French braid her doll's hair. She'd hide scraps of paper in my room, with *Tag! You're it!* in her loopy, girlie handwriting. I'd hide them back, and when she found them, she'd collapse with shrieks and giggles.

After the accident, I tore up my room looking for one of those scraps of paper. I emptied every drawer, even pulled my freaking mattress off its frame. My dad had to physically restrain me, wrapping his arms around me and saying, "It a piece of paper, Eldon. It's just a piece of paper." It meant more than that, though I couldn't explain why.

I still haven't found one.

I still haven't wrapped my mind around the idea that all those moments Ebba and I shared, well, they're *it*. They're all I have, because there won't be any new moments. We'll never create new memories.

My entire history is tied up in my sister's. My life is a

slideshow of events that only she would understand. It's no use explaining our inside jokes to anyone. No one else has lived them. Every single memory Ebba and I shared is now mine alone.

The woman on the radio drones on about the yeti, and Robert Nash says, "*Yes, Mmm-hmm.*" I press my face into my pillow. When my eyes start to sting, when tears start to fall, I don't hold back. I let out all I have to keep hidden at school, at practice, at parties. I let myself need my sister. I let myself hate Fletcher Hale for slamming his car into her and taking her away from me. I let my loneliness rip me apart.

By the time I'm wiping my eyes and blowing my nose, Robert Nash is signing off for the night. I turn off the radio and leave my room. I linger outside Ebba's bedroom and pretend it's not negative space. Pretend I can swing open the door and step into a few months ago, before any of this happened.

I've never been good at pretending.

I take a breath to steady myself, trying not to break down again, and continue down the narrow hallway.

I'm standing in the kitchen, filling a glass with cloudy tap water, when I hear a noise outside. Something bangs against the side of the house.

I turn off the water and listen. It's not the wind, no question about that. There's someone outside.

If this were a different house, if my dad loved another sport, there might be a baseball bat within reach. But there are only foot-balls in our house. Hardly protection against criminals. I take the next best thing—my mom's cast-iron skillet.

I step out the back door and into the warm desert night with its howling wind and howling coyotes.

The noise comes again.

I creep slowly alongside the house, the skillet gripped tightly in my hand. Really, it may be a better weapon than a bat. Harder to wield, yeah, but much more powerful.

There's only a sliver of moon, but the light seeping out of the kitchen and coming from Merrill's house next door is enough to see by. Carefully, I step around the corner.

And sure enough, there's a man standing in the shadows.

I don't swing the skillet. I sigh. "Barnabas."

Barnabas Fairley looks up from rummaging in the trash can. His long gray beard is tangled, his hair in matted dreadlocks. He winks at me.

"It's late," I say. "You're going to wake up my parents."

He's already gone back to sorting through our trash. Barnabas's bicycle is likely parked in the front yard, his oversize bag of aluminum cans—and who knows what else—tied to the seat. After tonight's prowl, that bag will grow bigger and bigger until it looks ready to burst. Then Barnabas will take his junk to wherever he sells it, the bag will deflate, and the whole process will start again.

"You won't find much," I say. Our trash is mostly scraps of paper from Ma's coupon cutting.

That doesn't deter Barnabas.

I watch him for a minute.

"Hey, Barnabas, will you tell me about your wish?"

The grizzled old man who dresses in rags and rides his rusty bike around town, never speaking to anyone, turns to me and raises himself to his full height. He meets my gaze.

"My wish is soon," I continue. "I'm trying to figure out what to wish for."

He smiles the saddest smile I've ever seen, clears his throat, and speaks.

"My wish…" Barnabas begins. His eyes get misty. The sad smile comes again. "My wish was a mistake."

"Tell me," I say.

And he does. He tells me the whole thing, pausing only to clear his throat and wipe his eyes. I listen, and even though I've heard the story before—parts of it, at least—it's different coming from him. It twists my gut in knots. Makes me want to take Barnabas inside with me, give him a family.

When he's done talking, he ducks his head and goes back to pawing through the trash.

"Thanks," I say softly.

He waves a hand at me. I don't know if he's saying *you're welcome* or telling me to leave. I watch him for a moment longer.

"Hey, Barnabas?" I ask. "You want this skillet?"

He looks back at me, and his eyes light up like I offered him a second chance at wishing. I hand over the skillet.

My mom is going to be pissed.

* * *

I'm surprised to find Ma in the kitchen. My eyes go to the peg where her skillet usually hangs, but she doesn't mention its absence.

"Do you want tea?" she asks, lifting the kettle from the stove.

I nod and slide into my usual place at the kitchen table.

The scent of mint and chamomile fills the room. It's what my mom always drinks when she can't sleep. If honey is selling cheap at the Tuttle farm, she'll add that too.

"Barnabas is out there," I say.

"I heard."

"Did he wake you?"

"I wasn't sleeping."

She places a steaming mug in front of me and sits down.

"He told me about his wish," I say.

My mom laughs. "The entire town knows his wish."

"I've never heard it from him."

Ma sighs, like she can't understand me. "It's all the same, Eldon."

It's not. It's not the same at all. When you hear a story through the grapevine, you can distance yourself from it. You can tell yourself it's only a story. You don't have to *feel* anything.

"Don't you think it's sad?" I ask. "He's so lonely."

"Lots of people are lonely."

From her sharp tone, I get the feeling she's talking about herself. Which is ridiculous. Her wish basically guaranteed she'd never be alone.

"Are *you* lonely?" I ask incredulously.

She takes a sip from her tea. I have my own mug clasped in my hands, so I know the tea is hot enough to burn, but Ma doesn't wince.

After a long pause, she says, "It's been a long time since I've had real friends."

I hesitate. I'm treading in dangerous water. "Because of your wish?"

She nods curtly. "This town has never looked at me the same. Sure, people talk to me in the grocery store or invite me over for coffee. But I'll always be pathetic to them. The girl who had to trick someone into loving her."

"I don't think that's true."

"It *is* true," Ma says. She taps a cigarette from her pack and pulls a chipped, clay ashtray toward her. "And I've accepted it. My only hope is that you learn from my mistakes."

"I am learning. From *everyone's* mistakes. I'm collecting wishes."

"I suppose that means you're still trying to decide on a wish." She exhales, and smoke mingles with steam rising from the tea.

I don't respond. I focus my gaze on the ashtray, which is an

Ebba original. My sister loved giving people handmade gifts. I can't even count how many macaroni necklaces she made for me. I threw all that stuff out, because I always assumed there'd be more coming. I didn't know how little time we had left.

"Eldon," Ma says when the silence has stretched on for too long.

I wait for more. But that's all she says. My name, in a weary tone. A tone filled with disappointment.

"You don't even know if it will work," I say. "If I try to save Ebba."

"No. I don't know. But I need you to try."

"The doctors said there's nothing—"

"Those doctors aren't specialists," Ma says sharply. "If we had the money to fly in specialists, to put her in a better facility, she might have a chance."

If only Sheriff Crawford hadn't rushed Ebba to Vegas immediately after the accident. If he'd kept her in Madison, maybe I could have wished for her health. It's too late for that now—it would break the golden rule of wishing. Money is our last hope, but I don't think it's enough.

I watch my mom. She watches her cigarette burn. I can feel the words she'll never dare say: *Ebba would do it for you.*

And she would have. Ebba would have done anything for anyone.

But that doesn't mean it's the *right* choice.

I have to wonder, if I don't make the wish my mom wants me to, will she ever forgive me? And if she doesn't, will my dad side with her? He will, of course. He has to. What will life be like if my entire family is lost to me?

One day, I might end up as alone as Barnabas Fairley.

CHAPTER 10

THE WISH HISTORY: BARNABAS FAIRLEY

C rack open that history book again.

And dig this:

We're taking our time machine way back, rewinding to the tail end of the psychedelic sixties.

Take a look around town. Even in Madison, kids are turning on, tuning in, and dropping out. Check them out, all these teenagers with flowers in their hair. These kids, they think they can change the world. After all, if a man can walk on the moon, anything is possible.

Skim past the Summer of Love. Browse through pages of peace signs and fringed vests. Take a look, but don't linger too long.

Because this is Barnabas Fairley's story.

And he's not feeling groovy.

The dude can't pick up a newspaper without a growing sense of dread.

Riots in New York.

A doped-up, murderous cult in California.

And the war.

Most of all, the war.

The year is 1969, and if you ask Barnabas, the world is terrifying.

Look at him, alone in his room, studying for Friday's physics test. Seventeen-year-old Barnabas Fairley, who's still rocking his 1950s flat-top. Kids at school joke that his mom picks out his clothes. Which, you know, she does.

Let's dive from the pages of this book into Barnabas's mind. Right now, it's not the scary, mixed-up world that's making Barnabas hyperventilate.

It's the thought of failing.

Good going, Mr. Walsh. You just had to give your students that lecture about the importance of Friday's test. How it's a huge part of their final grades. How if they fail the test, they'll probably fail the class.

Fail, fail, fail.

Never mind that Barnabas is one of the top students at Madison High School. Never mind that Mr. Walsh is overly dramatic and makes every test sound like the most important exam ever.

Barnabas isn't thinking clearly.

No, he's having a complete breakdown. The fear of failing grows and grows until no rational thought is left inside his head.

Until it isn't only his mind that's impacted.

It's his heart.

His lungs.

The fear of failing takes over his entire body until he's sure he's having a heart attack.

Until he becomes a hundred percent convinced he's dying.

He's not dying, of course.

Flip ahead to the next page in Madison's history. Stop on the part where his panic starts to recede.

Watch as Barnabas's heart rate returns to normal. As his vision clears. As his lungs suck in air and push it out. Exactly the way lungs are supposed to.

Scan ahead to Barnabas picking up his textbook again and studying, as if nothing strange has happened.

And notice what Barnabas doesn't do.

He doesn't say a word about what happened. To anyone.

Can you blame him? After all, this is 1969 Madison. There's no Mr. Wakefield running around school, making sure everyone's mentally sound. People in town don't know what a panic attack is. No one's going to sit with Barnabas and explain anxiety disorders.

This isn't the first time Barnabas has had a heart-attack-that's-not-a-heart-attack. It's not the second. Or the tenth. And it certainly won't be the last.

Read page after page of Barnabas's anxiety. Sometimes over things that matter, and sometimes over nothing at all. Because that's the cruel way anxiety operates.

"Boy's all wired up," Barnabas overhears his dad say to a neighbor. "Never seen someone so nervous in my life. Say boo, *and he'll pass out."*

But if you jump ahead, you'll learn news that Barnabas's dad doesn't know. Maybe, for the first time in his life, Barnabas has something serious to worry about. Something that's keeping even the most cool and collected of his peers up at night:

The draft.

The draft, draft, draft, draft.

It was bad enough when it was simply war.

The war is distant. Barnabas can lock it in a box and put it on a shelf in his mind. The war has nothing to do with him, with his life in Madison. He worries about it, of course *he worries, but if he tries his hardest, he can pretend it'll never touch him.*

But the draft? There's no locking that *in a box. There's no escaping it.*

Lucky for Barnabas, his wish day is approaching. It's his way out. He can't stop the war, as that would be against the rules. You can't wish for anything that'd impact the world outside Madison. *But maybe, just maybe, he can stop himself from being drafted.*

Are you ready to see how that turns out? Skim until Barnabas is in the wish cave.

And see how, once he's on the brink of wishing, he starts to get anxious.

He can feel Old Mayor Fontaine watching him. And yeah, the mayor is a good guy. He's not the judgmental type. But let's not forget, this is Madison, where life is football and mining and the American flag waving in the breeze. Sure, it's the sixties, but the old timers aren't exactly onboard with the dirty hippies and their peaceful ideals.

Mayor Fontaine believes in bravery and honor.

And here's Barnabas Fairley, about to dodge the draft.

Who cares that it's through a wish? Who cares that no one will ever report him? As far as the world will know, his number simply won't be called. *The wish might not even work. Barnabas isn't positive it won't break the rules of wishing.*

But all Barnabas is thinking about is how Mayor Fontaine will look at him. Of how disgusted he'll be.

And for the rest of Barnabas's life, the words *draft dodger* will hang over his head.

Barnabas's chest constricts. His heart beats faster and faster and faster until he feels like it's going to explode.

"Mayor Fontaine," Barnabas says. The echoing sound of his voice makes him jump.

"Yes, Barnabas?"

What can he say?

He wrings his hands. It's all wrong. Everything's wrong. He's been planning his wish for so long, and now he can't do it.

"Do you..." It's so hard to make the words come out. The kid can hardly breathe. "Do you think...do you think you could..."

His voice shakes. His hands shake. How much time does he have left? Can his wish expire? He has to say the words. But no, not with Mayor Fontaine staring at him. The mayor has to leave.

Will that make the mayor angry? It's hard to say. No one has ever wished in private before. Barnabas doesn't want to be the first. But more than that, he doesn't want to go to war.

"I can't, with you watching, I can't..."

"Spit it out, Barnabas," the mayor says. He doesn't say it unkindly, but Barnabas knows even the most patient people have a limit.

Barnabas needs to be strong. On this one day, this one moment in his life, he needs to fight through his anxiety.

It comes out in one burst, the words exploding before he can think them through. "Mayor Fontaine, please, with you watching, I can't... I wish you'd give me space. I need to be alone."

Look closely at the mayor's face. See the horror and pity.

Still, he does what Barnabas asks and backs down the tunnel.

And Barnabas feels relief.

Until he doesn't.

Maybe you've already guessed: the look on the mayor's face isn't because he sees Barnabas as weak. No, his sadness comes from what Barnabas said.

I wish.

I wish you'd give me space.

Wish, wish, wish.

If Barnabas was dizzy before, well, that's nothing compared to what he experiences now. A dark feeling spreads through him.

The mayor's gone, and Barnabas holds onto a desperate hope that his wish is intact. Quickly, stumbling over his words, he makes his real wish.

But it's too late for Barnabas Fairley.

In 1969, a new wish rule is put into place. All wishers will enter the wish cave alone. This is Barnabas's legacy: every wisher will get space.

Barnabas isn't around to enjoy the outcome though. Less than a year after his wish, Barnabas Fairley is drafted.

Keep going, and watch him come home from the war.

Or does *he come home?*

A man named Barnabas Fairley returns to Madison. But can you really say he's the same boy who left?

Look at the hollowness in eyes. Dive into the darkness in his mind. Did the war change him? The things he saw, the things he did—will they ever leave him?

Would his story have been different if he came home to a town that loved and supported him? Maybe, but we'll never know. Because Barnabas Fairley wished for space, and space he'll have. Forever.

It's the 1970s, a new decade, a new outlook. But Barnabas's life remains a struggle. Maybe it's due to his anxiety. Maybe it's the memories of war or the devastating consequences of his wish. Maybe a combination of all the above.

In the end, does it really matter?

All his life, Barnabas Fairley was a worrier. He obsessed over the terrible things happening in the world. He imagined all the misfortune that might befall him. But what Barnabas didn't consider is this: when the misfortune you've been dreading comes to pass, the story doesn't end. In fact, the pain is only beginning.

Can you dig it?

CHAPTER 11

COUNTDOWN: 17 DAYS

I pound on Merrill's front door for a good minute before it swings open. But instead of Merrill, Royce Delacruz stands in front of me. He blinks at the sunshine like he's been living in a cave. Which, in a way, he has. It's been years since Royce regularly left his bedroom.

"Your brother here?" I ask.

Royce looks around sleepily, like maybe Merrill's joined him in the last three seconds. Seeing nothing to confirm this, Royce shrugs.

"Can I come in?"

"Yeah, man." Royce steps away from the door and lets me into the house.

"How've you been?" I ask.

Royce shrugs again. "It's all the same around here." He wanders away, leaving me alone in the living room.

Well, not completely alone. Benny Delacruz is passed out on the couch, snoring. His feet hang over the edge. Before he made his wish, Merrill's dad was the shortest guy at Madison High

School. Now he towers over all of us. Or he would if he ever stood up.

I make my way down the hallway, a mirror of the hall in my own house, and walk into Merrill's bedroom without knocking. It's a wreck. Clothes and books and video games are everywhere. Merrill's such a freaking slob.

His walls are covered with planes—posters, drawings, photos. But as always, my gaze immediately goes to a framed picture on his nightstand. It was taken at an air show at Nellis Air Force Base when Merrill was six. His whole family went, but it's only him and his mom in the photo. She has her arm wrapped around Merrill's skinny shoulders and is pointing to something in the sky. Merrill's looking in that direction, absolute wonder on his face. That was the day he fell in love with planes.

What gets to me the most is that Benny Delacruz must have taken the photo. It's hard to remember what he was like before Merrill's mom died. But apparently, he was a man who went on family outings. A father who saw a moment between his son and his wife and felt compelled to capture it forever.

I don't know how Merrill can look at that picture without crying.

I pick up a shoe from the ground and toss it at the bed where Merrill's still sleeping. "Morning, sunshine."

He groans.

"Are you coming to wish class with me?" I ask.

Merrill rubs at his eyes blearily. He reaches out to his night-stand and feels around for his glasses. "Dude, I got home, like, an hour ago."

"That's a no then?"

He sits up and slides his glasses onto his face, appraises me for a moment. "What did *you* do last night? You look as bad as I feel."

Oh, I cried in my room for a while and listened to Barnabas Fairley's sob story. Then drank tea with my mom while feeling like the worst son and brother in the world.

"Nothing," I say.

"Dude, the hot springs were wild last night. You know that quiet freshman girl with red hair? Well, her boyfriend showed up while she was hooking up with—"

"I need to get to class," I tell Merrill.

"All right, all right," he says, holding up his hands. "So much for keeping you up-to-date on Madison's ever exciting social drama."

I laugh and roll my eyes. "So you're not coming?"

"Dude. I can't deal with Mr. Wakefield this morning."

I don't blame him. I can think of several ways I'd like to spend my Sunday morning, and wish class isn't one of them.

❋ ❋ ❋

Penelope and Archie arrive at the community center before me again. Which isn't surprising, since I'd found myself *sans* ride.

"Where's your faggot boyfriend?" Archie asks as soon as I walk in.

Penelope whirls around in her front-row seat. "Archie. That *word*."

"Don't mind him, Penelope," I say. "Degrading people is the only way he can make himself feel important."

Penelope smiles triumphantly, happy someone sided with her, I guess. Archie glares at me. I ignore them both and slide into my seat.

I yawn and rub my eyes while Archie stalks around the room trying to look menacing. I hope he feels like a jackass when I don't act threatened.

Archie gives up and sits down when Mr. Wakefield breezes in on the balls of his feet, singing "*Hello*, wishers!"

"How are you today, Mr. Wakefield?" Penelope asks. If anyone else talked all syrupy-sweet, it would sound mocking. But Penelope is only being Penelope.

"I'm good, I'm good." He stops at the front of the room and gives Penelope a big smile. "And how is our wish girl?"

Penelope babbles about how excited she is. Her birthday is on Friday. She's about to pass to the other side and join the ranks of people who know what it's like to live postwish.

Penelope isn't my favorite person or anything, but still. I wonder if she'll be happy at the end of the experience. I hope so.

"Today," Mr. Wakefield says theatrically, "we're going to discuss *That Which Cannot Be Wished For*."

How long had it taken him to come up with that title? The guy has the biggest flair for the dramatic.

"In life," he begins, "there are rules. Wishing is no different. There are things that can't be wished for."

As if we're all sitting around thinking wishing is a giant free-for-all. We're well aware of its limitations.

"And who knows the *golden* rule?" Mr. Wakefield asks.

Penelope's hand shoots up.

"Yes, Miss Rowe?"

"Never let an outsider find out about wishing."

"Bravo, Miss Rowe! That's exactly it. Under no circumstance are we to allow wishing to become public knowledge."

Of course we aren't allowed to tell outsiders. People would travel from all over the world to make wishes of their own. Not that they'd definitely be able to. Only people born in Madison have ever made a wish in the cave. For all we know, whatever magic is there wouldn't work for an outsider.

Either way, wishing is ours. And Madison's not big on sharing.

"And how do we go about upholding that rule?"

Penelope raises her hand again.

"Let's hear from someone else," Mr. Wakefield says. "Mr. Kildare, perhaps?"

Archie sighs as if he can't be bothered. "We don't wish for dinosaurs and shit."

I laugh.

Mr. Wakefield makes a sour face. "I believe what Mr. Kildare is saying is that we never wish for anything that would impact the world as a whole. We're careful to keep our wishes in Madison."

More stuff we already know. You can wish to be the best football player in Madison, but you can't wish to be the most famous football player in the world. You can wish to be rich or talented or intelligent, but after that, you have to make your own way in life.

You can't wish to stop wars or gain superpowers or, as Archie mentioned, have dinosaurs put back on the earth. Anything that might attract the attention of outsiders is off-limits.

Other rules: You can't physically harm someone, so mass murder is off the menu. You can't reverse time, wish for more wishes, or bring someone back from the dead. Wishes have to be kept small-scale.

"Do you have anything to add, Mr. Wilkes?"

I think for a second. "I guess I'm wondering what happens if you make an illegal wish. Does your wish get forfeited? Or does it come true with some spectacularly bad result?"

Mr. Wakefield's hesitation tells me he has no freaking clue. I'd already assumed as much.

"Well, I suppose we don't know, because it's never happened."

I wish Merrill was here. I know exactly how he feels about this subject. In fact, he ranted about it in the middle of the cafeteria a couple of weeks ago.

"Bullshit!" he'd said. "They're trying to tell us that never once, in the hundred-year history of this town, has anyone *ever* made an illegal wish?"

"That seems to be what they're saying," I'd said.

"You know what? Maybe there's no such thing as an illegal wish. Maybe that's a lie they tell to keep us in line, to make sure we only make pretty, happy wishes. But there are always rebels, Eldon. There are always people who are going to do exactly what you tell them *not* to. You think that hasn't happened? Of course it has. So ask yourself why we don't know about it. Ask yourself what happened to those people. Where did they go, Eldon?"

I'd kept my mouth shut until Merrill caught his breath and his face returned to a normal color. "Are you saying the mayor murdered them or something?"

"Of course the *mayor* wouldn't kill them. He'd have his goons do it."

"Murder people."

"*Yes.*"

"You're saying the mayor has anyone who makes an illegal wish killed."

"Yes, Eldon, that's what I'm saying. Why is this so hard for you to grasp?"

"I don't think that's happening, Merrill."

Merrill had sighed deeply. "No. You wouldn't."

I return to the present. Mr. Wakefield looks anxious to change the subject. I'm not quite ready.

"I heard about this guy in the eighties who wished to cure AIDS. No one knows what happened to him."

Mr. Wakefield says, "As far as I know, that's an urban legend."

I'm not so sure.

"I have another question," I say.

"Go on."

"Do you think maybe it's not the cave that made the rules but that someone *wished* them into place?"

"I don't know, Mr. Wilkes. There's so much we don't know about wishing. If you went to the wish museum, they'd be able to answer these questions much better than I."

He's brushing me off. We both know they won't have answers for me either. I don't call him on it though, and he continues with his lecture, talks about how wishes are confined to Madison.

Yeah, yeah, we know. Wish for money, and for the rest of your life, you'll have cash in your account at the Bank of Madison—no matter how much you withdraw. You can carry that money across town limits, no problem. But try to use an ATM somewhere else, you get nothing.

He babbles on for about five years, telling us information

we've known our entire lives. All wish class has taught me is that no one really knows a damn thing about wishing. I zone out until the door opens.

"Oh," Mr. Wakefield says as Mayor Fontaine steps into the room. "What an unexpected surprise."

From the tone of his voice, it's definitely not a *pleasant* surprise. I couldn't agree more.

The mayor surveys the room with his beady eyes. He's overweight and greasy looking, his hair slicked back with too much gel. His fingers are loaded with enough gold rings to purchase a small town. The worst part is the way he talks to people though. Like we're all inferior to him, and he's doing us a favor by giving us the time of day.

"I wanted to look in on our new wish makers." Mayor Fontaine smiles, but there's zero warmth in it.

"We're wrapping up," Mr. Wakefield says. "In fact, I was about to remind our wishers about meeting with you."

"Good. I trust you've all scheduled appointments with my secretary?" he replies, addressing us.

Penelope, Archie, and I nod.

"We're on top of things here," Mr. Wakefield says briskly. "Everything's shipshape."

The mayor gives Mr. Wakefield a penetrating look. "So you've been dealing in practicalities, not psychology?"

Mr. Wakefield pales. "Well, ah, of course psychology *is*

practical, considering the enormity of wishing and the impact it has on young—"

The mayor interrupts. "A straight answer will do."

"Yes, but in terms of wishing, nothing is ever *truly* straight-forward—"

"Wakefield, I've told you on multiple occasions that I don't want you bringing that nonsense into the classroom."

My hands clench into fists. I can't believe the mayor is cutting down Mr. Wakefield in front of us. Apparently, Penelope can't believe it either.

"Mayor Fontaine, with all due respect, Mr. Wakefield is an excellent teacher and has *very* adequately prepared us for our wish days."

The mayor smiles patronizingly at Penelope. "Yes, dear, I'm sure you're very fond of Mr. Wakefield. But wish classes serve a specific purpose, and my job as mayor is to see that purpose is achieved."

Penelope squirms in her seat. I don't blame her. Just being in the same room as Mayor Fontaine gives me the creeps.

He turns back to Mr. Wakefield, still using his I'm-talking-to-an-idiot voice. "Now, you *know* I'd like to teach these classes myself. But I'm a busy man. I simply don't have *the time* to handle every wish class on my own, which is why I've placed my trust in you to serve as my ambassador."

"I understand," Mr. Wakefield says quietly.

"Then see that you do the job properly."

With that Mayor Fontaine turns and leaves, slamming the door behind him. I guess he's never heard that it's generally polite to say *goodbye*.

Mr. Wakefield clears his throat and straightens the collar of his shirt. "Well then."

"Don't let him get to you," I say. "Penelope's right. You're doing a great job."

Mr. Wakefield looks surprised and maybe a little cheered up. "I appreciate you saying so, Mr. Wilkes."

"Is it true that the first Mayor Fontaine was totally different from the *current* Mayor Fontaine?" Penelope asks.

"Ah, yes," Mr. Wakefield says. "The old mayor was...quite dissimilar to his son."

"You mean he had a soul?" I ask.

"There's no need to be rude," Mr. Wakefield says, but I think he has to hide a smile. "It's actually very interesting the way different personality types manifest within the same family unit—"

"Aren't you supposed to stop talking about that crap?" Archie asks.

I glare at him.

"Indeed." Mr. Wakefield hesitates and looks at the clock. "I would love to have infinite hours with you wishers, but alas, we appear to be out of time."

As we gather our things and prepare to leave, he adds, "And

again, please don't forget your prewish appointments with Mayor Fontaine."

"I can't wait for *that*," I mutter.

"I know, I know," Mr. Wakefield says. "I assure you, no one is trying to police you. The mayor just wants to be certain your wish is legitimate so it will come true."

Spoken word-for-word from Mayor Fontaine's instruction manual, I'm sure. He'd be pleased.

I'm at the door when Mr. Wakefield says, "Mr. Wilkes, perhaps you'll stay for a moment and update me on your project?"

Penelope jumps in, "Actually, I wanted to talk to you about something too, Eldon."

"Sorry, guys. Have to be somewhere."

I hurry out of the community center. Being around Mayor Fontaine, and the reminder about my upcoming meeting with him, put me in a foul mood. I need space to chill out.

* * *

My dad and I are in the garage. He's alternating between instructing me on the craft of sink-building and dropping bits of football wisdom.

"You see," he says proudly, after successfully cutting the old copper pipes off the sink. "Told you this saw could cut through anything."

I nod and resist the urge to roll my eyes. The reciprocating saw is one of Dad's prized possessions. My mom bought it for him ages ago, back when she still made an effort. Which, if you ask me, makes the saw a depressing reminder of how their marriage has changed.

"Now all we need is the new fittings..." He trails off, scanning a piece of paper with roughly a million measurements.

My attention wanders to the TV where a newscaster out of Vegas is talking about Rachel. It throws me. Usually, no one notices this part of the state. I reach over and turn up the volume. Apparently, there's some kind of UFO festival coming up. It sounds absurd. It also means we'll have a lot of tourists passing through Madison to get there.

"Anyway, as I was saying earlier," my dad says, not the least bit interested in the news report, "when it comes to football, talent will only get you so far. That's where the hard work comes in. If you have dedication and ambition, then you're already doing better than most of the guys out there."

I nod.

"You have to shoot for the very top, Eldon. Even if you don't make it, you'll be better than if you never tried."

"Dad?"

He looks up from his measurements.

"What exactly do you think is going to happen next year?"

I've been wondering for months but haven't had the courage to ask. He's had enough bad stuff to deal with.

"What do you mean?"

I hesitate. "I mean with football. You know I'm not going to go pro."

He opens his mouth, like he's going to say of course I can, I can do anything I want, or some other lie like that. But then he shuts it again.

"Like, what are you even *hoping*?"

If we lived in another town, he'd want me to get on a good college team. I'm not going to college though. Only a handful of people in Madison do. It's weird to even think about the whole "turn eighteen and go to college" mentality. We turn eighteen and make a wish. It's all the same in the end. A significant event that determines what direction your future will take. Except in Madison, we skip the long years of toil.

"What's more important is what you're hoping," my dad says.

Maybe I was wrong to assume he hadn't been thinking about my future. He probably hadn't wanted to bring it up and hurt me, the same way I was trying not to hurt him.

"What are you boys up to?" my mom asks, coming into the garage and abruptly ending our conversation. She must have just gotten home from Uncle Jasper's apartment. She'd gone over to have another chat with him about his life choices. I can tell from the dark circles under her eyes and the way her hair is slipping from her bun that it didn't go well.

"Getting this hooked up," my dad says, patting the sink.

His grin wavers when Ma says, "I don't see the point of having a sink out here."

The point is that he *wants* a sink. The point is that he likes having projects. That it makes him happy to turn something broken into something useful.

But I keep my mouth shut.

"I..." My dad falters, looking lost. "I thought you would like it. You always complain that I track sawdust into the house. I thought if I had a place to clean up..."

I look at my dad in disbelief.

Ma loses interest and turns to me. "How was wish class?"

"Fine."

"Learn anything new?"

The unspoken: *What are you going to wish for?*

I want her to leave. The garage is not her space.

"We talked about this kid who tried to cure AIDS."

"I think I remember him," my dad says cheerfully, apparently not at all upset about getting blown off. "His name was John something."

My mom shakes her head. "You're getting him confused with John Dodge. He went to high school with us and wished to never catch a cold."

"Hmm. Maybe."

The AIDS kid is probably another one of Madison's tall tales. But I'm really starting to wonder.

"Harmon, could you take the day off tomorrow?" my mom asks.

"I really shouldn't. The Clash is only a few weeks away, and you know how tough those Tonopah kids are."

Ma frowns at him.

"Why?" he asks.

"I want to drive down to Vegas."

She doesn't say she wants to visit my sister. She speaks Ebba's name as infrequently as possible. But that's the only reason she'd be going to Las Vegas.

"Should *either* of us really be taking time off work right now?" my dad asks carefully. "With money being so tight…"

"I don't care," Ma says forcefully. She squeezes her eyes shut for a long moment. "Do you know what it's like to sit at the doctor's office all day, helping sick people, when my baby is alone in another town and sicker than any of them?"

Dad takes a step to comfort her but pulls back, like he doesn't know how.

"I'll go with you," I offer.

Ma collects herself. Some of the sadness leaves her face, and the frown I've gotten so used to reappears. "You have school."

"And we need you at practice," Dad says.

Only one of those statements is true. "I want to go. I haven't seen Ebba for a while."

My mom shakes her head. "Not on a school day. You can go next time, OK?"

So it's OK for you to skip work, but I can't skip school? How is that *fair?*

But I only say, "Fine."

It's not fine though. My mom wants to keep Ebba to herself. She wants to keep her *sadness* to herself. I overheard her on the phone once, telling the person on the other end, "There's nothing worse than a mother losing her daughter."

Yeah, it's shitty. I get that. It's so shitty that you feel like life is pointless, that maybe you want to give up, because being dead would be better than the constant pain you're in. But just because Ma's in pain, it doesn't mean the rest of us aren't.

Maybe if we let ourselves hurt together, we'd feel like a family again.

After my dad agrees to take the day off work, like we all knew he would, Ma leaves the garage.

Dad goes back to his workbench. I should help him. I can't quite shake what happened though. I'm feeling tense and edgy, and I want to go after Ma and shout that Ebba belongs to all of us.

Since I can't do that, I turn on my dad instead. "Why'd you let Ma make the sink about *her*? Why can't anything be yours?"

I regret it as soon as the words are out of my mouth. Dad looks sad and confused. He has no idea how to respond.

It's not his fault, I remind myself. *Don't get mad at him. He didn't ask for this. Besides, that's not really why you're upset. Remember what Mr. Wakefield said about misplaced anger.*

"Forget it," I say.

"Eldon—"

"So what's the next step?" I interrupt, gesturing to the sink.

Dad's face brightens, and he sits down next to me to show me his plans. And we talk about pipe fittings and water lines so we can avoid the conversation neither of us know how to have.

CHAPTER 12

COUNTDOWN: 16 DAYS

I know it's going to be a bad day when Penelope accosts me before I've even opened my locker.

"Eldon! *Hi!*"

"Hey, Penelope."

"Why'd you run off so fast yesterday? Look, I have a question. Well, it's actually a favor. Teensy-tiny."

She's wearing her cheerleading uniform, emblazoned with our football-playing fruit fly, and has a clipboard tucked under one of her arms. We all know to bolt in the opposite direction when we see her like this.

I sigh. "What is it?"

"Clem Johnson was supposed to work our bake sale table after school tomorrow, right? But something came up, and he's not going to be able to make it, and I can't find anyone else last minute, because other people have already taken the other shifts. It would be cool if you could fill in."

I look down at her uniform. "Is this a cheerleading fund-raiser?"

"Oh, no, the cheerleaders are collecting money for the new library. The bake sale is for Key Club. Totally different fund-raiser. So what do you say? Yes?"

"I'm kind of busy tomorrow."

"We're raising awareness about underage sex workers."

"Here in Madison?" I ask incredulously.

"No, silly. It's a national issue, duh."

"Look, Penelope, it's great what you're doing, and I'd love to help, but—"

"We really need you, Eldon. It would make everyone in Key Club so happy." She pauses and gives me a sly smile. "Juniper too."

"That's not really an argument that works on me anymore."

"Do it anyway? Please? Pretty please? Pretty, pretty pl—"

"Fine." People are starting to stare.

Penelope squeals and hugs me. Then she skips down the hall, her eyes fixed on her next victim.

It isn't a good start to the day at all.

* * *

If it wasn't for my conversation with Penelope, I wouldn't have been in the hallway when Mr. Wakefield walked by. And if Mr. Wakefield didn't ask a million questions about how my wish was coming along, as if something had changed since yesterday, then I could have gotten to first period on time.

"I'll walk you there," says Mr. Wakefield when I tell him I really need to get to class.

I try to say it doesn't matter, it's a pointless art class I'm taking for an elective credit, and Ms. Dove won't make a hassle about me being late. But Mr. Wakefield insists.

He keeps talking and talking, and by the time I get to class, everyone is already sitting in pairs.

"Please excuse Eldon's tardiness. He was with me," Mr. Wakefield says. "I'm afraid I talked his ear off!"

Ms. Dove gives me a sympathetic look, as if she's been cornered by Mr. Wakefield a few times herself.

"We're pairing up for our final project," she tells me.

My gaze skips around the room, looking for anyone who doesn't already have a partner. There's only one person sitting alone.

"It looks like you and Fletcher will be working together," says Ms. Dove.

Oh, fantastic.

Fletcher Hale and I eye each other. I consider refusing, but I know the other kids are waiting for my reaction. They want me to make a scene.

And the thing is, no one would blame me for it. They'd side with me and say I was totally right for snubbing Fletcher. But that doesn't change the fact that their stares make me feel like an animal in a cage.

So I cross the room and slide into the seat next to Fletcher.

"Hey," he says nervously.

I'm silent.

He lowers his voice. "You can ask Ms. Dove to switch part-ners. She won't care. Or I can do the work by myself. I'll put both our names on it."

I look down at the desk. My jaw is clenched tight. I know people are still watching. I know Fletcher is watching me too, waiting for a response. I slowly begin counting to ten.

"OK, well, I'll start brainstorming ideas, and if you want to jump in, you can."

And Fletcher does exactly that.

I watch him from the corner of my eye. It's been a long time since I've looked closely at Fletcher. Even when I beat him up, I wasn't really *seeing* him.

There are dark circles under his eyes. His hair is neatly combed, but it doesn't look like he's washed it for a while. Or washed at all, maybe. I don't remember him having so much acne before. Maybe it's his body's way of punishing him.

Fletcher glances up and meets my gaze. He can't hold it though. He ducks his head and speaks with his eyes fixed to the papers in front of him.

"Look. I never said I was sorry," he says.

"I know."

"I am. Sorry."

"That doesn't change anything," I say.

"I know," Fletcher agrees.

"Let's just do the work."

I look over the papers Ms. Dove handed out, but I can hardly concentrate. The project is something about showing how we've changed since starting high school. We can do whatever we want, as long as it's in one of the artistic mediums we learned in class.

"I can't really draw well," says Fletcher. "What about you? Are you any good?"

"No."

"Sculpting?"

"No."

"Photography?"

"Any idiot can take a picture," I say.

"Um, I don't know if that's true."

"Fletcher, I really don't give a fuck what you think."

Anyone else would have been deterred by my attitude. But Fletcher barrels on. "OK, right. We can put photos on the maybe list."

I sigh deeply. I know I'm being a dick, but I can't help it. It's either that or bash his face in.

"Maybe we can make some kind of collage?" he suggests.

I'm silent for a long moment. "Maybe we should go back to that idea where you work and I sit here. Because honestly, the more you talk, the more I think about how much I hate you."

"OK," Fletcher says. "OK, we can do that."

He goes back to working. I go back to doing nothing. When class ends, I leave without saying goodbye.

* * *

It's too much.

It's bad enough I have to pass Fletcher Hale in the hall and sit in the same classroom with him. But now, a project? Actual conversation? *Teamwork?*

It's just too freaking much.

I feel something stir inside of me. Maybe anger. Maybe hysteria. It feels like my heart is beating poison through my veins.

"What the hell is wrong with you?" Merrill asks at lunch.

I shake my head.

"You're freaking me out," Merrill says.

I'm freaking myself out. I feel like I'm going to snap.

"Eldon," my dad shouts at football practice after I—literally—drop the ball again, "get with the program!"

I try. I really do.

We're running a ladder and catch drill, repeating the same quick movements over and over. Sidestep, catch, sidestep, catch, sidestep, catch. Easy stuff. I shouldn't even have to think about it. But the tension in my body is making it impossible for muscle memory to take over.

When I drop the fifth pass in a row, Calvin Boyd smirks at me. "You having your period, Eldon?"

That's the nail in the coffin.

I walk over to Calvin and shove him as hard as I can. He stumbles back, trips over his own feet, and lands hard on his ass.

"What the hell?"

My dad runs over. "Jesus, Eldon, what's the matter with you?"

They're all watching me. The field is silent. And I can tell everyone's thinking the same thing, wondering what my problem is, wondering why I can't take a joke, wondering when I turned into such a little bitch.

Right there, on the football field where I used to be king, every single one of my teammates is secretly laughing at me. Or feeling sorry for me. Or feeling glad they're not the one being judged.

"He started it," I mumble, nodding at Calvin. And yeah, I realize I sound like a five-year-old.

"Get out of here, Eldon," my dad says.

"What?"

"Go. Right now."

My own dad is kicking me out of practice. It's too ridiculous for words. Will he suspend me from the Tonopah game? No way he'll do that... Will he?

"Dude," someone says softly.

Someone else clears their throat.

Everyone stares at me. And stares. And stares.

"Fine," I say.

I head toward the locker room. I don't look back.

* * *

The hot wind lashes my body as I walk home. That's OK. I rolled my ankle at practice, so I'm limping like my dad. Every step hurts, but that's OK too. Better than OK. It's good. It distracts me. The more I hurt on the outside, the less I feel inside. I know it isn't a real fix. Kind of like taking aspirin for a headache. It doesn't make the headache go away, only masks the pain for a while. But sometimes, that's enough. Sometimes, you need that aspirin to get through the day.

A car pulls up behind me as I trudge along the cracked sidewalk, but I don't turn around.

The car honks.

It has to be Merrill. I don't want to see Merrill. I don't want to explain why I'm not at practice. He'll probably tell me the whole thing was my own fault and, you know, he'd be right.

The car honks again.

It isn't Merrill. It's Norie Havermayer.

"You look like you're on death row," she calls from the driver's seat.

"I feel that way too."

"Want a ride?"

I open my mouth to tell her no. Stop. Nod and get in the car.

"So?" says Norie once we're driving.

"So what?"

"What's wrong? And don't say nothing. Clearly, something is wrong. It's not Juniper again, is it?"

"No, not Juniper. I just had one of those days."

"What does that even mean? One of *what* days? People always say that like you're supposed to know, like you're so in tune with them, you understand exactly what *one of those days* is."

I regret getting into the car.

"It's only a saying. You don't need to analyze it."

"That's the problem with the world. No one wants to analyze anything."

I've learned two things. The first is that Norie is as weird as she seems. The second is that she and Mr. Wakefield probably adore each other.

"Personally," I say, "I'd rather not think at all."

"That's true, isn't it?" Norie says, glancing over at me curiously. "You're one of those people who works purely on instinct."

I groan and rub at my eyes. "Please stop."

Norie laughs. And the unbelievable thing is, I can't help but smile a little too.

I have to give Norie directions to my neighborhood. She lives in one of the big houses on the hill—both her parents wished for money. She doesn't know her way around my crappy section of town.

"Did your parents buy you this car?" I ask.

I run my finger along the upholstery. It doesn't have a single tear in it. The car isn't fancy—it's a midsize sedan—but it's newer and nicer than anything my family has ever owned.

"No, it's my mom's. I just borrow it." Norie smiles ruefully. "Despite their wishes, my parents live in dread that one day, their cash flow will dry up. They're obsessed with saving money."

I don't tell Norie that being able to save money is a luxury to some people.

"Speaking of wishes," she goes on, "have you made the big decision yet?"

"Not yet. I'm researching other wishes. Maybe it'll help me make my choice."

"How's that going to help you?" she asks. "A wish being good or bad for someone else doesn't mean it'll be good or bad for you."

"It's all I've got right now, OK?"

Norie shrugs and makes the turn into my neighborhood.

"What did you wish for?" I ask.

"I told you. It's private."

"You haven't told anyone?"

"Not a single person."

I pause and wonder if I'm about to say the wrong thing. But I push forward anyway. "Was your wish about God?"

Norie laughs. "What? No. It wasn't about God."

"But you believe in God, right?" I prod.

Norie glances at me. She doesn't answer right away. "Yeah. I believe in God."

"That's weird."

"Is it?"

"In Madison it is."

"In my opinion, Madison is missing out."

She pulls up to my house. I stare bleakly at the front door. The minivan is in the driveway, so Ma's already home from work. She's going to wonder why I'm out of practice early, and there's no point lying. My dad will give her the full report the second he gets in.

I turn back to Norie. "How do you pray without churches?"

She bursts out laughing. "Eldon, you can pray anywhere."

"I guess I always assumed there were rules."

"Well, there are. Sort of." She bites her lip. "I don't know if I'd call them *rules* exactly. Different religions worship in different ways. But in Madison, I'm kind of stuck praying on my own."

I'm still not ready to get out of the car. I don't know if it's because I dread going inside, or because Norie might be the most unique person in the entire town. "So what religion are you?"

"Officially, I'm not anything. I haven't been baptized yet."

"Unofficially?"

"Unofficially, I believe in the doctrine of the LDS church." Norie reads the blank look on my face and says, "Latter-day Saints. That's what LDS stands for."

She reaches into her glove box, takes out a small blue book, and hands it to me. I look at the cover. *The Book of Mormon*.

I raise my eyebrows. "You believe in polygamy and shit?"

"The LDS church hasn't condoned polygamy for a *long* time," she says, rolling her eyes.

"But…isn't it sort of a cult?"

Instead of looking insulted, Norie smiles at me. "What do you know about it besides what you've seen on TV?"

"Nothing," I admit.

"That's what I thought. You can keep that if you want," she says, nodding at *The Book of Mormon.*

"I'm cool." I hand it back to her before she can try to convert me. "You really won't tell me your wish?"

"*You* really won't tell me what happened to you today?"

We look at each other for a moment, then we both laugh. We make a silent agreement to keep our secrets.

I thank Norie for the ride and tell her goodbye. Then I walk into my house, hoping my mom is in her bedroom, so I can sneak by.

No such luck. She's in the kitchen, chopping vegetables for dinner.

"What are you doing home so early?" she asks.

I wonder if I can get away with telling her *it was one of those days.*

CHAPTER 13

COUNTDOWN: 15 DAYS

It's a hundred and three degrees, wind is whipping through the valley, and no one wants to buy baked goods.

Penelope will probably blame that on me. If *she'd* been working the table, all the items would've sold already. She'd slam everyone who walked by with earnestness until they threw money at her.

It's too late for anything with icing. Those items may have started the day looking attractive, but that time has long since passed. Icing drips down the sides of cupcakes; glaze leaks off cookies. People in Madison should know better than to bake anything that could melt. Penelope should know better than to set up the table outside in this heat. *I* should have known better than to give up my afternoon.

I can't do anything about it now though. So I sit in front of the supermarket like a freaking Girl Scout, watching desserts melt and not selling a thing. There's an empty chair next to me, as if I started with a buddy but the heat liquefied him too.

Not that I have any other big plans, like football practice, for the afternoon. According to my dad, I need to "take a few days off to think about teamwork." Yeah, I'll get right on that.

Instead of thinking about teamwork, I'm thinking about something Penelope said when I arrived at the supermarket. She was arranging the table, moving muffins around to get the display perfect, like it was going to be photographed for a magazine.

"I appreciate this so much," she said, moving a plate of fudge an inch to the left. "I know it was totally last minute, but Clem had a dentist appointment, something with his wisdom teeth. He's in a lot of pain, I guess. Anyway, there was really no one else, and I was thinking I'd have to do it myself, but then I'd miss my Young Citizens of Madison meeting, and they really fall apart when I'm not there. You know how it is."

I nodded, like I did know, as if I'd been to a Young Citizens meeting or had any idea what they do there.

At the time, I was anxious for Penelope to leave, because her constant stream of do-gooding was making me feel ill. But after an hour in the hot sun, with nothing to think about but waving away the flies that are buzzing around, something else occurs to me.

I wasn't Penelope's first choice. I'm a last resort, the person you call when someone backs out and no one else is free. A year ago, that probably would have thrilled me. Penelope was up my ass once a week about doing charity work. She always wanted me back then. Everyone wanted my time.

Not anymore. She picked Clem Johnson over me. *Clem Johnson.* The dude can hardly form a complete sentence. Yet Penelope wanted *him* to represent her Key Club combatting underage prostitution fund-raiser. What's *that* about?

The sun is making me dizzy, and I'm pissed off about Clem, and still pissed off at Calvin Boyd from yesterday, and pissed off at myself. I haven't sold anything but two cookies and a loaf of banana bread in the entire time I've been sitting here, and even those seemed like pity buys.

When Merrill's car pulls up, I'm relieved. I need a distraction.

"Penelope doesn't want you here," I say as he approaches the table. "Like, she specifically mentioned it to me."

"Do you think she's worried my good looks will scare people away?"

"I think she's more concerned with your personality. Abrasive, I believe was the word she used."

Merrill grins and sits down next to me. "Eldo, let me tell you something about Penelope. Beneath that good girl façade, she's kind of a bitch."

"This is probably why she doesn't like you."

"If anything, my presence is an asset. I'm *quite* the savvy salesperson. Hey!" Merrill shouts to a woman pushing a cart into the grocery store. "We have cookies! You want some?"

The woman ignores him.

"Nice try," I say.

"Look at this mess. No wonder no one's buying anything." Merrill picks up a cupcake with melted chocolate icing and peels back the wrapper.

I open my mouth to protest. Penelope would flip out and give us a speech about how the cupcake is meant for saving sex workers, not us. But I change my mind. Merrill's right. No one's going to buy these cupcakes. I pick out one for myself.

"So when were you gonna tell me about yesterday?" Merrill asks through a mouthful of chocolate.

"Practice, you mean?"

"*Yeah.* You sat through a car ride, lunch, and government class and didn't say a word. I had to overhear Calvin talking about it in sixth period."

I shrug and stare at the parking lot. "There wasn't anything to say."

"Not how he makes it sound. He's telling people you attacked him."

"Attacked? Jesus. I pushed him. Not even that hard. He's a freaking baby." I shove the rest of the cupcake in my mouth.

"Was it about Juniper?"

"No."

"Look, Eldon—"

"Can we not talk about this?"

"I kinda think we should."

I hate the way Merrill's looking at me. Like I'm his little

brother and in desperate need of a shoulder to cry on. Like I'm *weak*. Merrill's going to lose respect for me. The whole town is going to lose respect for me. I'm not even first choice for the bake sale. Once upon a time, every girl in school would have stopped by for cookies and Bundt cakes simply because I was the one selling them.

"I had to pair up with Fletcher in art class," I say finally, keeping my eyes on the sprinkles that are cutting gorges through melted icing.

Merrill sighs. "How did *that* happen?"

"I was late for class, and everyone else had a partner and...I don't know. It just happened."

"Why didn't you say no?"

"Seemed like too much effort."

We're silent for a long time. Finally, Merrill says, "It's OK to hate him, you know."

"I know."

"Then why are you acting like everything's cool, then beating up on Calvin Boyd?"

Merrill and I aren't supposed to have this kind of friendship. We're supposed to joke and go to parties and give each other crap for things that don't actually matter. Like, he'll make fun of me for playing football, and I'll say he's jealous that he isn't good enough for the team. Or I'll make fun of some nerdy video game he's playing, and he'll say I've been hit in the head too many times to understand it. *That's* what our friendship is supposed to be. Not talking about our *feelings*.

Luckily, I'm saved from taking the conversation any further, because Mrs. Lynch comes over and browses the table. She's the local real estate agent, and her job is mostly helping people who wish for money move into bigger houses. And, of course, telling people who are thinking of moving to Madison from elsewhere that sorry, no homes are available for purchase right now. I guess she's pretty good at her job, because her wish was to be charismatic. Even at seventeen, she knew she wanted a job in sales and gave herself the skills to make it happen. It must be nice to have such a clear vision for your future.

"I promised my daughter I'd bring something home," Mrs. Lynch says.

Merrill grins and gestures at the table of melting baked goods. "As you can see, we have quite the enticing selection."

She ends up buying a stack of pizzelles, which have weathered the heat—but not before trying to talk down the price.

"Pay whatever you want for them," I say with a sigh, and she looks a little disappointed about getting her way so easily.

Once Mrs. Lynch is gone—looking for some other negotiation to conquer, I'm sure—Merrill and I lapse back into silence.

Eventually, I say, "Could you get the car this weekend? Sunday?"

"Sure. Why?"

"I want to go to Las Vegas."

Merrill raises his eyebrows. "That's different."

"I'll pay for gas."

"You don't need to pay for gas."

"I want to see Ebba. Without my parents around."

Merrill nods. I know he has questions, but he isn't going to ask them. "No problem, Eldo. We'll go to Vegas."

* * *

Night comes early in the desert. The sun drops behind the mountains and throws the landscape into shadow long before it would in other places. Merrill is gone, and I expect Penelope will arrive any minute to help me pack up, clucking her tongue at how little I sold.

A dusty pickup truck pulls up to the front, but it's not Penelope. She probably wouldn't accept a ride in it without doing a top-to-bottom clean.

Gil Badgley leaves the truck idling at the curb and climbs out. His dog sits in the passenger seat—Tuco the fourth or fifth. I can't remember what number he's on these days.

As he wanders over to me, Gil's cowboy boots clip-clop on the ground. As far as I know, he's the only coach in the history of Madison to wear cowboy boots on the football field.

"Hey there, Eldon," he says, hitching a thumb in his belt.

"Hey, Gil."

He surveys the treats on the table. "I ran into that girl from your school. She told me to come spend some money to stop kiddie porn or something."

"Yeah, something like that," I say.

He frowns at the dusty, gooey selection. "How about I give you ten bucks and we call it good?"

"Works for me."

Gil hands me the money but doesn't leave. He spits tobacco juice into the tin can he always carries around with him.

"How's the family?" he asks.

"Good. We're good."

"You all recovering? It's a damn shame what happened."

I don't say anything.

Gil shifts the lump of tobacco in his mouth to the other side. He's always talking around his tobacco. His teeth are stained brown.

"You know," he goes on, "I was thinking about your dad and the old days last week."

"He talks about those days a lot too."

"He was the best I ever coached, you know. A hero out on the field."

"I know."

"Same as you," Gil says.

There's no reason for us to pretend with each other. "Not anymore."

Gil sighs. He spits. "That's what wishing will get you."

"You happy with your wish?" I ask, nodding to his truck.

Gil turns and gazes at the truck for a long time. Tuco's nose is pressed to the window, a long string of drool hanging from his mouth. "You could say that."

"It always seemed weird to me," I say. "You wishing for a truck when you could have wished for enough money to buy a hundred of them."

Gil smiles. "You got a good head on your shoulders."

I shrug.

"Why you so interested in my wish?"

"Mine's coming up," I say, and Gil nods like he understands.

He thinks for a moment and spits tobacco juice into his can again. He says, "I'll be at the Last Chance tonight. Why don't you stop by after you're done with this?"

"Sure. I can do that." I try not to sound as curious as I am.

Penelope shows up a few minutes later.

"Did you sell *anything*?" she asks, surveying the table.

I can tell she isn't thinking I let *her* down but every underage sex worker in the country. In Penelope's mind, it doesn't take more than a few cupcakes to save a person.

*   *   *

The Last Chance Saloon has been around since Madison's mining days. Back then, it was on Main Street. Later, in the forties, when the town got serious about keeping wishing a secret, people wanted to tear down the bar and move it somewhere else. Couldn't risk a traveler stopping in for a cold one.

But there were enough Madison residents who cared about history, who couldn't bear the thought of destroying the old saloon. Instead of moving the bar, they moved the road. These days, people who take the new highway through Madison pass within a few blocks of the Last Chance but never know it's there.

I step inside and let my eyes adjust to the dark. Gil Badgley is at the bar, and I make my way over to him. It's musty inside the building. Smells old and stale, the way everything in the desert does after a while. It's clean though, all gleaming dark wood.

In Las Vegas, video poker machines line every bar. Not the case in Madison. Gambling is another one of those diversions that draws people in, invites them to invade our private world. Madison is one of the few towns in Nevada where gambling is outlawed.

Juniper's dad is behind the bar, same place he is most days of the week. Back when he was in high school, there'd been renewed talk of tearing down the Last Chance. His wish had been to save it—though from dating Juniper, I know the bar is struggling.

"Eldon," Mr. Clarke says. "I may be mistaken, but I don't remember you being of drinking age."

"Come off it, Hollis," Gil says, waving away Mr. Clarke. "The boy's with me."

"You watch this young man doesn't get into trouble," Mr. Clarke says, winking at me. "Though you keep drinking, Gil, and it might be the other way around."

Mr. Clarke and I talk for a few minutes, meaningless how-you-doing stuff. I don't ask about Juniper, though I have a million questions about how she's been. Finally, Gil puts a stop to our conversation.

"Two more of these," he says, nodding to his empty bottle.

"You know I can't serve the kid, Gil."

Gil grins. "And I'd never ask you to. They're both for me."

Mr. Clarke passes two beers down the bar. Gil picks them up, and I follow him to a booth in the back corner, the quietest and darkest spot in the building. As soon as we sit down, he slides one of the beers to me.

"Your pa was always my favorite," he says. "Kid could have done anything he wanted to. Even if it weren't for that thing with your mama, he could have been great."

"I know," I say.

"No, you don't. You only know him after he got hurt, and I'm telling you, he's a different man."

"OK," I say, but I'd already figured that much on my own. No adult is the same as when they were my age. With the possible exception of my uncle Jasper.

Gil takes a long swig of beer. "Always felt like I could've done something to prevent it. I didn't do right by your pa back then. All I thought about was winning."

"Are you trying to tell me to make my wish about football?" I ask.

"No. God, no."

I'm confused. "What are you saying then?"

Gil sighs and spits into his tin can. "Maybe I wasn't there for your pa," he says. "I pushed him too much. Made him think foot-ball was everything."

I wait.

"Look, I heard around town that you're asking people about their wishes. Wanna find the best wish for yourself. So I thought maybe you'd want to hear mine."

"About your truck?" I ask.

Gil laughs, long and deep. "I can't believe people still believe that old story."

CHAPTER 14

THE WISH HISTORY: GIL BADGLEY

Y ou'd think after the free love of the previous decade, 1970s
Madison would be a pretty open-minded place, yeah?

Open up the history book, and find out just how wrong you are.

Gil Badgley knows what people say about homosexual kids—how
they're always playing with their sister's dolls or wearing their mama's dresses.

And for Gil, well, it's not like that. He's as much a boy—a man—as
any other in Madison. Hell, he's more of a man than a good lot of them.
He's never cried after losing a football game like Irvine Griffin. He's not
scared of his own shadow like Barnabas Fairley. No, Gil isn't a pansy.
He's a freaking cowboy.

Take a look at him: seventeen years old and already ruggedly handsome. When football practice ends, he changes from his cleats to his cowboy
boots. Gil Badgley hasn't a clue that manliness and sexuality don't have
much to do with each other. That not every cowboy is looking for a cowgirl.

Gil figures, if he was homosexual, wouldn't he be sure? Would he
have to spend so much time wondering? On the other hand, Gil thinks
constantly wondering if you're homosexual is pretty telling.

Deep down, Gil knows who he is and can't remember a time when he didn't. When you get right down to it, even pansy kids like Irvine Griffin want to fuck girls. And no matter how he comes at it, Gil Badgley just doesn't.

Sure, he asks girls on dates. But it never goes further than a quick kiss on the front porch. The bizarre thing is, that makes the girls like him even more. They watch him, waiting for him to choose someone to get serious with. After all, graduation's right around the corner, and after that, marriage, children.

A guy like Gil, his whole life was planned out for him from day one. But in a place like Madison, life doesn't often go the way one anticipates.

So it's no big shocker: Gil doesn't tell anyone he's gay. While other kids enjoy high school and think about the future, Gil focuses on keeping his secret under wraps.

He plays football.

He drinks beer.

He spends hours in front of the TV, watching his favorite movie over and over again. He pretends he's the hero of it, the Man with No Name.

He buys a cowboy hat and takes up chewing tobacco.

He watches the movie again.

He learns to be silent, to look instead of speaking.

He watches the movie again.

And again.

And again.

Look closely at Gil Badgley. Do you think his attempt to blend in *is working? Or can you see the loss in his eyes, the understanding that something is missing from his life? Look at him, watching his friends go on dates, imagining what it's like for them. What it would be like to fall in love.*

Then Gil watches the movie again and reminds himself the Man with No Name doesn't need love. He only needs himself, and that's enough.

Don't you wish we could ask seventeen-year-old Gil why he wouldn't want more out of life? Judging from that look on his face, maybe he's already asking himself the same question.

Here's one thing we can say about Gil: these feelings, they've never made him hate himself. He's got no time for self-loathing. No, his situation makes him hate the world around him. But he can't change the world.

Himself though, that's different.

In Madison, everyone has one chance to change him or herself.

Take a look at Gil Badgley planning his wish. People are gonna ask about it, and Gil can't exactly tell them he wished away his gayness.

What to do?

He'll say he wished for a truck. He's always wanted a truck. Really, he wants a horse like the Man with No Name, but even in Madison, that's impractical. So a truck, a big Ford that'll leave clouds of dust in its wake. Exactly what people would expect from a guy like Gil.

But he can't make a truck appear from nowhere.

So he'll say he wished for the money to buy the truck. The whole town will act like he's an idiot for not wishing for unlimited money. But Gil's never tried to present himself as especially bright, and in this situation, it'll work in his favor.

Flip to the next page, and watch Gil save all the money he makes at the gas station. Watch him work all year to make enough for that truck, and see how he acts like he's blowing his paychecks on beer.

That's what people expect anyway.

Sometimes, people's shitty expectations can be a blessing.

Look how pleased Gil is. His plan is going exactly how he wants it to.

Now turn to the page where Gil makes his wish. He goes into the cave alone—thanks for that, Barnabas. He navigates through the dark, a candle lighting his way. He reaches the end of the cave, and in a spot that's been carefully described to him, seventeen-year-old Gil Badgley wishes for all his homosexual feelings to go away.

And they do.

The end.

Except you don't really believe that, do you?

Skim ahead to when Gil gets paired with Emerson Carby on a science project. These two kids hardly know each other. They don't have the same social circles. Emerson is a quiet, nerdy kid who keeps to himself. A kid who's probably written off Gil as a dumb jock.

The two of them couldn't be more different from one another. Yet after two weeks of working together, Gil knows with more certainty than he's ever known anything in his life that Emerson Carby is the person he's meant to be with.

Gil never knew it could be so easy to be around another person. For the first time in a long time, Gil doesn't need to be the Man with No Name. He's happy being himself. Even if being himself means wanting to be with another man.

Only, something is wrong.

Emerson is handsome in a way Gil can recognize but not feel.

Because the wish.

The wish.

Gil knows all about wanting. He spent the first eighteen years of his life wanting the simplicity of wanting girls. But that hadn't prepared him for Emerson, for knowing he should love Emerson, and that a few months prior, he would have loved him.

But knowing something and feeling something aren't the same.

The wish worked too well.

Look at overly optimistic Gil Badgley. He tells himself that his wish is only as strong as his determination for it to be true, and now that he sees this chance for happiness, it can be reversed.

"Gil," Emerson says when he's spending the night at Gil's house. "I need to talk to you about something."

"Sure," Gil says.

He sits there in his cowboy boots, looking at Emerson.

"We've been hanging out a lot, and…"

Gil waits.

"You know I'm gay, don't you?"

Gil doesn't say a word. Instead, he leans in and kisses Emerson full on the mouth. Emerson kisses him back hungrily. It's a long, deep kiss. *All those front porches, all those girls, and Gil never kissed anyone like this.*

It should have been the most perfect moment of his life.

Except he feels nothing.

It's not that there's anything wrong *with the kiss. It's enjoyable enough. But it's empty. There's no pleasure in it, only a sense that there* should *have been pleasure.*

The kiss over, Emerson stares at Gil expectantly. Watch how, for the first time since he was a young child, Gil Badgley cries.

Turn the page, past Gil's long and teary confession. Stop when Emerson slowly and sadly says, "So you like girls now."

"No," says Gil. "I don't. I don't like anyone."

That hadn't been his wish, after all. Despite the preplanning that went into it, Gil never considered that attraction wasn't an either-or scenario. Wishing to not like boys wouldn't make him like girls.

Gil also hadn't considered that wishing away an essential part of who he was would leave a hole. This lack of desire, it's not so bad. He doesn't need sex. *But his sexuality belonged to him. These days, he feels like there's an imposter living in his head, his heart.*

"We could still try," Gil says to Emerson. He can't shake his optimism. There must be a loophole; he can love Emerson's company even if he can't love him physically. After all, there's more than one way to love someone.

But Emerson shakes his head. "I want more than that."

If Gil met Emerson sooner, or made his wish later, or wished an entirely different wish, their story could have ended differently. Even if people in Madison never accepted them as a couple, they could have gone to a town where people were different. But it's too late.

Gil suddenly understands that the Man with No Name would have never made the same wish. He would have never run from what he was afraid of.

And Gil realizes he's a pansy after all.

Flip forward through the years.

Gil still sees Emerson Carby around town, and they wave to each other, make a few minutes of small talk. But they never discuss what happened between them that night in Gil's room. They never discuss the life they could have had.

Keep skimming.

See that Gil never marries. He has his truck; he gets a dog he names Tuco. He learns to let that be enough. Gil coaches football and spends his nights drinking in the Last Chance. He stops trying to find interest in either sex.

That life, those emotions, aren't for him.

Gil Badgley isn't the Man with No Name.

He's the Man with No Desire.

CHAPTER 15

COUNTDOWN: 13 DAYS

Having art class first thing in the morning feels like a curse. I'm forced to start every single day with Fletcher Hale in my face.

Thankfully, he mostly keeps to himself. I have no idea what he's working on or if we'll have a project to hand in at the end, but I can't make myself care. Occasionally, Ms. Dove wanders over and asks how we're doing, and I grin and tell her we're perfect.

"So I was thinking of taking the pictures this weekend," Fletcher says hesitantly.

"What?"

"For the project. We can tell Ms. Dove you came too."

I shrug. "Whatever."

Fletcher looks baffled. He's never blown off a school assignment. "You don't want to miss graduation because you failed an *elective*."

"No, *you* don't," I say. "*I'm* not going to Harvard in the fall."

At least he has the decency to look guilty.

"It must be nice," I say, keeping my voice low so no one else can hear. "Knowing you get to leave town and forget everything that happened here."

"I'm not going to forget," Fletcher says quietly.

But he will. He'll run away and start over and pretend Madison was nothing but a bad dream.

I say what I've been wanting to say for months. "You could have taken it back. If you really wanted to, you could have made it like the accident never happened."

Ebba was rushed to Vegas almost immediately. By the time my family showed up, the ambulance had already left for the hospital, and there was only a crowd of onlookers, Fletcher's car, and Ebba's mangled bike. And blood. Not a lot of blood, but some scattered drops on the road. Enough to tell us the story of what happened.

But even though the first responders were fast, even though Ebba was on the road to Vegas when Fletcher made his wish, he had time to fix it. And he didn't.

Fletcher looks away from me. His voice cracks when he speaks. "I know. I wasn't thinking."

"You expect me to believe that?" I snap. "All you *do* is think. You weren't willing to give up your wish."

I'm pushing him, and I know it. Maybe I want to piss him off. Maybe I want a fight.

When he responds, he doesn't seem angry. Just sad. "That's not what happened."

"You know what I hope, Fletcher?" I say. "I hope you get to Harvard and enjoy your fancy classes and have everything you ever wanted. Then I hope something happens to take it all away. Because you don't deserve happiness. You don't deserve *anything*. I want you to spend every second of the rest of your life remembering that."

A look I can't interpret crosses Fletcher's face. For a moment, I wonder if he's *already* thinking that. If maybe it's too late for him to make a run for it. For a second, I feel almost guilty. Almost.

*   *   *

I'm still thinking about Fletcher at lunch. It means I'm not paying attention to Merrill, and that makes him impatient.

"Do you even care that we're being lied to by everyone who has power in this town?"

"Come on, Merrill. I'm not in the mood."

"You're *not in the mood*? Well, OK, Eldon, I guess we'll let the corruption continue because you're *not in the mood* to deal with it."

I sigh. "Fine. Go ahead. I'm listening."

So are half the kids at our table, mostly football players and cheerleaders. Merrill either doesn't notice or doesn't care. I'd put money on the latter.

"It's the rules, Eldon. Who decided the rules? Have you ever stopped to think maybe this eighteenth birthday bit is bullshit? For all we know, everyone has infinite wishes. Who's to say we don't? Who's to say the mayor isn't going up there once a week to wish for whatever he wants? They keep those bars on the entrance and say no one can get in, but has anyone tried? Have you heard the story of Silas Creed?"

I have, but only because Merrill brings him up once a month.

"Let me tell you, *he* knew the whole setup was a lie. It's not about wishing. It's about *control*. This whole town is trying to keep us placid. Silas Creed took matters in his own hands, and he went up there and cut through those bars. And you know what happened to him?"

I do, because Merrill has already told me.

"He was found in the river two days later with a bullet in his head. Shot execution style. And do you know what happened to the cave?"

His voice is getting higher and higher, and soon, he'll run out of air. Then he'll pound his fists on the table and draw in a big gasping breath. Then he'll start again.

"They put up new bars. Bars that are thicker than before. The game is rigged, Eldon. Something is very wrong in this town, and the powers that be are making sure we never find out what exactly it is."

Everyone around us has turned to stare.

Merrill shoots them a dark look. "We're screwed," he says simply. "We can't get the upper hand."

"Were you smoking with Royce this morning?" I ask.

"Was I... What the hell? No, I wasn't smoking with Royce. This isn't some drug-induced paranoia or—"

"People can hear you on the other side of the cafeteria, you know," says a voice behind me.

Merrill and I both look.

"Oh great, Norie Havermayer's here to tell us it's all part of God's plan," Merrill says.

Norie rolls her eyes and gestures for me to scoot over. Which is weird, because wherever Norie usually sits at lunch, it sure isn't with us. I make space for her on the bench, and she puts her lunch tray down next to me. "You really believe all that stuff?"

"Nah," I say before Merrill can answer. "He just gets off on the idea of being the one to blow open a big conspiracy."

"Well, you're probably right on some level," Norie says to him.

Merrill and I both look at her, surprised.

"I don't think it's as dramatic as you make it sound though. It's not some grand plot or anything. But we're definitely not told the whole truth about wishing."

"Thank you, Norie," Merrill says smugly. "Have I mentioned how much I value your opinion?"

"I must have missed it. Was that before or after you insulted my beliefs?"

I laugh. Maybe Norie sitting with us isn't so bad. Especially when I catch the glance Juniper gives us from a few tables over.

"No one knows if Silas Creed was a real person," Norie says.

"I'll ask at the wish museum," I offer. "I'm going there after school."

Merrill takes off his glasses and cleans them on his shirt. "I can't imagine a more boring way to spend an afternoon."

"They'll probably have more answers than anyone else in town. Plus, my dad's keeping me out of practice until next week."

"I'll go with you. I haven't been there for a while," says Norie.

"Why have you been there *at all*?" Merrill asks.

Norie takes a sip of water before responding. "It's amazing. With all your conspiracy theories, you're not actually willing to learn real information to back them up. Or maybe you're worried that they'll be disproven?"

Merrill grins, accepting the challenge. "The lady's right, Eldo. Let's get educated."

Even though I'm out of football practice for the day, I still feel like I'm part of a team.

* * *

Madison isn't filled with rocket scientists, but we're not dense either. The wish museum doesn't have a sign, doesn't even have a real name. It's in a house on the edge of town, set back from the street, where no tourist will stumble into it.

The house was built when Madison was a new town, so it's not stucco like most of our buildings. It has wood siding and a wide front porch. It looks like a house out of a western movie, a place the town sheriff might live. In real life, it's occupied by the Samson sisters.

One sister is named Marla, and the other is Eulalie, though I never remember which is which. They're both old and gray haired. One is tall and one is short; one is thin and the other is pudgy. But when you're with them at the same time, all their features blend together, and they become a blur of a person, one being speaking with two voices.

"Come in, come in," says one of them when we knock on the front door.

"Young people! We rarely get young people!"

"Don't just stand there, come in!"

"Come in!"

They're like witches from an old fairy tale. Except, as far as I know, they don't cannibalize children. I hope.

We go inside. It's dim and run-down but clean. The entire downstairs has been turned into a museum, and the sisters live above it.

"It'll be two dollars each," one of them says.

"Yes, just a bit to keep us going. It's not much."

"Not much at all."

"I got it," Merrill says, pulling out his wallet. I try to protest, but he waves me away.

The three of us split up and look around. There are a few items on display, an old journal, some mining equipment, but it's a museum of photos. They go back nearly to the beginning of Madison. I see pictures of the wish cave from before they barred the door. The Last Chance Saloon when it was still brand-new. The first Mayor Fontaine when he was a kid, dated 1942.

"It's such a *lush* history," Marla or Eulalie says.

"Oh, yes," says the other. "In some ways, Madison is a typical Nevada mining town, but in others, it's *so* very unique."

"What's the story on Silas Creed?" Merrill asks.

"Oh, Silas, what a fun old rumor."

"They say he was shot, but *we* have no record of it."

"You know how these old stories are. So much is conjecture."

While Merrill tries to pull out more info about Madison's rogue wisher, I wander to a pedestal with a huge book on it. It's one of the few items in the museum that looks new.

The cover is blank. I open it to find pages and pages of precise cursive. Dates and names and, after those, wishes. The entire wish history of Madison.

I flip to the last page with writing, and there it is. My birthday, my name, and a blank space after it. They're ready to add my wish.

I go backward, January of 1992.

Harmon Wilkes: Increased football prowess.

Forward a few months.

Luella Maylocke: Love (Harmon Wilkes).

Back even further, 1969.

Barnabas Fairley: To be left alone (accidental).

It's all there, every wish that's been made in Madison. After people started tracking wishes, at least. The first few pages in the book are spotty, with random dates and a lot of question marks.

I run my finger down the list of wishes. Wishes that helped people and ruined people. Wishes for material goods and wishes for stuff you'd never be able to see or touch. It feels like you could learn everything there is to know about a person by finding out how they spent their only wish.

That gives me an idea. I turn back to the current year. February.

Eleanor Havermayer: Unknown.

So Norie is a mystery to them too. Before I can turn the page, my eyes land on a name a few spaces below Norie's.

Fletcher Hale: Materials facilitating acceptance to Harvard University.

The anger comes again, thick and cloying. Fletcher couldn't wish himself directly into Harvard, but he made his transcripts good enough to guarantee acceptance into any top-tier college. He has a future beyond this place, this life. And it makes me want to kill him.

Before I completely give in to my rage, I flip through the book again. I go back into the end of the sixties, but I don't see what I'm looking for. Go forward a little bit, to 1970. There it is.

Gil Badgley: "Truck."

It's the only wish in quotes. The sisters know. How the hell do they know?

"Do people tell you their wishes?" I ask, interrupting the sisters' conversation with Merrill, which is starting to get heated.

"Oh yes, some do."

"Some, but not *all*. We hear many rumors though."

"You can hear *so* much if you listen hard enough."

"Check this out," I say to Merrill.

He crosses the room and joins me at the pedestal, peers over my shoulder as I flip through the pages.

"It's a record of every wish. Wanna see yours?"

"I don't need to see my own wish," Merrill says. He nudges me out of the way and goes back a few years. "What's my brother's say?"

Royce Delacruz: Unlimited supply of an illegal substance.

Merrill and I laugh.

"What's so funny?" Norie asks, wandering over from the other side of the museum.

"My brother."

Norie follows our gaze. "That's actually more sad than funny."

"You antidrug or something?" Merrill asks.

"Well, *yeah*. But besides that, it's a waste."

"You shouldn't think of it that way," says Marla-Eulalie.

"No," agrees Eulalie-Marla. "A wish is never a waste if it feels right to the wisher."

"Anyway," I say before we get too off track, "we're trying to find out more about wishing. Like how it started."

"No one knows *how* it started, of course."

"Just that it *did*, and for that, we can be thankful."

"So very thankful."

It figures.

"I guess I was hoping you guys had some idea," I say.

"Well, *of course*, we have ideas."

"The cave walls are so *very* smooth, you see."

"And there are holes. Not many, but some. We call it a cave, but it's probably a *mine*."

"Almost *certainly* a mine."

"And if a miner happened to be there at the right time—"

"And said the right thing—"

"Then perhaps a wish occurred, all on its own."

Merrill snorts. "Not only would that be a massive coincidence, but how would this original miner dude even *know* his wish coming true had anything to do with the cave?"

"God works in mysterious ways," says Norie.

"Not God, dear. *Wishes*," says Marla-Eulalie.

"But all this is speculation, of course. We don't really *know*," says Eulalie-Marla.

"I can see our trip here has been immensely helpful," Merrill deadpans.

I turn back to the wish history, flip through it for a few more seconds. Wish after wish after wish. It's all here.

Or is it?

The wishes are listed, yeah? But what about the stories behind them? What does it matter if you know someone's wish if you don't know why they wished it? If you don't know *what happens next*? A wish can't be reduced to a few words.

It makes me think of the people I've been talking to, the wishes I've heard directly from the sources. Those are *real*. Those are the true wish history of Madison, Nevada.

I turn away from the book, wander the museum for a while longer, the sisters trailing behind me and offering useless bits of information. I hate to admit it, but Merrill is right. We wasted an afternoon.

"What about Othello Dewitt?" I ask the sisters.

They look at each other before answering.

"A very odd case."

"The *most* odd."

"The only time in the history of Madison someone chose to give up their wish."

"So it's true?" I ask, and they nod in unison. "Why?"

"Well, I'm sure *we* don't know."

"Certainly not."

"But you can ask him."

"Oh yes, if he'll talk to you."

"He's a hermit, you know."

"Thinks he's Henry David Thoreau."

"*My Life in the Woods.*"

"*My Life in the* Desert."

They both giggle. They sound like girls I go to school with, only coming from them, it's kinda disturbing. Merrill and I glance at each other. He shudders.

"Well, OK," I say. "Maybe we'll talk to him."

I'm ready to get out of here before I'm infected with whatever wish mania has taken over the Samsons. I thank them, and we make our way to the door.

Norie turns back. "What did you two wish for?"

"Why, the museum, of course," says Marla-Eulalie.

"We always fancied ourselves historians," agrees Eulalie-Marla.

"Yes, *always.*"

"You *both* wished for the museum?" asks Norie.

They nod.

"But once one of you had it, didn't you both?"

"It wouldn't have been fair, you see," says one of them.

"It wouldn't have belonged to *both* of us."

We say our goodbyes pretty fast after that.

"Well, that was creepy," Merrill says as we walk back to the car.

"They're not creepy," Norie replies. "They want something to believe in."

"And they have wishing," I say.

Norie looks at me. "Wishing isn't enough."

We get into the car, and Merrill starts it. He glances at me before shifting into drive. "So I assume we'll be paying a visit to Othello Dewitt?"

"You assume right," I say.

CHAPTER 16

COUNTDOWN: 12 DAYS

It's Penelope Rowe's birthday, and she's determined everyone knows it. And *cares* about it. I'm hardly through the school doors when she assaults me.

"Eldon, *hi*! Can you believe it?"

"Um. No?"

"You don't even know what I'm talking about, do you? That's OK. I know you have your own big day coming up, and you're probably totally distracted. I know I've been completely out of it for, like, *days*."

Ah, right. Wish day.

"Happy birthday, Penelope."

"Thank you!" She beams. "I can't believe it's finally here. I've been waiting my whole life for this. Well, not my *whole* life, because when I was a baby, I obviously didn't know what wishes were, so it's not like I was excited back then."

That's when I notice Juniper a few steps behind Penelope. It's pretty shocking that I hadn't noticed her immediately, since she looks freaking amazing.

"He knows what you mean, Penny," Juniper says and gives me an amused smile. The same kind of smile I used to get from her all the time, the one that said we knew exactly what the other was thinking.

While I'm gazing at Juniper and reminiscing, I hear Penelope say, "Dessie, *hi!*"

Shit. I've been avoiding Dessie Greerson since that night at the hot springs. Judging from the way her eyes narrow in my direction, she's not exactly thrilled to see me either. I have a sudden, horrifying vision of Dessie bringing up what happened between us in the cave while Juniper listens in.

"Look, I need to get to class," I say. "But good luck with your wish, Penelope."

"I won't need it, but thank you," Penelope replies with her megawatt smile.

I quickly make my exit.

Penelope's day will unfold like it does for most kids on their wish days. She'll wait all day, excited, nervous. Depending on what time her wish is scheduled for, she might go home and have a nice meal with her parents. Eat cake. No candles of course. No kid in Madison has ever wished on birthday candles. There won't be gifts either. Kids don't get gifts on their wish birthdays. I guess people figure they're already getting the biggest gift there is.

It's kind of sad. After you make your wish, your birthday stops mattering. Nothing is ever going to top the year you turned eighteen. So everyone stops celebrating, and it becomes just another day. I was probably five before I even realized my parents had birthdays too.

I go to art class and take my seat. Fletcher isn't here yet. The bell rings, and Ms. Dove talks for a while, and Fletcher still doesn't show. Fletcher's never late, not anymore. He must be out sick.

That should make me happy, yeah? Because I don't have to see his face first thing in the morning. But he's been doing our assignment on his own all week, which means I have no idea what to work on. Ms. Dove will definitely notice if I don't pretend to do something in class.

So I take the only obvious course of action. I tell Ms. Dove I have an appointment with Mr. Wakefield.

* * *

"I can't tell you how much it means to me that you sought me out," Mr. Wakefield says when I'm settled in his office.

I shrug.

"Why don't you tell me what's on your mind?"

"Oh, you know…"

Mr. Wakefield has a serious look on his face and nods like he understands. Which is impossible, because I don't even know what I meant.

We sit in silence. I wonder if it's the first time anyone has willingly entered his office. He's probably at a loss for what to do.

"Have you had any dreams lately?" he asks finally.

"Everyone has dreams."

"Yes, but any you remember?"

"No."

Silence again.

"What would you like to talk about today, Mr. Wilkes?" Mr. Wakefield asks tentatively.

"I don't really know."

"That's fine," he says. "Perfectly all right. Sometimes, we simply need to be in the presence of another person. Someone who understands."

"Actually, there *is* something," I say, because I'm not cool with Mr. Wakefield thinking we're sharing a comfortable silence.

"That's OK too. It's *great*, in fact. Go on."

He leans forward, anticipating some huge revelation, I guess. My mind flashes to Penelope, prancing around and getting ready to wish for some important cause or another.

"I'm concerned about underage sex workers," I blurt out.

Mr. Wakefield pauses and tilts his head. "Ah, I see… Do you *know* an underage sex worker, Eldon?"

Is he freaking kidding me? We live in Madison. *Of course* I don't know any underage sex workers. And Mr. Wakefield must be aware of that but is giving me the benefit of the doubt anyway.

Which makes me feel guilty.

"I really shouldn't say," I reply vaguely.

He leans in even closer. If he scoots forward any farther, he'll fall out of his chair. "Eldon, these are very serious allegations. If you're not *certain* about this…"

What have I done? I start to sweat. Surely, Mr. Wakefield knows I'm lying. Is he going to call me on it?

"Yeah, I know," I mumble. "Maybe we should forget this conversation?"

"No, no," Mr. Wakefield says quickly. "If there's something you need to talk about, by all means, do so. This room is a safe place."

I want to groan and bury my head in my hands. Instead, I say, "It's cool, really. The situation is under control."

Mr. Wakefield stands up and walks to the window. Gets into his thinker pose. When he turns, his face is set, like he's made a decision.

Apparently, that decision was to trust me. Because that's the kind of guy Mr. Wakefield is. He has faith in everyone, even selfish jerks like me, who take that trust and use it against him.

"Eldon, sometimes, we think we can handle a situation on our own. Sometimes, we think that's the adult thing to do. And it's admirable, it is. But if you know that someone is in pain, you need to share. You can't place the entire burden on yourself."

"It's really not my place to talk about this."

"Whatever you say here will be kept in the strictest confidence." Mr. Wakefield walks back and sits in the chair next to me. "Is it one of your friends?"

I shrug, because I can't think of how to respond.

No, that's not true.

I know exactly what I *should* say. *Look, Mr. Wakefield, I was trying to get out of class, and this sex worker thing was the first excuse that came to mind. I'm a dick, yeah? But I promise, there's no secret prostitution ring in Madison.*

I can't make the words come out though. I imagine the disappointment on his face. The realization that all his suspicions about me are correct. That I'm an awful person.

"OK," Mr. Wakefield goes on, his brows knitting. "Let's come at it from a different angle. The demands that society places on young women can be very damaging. Your friend is female, correct?"

I cringe at the thought of Mr. Wakefield calling every girl in the school to his office to ask if she's a prostitute. I have to put a stop to this.

"Uh, no, it's actually not." *What is coming out of my mouth?*

His eyes widen. That look comes across his face again, the one that says deep down, he suspects this is bullshit. "It's not? Well. OK. I suppose it was presumptuous of me to think so. Of course young men face challenges too."

"They do," I agree.

"Is this person on the football team with you?" Mr. Wakefield asks.

"No."

"Eldon…you're not talking about *yourself*, are you?"

I almost laugh.

"Sometimes, we say something is happening to a friend because it's easier than—"

"Mr. Wakefield, I promise, no one's paying me to have sex with them."

He nods earnestly and opens his mouth to ask another question, but the bell rings.

I jump up. "Thanks for the chat. This was really helpful."

"But—"

"Talk to you later."

I hurry out of his office, guilt churning in my gut.

Sometimes, you do something bad without realizing you're doing it. And that sucks, but can you really be blamed? Other times, you know you're being terrible. You know it, and you do it anyway.

What's wrong with me, that I didn't put a stop to this? What's *wrong* with me?

✻ ✻ ✻

Merrill and I leave campus for lunch. As soon as we get back to school, I know we missed something. No one's in class. The entirety of Madison High School seems to be packed in the hall whispering to each other. A few girls are crying.

For a second, I have the horrified thought that Mr. Wakefield went overboard trying to solve the case of the teenage sex workers. But I quickly decide that's unlikely. That wouldn't be dramatic enough for people to act like wishing was outlawed.

Merrill and I glance at each other.

"I must admit," he says, "I'm feeling a little out of the loop."

Norie is down the hall at her locker, one of the few people not clustered in a group. Merrill and I start toward her, but I get distracted.

Juniper.

She catches my eye and heads in my direction. Which is how I know something big is happening. It's been a while since Juniper willingly approached me.

"Have you heard?" she asks.

"No."

"It's Fletcher Hale. He tried to kill himself last night."

I don't know what I was expecting. Certainly not this. I glance at Merrill, but he's still making his way toward Norie. I look back at Juniper's worried face.

"Tried?"

"He's alive. For now. He's at the doctor's office, and they're doing what they can. But people are saying he won't make it."

I wish I had something to hold onto. The ground beneath me doesn't feel stable anymore. "What happened?"

"It's gruesome," Juniper says.

"If you can handle it, I'm pretty sure I can."

Even then, even in the middle of the hall, with a kid nearly dying, with us having been broken up for months, Juniper takes the time to roll her eyes at me. "Don't be arrogant."

"*Tell me,*" I say.

"He jumped off a cliff near the hot springs."

"Jesus. And he's *alive?*"

"Like I said, barely. Some stoner kids skipped class and went down there to smoke this morning. That's how they found him. People are saying it's a miracle he lasted the night."

"A miracle?" It has to be the shittiest miracle ever. Dude tries to kill himself, fails, and ends up lying outside all night, completely messed up. To me, that doesn't sound like a miracle so much as a *punishment.*

"Are you OK?" Juniper looks at me with her perfect golden eyes.

I'm not OK. I don't know what I am. Shocked. Horrified.

"Why wouldn't I be OK?" I try to sound casual but fail.

"Eldon."

Just that. Just my name. But in her voice, there's so much more. She knows me so well. It's as if all the feelings running through me are appearing in thought bubbles above my head, and only Juniper can see them.

And yeah, let's not pretend here. I'm thinking about what

I said to Fletcher yesterday. Thinking about how cruel I was. Wondering if maybe I'm what made him do this. I feel light-headed. I have no idea what to do.

Suddenly, Merrill's back at my side.

"Dude," he says.

"Juniper told me," I tell him.

"They canceled classes for the rest of the day," Juniper says. "Everyone's going to the community center."

"Why? That's not gonna do Fletcher any good," I reply.

She shrugs. "I don't know. It's something to do."

People gather in the community center anytime something goes wrong. Anytime someone dies. It isn't usually someone so young though. And I can't remember a suicide.

"You wanna go?" I ask Merrill.

He looks at me closely. "Are you OK?"

"You guys can stop asking me that."

"All right," Merrill says.

But I see the way he and Juniper glance at each other. Neither of them believe it. *I'm* not the one who needs their concern though. I'm not the one on the verge of dying.

☀ ☀ ☀

The last time the whole town gathered at the community center was after Ebba's accident. Which sort of makes me feel like I should be glad we're here because of Fletcher. Because of justice, or vengeance, or whatever. I'm not glad though. I hate the guy, but I don't want him to *die*.

All the wishers—past, present, and future—are crammed together. Penelope runs around handing out tissues and offering words of comfort. The Samson sisters are in the back of the room, watching the goings-on but not participating. I pass Archie Kildare giving a speech to his thuggish friends, saying if he ever tried to off himself, no way would he fail.

I nod to my dad, who's talking to Gil Badgley, but I don't go over to him. Instead, I sit on the floor in a back corner with Merrill and Norie and pull out my phone.

I text my mom, Are you still at the doctor's office?

Yes, she responds.

How's Fletcher?

Her response comes fast. Not good.

I'm typing out another meaningless question when Ma texts again.

I love you, the message says.

I stare at my phone. Three short words, unrelated to the current situation, but they tell me everything I need to know.

They say, *The situation is bad.*

They say, *Fletcher is going to die.*

They say, *Now is the time to remember how fragile life is, to pull your loved ones close and remind them how much they mean to you.*

My eyes sting, and breathing becomes harder. I text my mom back. Love you too.

The conversation I had with Fletcher yesterday races through my mind, no matter how hard I push it away. If he tried to kill himself because of it, because of *me*, doesn't that make me a murderer?

"Dude, this is intense," Merrill says, scanning the room.

Norie's watching me. "It's not your fault," she says again. She and Merrill have been repeating that since we drove over and I admitted I'd torn into Fletcher the day before.

"You know how many times I wished something bad would happen to him?" I ask. "I hated him."

Norie squeezes my hand. "You could never hate Fletcher as much as he hated himself."

I don't respond, because what could I possibly say?

"He was miserable, Eldon," Norie goes on. "He never stopped thinking about the accident."

I frown. "Did you talk with him about it?"

"Yeah, sometimes."

I look at her for a long moment.

"We weren't close," she says. "Just a few classes together. Honestly, I think he would've talked to anyone who listened."

The old bitterness creeps up on me. Why should Fletcher Hale have someone to listen to his thoughts? His situation is his own fault. *I'm* the one who's needed someone to talk to these past few months.

But I try to push away that resentment, because the situation has changed. It doesn't feel right to be bitter, to be pissed off, when

Fletcher is broken in pieces. And whatever I feel toward him, I really, really don't want the kid to die.

There's a murmur in the crowd, and I look over to see that Mayor Fontaine's arrived. He has some of his men with him, the guys Merrill calls goons. Which I guess is as accurate as any other description. They're regular guys from town, but they're big and mean, and they strut around like they've got something to prove.

Sheriff Crawford bumbles along two steps behind the mayor, as always trying—and failing—to look like he's in control. I wonder if he knew when he took the job that being sheriff in Madison is only show.

I assume the mayor will make a speech, but instead, he goes around talking to people quietly. Trying to score points, probably. No matter what time of year it is, he's always focused on the next election. He starts campaigning the day after a win. Like it matters. He's going to be reelected no matter what.

"If we lived in another place, everyone would be praying right now," Norie says.

"What good would that do?" I ask.

"It would make people feel like they were helping."

"But they wouldn't actually be helping. So what would it matter?"

Norie squeezes my hand again. "Prayer *does* help, Eldon. You might not be able to see it working or know how it works, but it does."

"You pray then. You can do the praying for all of us."

And Norie does. The rest of us wait. We wait and wait, and hours later, there's still no news.

* * *

Madison doesn't have a hospital. Not a real one anyway. There are some rooms at the doctor's office that get used as a makeshift hospital when it's needed. Mostly though, people go to Vegas when they're really sick or hurt. But there's no time to get Fletcher there. His injuries are too bad to move him.

At least, that's what people say. That's what *the mayor* says.

"It's bullshit," Merrill whispers. "They don't want Fletch to go to Vegas, because then people will start asking questions, and maybe they'll realize something is off about this town, and maybe they'll even connect Fletcher to Ebba and wonder what the hell—"

"Give it a rest," I say, and I'm shocked when he does.

The three of us are still in the corner, keeping tabs on the action but staying out of it. Every half an hour, I text my mom, and she texts back that there's no improvement.

I'm having flashbacks to Ebba's accident, and it's making me slightly hysterical. I count to ten, then to twenty, then thirty, but it doesn't calm my racing heart or take away the feeling that I need to *do* something. I give up counting and watch the room.

Mayor Fontaine makes his rounds. Uncle Jasper sneaks out his flask when he thinks no one's looking. Juniper blots her eyes with a tissue while her dad comforts her. Barnabas Fairley, drawn by all the action, stalks around the room like he has someone whispering marching orders in his ear. It's a freaking circus.

My phone buzzes in my pocket. I pull it out and read the message from my mom. He's fading fast. The Hales are saying their goodbyes.

My breath catches in my throat. I can't bring myself to repeat the message, so I pass the phone to Merrill and Norie and let them read it for themselves. None of us speak.

A few minutes later, Mr. Wakefield comes over, more somber than I've ever seen him. "Mr. Wilkes, could I speak to you for a moment?"

I don't have the energy to roll my eyes at him. I stand and follow him away from my friends.

"It's very important you answer me honestly," he whispers.

"OK."

"Was Mr. Hale the student you were talking about earlier?"

"What?" I ask, baffled.

"With the, ah, sexual abuse."

Shit.

I study Mr. Wakefield's face. The doubt from earlier is gone. He's no longer questioning my trustworthiness. Sometime between this morning and now, he's accepted that someone in Madison is being taken advantage of.

Which is true. He just doesn't get that it's *him*.

"No," I say emphatically. "I wasn't talking about Fletcher."

"Because if you were, you need to tell me. It's important that we prevent this from—"

"I promise, Mr. Wakefield. Seriously. I wasn't talking about him."

He doesn't seem entirely convinced, but he lets me retreat back to the corner.

Outside, the sun is sinking. Inside, everyone is afraid to speak louder than a whisper. As if our voices might give Fletcher that final push over the edge.

"It sucks that this is happening," Merrill says. "But honestly, can you blame the guy?"

Neither Norie or I respond. For once, Merrill's being serious, not trying to shock us. Besides, I don't know what to think. I understand why Fletcher did it, but at the same time, I disagree with his choice. I feel conflicted about a million different things.

I'm about to suggest that we get out of here. We aren't doing Fletcher any good by sitting around. But then I see something that gives me pause.

Penelope Rowe and Mayor Fontaine. They're off to the side of the room, and from the way Penelope is talking and gesturing, she probably pulled him over there. The mayor shakes his head, but every time he starts to speak, Penelope plows ahead.

I nudge Merrill and nod in their direction.

They argue for a bit longer. Or Penelope argues anyway.

Sheriff Crawford tries to step into the conversation, but the mayor holds up a hand and gives him a sharp look. The sheriff backs off, resigned. Finally, Mayor Fontaine nods. He whispers something to one of his entourage. Then he and Penelope leave the community center together.

"What the hell was that about?" I ask.

Norie doesn't even have to think about it. "Penelope's wish."

"Seriously? You think she's concerned about *her wish* right now? How selfish is that?"

"I wonder…" Norie says thoughtfully.

I wonder too.

CHAPTER 17

COUNTDOWN: 11 DAYS

Y ou can only wait around for so long. Eventually, everyone realizes we aren't going to get any more of an update anytime soon. So we go home and climb into our beds and wait until the next morning to find out if Fletcher survived the night.

A weird hush has fallen over Madison.

"Does that mean he's alive?" I ask my mom in the morning.

"He was when I left last night."

She's dressed in work clothes and has her purse in hand, clearly on her way back to the doctor's office. It's one more reminder of how serious the situation is. Ma never goes into work on Saturday unless she absolutely has to.

"Would someone have told you if he died overnight?" I press.

She closes her eyes and rubs at her forehead. "I don't know, Eldon."

I refrain from asking the question I most want an answer to.

Do you want *him to live?*

I'm certainly not the only member of the Wilkes family who has complicated feelings about Fletcher.

I take a glass from the cabinet and turn on the tap to fill it, but nothing happens.

"Your father turned off the water," Ma says.

"I guess he's making progress on the sink, huh?"

"Apparently."

I put the glass down, check to make sure my keys and phone are in my pocket, then head toward the door.

"Are you working today?" Ma asks.

I nod.

"I'll give you a ride."

I sort of would've preferred walking to the gas station. I want time to think. But the way my mom was standing in the middle of the kitchen looking lost and unsure makes me think alone time is the last thing *she* wants. So I say, "OK, thanks."

We make our way through the house, but Ma pauses as she's about to open the front door.

"Eldon?"

"Yeah?"

"Have you seen my cast-iron skillet?"

Really? *Now* is the time she chooses to bring this up?

I hope my expression doesn't give me away as I tell her I most definitely have *not* seen it. What would I want with a cast-iron skillet?

* * *

Around ten in the morning, Penelope Rowe pulls her yellow VW Beetle up to the gas pump.

I wave hello, but she isn't looking at me. Her eyes are fixed straight ahead; her hands clench the steering wheel. I get the gas pump started, then walk over to the driver's window and knock.

She only rolls down the window a couple of inches. I'm not feeling too good about the situation. At this point, even the most oblivious person in the world would have a sense of foreboding, yeah?

"I can't talk right now, Eldon. I'm sorry, but I can't."

"It seems like you need to," I say.

"Well, I can't."

But she doesn't roll up the window.

"Where you coming from?" I ask.

Her response is almost a whisper. "The doctor's office."

"Were you visiting Fletcher?"

Nothing.

"Penelope. Why don't you tell me what's going on?"

She sniffs and wipes her nose. "I wanted to do the right thing."

"What did you do?" It comes out slow and patient, like I'm talking to a child.

She doesn't respond, keeps staring blankly ahead.

"Penelope. Hey, look at me."

She meets my eyes. She's been crying.

"Penny, seriously. What's going on?"

Her face crumples. It's like she held herself together for as long as possible, but now she's finally breaking. Her eyes are locked on mine, and in them, I see a world of regret.

"Hey, it's OK," I say when her tears start falling. "It's going to be OK."

She shakes her head. "Eldon," Penelope says, her voice trembling. "I think I made a very serious mistake."

✹ ✹ ✹

I almost stay home that night. I keep thinking about Fletcher and Penelope, which doesn't exactly put me in the mood to party. But I don't know what else to do. So once it starts to get dark, I walk through my ghost neighborhood until I get to the skeleton house.

Merrill is already there, which isn't abnormal. The surprising part is that Norie is with him. It's weird, them hanging out without me. I wonder what they've been talking about.

Probably about Fletcher. That's all anyone's talking about tonight.

"Hey," I say, climbing up to the top of the house. "You going to the hot springs with us, Norie?"

"I guess. I've made an effort to stay away from there, but what the heck. We're graduating soon. I might as well experience it once."

I sit down next to them. If they *were* talking about Fletcher, they don't resume their conversation. Instead, we swing our legs over the open space, talk about stuff without really talking about anything at all. I start to tell them about my run-in with Penelope a few times but keep changing my mind. It's not really my news to tell. And besides, I don't want to ruin the moment.

There's something easy about this. About being with the two of them. Uncomplicated, amid a million things that are anything but. I feel like the three of us have been friends forever, that we'll always be friends. Eternity is sitting in a half-built house, saying more in the silences than when we talk.

But eventually Merrill says, "Wanna head to the party?"

I don't. At all.

But what are you supposed to say? *Nah, let's sit here and contemplate our friendship for a while.*

I tell him I'm ready. We go to the hot springs.

* * *

I guess it's morbid, yeah? Going through the canyon right after Fletcher tried to kill himself there. But everyone needs a release, and we don't have anywhere else to go.

"There's seriously not an easier way in?" Norie asks when we get to the rope.

"This *is* the easy way," I say. "Unless you're good at scaling walls."

When we get to the springs and the party, Norie surveys the area. "Well, this is exactly what I was expecting."

I laugh. "If you stop being judgmental for a few minutes, you might actually have fun."

"She's religious," Merrill says. "Judgment comes naturally to her."

"Wow, you guys have a whole comedy routine."

We laugh and wander to the cooler. Merrill offers Norie a beer, but she shakes her head.

"Seriously?"

"I don't drink."

"Because of a health thing?" Merrill asks.

"Because of a Word of Wisdom thing."

"I'm gonna need a few of these before I get into *that* with you," Merrill replies, cracking open his first beer of the night.

We circle the party to see who showed up. I keep looking for Penelope, though I'm pretty sure she won't be here.

To Norie, this might seem like a typical night at the hot springs, but it's not. Even with the music and talking and drinking, it's somber. Fletcher is on everyone's minds. Or maybe I'm *projecting* like Mr. Wakefield talks about.

When Merrill wanders away to get more beer, I ask Norie if she wants to go sit by one of the pools.

"Shouldn't we wait for him?"

I shake my head. "He'll get distracted and spend the rest of the night trying to convince a freshman the mayor is the reincarnation of Hitler or something."

So we go to one of the springs away from everyone and stick our feet in the water. It's a nice night. The temperature hasn't dropped below ninety, but there's a breeze. The moon is bright, and the air feels rich. You can almost pretend someone didn't try to kill themselves farther up the canyon.

"I never pictured you as the guy who goes off on his own at parties," Norie says.

"I'm not feeling it tonight," I say.

"Because of Fletcher?"

"Because of everything."

Norie doesn't ask more, for which I'm grateful.

"What's your deal?" I ask her. "Why haven't you ever come here before?"

"This isn't exactly my crowd. Obviously."

"Do you *have* a crowd?" I ask.

Norie laughs. "What, you think because I don't hang out with the popular kids I don't have friends?"

I hadn't considered it one way or another, because I hadn't paid attention to her until she started hanging out with us. Norie was just another person at school, someone who wasn't in the same social circle as me.

"That's not what I meant," I mumble.

"No?" Norie raises her eyebrows. "Here's the thing about the people you hang out with: you think what you're doing is so important and special that you can't imagine there's a whole other world happening behind you. Or *below* you, as you'd probably think of it."

I try to read her expression. Is she angry, insulted? She just looks matter-of-fact.

"So who *do* you hang out with?"

"A bunch of different people. We don't all fit into neat little cliques the way you think."

"Stop telling me what I think," I say, my voice rising a little.

She looks surprised. "You're right. Sorry."

For a while, we watch the party without talking. Juniper shows up, hanging all over Calvin Boyd. I sigh.

"What's your deal with her?" Norie asks.

"You gonna tell me how much better I can do?"

"No. I think Juniper's really nice."

I didn't realize she even *knew* Juniper, but I know better than to say so.

"I don't know what it is," I say to Norie, keeping my eyes on Juniper and Calvin. "She's special. Even before her wish."

"Her wish?"

"Yeah. To be beautiful."

Norie laughs. "Are you kidding me? Juniper didn't wish for beauty."

This gets my attention. "She didn't?"

"She wished to keep her dad's bar running. It was about to close, you know."

I can't wrap my mind around this.

"But…after we broke up, it was right around her wish. I swear she changed."

"Maybe you saw her differently because she was the first

girl to break your heart. You'd never been dumped before, had you?"

I hadn't.

"If that's true, why didn't she wish for money? They could've been rich enough that her dad didn't need the Last Chance."

"That's your problem, Eldon," Norie says. "You reduce everything. Try to make life too simple. Like thinking every girl at school only wants to be beautiful. People want more than that, you know. Juniper's dad doesn't care about money. He cares about the *bar*. That's why he wished for it in the first place. It's his passion."

I think about that for a minute. I wonder what it must feel like to care about something so strongly that you want it simply for the sake of having it in your life. Then I think of my sister, and I realize I already know.

It's like Norie reads my mind. "Haven't you ever been passionate about anything?"

"I guess so," I say. "What about you? What are you passionate about? God?"

"Oh jeez. Why does it always have to be about God?"

"Because you're the only person in this entire town who's religious," I say. "It's sort of a huge deal."

"First of all, I may be the only person in Madison who believes in God, but I'm not the only one who's religious."

"Name one other person," I challenge.

"Don't you get it? *Wishing* is a religion here. For me, that's not enough."

"Why?"

Norie thinks for a long moment. She twirls the ring on her finger. "My whole life, I felt like something was missing. I was convinced there was a bigger picture, more to the world than what I was seeing. More than just *wishing*. It seemed as if everything happened for a reason, but I didn't know what the reason was."

She looks at me, and I gesture for her to go on.

"A few years ago, I was in Las Vegas for a Varsity Quiz event. I snuck away for a while and spent time wandering around and…I don't know, imagining what it would've been like to grow up somewhere else. That's when I ran into Elder Jansen. We got to talking about Mormonism, and it clicked for me. All I'd been confused about came into focus."

"That must have felt good," I say.

Norie narrows her eyes as if I'm teasing. I'm not. "Yeah. It did."

"But the whole *God's plan* thing, don't you ever feel like it's a cop-out? An excuse to never take responsibility for your actions?"

Norie snorts. "And how is that different from the way people treat wishing?"

"I guess you're right."

"There's one big difference though," Norie says. "Religions encourage you to help others and be the best person you can be. With wishing, you get your heart's desire handed to you without effort. It doesn't matter if you're mean or selfish or lazy. In fact, wishing *encourages* that behavior "

She isn't wrong. I've heard my fair share of spiteful wishes. That's one of the reasons we have to get wishes approved by Mayor Fontaine.

"You see my ring?" Norie asks, holding out her hand.

I lean over. It's a simple band with a shield on it. Stamped on the shield are the letters CTR.

"It stands for choose the right." Norie pulls back her hand and examines the ring herself. "It's a reminder. Life is full of tough times and hard decisions. But as long as you choose to do the right thing, you'll be OK."

Sounds fine in theory. "But how do you know what's right?" I ask.

Norie smiles at me. "You just know, Eldon. Even when you think you don't."

I don't buy it. Maybe *Norie* knows. Maybe all she needs to guide her through life is a ring. But I'm looking for a little more direction than that. I need a clear path.

"I refuse to believe this is all there is to life." Norie gestures to the party around us. "And I refuse to let my future be dictated by wishes."

I watch my classmates. Norie's right. They're held hostage by wishes. Drinking away their nights to escape boredom, counting down the hours to their wish days, thinking that's when their life starts. And after that, after their wishes are made, counting down the hours until they die, because their moment has passed. No one's living—they're *waiting*. What they're waiting *for* is the only part that changes.

"Really, Norie," I say. "What did you wish for?"

Knowing the answer is becoming more important by the day.

"I'll never tell," Norie says with a serene smile.

I sigh. "You know, the longer you hold out, the more invested I get."

"Are we still talking about wishing?"

The joke catches me off guard, and I laugh.

Norie laughs too and nudges me with her elbow. "My wish won't help you, Eldon. You need to come up with your own."

"Yeah." I frown. "I know."

On the other side of the party, Merrill is holding court, regaling a group of people with God knows what story. He gestures wildly and spills his beer but doesn't notice.

"I can't let him get too drunk," I tell Norie. "He's supposed to drive me to Vegas tomorrow."

"For what?"

"I'm visiting my sister."

"Ah," Norie says. "You do that often?"

"Not as often as I want." I turn to her. "Wanna come with us?"

"Yeah. I'd like that."

A melancholy silence falls over us. Or maybe it's only

melancholy for me. I wonder if I'll ever be able to talk about Ebba without feeling like someone's stomping on my heart with football cleats.

Thinking of Ebba leads me right back to Fletcher Hale. For the rest of eternity, the two of them will be linked in my mind. The accident created a union between them as strong as marriage vows.

I guess Penelope's wrapped up in that too now.

Word hasn't gotten out about Penelope's wish. If it had, the entire party would've been buzzing about it. It's only a matter of time though. You can't keep secrets in a small town. And even the most oblivious of Madison's residents will find it pretty hard to miss a dead guy walking among us.

CHAPTER 18

THE WISH HISTORY: PENELOPE ROWE

O pen up the wish history and flip to the latest entry.

Penelope Rowe. Look at her, bursting with sunshine and rainbows, doing her best to change the world.

See how people mistake her optimism for naivety?

Nothing could be further from the truth.

Penelope Rowe knows the world is far from perfect. There are so many terrible people. There are so many terrible things that happen to good people. The world can be a dark place, and nothing will ever change that.

But Penelope also knows moping around and feeling sad isn't going to help anyone. And more than anything, Penelope wants to be helpful. She may never change the world. But that doesn't mean she won't try.

Turn to the page where eight-year-old Penelope first realizes she can Make a Difference.

She's watching the news—a broadcast about a flood on the other side of the country. Look closely at the horror on her face as she hears about people who are dead or missing or now homeless. Watch the tears pour down Penelope's cheeks as a flood victim on TV cries about not being able to find her dog.

Little Penelope Rowe scoops up her cat and snuggles her as tight as she can. When Penelope has a really bad day, like when she gets a B on a test or doesn't get the lead in the school play, hugging her cat is what makes her feel better.

Those poor flood victims. They've lost so much and don't even have their pets for comfort.

This is the moment. You can see it on Penelope's face. She's having a revelation.

If the flood victims had their animals, could hug their puppies and kittens, they'd feel better too. It wouldn't undo the flood, of course. But maybe it would make the coming days a little more bearable for them.

That weekend, Penelope sets up a lemonade stand in front of the supermarket. She mixed the lemonade all by herself. She carefully painted the sign:

FIND THE MISSING FLOOD ANIMALS!

Let's watch as she stops every person who walks by. Tells them how important it is to Make a Difference.

"This is a fund-raiser to locate and return displaced flood pets to their owners," she tells Gil Badgley.

Gil scratches at his beard. "Dontcha suppose they need homes more than their pets?"

Eight-year-old Penelope, she's brimming with earnestness. "How would you feel if Tuco was out there, lost and scared, with no way to get back to you?"

Gil buys a cup of lemonade.

All day, people pass Penelope's table, and she says, "Don't you love animals? Don't you want to contribute? Don't you want to Make a Difference?"

At the end of the day, Penelope's earned forty-two dollars. Her mom helps her seal it in an envelope addressed to the flood relief program, along with carefully worded instructions for how the money should be spent. That night, Penelope goes to sleep knowing that she may not have changed the world, but she tried.

Turn to the next page of this history book.

There's Penelope brainstorming fund-raiser ideas, giving money to charities.

She keeps loose change in her pockets in case she runs into Barnabas Fairley.

She has her mom drive her to Las Vegas so she can volunteer at the women and children's center.

Year after year after year of helping people, and Penelope's desire to Make a Difference grows.

Sure, it's admirable.

But what Penelope doesn't understand: some people don't want to be helped.

Let's read ahead. Penelope, now seventeen, has her prewish meeting with the mayor. In his office, she holds her head high and tells him she's going to wish for money.

Mayor Fontaine listens from the other side of the most massive desk

Penelope has ever seen. She thinks about how much wood was wasted, how many trees were killed to build that ridiculous desk. She thinks about taking an ax to it and how the kindling could keep homeless people from freezing to death during harsh winters.

"A sound choice," Mayor Fontaine says. "The best way to ensure a comfortable life."

"Oh, it's not for me," Penelope replies. "It's to send to charities and relief funds. I can't actually wish to change the world outside Madison, so sending money to support causes is the best I can do."

The mayor peers at Penelope with his tiny, black eyes, making her squirm.

Penelope figures the mayor thinks she's lying. But she doesn't care what he thinks. Though she'd never admit it, Penelope doesn't like Mayor Fontaine. He never contributes to her bake sales and probably hasn't helped anyone in his entire life.

"Whatever it's for, the wish is straightforward," the mayor says. "Let's talk about wording."

They talk, and plans are put in place.

But this is Madison, where life seldom goes according to plan.

The night before Penelope's scheduled to make her wish, Fletcher Hale throws himself off a cliff.

Penelope isn't exactly close to Fletcher. But she knows him, because she's made an effort to know every person at their school.

She definitely doesn't want him to die.

She wants him to be happy.

She wants to help *him.*

Penelope scurries around the community center, handing out tissues and offering comfort. She calls Fletcher's parents, offers to assist them with anything they need, anything at all. There are so many people who need her right now.

Except the person who most *needs help is out of reach.*

What can she do for Fletcher?

Penelope thinks of a documentary she saw once, about people who tried to kill themselves by jumping off the Golden Gate Bridge but failed. Every one of those people said that, as they were falling, they regretted their decision.

It's not human nature to want to die, Penelope knows. All over the world, even in the most dire circumstances, humans instinctually fight to live.

At the community center, Penelope wanders to the corner where a friend of hers sits. Her sad, mixed-up, fool of a friend.

"Are you OK?" Penelope asks him.

He runs his fingers through his hair. "I don't know. I guess. I mean, I hated the guy, but I never wanted this."

Of course you didn't, *Penelope thinks.*

No one did.

Not even Fletcher, not really.

And that's when Penelope Rowe takes the situation into her own hands.

She pulls the mayor away from the people he's talking to.

"About my wish," she says.

"Don't worry, I haven't forgotten. You'll still get your wish." He

smiles at her with understanding, seeing his own wish-greed reflected in her eagerness.

Penelope shakes her head. "It's not that. I want to change it."

The mayor listens to what she wants to do. The understanding fades from his face. He argues and tells her it's a waste, it's unnatural. He reminds her that there are rules against wishing someone back from the dead.

"He's not dead yet," says Penelope. "But he will be if we don't hurry."

Astonishingly, the mayor relents.

They go to the wish cave.

And Penelope wishes for Fletcher Hale to live.

She wants to see him right afterward, but Mayor Fontaine convinces her to wait out the night. After all, no one's ever attempted to save someone this close to death. No one knows how it'll work, or if it'll work.

Turn to the next page in the history book. The following morning.

Watch Penelope get up early and hurry to the doctor's office. See how kindly she smiles at poor Mrs. Wilkes who's slumped behind the reception desk, looking like she hasn't slept for days.

Mrs. Wilkes says, "Yes, Fletcher's alive."

She continues, "No, honey, I don't think it's a good idea for you to see him."

But as we know, Penelope Rowe is nothing if not persistent.

"Fletcher?" she says softly, stepping into the dim room.

His face is turned away from her.

Penelope moves closer, and she's glad Fletcher isn't looking at her, because she's not able to mask her horror.

His body is broken, bruised.

"Hi, Fletcher. It's Penelope," she whispers.

"Are you the one who did this?" he asks.

His voice is bitter. No one's ever spoken to her with that tone before.

"Yes. I wished for you to live."

Fletcher shifts to look at her. His eyes are dead, hollow. And more than anything, Penelope wishes he would turn away again, because she can't bear to see his pain.

"You should have let me die," Fletcher says.

"I…I thought—"

"This wasn't your choice to make."

Then he tells her to get out, which Penelope is happy to do.

She's shaking so much, she can't trust herself to drive. She pulls over at the gas station. There's her friend. He can tell something is wrong. He speaks with such concern it's as if, for once, he cares about someone other than himself. Penelope can't help herself—she spills everything.

And as she talks, Penelope has a new revelation. Helping people is good. But it's also a two-way street.

You can't save someone who doesn't want to be saved.

CHAPTER 19

COUNTDOWN: 10 DAYS

Sometime during the night, Uncle Jasper found his way onto our living room couch. His mouth is hanging open, and I have the urge to throw something in it, see if it'll rouse him from his drunken stupor.

In the kitchen, my mom is in a coupon-cutting frenzy. Scraps of paper fly around like confetti.

"Looks like Jasper had a rough night," I say to her, crossing to the fridge for a glass of orange juice.

"As usual," Ma replies in a clipped tone.

"Why do you always rescue him? Maybe it would do him good to fend for himself."

"Because he's *family*, Eldon," she says. "I may not always like what Jasper does. I may not always like *him*. But I love him, and you do everything you can for the people you love."

Ma's speaking in an even tone, but it sounds like she's barely holding back rage. Uncle Jasper doesn't usually get her so worked up.

"Uh...is everything OK?" I ask.

Ma slams down her scissors. "Did you know about Fletcher?"

I guess the secret is out.

She glares at me with eyes that are red and glassy and burning with fury. "Did you know he got a second chance? A *stranger* gave him a second chance, and my own son won't do the same for his *sister*."

I don't speak. Because what could I possibly say?

I'm sorry, I think. *I'm sorry, I'm sorry. I'm sorry I'm letting you down, but I can't save Ebba, and the longer you pretend I can, the more painful this is going to be.*

"Ma—" I begin quietly.

"Don't, Eldon. I don't want to hear it." She rests her elbows on the table and puts her face in her hands. I expect to hear sobs, but she's silent. She's waiting for me to leave. She can't even stand the sight of my face.

I slip out of the kitchen without getting my orange juice. I couldn't have stomached it anyway.

*   *   *

"It's like he was *resurrected*," says Merrill.

We're on our way to Vegas. I'm sitting shotgun, and Norie's in the back seat, leaning forward to hear us better.

"He wasn't resurrected," I say. "He wasn't dead yet."

"From what I hear, he was pretty goddamn close. What was Penelope *thinking*?"

"I think it's honorable," Norie chimes in from the back seat. "Penelope made a huge sacrifice for Fletcher."

"How can you say that?" Merrill replies, swerving a little. I consider asking him to pull over so I can drive. "She *played God*. You can't possibly be cool with that."

"Or maybe God wanted Fletcher to have a second chance."

Merrill glances over at me. "Come on, Eldo. Back me up here."

I haven't worked out my feelings though. I think about Penelope's haunted expression. The fear and regret that she couldn't hide with an optimistic smile. We always assumed you couldn't wish to resurrect or kill someone because it's too complicated. Like the wish cave doesn't have that much power, yeah? But maybe there's more to it than that.

Right before Fletcher jumped, he must have been dead in his own mind. Did Penelope's wish get him stuck in some strange in-between? His body may be alive, but what about the rest of him? Maybe Penelope screwed him up even worse than he was before.

On the other hand, isn't this what I wanted for Ebba? If I could turn back the clock, wouldn't I want Fletcher to use his wish to restore her health before she was whisked out of town?

Is it different because Ebba didn't *choose* to end her life?

Realizing he's not getting help from me, Merrill goes on. "Everyone has a right to make their own decisions. None of us know what Fletcher was going through. Penelope overstepped."

"And what if next week, Fletcher would have felt differently?"

Norie asks. "Just because he was in a dark place a few nights ago doesn't mean he'd stay there forever. Penelope may have prevented an outcome Fletcher didn't really want in the first place."

I imagine this same argument is happening all over Madison. But what's the point? It won't change what happened. Why debate what's already done?

I tune out Merrill and Norie, gaze out the window, and watch the desert roll by. Dirt and Joshua trees and tumbleweeds, mountains in the distance. The landscape all looks the same: one great big wasteland, with Madison lost in the middle of it.

An hour and a half later, Las Vegas appears in the distance. It's always jarring to first see in on the horizon. You're driving through a barren land, when suddenly, there's a pyramid, a castle, the Eiffel Tower, the New York skyline.

When I was a kid, my family took day trips to Vegas a few times a year. We'd eat at a buffet, then wander the Strip. Watch sharks swim through a shipwreck at Mandalay Bay or play midway games at Circus Circus or laugh at people in togas at Caesar's Palace. As if it was totally normal, all those things being together in one place. The Strip is like an eccentric fantasy.

But Ebba isn't on the Strip. Obviously. No fantasyland for her.

Merrill drives to a sketchy part of town where there's nothing but medical buildings and homeless people. He pulls into the parking lot of the nursing home where Ebba's lived—or *sort of* lived—for the last several months. It's an unimpressive building that reeks of hopelessness.

Before the accident, I thought nursing homes were only for old people. Not the case. Yeah, they're for people who need long-term care they can't get at home. But they're also for people who can only stay alive with the help of machines, people who got kicked out of the hospital. The hospital only lets you stay if there's a possibility you'll get better, and a nursing home is where you stay, old or young, while you slowly wait to die.

"Want us to go in with you?" Merrill asks.

I shake my head.

He points at a Del Taco across the road and tells me they'll wait for me there.

It's been a while since I visited Ebba, but the woman at the front desk remembers me. I remember her too, because she always tries to flirt with me, which is extremely off-putting. She's several years older than me, and also, who goes to a nursing home to get a date?

"Your sister will be so happy to see you," the woman says, smiling and twirling her hair around her finger.

I resist the urge to roll my eyes.

My sister *won't* be happy to see me. She won't even know I'm here. I want to shout at the front desk lady, but I don't. There are a couple of other people in the waiting room, and they don't want to hear that shit. They have loved ones here too. And even though we all know it's a stopover place, a preparing-to-die place, I'm not gonna say it out loud.

The wait isn't long, but it feels like a million years. It's enough time for me to get angry. I shouldn't have to wait to see my sister. I shouldn't have to travel to a *nursing home* to see my sister. She should be at home, where she belongs, living the life she deserves.

It's not fair. Nothing about the situation is fair. Sorrow rises in my body, wrapping around my throat, trying to choke the breath out of me.

When a nurse finally leads me into Ebba's room, my hands are sweaty, and my mouth is dry.

Ebba looks the same as last time I saw her. The exact same. Her tiny body is lost in the hospital bed. She's just a kid—we celebrated her thirteenth birthday here a month ago. Before the accident, Ebba gushed about how she couldn't wait to be a teenager. She was more eager to grow up than anyone else I know, and now she never will.

Life is nothing but a cruel joke.

"Hey, Ebs," I say, pulling a chair next to her bed.

Her eyes are closed, but she doesn't seem peaceful. The old Ebba, Ebba before the accident, smiled constantly. Even in her sleep, she'd have a half smile on her face. Without it, she doesn't look like she's in a coma—she looks like she's already dead.

I pick up her hand and squeeze it. I listen to the machinery that's keeping her alive. I have no idea what to say.

"Fletcher Hale tried to kill himself."

That's totally the wrong thing to share. If Ebba was herself, she'd tease me about my shitty bedside manner. More than anything, I want her to wake up and make fun of me. She could mock me for the rest of our lives, if only she'd *wake up*.

"My wish is soon," I try instead. But that doesn't feel right either.

I imagine Ebba rolling her eyes. She was big on rolling her eyes. And she'd say something like, "Oh *gawd*, Eldon, it's only a wish. Don't have a major freak-out."

Then I would've mimicked her in a high-pitched voice, "*Oh gawd.*"

She would have shrieked with laughter.

And it would have made me laugh too.

And our parents would come in the room asking what's so funny, but we'd be cracking up too hard to answer, and it wouldn't be their business anyway, because they aren't a part of that secret club siblings have.

"I've been listening to Robert Nash," I tell Ebba. "He's getting weirder. The other night, he did a show about how George Washington was an alien abductee and our whole political system is actually based on an extraterrestrial government."

Laugh, I will Ebba. *Please crack a smile. That radio show is one of your favorite things in the world, and I know you must miss it. I know you want to squeal over some ridiculous conspiracy, slug me in the arm when I tell you it's crap.*

But her face doesn't change. There's no sign that my sister is still inside her body. I keep looking for her, but she's not there. My mom says she can feel Ebba with us, and I nod like I agree, but the truth is, I never have. For me, she was gone the second she was hit by Fletcher's car.

"Tag, Ebba. You're it," I say. "Now it's your turn. You have to tag me. You have to leave me a note." My voice cracks. I'm completely losing it.

I lean forward and rest my forehead against the edge of her hospital bed. I can't do it. I can't sit here and talk to an empty room. I won't bustle around like my mom, arranging stuffed animals, hanging posters, chatting away like Ebba's sitting in bed taking notes.

"I miss you so much, Ebs." My voice catches, and tears start to fall like someone turned on a tap.

I try not to cry at the nursing home. My mom hates it when I cry, thinks it's a sign that I've given up. And what if Ma is right? What if Ebba is here, watching us? I don't want her to hear me sobbing, know how miserable I am. She's fighting a battle that's hard enough without my pain adding to it.

Deep down, I know she's not fighting a battle though. She's not. I can cry tears to wash away the entire nursing home, and Ebba will never know any different. *She's never going to wake up*, the doctors have told us over and over again, gently at first but more firmly the longer my mom refuses to believe them.

So I don't try to fight it. I let myself cry.

I'm never getting my sister back. Everything that we shared, that we were supposed to share in the future, is gone.

And it's my fault. I wasn't the one driving the car, but I should have been there for her. Ebba should have never been riding her bike that day. I'm her big brother, and it was my job to protect her, and I didn't. I let her down. I let my whole family down.

For as much as I hate Fletcher Hale, as much as I blame him for Ebba's accident, there's no denying that I hate and blame myself too.

* * *

"How is she?" Merrill asks when I join him and Norie at Del Taco.

I sit down at the table, take one of Norie's fries. "The same."

"I'm sorry, man."

Silence descends on us as we all contemplate topics that are way too heavy for a fast-food joint. I'm having trouble pulling myself out of Ebba's room. It's always hard to walk out of the nursing home and back into normal life.

"Is there any chance of recovery?" Norie asks carefully, like I'm so fragile, her words might shatter me.

I don't respond, because I'll break down again, and sobbing in the middle of Del Taco isn't high on my to-do list. Thankfully, Merrill answers for me, speaking in the same gentle voice.

"Not really," he says, glancing at me quickly to make sure it's

OK. "Eldon's parents, they just don't want to…you know, pull the plug yet. Not until Eldon's wish."

"I see," Norie says. And she *does* see. She looks at me as if she suddenly knows everything about me.

I clear my throat. Concentrate on wishing instead of Ebba in that terrible room. "My mom thinks I can save her."

"Can't you?" Norie asks.

"Maybe if she was in Madison." Though the situation with Fletcher has me questioning that. "But even if I could wish for her to get better here, it won't go unnoticed. The doctors know how bad she is, and if she suddenly recovers, it'll be a miracle. Like, articles in medical journals and segments on the news. It would break the rules of wishing."

"Can't you bring her home to Madison then?" Norie asks. "Right before your wish?"

"She wouldn't survive the trip."

"Besides," Merrill says, "what then? People here know about her. Someone would find out she'd been magically cured. The other option is that the whole town fakes her death. And even in Madison, that charade is too much."

"It was a mistake bringing her to Vegas in the first place," I say. "But no one knew how bad it was. We thought she would be in the hospital for a week or two."

Though truthfully, right after it happened, no one knew *what* to think. We were all so upset, it was impossible to make smart choices. Sheriff Crawford rushed Ebba to Vegas, and maybe we could have called him back in time, but no one *knew*.

Norie frowns and twists her ring around her finger. "I don't get it then. What exactly does your mom want you to wish for?"

"Money. My mom thinks if we throw enough money at people, we could get Ebba into the best hospital in the world, and they could find a way to make her better."

"What do you think?" Norie asks.

"I think there are some problems money can't fix."

And deep down, I think my mom knows it too. She knows that what she's doing is terrible, prolonging Ebba's life when the outcome has been inevitable from the start. No amount of wishing can change what happened.

I also know that if I don't try, my mom will hate me forever.

The easiest choice would be to do what Ma wants. Wish for money. But how long will this go on? How many specialists will she fly to Vegas? How many years will pass before the doctors say enough is enough? Ebba deserves better than that. I don't want her hovering around in some kind of half-life. I want my sister to be at peace.

I can do what's best for my mom or what's best for my sister. What's best for *me* has never even been a factor.

"Let's go," Norie says.

"Back to Madison?" I ask.

She shakes her head. "Let's do something fun. You should get your mind off all this for a while."

I don't know if that's possible, but I'm willing to try.

* * *

Merrill wants to ride the High Roller. It's a new addition to the Las Vegas playground and supposedly one of the tallest observation wheels in the world.

"Isn't it expensive?" I ask. I don't have much cash on me.

"I'll spot you," Merrill says.

So we end up on the Strip after all.

At the top of the High Roller, we can see the whole city spread out below us, a grid of houses and streets extending right up to the mountains. I think of my own town, farther out in the desert. Hidden in the middle of the Mojave and more magical than the entire city of Las Vegas.

Merrill leans forward, taking in the view. His eyes shine, and he's got a huge grin on his face.

"It's like flying," he says.

"Have you ever been in a plane before?" Norie asks him.

"Well, no," Merrill says. "But this is how I imagine it. Looking down and seeing the whole world below you and feeling *free*."

Norie smiles at Merrill. "You'll fly one day."

"Damn right I will."

I'm not trying to ruin the mood, but I'm having the opposite reaction of Merrill. Seeing the world from above doesn't make me feel free. It makes me feel small. Insignificant. There's a whole city down there filled with people. And each one of those people has their own problems, their own pain. What does my life mean in the mix? "I don't know," I say. "It doesn't really look special when you see it from here."

"Nothing looks that special when you see it from above," Norie replies.

Merrill laughs and nudges Norie. "Don't you ever give it a rest?"

After the High Roller, we get hot fudge sundaes at the Ghirardelli ice cream shop. We push our way to the front of the crowd to see the water show at the Bellagio. Merrill wants to ride the roller coaster at New York–New York. Norie wants to see the white tigers at the Mirage. I don't care what we do. I'm happy to go along for the ride.

Security kicks us off the casino floor at Treasure Island. We go back outside and walk the Strip, rubbing elbows with tourists who are beating the heat with two-dollar margaritas.

"Wanna see if anyone will serve us?" Merrill asks, stopping at a bar.

"Dude, we're not in Madison," I say.

"Maybe I should have wished for a fake ID."

Norie rolls her eyes. "It's possible to have fun without being inebriated, you know."

Merrill laughs and wraps an arm around her shoulders. "Who says I'm not having fun?"

Believe it or not, I'm having fun too. If I'd been knocking

back cheap margaritas, I probably would have thrown my arms around Merrill and Norie and thanked them for being such amazing friends.

Instead, I say, "You guys hungry?"

The sun is setting when we return to the Mustang. All three of us are sunburned and exhausted and a little dazed from all the lights and noise and activity.

"Can we make one more stop before we leave town?" Norie asks.

"I'm not in any rush to get back to Shitsville," Merrill says.

Norie's directions take us away from the center of the city. We pass through residential neighborhoods and work our way to the edge of town, until a majestic white building appears in front of us. The expertly—and probably expensively—manicured lawn looks ridiculously out of place against the backdrop of the mountains. I lean forward and crane my neck to see where the building's spires touch the sky.

"What the hell is this?" Merrill asks.

"The Mormon Temple," Norie replies.

We should have known.

Merrill groans but parks the car without argument. We wander up to the building, and Norie looks at it in awe. I imagine the expression on her face isn't so different from when a kid sees the wish cave for the first time.

"You gonna go in?" Merrill asks.

Norie shakes her head. "I can't. There are steps you have to take first."

Merrill raises his eyebrows. "That's pretty messed up."

"It's a sacred place," Norie says. "I don't think it would be right for just anyone to be allowed to waltz in."

"Like us heathens?" Merrill jokes.

Norie grins at him. "Something like that."

I can't help but ask the obvious. "So, uh, why are we here then?"

"I wanted to see it. And walk the grounds. I don't need to go inside to feel close to God here."

"Well," Merrill says, "while you're having a moment with God, I'll be over there, having a moment with rest."

Merrill wanders to a tree and collapses beneath it, stretching out on his back in the grass. I shrug at Norie and follow him.

"I can't believe *this* is where we're spending our last moments in Sin City," Merrill says while Norie starts away from us down a flower-lined path.

"It was either here or home." I'd happily stay at the temple forever if it meant not facing what is waiting for me in Madison.

"Good point, Eldo. Good point."

Merrill takes off his glasses and tosses them in the grass. I pick them up and put them on my face. I did this all the time when we were kids. Merrill and I figured if he had his glasses off and I had them on, we were seeing the world in the exact same way.

"Do you get any of this?" Merrill asks, waving a hand toward the temple.

"No." I take off the glasses and set them down. "But I bet the people who pray here wouldn't get wishing."

Merrill props himself up and looks around dramatically. "Did Norie come back? Because I'm pretty sure those are her words coming out of your mouth."

I shove him playfully, catching him off balance so he falls back. "Maybe Norie knows what's up."

"Please don't get religious on me," Merrill says. "I don't think I could handle you adopting a puritanical lifestyle."

"No worries on that front. I'm probably more likely to end up with a substance abuse problem like my Uncle Jasper."

"Dude," Merrill says, his voice suddenly serious. "Don't even joke about that. You're never going to be like Jasper."

He's right—at least, I *hope* he's right. I want to be *something*. I want life to take me *somewhere*. It's past time for me to figure out what or where that is. The longer I hesitate, the more likely a path will be chosen for me without my consent. And I'm pretty freaking sick of not being in control.

"You know, part of me hopes Norie's right about all this," I say, nodding at the temple.

Merrill doesn't say anything. Then he sits up and puts his glasses back on. "Hey, Eldo, speaking of Norie—"

"Why are you speaking of Norie?" Norie asks from behind us.

Merrill hesitates but recovers quickly, grins at her. "Just wondering how your chat with God was going."

Norie rolls her eyes. "Come on. Let's go home."

I let Norie ride shotgun on the way back to Madison. I crack open my window and close my eyes, enjoy the air on my face as the world rushes past us. Merrill turns on the radio, and I smile when I hear, "*Live from the loneliest corner of the Mojave, you're listening to Basin and Range Radio, where we keep an eye on the night sky. This is your host, Robert Nash.*"

I hope, wherever Ebba is, she has her own version of Robert Nash to listen to. I hope she's surrounded by everything she loves.

"Was the temple all you were hoping?" Merrill asks Norie, so quietly I can hardly hear him over the radio, over the wind whipping in from outside.

"Yeah," she replies. "Sometimes, when you go to a good place, you feel lighter from simply being there."

I listen to Robert Nash talk about crop circles. I listen to the low hum of my friends' voices from the front seat. I *do* feel lighter than I did earlier. But it doesn't have anything to do with the temple. It's because of Merrill and Norie. Because I have people in my life who will try their hardest to make me feel better, even though we all know it's hopeless.

I fall asleep and don't wake up until we're back in Madison.

CHAPTER 20

COUNTDOWN: 9 DAYS

Fletcher Hale is only *technically* alive.

He limps into art class on Monday morning, dragging one of his legs behind him. His breathing is labored. One of his ears is mostly gone, and a huge scar runs up that side of his face. Penelope's wish fused Fletcher's bones back together, but from the jerky way he's moving, I'm guessing he's not exactly good as new.

It's his eyes that are the worst. I've never seen a person look so empty. So resigned. No wonder Penelope was terrified.

The entire classroom watches him make his way to his desk. He sits down stiffly.

"OK, class, let's talk about the progress we've made on our projects," Ms. Dove says, like it's business as usual. But her face has gone completely pale.

I stare at Fletcher. I can't *not* stare. I try to keep myself from shuddering.

"You have something to say? Then say it," Fletcher snaps.

I look away guiltily.

When Ms. Dove gives us time to work on our projects, no one does. Everyone pretends to work while shooting glances at me and Fletcher. I have no idea what to do.

"We should probably talk about the project," I say.

Fletcher gives me a long look. "What could possibly make you think I give a shit about the project?"

"I don't know. Harvard, I guess."

He starts laughing. It's a horrible, choked sound. "Yeah, Harvard. Can't wait. I'll be the most popular dead guy on campus."

I clear my throat. "So, the project. Maybe we can go out this week and take some pictures after school?"

"What, you and me together?"

I nod.

He laughs again. "Now we're best buddies, huh? You feeling guilty? Spend too much time wishing something like this would happen?"

I take a deep breath and remind myself that, considering the circumstances, I should be patient.

"I'm trying not to make the situation worse than it already is," I say evenly.

"Too late, Eldon. That bitch screwed me out of the one thing that could have made me happy."

"Penelope only wanted to help you."

"Well, she didn't," Fletcher says. "It was my choice. *Mine*. I'd spent months thinking about it. I'd made my decision. And she wished it all away like it was nothing."

"But…this is a second chance," I say, still unsure if I believe it myself. "You can start over."

Fletcher snorts. "Jesus, you really *are* as stupid as you look."

That's when I discover that even an almost-dead kid can piss me off. "Do it again then. If you want to die so bad, why are you sitting in art class?"

"Because Penelope Rowe didn't wish for me to *live*," Fletcher says. "She wished for my suicide to *fail*."

Oh. I get it.

Penelope's wish doesn't only apply to Fletcher's recent suicide attempt; it would apply to *all* of them. No matter how many cliffs Fletcher Hale throws himself off, no matter how many pills he takes, no matter how close to the brink of death he steps, he'll come out of it at the end.

Suicide is no longer an option.

You've gotta hand it to Penelope Rowe. When she decides a job needs to be done, she sure does it well.

✶ ✶ ✶

The entire school spends the day whispering about Fletcher and staring at him while trying to make it look like they're not.

I pass Penelope in the hall and stop her, ask how she's doing.

"How am I doing?" she asks blankly. "Who cares how *I'm* doing?"

I shift back and forth, try to think of something to say. "You have any fund-raisers coming up?"

"Yeah, because it worked out so well last time I tried to help someone."

"Maybe it did, Penny," I say. "Give Fletcher some time to process before you beat yourself up."

Penelope's eyes fill with tears. "People keep praising me, Eldon. They're telling me I'm a hero. But I look at Fletcher and how devastated he is, and I know that *I* caused that. *Me*. I'm not a hero. I'm a monster."

"No," I say. "Fletcher was depressed before any of this. Your wish didn't do it to him."

Penelope shrugs and wipes her eyes.

"Can I ask you something?" I say gently. Penelope nods, and I continue. "If you had the chance to do it over again, would you make the same wish?"

She thinks about it. The bell rings, and the hallway clears out, everyone except us making their way to class.

"Yes," Penelope says quietly. "Yes, I'd make the same wish."

I suspected as much. Even with Fletcher's anger and bitterness, Penelope feels deep down that she did the right thing. And you can't help but admire that, yeah?

I give Penelope a hug and tell her again to give it some time.

She'll bounce back, I know. Penelope's resilient. Eventually, she'll work through her guilt and come out of this situation OK.

As for Fletcher, whether or not he'll bounce back... Well, that's anyone's guess.

* * *

In the locker room after school, a lot of zombie jokes are tossed around.

"Hey, you think Fletcher craves brains now?" Otto Alvarez asks, and the other guys laugh.

"This is a blessing for him," Calvin Boyd says. "I mean, dude had no chance of getting a prom date before this. Now he can go to the cemetery and dig one up."

More laughter. Except from me. I slam my locker shut.

"What's your problem, Wilkes?" Calvin asks.

As if he can't imagine why I'm not joining in on their good time. As if he's the king of the freaking world, and I, his loyal subject, should be honored to be included in their festivities.

"I just don't think this is funny," I say.

Calvin raises his eyebrows. "I'd think you, of all people, would find this situation *hilarious*."

"I don't."

There's nothing funny about dying or *almost* dying or whatever it is that Fletcher did. There's nothing funny about the state he's in right now.

"Well, don't get all butt hurt about it," Calvin says.

I continue to suit up and steady myself with a deep breath. This is my first day back at practice. Pounding the smirk off Calvin's face is definitely not in my best interest.

The conversation moves away from Fletcher and to prom. It's this Saturday, and even though Madison's proms are nothing fancy, not like you see in movies, it's still an excuse to party. The after-prom parties at the hot springs are a huge deal.

There's a lot of talk about how far everyone will get with their dates. Spoiler alert: most of the guys will end up lingering around first base. I don't call anyone on their shit though. I'm just glad to be back in the locker room. Missing out on a week of football practice kind of sucked.

Except for the part where I didn't have to see Calvin.

"Juniper's asking for it," he gloats. "Trying to drop hints or whatever, but you can see through it. She might as well come out and tell me how much she wants me to fuck her on prom night."

I tense up. Take another deep breath. I'm not going to let him get to me.

"Who're you going with, Eldon?" someone asks.

"Just friends," I say.

I can feel Calvin's smirk even with my back turned. The dude is smothering the whole locker room with his smugness.

Luckily, my dad comes in before I have to hear anything more about what Juniper does or doesn't want Calvin to do to her on prom night.

"I don't need to tell you what a big week this is," my dad says.

"Sunday isn't only our game against the Tonopah Muckers. For some of you, it's the last time you'll be on the field. That means you owe it to yourselves to play harder than ever before."

Everyone cheers, and my dad launches into a long speech about how much the Clash means, how the Madison Drosophilae are going to make the Mucker Fuckers wish they'd never been born. He's trying to get everyone pumped up, and I guess it works. We all play hard.

"Glad to have you back, son," my dad says, clapping me on the back during a break.

It's good to *be* back.

It's good to feel like part of my life is normal again.

Norie's waiting for me outside the locker room when I get out of practice. Some of the guys nudge each other and laugh. Norie rolls her eyes at them.

"What's up?" I ask.

We walk down the hallway and out of school. The wind's picked up since practice ended, and we get slammed in the face with dirt as soon as we step outside. So much for the shower I just took.

"I wanted to see how you are," she says. "After yesterday, and now with Fletcher being back."

"I'm all right."

She studies my face. "You don't need to lie to me, you know. I'm not like the rest of them."

We stand on the steps of the school. Everyone else is getting into their cars and driving away or getting ready to walk home with the hot wind for company.

I know Norie's telling the truth. She doesn't need me to be anyone but who I am.

"I'm kind of messed up about the whole thing," I admit.

"You're allowed to be."

"Thanks." I hope she knows I mean it.

"Need a ride home?" She's already moving in the direction of her car.

"Let's go somewhere else."

"Where?"

"Anywhere."

* * *

One of the few places with greenery in Madison is the Tuttles' farm. It isn't lush, but there's some grass and bushes and stuff. They have horses and a couple of cows, and they keep bees for honey. Sometimes they get enough to sell, sometimes not. It doesn't matter. At least three of their kids wished for money, so the Tuttles are doing fine.

There's a rock wall on the far edge of their property with a big mesquite tree next to it. Norie and I lie down in the grass under the tree, look up at the wind whipping though the branches. The Tuttles have enough acreage that they can't see us from the house.

They probably wouldn't mind us being here anyway. They're a nice family.

"This has always been one of my favorite spots in Madison," Norie says.

"How come?"

"Makes you feel like you're somewhere else."

"It's hard to imagine any place but Madison."

"No kidding."

We lapse into silence. I like that Norie doesn't need to fill every moment with words. I watch from the corner of my eye as she twirls her Mormon ring on her finger.

"I'm thinking of not wishing," I say eventually.

She looks over at me, surprised. "Really?"

"No matter what I wish for, it's gonna be messed up."

"Not necessarily."

"People are always telling me wishing is such a privilege," I go on. "Don't you think the real privilege is getting to *choose*?"

Instead of answering my question, Norie says, "We should go see that guy. Othello Dewitt. Find out how not wishing worked out for him."

"Tomorrow maybe? After practice?"

She nods. "I'll let Merrill know."

"I can text him," I say, reaching into my pocket for my phone.

"I was gonna call him later anyway," Norie says.

I shrug and put my phone away. Go back to staring at the tree above me, at the cloudless blue sky.

"Norie," I say after a while. "What did you wish for?"

I assume she'll be coy again. I've come to terms with the fact that Norie's pretty set on keeping her secret. But when she looks at me, her expression is grave.

"It's not something I want the whole town to know," she says.

My heart rate picks up. "I won't repeat it."

"Promise?"

"Of course I promise."

Norie sits up and pulls her knees to her chest, wraps her arms around them. I've never seen her vulnerable, and it makes me want to hug her.

"It's not so much that I don't want anyone to know my wish," she says. "But I have this superstition that if I tell people, I'll jinx it. And I want it to come true." She thinks for a moment. "No. I *need* it to come true."

I sit up too, my curiosity hitting an all-time high. Wishes are almost always instantaneous. "Your wish hasn't come true yet?"

"Soon," Norie says. "It'll come true soon."

CHAPTER 21

THE WISH HISTORY: ELEANOR HAVERMAYER

T his is Norie Havermayer's chapter.

But first, we're gonna take a step back, soak up decade after decade of Madison pride.

What's that?

You can't find any?

No kidding.

Instead, there's page after page of kids who hate this town.

They hate how it's tiny.

How it's hot.

How it's boring.

Hundreds of pages of hate, of kids insisting one day they'll get out. Pages with dreams of beaches and high rises. Of culture. Of adventure. Of a million attributes that'll never be found on Madison's dusty desert streets.

This town is basically a teenager's nightmare.

And these kids, they're ready to bust out of it, find their place in the real world.

Can you guess what happens next?

Do you need to read each individual story to know how their lives play out?

All these kids talking about how they're meant for so much more, well, they grow up. Make their wishes. Graduate high school. Get married and have babies, and then those babies get older and talk about how much they hate Madison.

This history book, it's the same story, over and over again.

Forever.

But occasionally, someone breaks the cycle. It's rare, but it happens. With enough determination, it can happen.

That's where Norie Havermayer comes in.

Norie knows few people leave Madison for good. All the big ideas kids have never amount to more than that, yeah?

She also knows there's a way to beat the system.

Look at her on her wish day.

Her parents don't drive her to the wish cave. Not that she expected them to. Bernard and Harriet Havermayer have never taken much interest in their daughter. They haven't taken much interest in anything besides the piles of money they're sitting on.

Norie makes her way up the trail, followed by the mayor and his men. See how hard she tries not to grimace at their nearness? Norie's all for keeping an open mind about people, but she can't see the good in Mayor Fontaine.

He doesn't care for her either.

Flip back a few pages to when Norie had her prewish meeting with

Mayor Fontaine. Check out his reaction when Norie refuses to tell him her wish.

That barely concealed outrage.

Norie doesn't miss it.

Mayor Fontaine threatens to not let her wish at all. "If you want to wish, you have to play by the rules."

Norie sweetly smiles back at him, calling his bluff. "Then I'll make up something, and you'll never know the difference."

He backs down.

Of course he does.

In the history of Madison, no one's ever been denied their wish.

Back to Norie's wish day.

It's a long hike to the cave. Not as treacherous as the hot springs—not that Norie would know, because she's never been—but much steeper. Mayor Fontaine starts huffing and puffing after a few minutes. He turns bright red, like an angry cartoon character.

Norie tries to push that unchristian thought from her mind.

They twist up the mountain, sidestepping rocks. The wind is fierce, and Norie ducks her head into it and says a prayer.

Heavenly Father, *she thinks,* I try not to ask for much.

But this once, I really, really need your help.

Please let my wish work.

Please, please, please.

Please don't let me get stuck here.

Finally, the mouth of the wish cave is in front of them.

It's unspectacular. A dark slit in the rock. A heavy, barred door prevents anyone from entering. Even that's not remarkable though. Tons of old mines in the area are blocked off in the exact same way for safety.

The mayor hands a heavy key ring to one of his assistants. The man steps forward and unlocks the door, swings it open with a loud screech.

"This is a momentous day," Mayor Fontaine says. "For the rest of your life, you'll look back and fondly remember the moment you made your wish. Choose wisely."

He's given the speech so many times that Norie doubts it still has any meaning. If it ever did.

One of the men hands her a candle and lights it. It's ludicrous, using a candle in the cave. Dangerous too. It could blow out, and you'd be lost in the mountain, alone in the dark. But the goal is to recreate the original wish as closely as possible, and back then, there were no flashlights.

Candle in hand, the mayor and his men waiting behind her, Norie steps into the wish cave.

And she prays, please, honor this one prayer.

Check out Norie Havermayer navigating through the cave. All those years of buildup, she's expecting an amazing sight. But it's a regular cave. Smooth walls, rocky ground, narrow in passages. Like so many milestones in life, the anticipation of the wish cave doesn't match the reality.

Norie knows where to go. She avoids the passages that branch off from the main tunnel. She's memorized her path.

She walks for about five minutes, twisting deeper into the mountain, candlelight flickering on the walls.

And what's she thinking about as she walks?

Is she wondering about those other passages, if there's magic waiting down them too?

Is she thinking of all the kids who had gone before her, about their wishes, wondering if they were afraid?

Or is her prayer still playing like a refrain through her mind?

Heavenly Father.

Please.

Please, please, please let my wish work.

Finally, she reaches an open cavern. On the far side, there's a pool of water. That's not unusual for caves. It's probably from an underground spring. Rain water couldn't make it all the way inside, not out in the desert where it only rains a couple of times a year.

Norie takes off her shoes and socks.

She takes a deep breath.

She wades into the water.

She spins the ring around on her finger, her reminder to do the right thing.

Then Norie Havermayer speaks her wish out loud:

"I wish, after graduation, to leave Madison and never come back."

Turn to the next page in the history book.

Norie exits the cave, refusing to tell the mayor what she wished for. Brushing off her parents when they halfheartedly ask about it. Shaking her head and staying silent through her classmates' barrage of questions.

It's not for them to know. It's Norie's secret. All her hopes are pinned on this one wish, and she's not going to jeopardize them by repeating her wish

Please, let this work, *she prays over and over again.*

Skim through the pages.

See how confident she is in her decision.

She won't be leaving anyone behind. Her parents will pretend to be sad, then they'll go back to counting their money. She has more acquaintances than friends. No loss there.

There's nothing, no one to keep her in Madison.

There's every reason to go.

Maybe she could have left town without wishing, sure. But it would've been risky. People usually come back. They go away but never put down roots elsewhere. Some head to college, like Fletcher Hale likely will. But Norie's sure he'll return to Madison with a degree and end up teaching high school English or something.

No, Norie Havermayer isn't leaving her future to chance. She wants assurance. On the day she drives out of Madison, she will be positive that she'll never return.

Now it's a waiting game.

Every night, she crosses another day off the calendar, one step closer to graduation.

Every night, she says a prayer.

Every night, she dreams of living in a place where people are free to make choices and have second chances and believe in something besides wishing.

She avoids thinking about that saying, the one about the grass always being greener. She doesn't want to consider that, all over the world, even in places where there's no wishing, people are bound to something.

No, Norie's too busy waiting for the moment her life will really start.

Here's what she hadn't considered: that in the month before graduation, a month before she'll blow out of Madison for good, she'd unexpectedly make friends. Friends who won't be so easy to leave.

"When are you going?" one of those friends asks her. The friend who's lost in a way that Norie's never been, who's waiting for someone, anyone, to tell him what to do.

Look at the two of them, sitting under the tree at the Tuttles' farm. Look at how important this is to Norie—the moment when, for the first time, she tells someone her wish.

"Soon," Norie says. "Right after graduation."

"I'll miss you."

Norie will miss him too, no question. She hadn't expected their friendship, but she's glad for it. These guys she's been hanging out with, they click with her. Almost like the click she felt the first time she learned about God. Some things you just know are right.

Look at the way Norie hesitates. At the hope in her eyes. "You can come with me, you know. You and Merrill. We can drive away from here and never look back."

Norie and her friend look at each other.

And they both know it's true.

This friendship between them, it doesn't need to end. There don't need to be goodbyes. *A door swings open, offers them possibilities they've never considered.*

"Maybe we can," Norie's friend says softly.

And maybe they will.

But this story's conclusion comes in another chapter.

Be patient.

We'll get there soon enough.

For now, feel the way the air around them has gotten thicker.

Ahead of them, barely out of reach, is the promise of another life.

CHAPTER 22

COUNTDOWN: 8 DAYS

I feel like I'm waking up from the longest dream ever. There are all these paths I thought I was supposed to take. All these ways I'd been told I needed to live my life. Now everything's changed.

Maybe I don't need to wish. Maybe I don't need to stay in Madison. Maybe I can do whatever the hell I want to do, because it's *my* life, and I'm the one who has to live it.

Even my mom can't kill the spark of possibility.

She's at the kitchen counter, packing herself lunch for the office. I try to slip past without her noticing me, but no such luck.

"Why didn't you tell me you visited your sister?"

Who ratted me out? Probably the creepy, flirty receptionist.

"I don't know. I thought you might tell me not to go. And…" I pause, swallow hard, and hope my voice doesn't let on how emotional I'm feeling. "I really miss her."

I brace myself, ready for a fight. I'm gonna get a lecture about driving all the way to Vegas without telling her, like my whereabouts are suddenly real important to her.

But Ma doesn't get upset. She finishes making her sandwich and adds it to her lunch bag. "I know you miss her. So do I."

"I know," I say, then I push my visit with Ebba from my mind, because thinking about it too much will depress me. And I'm not going to let anything get me down today.

I go to school, exercise award-worthy patience with Fletcher in first period, and stop to tell Penelope to call if she needs to talk. At lunch, I pop my head into Mr. Wakefield's office, let him know I'm taking a big step on my wish-collecting journey tonight. He beams. I even maintain my good mood when I see Calvin Boyd, that asshole, practically mauling Juniper at her locker.

It doesn't matter. None of it matters. School, Madison, wishing. I only see a great big exit sign. An invitation to step out of my life and into an entirely new one.

At practice, I play better than I have in months.

* * *

I'm the first guy out of the locker room. My hair's still dripping, but it doesn't matter. Being outside in Madison is more efficient than using a hair dryer.

Merrill and Norie are waiting for me in the parking lot, sitting on the hood of the Mustang, their heads bent close in conversation. The wind pushes my wet hair from my eyes as I make my way over to them.

"You find out where this place is?" I ask.

"I did," says Merrill. "And to be honest, I get the distinct impression we're walking into a horror movie–type scenario." He pulls up a map on his phone. "We take this dirt road here, see? It goes down a narrow canyon where there's a fifty-percent chance the car'll get stuck and we'll die. Assuming *that* doesn't happen, we turn here, cruise along the dry lake bed, and end up at the mouth of another canyon, probably one that has several bodies buried in it. That's where this Othello dude lives."

"Let's go," I say, moving toward the passenger door.

"Have you not seen *The Hills Have Eyes*?" Merrill asks. "Do you not know about desert people?"

"He's been going on like this for an hour," Norie says to me.

I look at Merrill. "If it turns out Othello Dewitt is a killer mutant, you can say you told me so."

I get into the car as Merrill says something about how he won't be able to tell me *anything*, because we'll be dead. He still slides into the driver's seat though. Still turns the key in the ignition.

But before he drives away from school, Merrill stops and turns to me like he remembered something. "Out of curiosity, Eldo, do you have any idea why Mr. Wakefield stopped me in the hall and asked if I'm a secret sex worker?"

I'm so surprised, I almost laugh. I hide it with a cough and give Merrill my most innocent response. "Nope. Beats me."

* * *

I don't know where Merrill got these directions to Othello's house—
Othello's Hideaway he calls it—but they're perfect. The drive takes
less time than I expected. Othello isn't that far out of town.

We pass a sign at the mouth of the first canyon. *Open air art
gallery ahead*, with a big red arrow pointing the way.

"So he's an artist," Norie says.

"Or it's a clever way to lure in victims," Merrill replies.

We drive through the canyon. It's a dirt road but well maintained. Most of the dirt roads around here are well maintained. We
don't have rain or snow to mess them up. We don't have enough
plant life for them to become overgrown.

The Mustang bumps along without trouble until, at the end of
the canyon, we arrive at Othello Dewitt's house.

If you can call it a house.

"Well," Merrill says. "This doesn't exactly reassure me."

The shack is pieced together with scraps. Plywood, a corru-
gated metal roof, all sorts of mismatched materials tacked together
and jutting out at odd angles. Still, it's probably as structurally
sound as the shitty houses in my own neighborhood.

But it's not the *house* that's the weirdest part—it's the art. And
I use the word *art* in the loosest way possible. At a glance, we've
wandered into a junkyard, but after closer inspection, I see it's
sculptures, not trash. Sculptures made of beer bottles, rusty car parts,
broken clocks, barbed wire. It's as if Othello took every broken bit
of Madison and tried to morph it into something beautiful.

There's another hand-painted sign in the front of the house that says *Visitor Center*.

"This is good," I tell Merrill. "He *wants* visitors."

Merrill shoots me a dark look.

We get out of the car and make our way through the sculpture garden but hesitate at the front door.

"I guess we knock?" Norie says.

So I do.

The door swings open, as if he'd been watching us through the dusty window, waiting.

"Welcome to Art on the Rocks!" says Othello Dewitt.

He's not what I was expecting. I had it in my head that he'd be this worn-down old dude, like Gil Badgley if he were a hippie. But Othello Dewitt is closer to my parents' age, maybe younger. He doesn't seem like a desert person either. Desert people wear camouflage and have guns on their hips and rant about the government. Othello is dressed in jeans and a T-shirt. His only eye-catching characteristic is his curly afro.

"Are you Othello Dewitt?" I ask.

"I am he! And you, you're Luella Maylocke's son."

He catches me off guard. "Luella Wilkes now, but yeah. Eldon."

"You're surprised, I see. They're always surprised. I may live outside town, but I'm in tune with what happens there. Come in!"

He holds the door open, and Merrill, Norie, and I cautiously step inside. The interior is as bizarre as the outside. It's one big room, part sleeping quarters and part workshop. There are piles of junk everywhere. Bits and pieces of supplies he uses to make his sculptures, I guess. A long table in one corner holds a few works in progress.

Merrill and Norie introduce themselves, but Othello seems to already know who they are as well.

"Please," he says, "step into the visitor center."

We look at him blankly.

Othello spins and takes a giant step toward the other side of the room. There's a small table with brochures fanned out for display and pictures hanging above it.

Merrill seems to be debating if Othello is dangerous. He steps over to the table and looks at me wryly. "Come on, Eldo. Join us in the *visitor center*."

I narrow my eyes at Merrill, silently telling him to cut it out, but Othello doesn't seem put out.

He laughs and says, "I know it doesn't look like much, but we don't *need* much out here."

"We?" I ask.

"*We* in the most singular sense."

Merrill looks entirely unamused.

Norie and I join them at the table. The brochures are black and white, printed from a home computer, and showcase the sculptures we saw in the front yard.

"This is Art on the Rocks," Othello says, gesturing to the

photos on the wall. "An open-air gallery of sculptures, murals, and other artistic pursuits. Take a moment to browse, then I'll be happy to guide you into the canyon. Free of charge, of course. No price can be put on creative endeavors."

Norie leans forward to examine the photos, and Merrill sneaks a look at his phone, probably checking to see if we have reception out here.

"Actually," I tell Othello, "we wanted to talk to you about your wish."

"Of course you did! And we'll get to that."

"Where do you get all this stuff?" Norie asks, pointing to a photo showcasing a sculpture made of rusty bike parts. I don't know what it's supposed to represent, but it looks like a misshapen uterus. "Do you go to a junkyard or something?"

"Ah, an excellent question. In fact, the *junkyard* comes to *me*. I'm in touch with a collector who sells me these wonderful materials for a minimal fee."

"Are you talking about Barnabas Fairley?" I guess.

"Yes, Barnabas! Delightful man. Very keen eye."

"What do you pay him?" Merrill asks skeptically, as if he's expecting the answer to be *cogs* or *thumbtacks* or something.

Othello laughs. "My work doesn't seem profitable, no? In fact, upcycled art is quite popular these days, and I'm able to connect with buyers through the power of the Internet."

"So you actually make money off all this?"

"A modest income. But I've always believed having *less* encourages *more*. So much of the creative process is making do with what you have. The greatest geniuses didn't come from wealthy backgrounds."

I'm pretty sure there are examples to disprove this theory, but I don't know any, so I let it go.

"What are you working on now?" Norie asks, and I honestly can't tell if she's only being polite or if she's genuinely interested.

Othello's face lights up. "A very special project! Though due to damage it sustained in the last earthquake, I've been set back quite a bit."

"I'm sorry to hear that," Norie says.

Othello waves his hand. "No cause for regret. Tremors are the earth's way of speaking to us, sharing its story."

"I guess California must be a gold mine of *stories* then, huh?" Merrill asks.

Ignoring him, Norie says to Othello, "Can we see it? Your work in progress, I mean."

"As much as I would love to share it with you, an artist should never unveil his soul before it's ready."

"Well, uh, we'll be looking forward to the unveiling," I say.

"In the meantime, would you like to see the canyon?" Othello asks.

"Yes," I reply before Merrill can say otherwise.

We follow Othello Dewitt out of his house and through the

narrow canyon behind it. Merrill shoots me death glares, but I don't feel the least bit threatened by Othello. I mean, the dude spends his life stringing soda tabs into angel wings and turning hubcaps into sunflowers. It doesn't exactly scream serial killer.

"Art has always been my raison d'être," Othello says as we follow behind him. "My goal was to have enough land to bring my dreams to waking life, which I accomplished shortly after graduation."

"But you didn't wish for this," I say. "This land."

"No, no. Achieving my goal through a wish would have cheapened it. True art comes from purity."

"Do you get lonely out here?" Norie asks.

Thanks for moving the conversation away from wishing, Norie. I give her a sharp look to convey this but only manage to stumble over a rock. I catch myself from falling, and Norie ignores me completely.

"Lonely?" Othello says. "No, of course not. Creative individuals can never be lonely. The ideas that live in their heads are constant companions."

"Yeah, but there's a difference between being a loner and a hermit," Merrill says, and he *also* pretends not to see my warning look. "Most people who live out in the desert come into town *occasionally*."

"Of course I visit town," says Othello. "Being an artist doesn't remove my body's need for sustenance."

"Why don't we ever see you then?"

Othello smiles kindly at Merrill, like he's talking to someone painfully naive. "Perhaps you're not looking."

The canyon ends abruptly, and I stop and suck in my breath. Next to me, Norie and Merrill do the same, but I'm too trans-fixed by the mural in front of me to pay much attention to my friends. The entire canyon wall is covered in a psychedelic swirl of colors and pictures. The earth and constellations, animals, Native Americans, Buddha.

I'm impressed by Othello's dedication. It must have taken ages to paint. He probably had to use rock-climbing gear to reach the top.

"It's the story of the world," Othello beams.

"Uh, what's with the aliens then?" Merrill asks, nodding to a flying saucer.

"They're *of the world* as much as you or I," says Othello. He looks heavenward. "Haven't you ever looked at the night sky?"

Merrill shoots me another look that I have no trouble reading. "I've lived here my entire life, and I've never seen a flying saucer."

"Perhaps you're not looking," Othello repeats.

"Are you one of those alien hunters who hangs out in Rachel?" Merrill asks, like it's the ultimate insult.

Othello laughs.

"I think the mural is beautiful," interrupts Norie. "Inspiring."

I walk to the canyon wall to examine the mural. What makes a person want to go to a hidden canyon, in the middle of a desolate desert, and paint the history of the world? What's wrong with *me* that I can't see beauty but a massive waste of effort and talent?

"Why didn't you do this somewhere else?" I ask. "Somewhere people would actually see it?"

"The solitude of the setting deepens the message of the piece," Othello replies. "Coming to this canyon was my destiny. The universe portended that this was to be the site of my most significant work."

Merrill squints at Othello. "Did you ever stop to consider that sometimes the universe is *wrong*?"

"So, about your wish," I break in before Merrill can offend Othello beyond redemption.

"Yes, my wish! But really, it was a nonwish, which I imagine you already know."

I turn to Othello, glad we're finally arriving at the point. "You're the only person in Madison who's turned down their wish."

"The only person in the records anyway," Merrill adds.

"Yes," Othello agrees. "There may have been others. Who can say? Unlikely though. It takes a strength of will that most don't possess to refuse an opportunity like wishing."

"What gave *you* the strength to turn it down?" I ask.

"It was a matter of trust."

No one's looking at the mural anymore. Merrill, Norie, and I stare at Othello, eagerly waiting to hear more.

"Accomplishment comes from toil," Othello says. "Growth is a result of sacrifice. Take art, for instance. Some believe it's the finished product that matters most. But it's also the *journey*. A finished piece is nothing without the labor and emotion of the artist behind it. I mistrusted the ease of wishing, the idea of receiving a gift I hadn't worked for and didn't deserve. You can only truly love art if you've bled for it."

"Wishing isn't always the end of the line," Norie replies. "Sometimes, a wish is a tool. It's what you *do* with it that matters. There's still hard work and sacrifice."

"Ah, yes, right you are! But as a young man, I didn't see it that way. I was certain wishing would devalue my life, keep me forever in doubt as to whether I *deserved* my accomplishments. So despite the protestations of those I knew, I chose to forgo my wish."

"And now?" I ask. "Do you think you made the right choice?"

"Choices, by nature, are not right or wrong. They are only different paths, all ultimately leading to the same end."

Norie looks captivated. I'm sure she's aching to show off her ring and engage Othello in a conversation about *choosing the right*.

Merrill, on the other hand, rolls his eyes and sighs deeply. "What Eldon's asking, if you don't mind me butting in, is if your alien pals reversed time and let you do it all again, would you still give up your wish?"

"I would not," Othello says.

That's not what I was expecting.

"Seriously?" Merrill asks.

"I couldn't say what I would wish for this time around. Only that I *would* wish."

Not that I'm all gung ho about modeling my life after Othello Dewitt's, but I assumed he'd give us some speech about not wishing being the best decision a person could make. Or maybe that's just what I *wanted* to hear.

"Why?" I ask.

Othello has the answer ready, as if he's spent countless hours in his shack pondering it. "I gave up my opportunity to become part of something infinite. A known magic, the rarest phenomenon. It's not the *wish* I missed out on but the *experience* of wishing. And what that experience might have made me."

"It probably would have made you regretful," I say.

"Ah, regret, that old demon. It creeps up when you're not looking, haunts your dreams. Wishers regret their wishes. I regret not wishing. We all have regrets, Eldon. It's human nature to fixate on the path not taken rather than the one you're walking."

And just like that, I feel as lost as before. I want answers. I want someone to tell me what to do. I want, instead of a wish, for some fairy godmother to show up and fix my life, wrap it up in a neat little package.

"That's not what I was hoping to hear," I say.

Othello Dewitt looks at me gravely. "That will be your downfall. You're looking for someone else to save you, when really, we can only ever save ourselves."

✳ ✳ ✳

"I hope that convinced you not to give up your wish," Merrill says as we're driving back through the desert, away from Othello's Hideaway.

I don't know what it's convinced me of though. Maybe that I'll be unhappy no matter what I do. Wish or no wish, I'm always going to wonder.

"Just because Othello regrets not wishing doesn't mean *you* would, Eldon," Norie says. "I think he was trying to tell you that it needs to be your decision either way."

Merrill snorts. "I admire your optimism, Norie. But I don't think he was trying to say *anything*. Dude also told us he sees flying saucers, so let's not take his word as law."

"Shit," I say. "That reminds me."

Merrill glances at me. "Please, go on. I'm dying to know what I could have *possibly* reminded you of."

"That UFO event is this weekend."

"Oh, right, the festival," says Norie.

"So?" Merrill asks. "No one's forcing you to attend. It's not even in Madison."

"Yeah, but people will be passing through Madison to get to Rachel. No way will I get out of work on Saturday. And it's prom, and the Clash is on Sunday."

"So it'll be a busy weekend," Merrill says, shrugging.

"Yeah. Which means I won't have time to even *think* about my wish."

"Maybe that'll be good for you, Eldo. Get it off your mind for a few days."

"I don't have *a few days*," I say.

As I speak the words, I realize how true it is. My wish is a week away. It's snuck up on me. It's only a week away, and I still don't know what to wish for and don't feel the slightest bit closer to knowing.

All that time spent screwing around and half-assed thinking about wishing. Playing football and going to parties and never recognizing how quickly time can pass when you're not paying attention.

My birthday is one week away.

My *wish day* is one week away.

I have one week to make the most important decision of my life.

That's about the time I start to panic.

CHAPTER 23

COUNTDOWN: 7 DAYS

I'm standing at the urinal when Archie Kildare yanks open the bathroom door. It makes me jump a little, which could have ended in disaster. Luckily, I recover and don't douse myself in my own urine.

"Wilkes," Archie says, pointing his finger at me. "Seven days."

"Is that a threat?"

He walks over to the urinal next to me, which is sort of breaking a code. "Why are you so uptight about this? You get to *wish*. You should be celebrating."

"I'll celebrate when I know what I'm gonna wish for," I say, because I have to say something, even though I'm pretty opposed to having conversations with other dudes while I have my dick in my hand.

"You *still* don't know? Bro. You've had eighteen *years*."

I finish up and go to the sink, desperate to get out of the bathroom as fast as possible.

"Me, I knew since I was a kid," Archie says. "Like, no question. I've been waiting for this."

I don't ask him what he's going to wish for, because I don't care.

"I'm going to wish to be a pro wrestler," Archie announces.

I stop and look at him.

"Archie, weren't you paying attention in class?"

"Screw wish class," he says, zipping up his pants. "I already knew all that shit, and I don't need to sit around and talk about my *feelings*."

I'm not going to tell him. He'll find out for himself in a couple of weeks when he has his meeting with Mayor Fontaine. He can't wish to be a pro wrestler. That would take his wish outside Madison.

"Glad you got it all figured out," I say and flash him a genuine smile.

I leave the bathroom and look for Merrill. He's gonna die laughing when I tell him Archie's wish. And joking about Archie will prevent me from thinking about my own meeting with Mayor Fontaine. It's scheduled for tonight, and I'm not looking forward to it. Not a bit.

✳ ✳ ✳

Everywhere I look, there's a reminder of wishing.

First period, Fletcher looking half dead, a reminder of a wish gone wrong. Juniper radiating happiness in the hallway, a reminder that wishes aren't always selfish. Calvin Boyd, with his arm around Juniper, a reminder that most of the time, they are.

At lunch, Norie and Merrill ask me questions: What do I want to do? Do I want to talk to more people? What am I going to say to the mayor?

And the reminders keep coming.

A freshman girl I pass in the halls, gossiping with her friends: "Seriously, I wish she would, like, disappear."

Mrs. Franklin, in English class, talking to Clem Johnson, who can't take his eyes off her tits: "I wish you would take this class more seriously."

My dad, in football practice: "I'm not gonna wish you guys luck against the Mucker Fuckers, because I know you don't need it."

I wish, I wish, I wish.

It's kind of astounding how often that phrase is used in everyday conversation. How the more you try to avoid a certain word, the more it haunts you.

The school, the town, the *world* is full of wishes. Why don't people stop wishing and start *doing*? Why is everyone so willing to wish away their lives? I want to scream at them to stop. There's more to life than wishes. Wishing never gets you anywhere.

Except, of course, in Madison, it does.

If you're lucky, that is.

Wishing either gets you everything or nothing. And it's a gamble everyone is willing to take.

* * *

"Mr. Fontaine will see you now," says the mayor's secretary, whose name I can never remember.

She's one of those people who looks scared all the time, which I figure has something to do with working for the mayor.

I trudge toward Mayor Fontaine's ridiculous office. It's probably the most expensive room in Madison, all shiny marble and dark wood. The bookshelves on the far side of the room are flanked by gold lion statues, and a chandelier illuminates the room. It's the kind of office you have when you're trying to prove something. The mayor probably has no idea how cheap all this richness looks.

"Come in, son," he says when he sees me hovering near the door.

I sit in a chair across from his massive desk. It's roughly the same size as my bed. If you ask me, no one needs a desk that big. Ever. But Mayor Fontaine strikes me as one of those people who believes the bigger your desk, the more important you are, as if that's all it takes to define a person's worth.

The guy's definitely compensating for something.

"So," he says, folding his hands in front of him, "the big day is almost here."

I nod.

"Why don't we chat about your wish?"

He's using his we're-all-best-buddies voice. I'm gonna need to shower after this.

"There's not much to talk about," I say.

That gives him pause. "And why's that?"

"I get that you're supposed to approve my wish and help me with the wording or whatever, but you can't. I don't know what I'm going to wish for."

He looks at me as if I spoke in another language. A long, uncomfortable silence stretches between us.

"That's not how we do things around here," he says finally. "Wishes are to be prepared at least a week in advance."

Who is *we*? As far as I know, he's the one who makes that rule.

"Sorry," I say with a shrug. "But you either know your wish or you don't. And I don't."

"Huh," he says. He leans back in his chair—leather, of course—and considers me like I'm an alien that hopped off a spaceship in Rachel and hitched a ride into Madison.

No. That's not right.

He wants to me to think he's concerned, like he's contemplating what I said. But that's a facade. There's emotion in his eyes, emotion he's trying to bury. Anger. I questioned his authority, and he doesn't like it.

Unfortunately for him, we all have to deal with situations we don't like.

"You know, son, wishing is a *privilege*. Do you know how many people in the world would kill to get a wish?"

"A lot, I guess."

"It makes me wonder why you're not taking this opportunity seriously. If I didn't know better, I'd say wishing didn't matter to you."

I return his gaze but don't speak. His beady black eyes bore into me. It's like the dude's trying to steal my soul.

"Well, what are we going to do with you?" he asks. He smiles, as if we're having a perfectly pleasant conversation. But the rage hasn't left his eyes.

"I have a week left," I say with a shrug. "I'll think of a wish in time."

"But that's not fair, is it? Everyone else needs to have their wish approved first. How would it look if you got special treatment?"

He's so calm, so reasonable. Like we're two guys having a chat. I guess those tactics probably work on some people.

"I never said anything about special treatment," I say. "I just don't get why you need an answer today when my birthday isn't for a week."

Then comes another smile, gentle, like I'm a foolish kid who's too silly to understand how the world works. "I know wishing is complicated for a lot of people. That's why *I'm* the mayor. I'm more than happy to offer you guidance."

"I guess I don't understand what being the mayor has to do with wishing." I'm putting on a voice of my own: the most inno- cent, earnest voice I can muster. I'm channeling Penelope Rowe, big time. "Seems to me, they're two totally separate roles."

For a second, his mask slips, and Mayor Fontaine's face contorts with wrath. Then, just as quickly, his patronizing smile is back.

"As mayor of this town, it's my duty to ensure the well-being of all citizens. That means helping people with wishes. People who sometimes don't know what's best for themselves, and the town."

"I know what's best for me. Thanks though."

Another stare-down. I'm trying to keep my expression neutral. If the mayor knows how fast my heart is racing, how much my palms are sweating, he'll eat me alive. Seconds tick away on a gaudy, gold-plated clock.

Mayor Fontaine breaks first. "I can see you're not yet ready for this meeting. Why don't you take a few days and think this over?"

I know very well he means think about my attitude, not my wish. But either way, I got what I wanted.

"Sure," I say, standing. "You've been really helpful."

He smiles, a tight smile that sure as hell doesn't reach his eyes. "That's what I'm here for."

* * *

I walk out of the office casually, cool as a cucumber, like Mayor Fontaine didn't completely creep me out. But I'm pretty shaken up, yeah? Suddenly, it seems like the best part of wishing will be never having to interact with the mayor again.

I envy my parents and all the other people who made wishes while the first Mayor Fontaine was in office. From everything I hear, old Mayor Fontaine was this kindly grandfather-type. He's in an old folk's home now. I wonder what he thinks of his son.

Once I get outside, into the heat and wind, I'm feeling a lot less cavalier. The mayor's a douchebag, but he's right. The clock is ticking. I need to figure out my wish.

Or I need to decide not to wish and be OK with that.

I need to try to save my sister and maintain my relationship with my family or be brave enough to risk losing everything.

One way or another, I need to decide *something*.

I want to talk to more people, hear more wishes, take notes. I was supposed to be doing that all along, not screwing around and riding Ferris wheels and wasting time. I have to talk to as many people as possible, and I need to do it ASAP.

I text Merrill and Norie and ask if they're cool with ditching school tomorrow.

CHAPTER 24

THE WISH HISTORY: A COLLECTION

We're flying through the wish history.

There's no time to leisurely peruse this book, not now.

Watch these three kids racing around town.

Listen.

Can you hear it?

The clock is ticking.

* * *

Adelaide Johns, 2003.

Adelaide Johns sits behind the circulation desk at the library, her voice a well-practiced whisper. "I wished for happiness. It was the only wish that made sense to me."

"Were you unhappy before?" asks the boy who'd come to see her.

Adelaide thinks about it. Look at her. You can see the wheels of her mind turning. Finally, she says, "Well, no."

"Are you happier now?" the boy asks.

She chuckles. "I suppose so. I'm not miserable anyway. But with nothing to compare it to, how do I really know? If I had to go back, I would wish for something I could quantify. It would be nice to know for sure whether or not my wish came true."

✸ ✸ ✸

Moses Casey, 1986.

"The gas station?" Moses Casey says to the kid. "You think I wished for the gas station?"

"You didn't?" the kid asks.

"I wished to be a businessman. It was the eighties, man. I was picturing Wall Street shit, running some huge company, wearing suits. Look at me," he says, gesturing to his grease-stained T-shirt and work boots. "Let that be a lesson to you. Don't expect the cave to work out the details for you. For fuck's sake, be specific."

"Got it." The kid turns to leave.

"Hey," Moses says, stopping him. "I need you for double shifts on Saturday."

"I can't. Saturday is prom."

"I don't care if it's the fucking apocalypse. We're gonna be up to our asses in loonies passing through for that UFO festival in Rachel. I need you here."

Moses Casey, he doesn't care that the kid is annoyed.

Moses has his own annoyances to deal with, and the kid is one of them.

✶ ✶ ✶

Jasper Maylocke, 1994.

"People were always saying I wasn't smart, and I guess it was true," Jasper says.

He takes a swig of beer, peers at his nephew.

Look at him, Jasper Maylocke, drunk before noon.

"All I know," he says, "is I got in the cave, and I knew all the things my ma wanted from me. She was still mad, you know, cause your ma wished for your dad. But still, all I could think of was the shoes. The basketball shoes, all the cool kids had 'em."

Jasper makes his way down the hall, staggering a little, his nephew in tow. The shoes are in the bedroom, sitting on a table like they're on display in a museum.

"They're nice shoes," says the kid.

"Damn right, they're nice shoes. They're the best shoes. Still fit, but I'm too scared to wear 'em. Don't want 'em scuffed, you know?"

"But if you wished for money like Grandma wanted, you could have bought the shoes."

"I know that now! But damned if I was thinking then. You get in that cave, and your brain goes all wonky, like hyperfocused, you know?" Jasper pauses. "Plus, I was a little drunk."

"Would you do it differently if you went back?"

Jasper laughs. "Boy, I ain't the smartest, but I ain't that stupid. What the hell kinda question is that?"

✶ ✶ ✶

Izora Walsh, 1990.

She almost tells them to leave her alone. The teenager and his two friends, the obnoxious boy and the strange girl.

She's busy. She's getting groceries. The toddler in the cart is crying, the seven-year-old is tugging at her sleeve, and who even knows where the twins have gone. The rest of them are waiting for her at home, all wanting something, needing something, needing her.

"We want to know what you wished for," the boy says. "For a big family, right?"

Izora laughs and laughs. It makes the toddler cry harder. The seven-year-old stops tugging on her sleeve and steps back, startled.

"Lord, no," Izora says. "I wished to be loved.*"*

The kids don't get to ask any follow-up questions, as the twins run up, both shouting, "Mom, Mom, Mom!*"*

✻ ✻ ✻

Marcus Boyd, 2009.

He writes in the bar, because he drinks while he writes. Writing and drinking go hand in hand.

He doesn't look up when the kids approach. Kids he knows—they go to school with his brother.

"I wished to be a writer," says Marcus Boyd, typing away, always typing. "I was going to be a novelist. The next great novelist."

"And?" asks one of them. He doesn't know which, because he doesn't bother looking up.

"I didn't ask to be a published writer. Or even a good writer. Hilarious, isn't it? Come see my house sometime. Stacks of books that no one will ever read."

And still he types and types.

Words that are for him alone.

※ ※ ※

Stella French, 1929.

They come to her in the old folk's home, where she's confined to bed. She's not used to visitors, and for a moment, she thinks it's one of her dreams. They're young, so heartbreakingly young. They ask her about her wish.

She speaks in a voice that's clearer and stronger than it has any right to be. "It was still so early in the life of wishing. There were no rules back then. We didn't know what we were dealing with."

The blond boy leans closer, captivated. How long since someone has looked at Stella that way, as if her words mattered?

"It seemed such an obvious choice: to wish for long life."

"Obvious doesn't make it right," the girl says gently.

Stella wants to reach out and touch her shiny hair. "Such a smart child. I wasn't. I didn't think about how everyone I loved would leave me, pass away into the next life while I linger in this one. There's no one left to visit me now."

She tells them how she watched the world change around her. How she'd slowly been forgotten. How she watched her body grow old while her mind stayed as sharp as ever. She tells them everything on her mind while she has the chance, because when will someone next listen to her words?

They all hug her before they leave, and it fills Stella with a sharp pain, a longing for the life she used to have.

If only she could be young again.

✹ ✹ ✹

And on it goes, and on and on.

They wished for huge houses, but they had nothing to fill them.

They wished for knowledge, only to realize some information was better left unknown.

They wished for love and looks and money and success, and they found none of that was enough.

There were selfish wishes and selfless wishes. Wishes that were trivial and wishes of great importance. Some wishes were spontaneous, and some were well planned. Each wish different from the last, but in the end, they all amount to much of the same.

Browse through the wish history of Madison, Nevada.

And consider:

Is there really such a thing as the perfect wish?

CHAPTER 25

COUNTDOWN: 6 DAYS

I've ended football games with more energy than I have tonight. It doesn't seem like that big of a deal, yeah? It's only *talking* to people. But it's exhausting to run around in the hot sun all day. Also, Mr. Wakefield's given speeches about how stress can wear your body down, and I've been a mess of tension and anxiety since the moment I woke up.

"I never want to speak to another person again." I groan.

My dad was nice enough to leave the garage and give Merrill, Norie, and me some privacy to hang out. I collapsed on the couch and downed an entire beer before we'd been here five minutes.

"I don't get why people are so *willing* to talk to us," Merrill says. "Like, *hey, how's it going? We don't really know each other, but let's share all our secrets, 'kay?*"

Norie's sitting on the couch between me and Merrill, spinning her ring on her finger. "I think people want to be asked how they're doing. *Really* asked. Everyone wants to know someone out there actually cares about their answer."

"Thanks, philosopher," Merrill says, and Norie gives him a playful shove.

I take a long swig from my bottle and run over the events of the day. All the wishes. Wish after wish after wish, and so few people satisfied with the outcome. Maybe dissatisfaction is human nature. Maybe there's no running from it.

"Everyone is so miserable," I mumble. "Everyone in this entire town."

"This is a broken place," Norie agrees.

"Maybe it's a broken *world*."

"I hope not."

"It's not the world," Merrill says, leaning forward. "It's Madison. It's everyone walking around like wishing is the greatest thing ever, because they think that's how they're *supposed* to act. Because that's the way it's *always* been. They're too terrified to be the first to speak out and—"

I can't help it—I start laughing. I lean my head against the back of the couch and laugh until I'm gasping for air.

"OK, Chuckles, settle down. What's so funny?" Merrill asks.

"You," I manage to say.

I look at Merrill over Norie's head. He raises his eyebrows at me. "I'm all for laughing at my own expense, Eldo, but you mind elaborating?"

I take another long drink, let the alcohol course through my body. I haven't eaten since breakfast, and it's hitting me hard.

"So what are the plans for prom night?" Norie breaks in.

"Don't change the subject," Merrill tells her. "I want to know what's so hilarious."

"Your little speech," I say. I should stop myself. I'm tired. I'm stressed. I'm already a little buzzed. But the words pour out of my mouth anyway. "Wishing is terrible. Everyone's a sheep. We should all revolt and take on the man. But when I say I'm not gonna wish, you tell me I'll regret it. When it's time for your wish, you don't even *consider* turning it down. You want everyone to think you're such a rebel, but you're the first to tuck your tail between your legs and step into line like everyone else."

Merrill is quiet for a long moment. "You know what, Eldon? I'm not laughing."

"Don't be pissed at me because you don't like the truth," I say.

"I think I'm done for the night," Merrill replies. He's calm, but I can tell he's not happy. He stands and moves to the door. "I'll see you later."

"Come on. Don't leave," I call out. But he's already gone. Whatever. Let him go. It's not my fault he's a hypocrite.

I finish my beer and walk to the fridge to grab another one. When I'm back on the couch, Norie says, "What was *that*?"

"What?"

"I know you're stressed, but don't take it out on the people who care about you."

"Please don't lecture me, Norie." I run my fingers through my hair. I'm feeling a little drunk but not numb. Numbness is the goal. "I can't deal with that right now."

Norie stares at me long enough to make me uncomfortable. It's like she's trying to read my mind. I silently tell her to stop.

"Can I ask you something?" she asks.

"You're going to anyway, aren't you?"

In response, Norie says, "Why do you hate wishing so much? Really?"

"I don't know what you're talking about." I tilt my head back and pour more booze down my throat, but it's not enough. Right now, nothing is enough.

"Is it because of Ebba?"

"What's it have to do with her?"

"If Fletcher hadn't been late to make his wish, he wouldn't have been speeding. And if he wasn't speeding, he probably would have been able to stop the car in time."

I shrug and drink more. And more.

"And maybe you feel guilty," Norie says.

I snort. "Why should *I* feel guilty?"

"Maybe you feel guilty that you get to make a wish and Ebba never will."

If I were a little drunker, I might tell her the rest of it. How that's not the only part I feel guilty about. How Ebba asked me to give her a ride that day, and how I said sure but forgot, and how if I'd been there, she wouldn't have taken her bike to her friend's house. If not for me, she never would have been in the path of Fletcher's car.

"Maybe," I say softly, and my irritation fades. I'm left with sadness.

"Are you going to wish for her?" Norie asks.

I stare down at my beer bottle for a long time. "You've seen Fletcher. *That's* what happens when you bring someone back."

"Fletcher's situation is different. Besides, I saw him yesterday. I think he's doing better."

"It's not only that," I say. "I can't wish for her health, you know that. The logistics are screwed up. And wishing for money... No doctor can save her, Norie. They've told us that a thousand times. I just want this limbo to be over. I want Ebba to be at peace."

And it's back—the wave of sorrow that's drowning me. The sudden, stabbing pain as I remember that my sister is dying, and my happiness is dying with her. For as long as I live, my grief will hit me like this, sneaking up, jumping out to break my heart again and again, until there's no hope of putting the pieces back together.

I press my fingers to my eyes and try to force back the burning sensation. The last thing I want is to cry in front of Norie.

"Maybe," Norie says quietly, "you feel guilty about that too. Maybe you think you should wish for her and feel guilty because you know you won't."

I raise my beer to my mouth, hesitate, put it down. It's not helping me.

"Eldon."

I look at Norie.

"It's OK to feel this way. It's OK to let Ebba go."

The way she's treating me, so open and honest, makes me feel like she really means it. Like she doesn't think I'm a complete monster for believing death would be better than the horrible in-between place Ebba's in now.

Norie smiles. She reaches over and squeezes my hand. "I'm on your side. OK? Merrill and I are both on your side. You don't need to go through this alone."

I get what Norie's trying to say. The way she's talking to me—like we're the only two people in the world—is the only part of my life that makes sense right now.

Before I can think about what I'm doing or talk myself out of it, I lean in and kiss her.

Her lips are warm and soft. I scoot closer, wrap my arm around her back. It isn't the most amazing kiss ever. The world doesn't explode. But it's nice. Like stepping into a warm room on a cold day.

"Eldon," Norie says, pushing me away. "Don't."

Or maybe not.

I pull back. I have no idea what the problem is. Is *kissing* another item on the long list of what her religion considers taboo?

"You don't really want this," she says.

"What? I wouldn't have kissed you if I didn't."

"You have a lot going on right now," Norie says gently. "You don't know what you're doing."

I still don't get it. Who cares how much I have going on? Kissing Norie has nothing to do with that. "Don't you like me?" I ask, even though she does. She obviously does.

"I like you a lot. Just not like that."

The shock hits me through my buzz. I study her for evidence that she's lying. A sinking feeling in my gut tells me she's not. "Seriously?"

"Yes," Norie replies, starting to get annoyed.

"Then what's all this been about?" I ask, gesturing between us. I try to remember any other time a kiss has ended like this, and I can't.

Norie gapes at me. "It's been about *friendship*."

I sit back on the couch, trying to straighten out my thoughts. It's not working. My edginess is back. I can't process anything that's happening.

"Bullshit," I say. "You want me. Since the hot springs, at least, maybe even before then."

I glance over at Norie, who's staring at me like I disgust her. "Are you kidding me? Do you think every female you know is waiting for the chance to jump into bed with you?"

"Experience doesn't lie," I say.

Norie shoots to her feet and grabs her bag. "You know, every-one is right about you."

"What's that supposed to mean?" I glare up at her through my baffled haze.

"You're egotistical. And selfish. And a jerk."

I get to my feet, and the room tilts. I try to steady myself. Maybe I'm a little more than *buzzed*.

"*Who* says that?" I demand.

"Everyone!" Norie says. For as angry as she is, she also seems disappointed. And maybe that's worse. "I thought it was just a show you put on for your football buddies. Or that maybe Ebba's accident changed you—taught you some humility. But I was wrong, wasn't I?" She shakes her head, like she can't believe I'd managed to fool her. "You're nothing but an arrogant jock."

Before I can respond, she leaves the garage, slamming the door behind her. I don't know what I would have said anyway.

I sit down heavily on the couch and put my head in my hands. I don't bother trying to calm myself. No deep breathing, no counting to ten. I already know it's not going to help.

Had I really misread her signals? I think back over all our conversations, try to pinpoint why exactly I assumed she was into me. I don't come up with any answers.

In fact, I hadn't really given it any consideration. I hadn't thought about kissing her until the split second before I did it. I'd kinda taken it for granted that she liked me and was waiting for me to make a move if I decided I liked her too.

Norie's right. I *am* an asshole.

I'm an asshole, and everyone knows it. Norie's speech could've come from the same script Juniper used when she broke up with me. I'm an asshole, and I'm selfish, and the only person who never thought so was my sister. Which is the shittiest twist of fate, because in the end, my selfishness killed her.

My stomach twists, and I'm sure I'm about to puke. I don't know what's making me more sick though—the booze or my messed-up life.

I lie down on the couch, not bothering to roll onto my side like I know I should. Who cares if I pass out and die like a rock star? That's probably the fate I deserve.

CHAPTER 26

COUNTDOWN: 5 DAYS

The next morning, I don't wake up on the wrong side of the bed, because I never made it to bed. I'm still on the couch. It's about nine hundred degrees in the garage, and my head is pounding.

Before I even open my eyes, I know it's going to be a terrible day.

I get ready for school hastily. Goal: avoid Ma, who's going to tell me we need to have a chat about my life choices, and Dad, who's all gung ho about the Clash, as if I give the slightest of shits.

While I brush the foul, morning-after taste from my mouth, I try to pinpoint what exactly I'm feeling. There's another emotion riding along with my depression and general pissed-off attitude, but I can't identify it.

Then I realize: it's embarrassment.

I'm freaking *mortified* about last night.

Number one on the list of things that doesn't help my mood? Archie Kildare passing me in the hall and holding up five fingers.

"Five days, Wilkes."

No kidding, Archie.

Maybe I'll wish for the entire fucking town to explode.

In first period, Fletcher's mood is about as fantastic as mine, which I take advantage of by asking if he's gonna treat us to a performance of "Thriller" at prom.

"Wow, you're hilarious, Eldon. How long did it take you to think that one up?"

Penelope tries to talk to me in between third and fourth periods. It's the first time she's seemed like herself since she added necromancy to her list of extracurriculars, but I blow her off. Pretend I don't see the hurt look on her face.

Though Merrill and I mostly ignore each other, at lunch, he tries to talk to me, asks me to meet him at the skeleton house after practice. I'm only half paying attention because I'm wondering where Norie is and if she's going to stop eating with us.

I'm even a jerk to Juniper when she tries to ask me how I'm doing. The thing is, she's hanging out outside the locker room, and it's right before practice, so I know she's waiting for Calvin Boyd.

"You don't need to act like you care," I say.

"I *do* care."

"You have Cal to care about. Go bother him. You're the one who broke up with me, remember?"

"Yeah," Juniper snaps. "Trust me, I remember."

What I'm saying is, I have a bad attitude before practice even starts.

* * *

We're on the field, and my dad is being a bitch, and I'm messing up so bad, it's like I've never seen a freaking football before.

"Eldon, you need to take a moment?" Dad asks at one point.

"No, I don't need to *take a moment,*" I say with a sneer.

Some of the guys laugh. I can feel my blood pressure shooting up.

"All right!" my dad calls, turning away from me and switching back into coach mode. "Let's run a weak side pick to Cal. Line up!"

As we head to the line, Calvin and I fall into step. "You ready for prom, Eldon?" he asks, smugness dripping from his voice.

"Go fuck yourself, Cal."

We get into position, and my dad blows his whistle to start the play. Here's how it's supposed to go down: I step forward and run into my defender—Otto Alvarez—and push him back. That leaves Calvin open to run behind me and to the left for a quick pass.

We've practiced this play a million times. Except, you know, it used to be me on the receiving end of the pass, while Calvin was the muscle. But still, role reversal aside, Calvin and I can run through this as smoothly as if we were ballroom dancing.

Except I'm not in the mood.

I don't feel like watching the ball land in Calvin's open arms. I might puke if I have to watch the rest of the team pat him on the back after he makes another great play.

Without really considering what I'm doing, I deviate from

the plan. Instead of pushing Otto straight back, I shove him to the left, into Calvin's path. Calvin slams full-force into him. They get tangled, fall hard onto their asses while the ball whizzes smoothly over their heads.

My dad blows his whistle.

Calvin gets to his feet first, breathing heavily.

"What the hell was that?" he asks, spitting out his mouth guard and pulling off his helmet. "You shoved him right into me!"

I glance at Otto. He's still sitting on the turf, none too pleased about being flung into a dude running full speed.

"My bad," I say casually, pulling off my own helmet.

"*Your bad?* That's *it?*" Calvin sputters. "How about a fucking apology?"

I shrug and start to walk away.

"What's your problem with me, Eldon?" Calvin shoots after me.

I should keep walking.

I should take a break. Go sit on the sidelines and calm myself. Count to ten.

Instead, I scan the field for my dad. He's out of earshot. I walk back to Calvin, who's surrounded by guys on the team like he's king and they're his court.

"My *problem*? Are you fucking kidding?" I'm losing it. I know I'm losing it, and I can't help myself. "You stole my position. You stole my *girlfriend*."

"I *stole* them? You didn't own them."

"Whatever," I say. "Enjoy my sloppy seconds."

Calvin doesn't flinch. No, that motherfucker *smiles*. He's having a grand time. Why wouldn't he be? He has everything I want, everything I *had*, and we both know it.

"Tell me something," he says like we're having a pleasant chat. "Why'd Juniper dump you anyway?"

I need to walk away. I need to not have the reaction Calvin is clearly gunning for. I need to get a grip.

"Sounds like you have a theory," I say.

Calvin's grin gets even wider. He's the freaking Cheshire Cat.

"I don't know for sure, 'cause Juniper's too classy to talk shit," he says, and though he pretends he's addressing me, his speech is clearly meant for the guys around us, who are hanging on his every word. "But my guess is that you couldn't get it up for her. Like what happened with Dessie Greerson. Now *that girl* has never kept a secret in her life."

I lunge toward Calvin faster than I've ever moved during a game.

And yeah, it feels good when my fist smashes into his face.

He goes down quickly, collapses on the turf. The other guys are shouting, and my dad blows the whistle, but I can't stop hitting Calvin. He tries to hit me back, except I have the advantage, and I'm not letting up. One side of his face is pressed into the turf, and I know it must burn. When it's more than a hundred degrees outside, that turf gets *hot*.

It's almost like I black out. I totally lose control. All that matters is destroying Calvin, using my fists to erase every smug smile, every jab he's taken at me in the past months. The field fades away. The rest of the team fades away. There's only me and Calvin and the rage that's coursing through my veins.

The next thing I know, someone—my dad, I think—is pulling me away.

"Stop it!" he keeps yelling.

I try to catch my breath. I close my eyes and wait for my heart to stop drumming in my ears. Sweat drips down my forehead, and I swipe at it. Regular sounds come back. I can feel my feet firmly planted on the field. The world becomes real again.

I open my eyes, and everyone is looking at me like I'm a monster.

Calvin staggers to his feet, blood running down his face. If I'm lucky, I broke his nose before my dad interfered.

"You're insane," Calvin says, pointing a finger at me. He sways, and Clem Johnson reaches out to steady him.

"What the hell is wrong with you?" my dad shouts, grabbing my shoulder roughly, forcing me to face him.

I shrug his hand off.

"Get off the field," he says.

I don't move. I'm disoriented, as unsteady as Cal, but no one's offering me a shoulder to lean on. I search my teammates' faces for any sign of sympathy, but I'm nothing but a sideshow attraction. *Step right up, and see a once promising football star entirely lose his cool! Grab a front row seat, and watch as he destroys everything he loves!*

"I'm not telling you again," my dad says coldly. "Get off my field."

I finally meet his gaze, which is a mistake. I've never seen anyone look so disappointed.

✼ ✼ ✼

I've got my head together enough to remember Merrill wanted to meet up. I text him, say practice ended early and I'm free.

The last of my adrenaline fades as I make my way to the skeleton house. I wish it would come back. At least when I was beating up on Cal, I wasn't *thinking*. I'd happily live in a rage-induced blackout if it means I'm otherwise numb.

The sun feels hot enough to melt my organs, and I'm already feeling sore from the fight. I try to hang onto my fury, but there's nowhere to direct it. I don't even know who I'm angry at. Maybe myself.

When I get to the house, Merrill's already there. He's not in our usual spot up in the eaves though. Instead, he's pacing what would have been the kitchen.

"What's going on?" I ask.

He stops and stares. "What happened to you?"

"Got in a fight."

"With?"

"It doesn't matter."

I wait for him to make a joke, but it doesn't come. He has a weird expression on his face. Maybe he thinks I'm a monster too.

"Look, I'm sorry about last night," I say.

He eyes me cautiously. "You are?"

"I shouldn't have called you a sheep. Can we move on?"

"That's actually not what I wanted to talk to you about."

"OK." I wait.

Merrill takes off his glasses. Looks at them. Puts them back on. Runs his hands through his hair. Shuffles his feet.

"You mean talk about it now or sometime next decade?" I ask. I'm trying to be chill, but I'm a little short on patience.

Merrill takes a deep breath. "Do you like Norie?"

I hope my cringe isn't visible.

"She told me about last night," he goes on.

I shrug, and pain shoots down my arm. Yep, I'm going to be paying for my fight with Calvin for a while. "I was drunk," I tell Merrill.

"That's all?"

"Yeah." I force a laugh. "Why? Do *you* like her?"

I only mean it as banter. He's supposed to joke back, restore the balance of our friendship. But Merrill keeps staring at me with that weird expression and goes a little pale.

You've got to be kidding me.

"Shit. You *do* like her, don't you?"

"Yeah, man," he says softly.

He turns away, gives me a minute to process the information. It's hard to wrap my mind around. How did I not notice this? What the hell else have I been missing?

"Wait a second," I say. "Has something been *going on* between you two?"

Merrill sighs deeply again, like this conversation is just *so difficult* for him. Like he's wanted to tell me for *so long*, and it's *killed* him to keep it from me.

"Something *has* been going on," I say flatly. "Behind my fucking back."

"It's not like that, Eldon."

"What's it like then?" I snap.

Anger flashes in Merrill's eyes, washing away his woe-is-me expression. "You don't get dibs on every girl we speak to, OK?"

"I never said I did."

Merrill snorts. His mouth curls in a smirk. "Sure you didn't, buddy."

My fists clench at my sides. It takes every bit of my willpower not to hit him. Which he sees.

"What, you want to beat on me? Is that gonna make you feel better?" He takes off his glasses and folds them, carefully tucks them into his pocket. "Go ahead. Believe me, I know how to take a beating."

I struggle to get control of myself. This is Merrill. It's not Calvin or Fletcher or some other douchebag. It's the guy I've called my best friend since I could speak. I'm not going to fight him.

I unclench my fists and take a step back. "Why didn't you tell me? If you didn't think anything was wrong with this, then why wasn't there any *oh, by the way, Norie and I have been hooking up for weeks*?"

"And what, you would have wished us well?"

"Maybe!"

We both know that's probably not true, and Merrill being right while I'm wrong—wrong about *everything*—makes me angrier.

"Look," Merrill says, sounding much more composed than I feel, "I had no idea you liked her. Norie's not even your type. I wasn't trying to screw you over."

"Gee, thanks for being such a pal."

Disbelief washes over his face. "You know what, Eldon? I've been a *great* friend to you. I've had your back through *everything*. And trust me, you don't always make it easy."

He's right.

Right again.

"Yeah, well, I never asked you to," I say.

I walk away from him and sit on the poured concrete floor, lean back against one of the beams that's keeping the half-built roof over our heads. I close my eyes and wait for Merrill's footsteps on the gravel, the sound of him walking away from me. It doesn't come.

I open my eyes, and he's still squinting at me like I'm a stranger. A stranger who he doesn't particularly want to get to know.

"What?" I ask.

His sadness is focused on me for what feels like an eternity. "Why couldn't you let me have this one thing?"

I don't respond.

After a moment, Merrill shakes his head, pulls his glasses from his pocket, and slides them onto his face. "Later, Eldon."

I don't respond to that either.

He walks away from the skeleton house, leaving me sitting on the dusty floor. Completely alone.

CHAPTER 27

COUNTDOWN: 4 DAYS

W hen I open my eyes the next morning, the only positive
thought in my head is that it's Saturday, so I don't have
to deal with school. Then I remember the UFO festival and my
double shift at the gas station.

Fantastic. *Exactly* what I'm in the mood for.

Ma's at her usual place in the kitchen, tearing through a flyer
for a grocery store we don't have in Madison, looking for ways to
save money on items she doesn't intend to buy.

"Where's Dad?" I ask, hovering in the doorway.

She won't even look at me. "In the garage. But I'd give him
space if I were you."

Probably good advice. But the longer I wait, the worse I'll
feel, so I go out to the garage anyway. He's slumped on the couch,
not even bothering with one of his projects. I take that as a very
bad sign. I wonder if I'm going to get Dad or Coach.

"Hey," I say, walking in and sitting down next to him.

The TV is on, news from Vegas again. Another drowning at Lake Mead, more kids cliff-jumping out there.

"I'm sorry," I say softly.

He doesn't respond, and I think maybe he won't. Maybe we'll sit here in silence until I take the hint and leave. But then he sighs.

"I didn't get to play in the Clash, you know. Got hurt about a month before the game."

"I know," I say.

"It was one of the biggest disappointments in my life. But when I had you, I knew I'd get to watch *you* play in it."

"Does that mean I'm off the team for good?"

My dad frowns, as if he can't believe I'd ask. "Eldon, I can't let you play tomorrow. Your behavior was unacceptable."

"I'm sorry," I say again. And it's true. I really am sorry. Sorry I let my dad down, at least. I'm not really repenting busting up Calvin's face.

"What the hell were you thinking?"

I can't meet his eyes. "I don't know. I was mad."

"You can't go around hitting people when you get mad at them. How can you be eighteen years old and not realize that?"

My dad seems to be having an internal fight of his own. His sadness and fury are locked in a battle, and I have no idea which emotion will win. Not that it matters. He loses either way and is stuck with a son he's ashamed of.

"The last game of the year," he goes on. "The last game you'll ever play. And you threw it away because some jerk made a comment you didn't like. Guess what, Eldon? There are a lot of jerks in the world. And they're gonna make a lot of comments. You need to learn self-control."

This is not the first time I've been told that. I guess if I weren't such a screwup, it would've sunk in by now.

"I have to get to work," I say, standing. "But I really am sorry."

My dad looks up at me. "When are you gonna stop apologizing and actually change your attitude?"

I wish I knew.

✻ ✻ ✻

The alien hunters are out in full force. Carload after carload of people, making the pilgrimage to Rachel to buy Area 51 coffee mugs and T-shirts and swap made-up stories about their encounters with UFOs. We've never had so many people pass through Madison before.

Mr. Casey is on edge from the moment I clock in.

"Swarming," he says, frowning at the tourists through the window. "All nosing around, looking for something supernatural."

"They're looking in the sky, not the mountains," I say.

"No matter. It's still a risk. Get 'em out of here as fast as you can, got it? I want you working all the pumps at once."

Yeah, sure. Seems easy enough.

"I've only got two hands," I say.

"Then grow a few more."

I wonder what the UFO hunters would think about *that*.

Cars roll into the parking lot without let up. I do my best, but I'm having trouble turning on the charm. I keep thinking about Merrill and how I can't remember the last time we had a fight. A real fight, over something that matters. A girl coming between us is pretty high on the list of crap I never expected.

A car pulls up. I smile, flirt with the women, talk aliens with them, tell them how boring Madison is, how Rachel is where everything's happening. Before that car is gone, another appears. Mr. Casey runs outside at one point to help me, which has never happened before.

"And you were worried about *prom*," he says.

"Well, it doesn't matter now," I reply. I'm not going to prom alone to watch Juniper and Calvin, Merrill and Norie. Madison High School is filled with happy couples these days. Even catering to alien-obsessed tourists is better than dealing with that.

The mass pilgrimage to Rachel is finally slowing down, and Mr. Casey has returned to his air-conditioned haven, when a beat-up car pulls into the gas station. At a glance, it looks so much like Merrill's Mustang that for a second I think it's him. And yeah, I guess I'm disappointed when it isn't.

Which is senseless. Because if it *were* Merrill, it wouldn't only be *him*. It would be him and Norie, on their way to prom, rubbing it in my face that they're part of a secret duo where there's no place for me.

The car stops at the gas pump, and the driver's window rolls down. Nope, definitely not Merrill. Unless he turned into a ridiculously hot girl.

"Hey there," she says, flashing me a crooked smile.

I grin back.

She's a few years older than me, college aged. She's got this bohemian look, a scarf wrapped around her head like she's some sort of hippie-pirate. You don't need to be local to tell she isn't from Madison.

"I guess this is what passes for a gas station around here," she says.

If another tourist made that remark, I would have been insulted. With this girl, I let it slide. "You guess right," I reply.

I move toward the gas tank. There are two guys in the car with her. I assume the one in the passenger seat is her boyfriend. They match each other, like they're extras on the same movie set. The guy in the back is a massive dude who looks like he'd be more comfortable on Madison's football field than crammed into the car.

I nod to the guy in the front seat. He smiles back. All three of them seem totally at ease. They're having fun. Madison is only a stopover on the way to a bigger adventure.

I'm hit with a pang of jealousy so sharp that it makes me pause in the middle of what I'm doing.

"You into this whole UFO obsession?" the girl asks.

"Not exactly." I fit the nozzle into the gas tank and look over at her. "You are, I guess?"

She and the guy in the passenger seat glance at each other and laugh. "Not exactly."

I raise my eyebrows. "Well, you didn't come to Madison for the awesome scenery."

"Oh, we're going to the UFO festival. But it's not the end goal."

"What is?"

The girl laughs again. "Dunno. I guess we'll know when we find it."

More jealousy. I want that life. I have the urge to jump in the car with them. To make them take me with them, anywhere. Drive the desert roads until we land in some mystery place, far from Madison.

"I'm Abby," the girl says, holding out her hand. "This is JP, and that's Sweet Pete in the back."

"Eldon," I say, walking over and shaking her hand.

Instead of letting go at the appropriate time, her grip tightens, and she pulls me closer to the window.

"Hey, Eldon," she says, lowering her voice, like we're conspiring. "Maybe you can answer a question for me."

"Uh, sure?"

She's still holding my hand. Her palm is warm and sweaty and alive.

"I heard a rumor that aliens aren't the only mysterious occurrence around here."

I pull my hand from hers and take a step back.

"What's that mean?"

"I *wish* I could say exactly."

She draws out the word. There's no mistaking it. She most definitely put emphasis on *wish*.

The guy in the front, JP, leans forward and watches me closely. The sun suddenly feels hotter. Dust rasps against my skin. I glance around the gas station parking lot.

"I don't know what you mean," I say.

Abby winks. "Sure you don't."

The gas pump clicks. They're done filling up, but I don't move.

"Who are you?" I ask.

"I guess you could call us explorers," JP says.

"Close enough," Abby agrees.

We stare at each other. My mind races. Who are they, and how do they know? *Do* they know? Am I misreading the situation?

"Look, we're not here to blow your cover or anything," Abby says. "We like mysteries. And it sounds as if this town has a pretty big one."

"Where'd you hear that?" I ask. My voice practically squeaks.

Abby laughs. "The same place you'd hear about UFOs or Bigfoot or crybaby bridges. Nothing to get worked up about."

I pull the nozzle from the gas tank and replace the cap, taking a moment to compose myself while my back is turned. This is the situation I've been hired to handle. I've been *trained* for this. Time to be charming and reassuring. Get them out of town. Make sure they don't notice my shaking hands or that's it's not the heat that's making me sweat.

When I look back at Abby, I give her a megawatt smile. "Unfortunately, you heard wrong. This is probably the least mysterious place in the world."

My act must work, because she shrugs and says, "OK then. Just thought I'd ask."

"Sorry," I say.

Abby suddenly lunges forward and grabs my arm again. I'm too caught off guard to pull away.

"Look, we'll be in Rachel for the night." She produces a pen and scrawls a phone number on my hand. "In case you change your mind."

A second later, I'm watching them drive away. What was *that* about? And how am I going to deal with it?

* * *

I guess it's one of those right place, right time scenarios.

Under different circumstances, I would've finished my shift and gone to prom and never thought about the kids in the car again. Probably, I would've told Moses Casey about them, and he'd alert the mayor, which is what we're *supposed* to do should a situation like this arise.

There's no prom for me tonight though. There's only anger and loneliness. There's my entire world crashing down around me and feeling like I don't have a place I belong anymore. Feeling like even the parts of my life that made sense have become twisted and strange.

Maybe that's why I don't raise the alarm like I'm supposed to.

Instead, I go home and lie in bed, stare at the ceiling, and don't say a word to anyone. I'm tired from work—worn out from my entire messed-up life, really. I certainly can't handle talking to Mayor Fontaine tonight, which is exactly what'll happen if I alert anyone to what happened.

Or maybe that's an excuse. Maybe the reason I don't snitch on the wish seekers is because I simply don't want to.

Because I'd rather mull over the kids in the car than think about my actual life. My two best friends getting ready for prom without me. My parents, who see me as a huge disappointment. My wish, which is mere days away. Contemplating Madison's leaked secret is a lot more appealing, yeah?

How did they know about wishing? Do other people know? Is our secret less of a secret than anyone realizes?

I get out of bed and pace my room, replay the conversation in my head. Did I imagine her inflection? They *did* know about wishing, right? I'm not inventing it. *Am I?*

After a while, I realize I'm not going to be satisfied until I know more. This might be the biggest happening in Madison since... well, since wishing began. And really, I shouldn't ignore the situation and leave loose ends. I owe it to the town to dig deeper.

That's what I tell myself anyway.

So while all my friends—or at least the people who called themselves friends—are at prom, I'm asking my parents if I can borrow the minivan. I'm speeding down the highway toward the Little A'Le'Inn.

I roll down the windows and crank up the radio.

"*Broadcasting live from the Rachel, Nevada, UFO Festival, this is Basin and Range Radio, and I'm your host, Robert Nash.*"

I'm being reckless. One hand on the wheel, the other texting Abby. I have no idea what I'll say when I get there. I have no plan, and it feels good. It feels like freedom.

I roll into Rachel half an hour later, and I'm quickly reminded why I seldom come here. It's gracious to even call it a town. It's nothing but a single restaurant and a handful of trailer homes dotting the desert landscape. There's a big sign on the way in:

Welcome to Rachel, Nev.

Population: Humans 98

Aliens: ?

They really take the whole alien thing too far. But I guess it makes sense. What else do they have?

A second later, I pull up to the Little A'Le'Inn. The vacant land surrounding the restaurant has morphed into a fairground. There are booths everywhere—more made-in-China alien merchandise than I ever hoped to see. Due to the lack of hotel accommodations, most festival-goers are set up in tents or RVs on the outskirts of the action.

I get out of the car and wander through the crowd, pass a stage where a familiar voice is being projected to an audience.

"…the fact is, ancient astronauts *did* visit Earth, and they *did* leave their mark. Can we blame our ancestors for mistaking aliens for divine beings? When we look at petroglyphs depicting star people or the appearance of unidentified flying objects in Renaissance paintings, can we really claim…"

I stop walking and turn to the stage where Robert Nash is doing his live radio broadcast. In all my years listening to him, I've never actually *seen* the guy. From his smooth, deep voice, I'd expected someone scholarly. Someone who demands respect. But he's got a ridiculous ponytail, his clothes look like he picked them up off the floor, and his glasses are so thick, they rival Merrill's. Dude looks like every other UFO hunter who spends their life camped out on a ridge, binoculars pointed at Area 51. I feel oddly let down.

I turn away as Robert Nash gears up for a lecture on how aliens built the pyramids.

Personally, I've always found that alien pyramid stuff insulting. Like, do people think humans are so incompetent, we can't erect buildings on our own? We need freaking *extraterrestrials* to help us? Whatever.

I pull out my phone while I wander through booths where people hawk food and crafts. I almost walk straight into a guy in full alien costume. Another guy passes me, literally wearing a tin-foil hat.

I'm here, I text Abby. I glance up. I'm by the flying saucer ride.

A few moments later, an arm wraps around my shoulder.

"I knew you'd come!" Abby grins wildly. "Come on. We have a table inside."

She pulls me into the Little A'Le'Inn. The small restaurant usually only has a couple of people in it at a time. Tonight, it's as packed as a Las Vegas club.

"It's too crowded. We can't talk here," I say over the noise. I eye the menu regretfully. I haven't eaten all day and could really go for a chili burger.

Abby raises her eyebrows. "You *do* have something to tell us, don't you?"

We end up piling into Abby's car, parked at the edge of the UFO Fest circus. It's like before, Abby and JP in the front. Only now I'm crammed in the back with Sweet Pete, who's making his way through a family-size bag of potato chips.

JP lights a joint and passes it to Abby. When she offers it to Pete, he waves it away.

"Gotta stay healthy," he explains.

I look dubiously at his bag of chips.

"Pete played football," Abby tells me.

"Will again too, when we get back," he says.

"*If* we get back," Abby says, her eyes sparkling. "Maybe we'll find a portal to another world and spend the rest of our lives dimension surfing."

"Maybe." Pete nods agreeably.

I take the joint when it's passed to me. "So what's your deal? Are you, like, conspiracy theorists or whatever?"

"No, no, we're not truthers," says JP. He nods at the fairground out the window. "This whole setup is cool but more of a novelty than anything else."

"We're legend trippers," Abby offers.

I certainly agree with the *tripping* part. "What's that mean exactly?"

"We find places where weird things happened."

"There are people who go looking for ghosts," JP says, twisting in his seat to see me. "They're purely interested in hauntings."

"And there are urban explorers," Abby adds. "They break into creepy abandoned buildings. Sometimes to take pictures and sometimes to destroy stuff and sometimes simply to soak up the atmosphere."

Back to JP. "We don't exactly belong to either of those groups."

The way they play off each other, I get the feeling this is an act they've performed a million times. I've never felt like such an outsider.

"We go where there are *legends*," Abby says. "Places where there are supposed to be vortexes and portals and poltergeists. You know, anything mysterious."

Is this what people consider recreation outside of Madison? I know I'm a little clueless about the outside world, but this seems bizarre. Or maybe growing up in the desert has made me immune to *the mysterious*. "And, uh, what exactly do you *do* in these places?"

Abby shrugs. "Wait for something to happen."

"Why?" I pass the joint back to the front of the car. When Pete offers me his bag of chips, I gladly take a few.

If Abby's insulted that I don't get it, it doesn't show. "I dunno. It's better than college, I guess."

"It's a different kind of summer road trip," JP says. "Some people go see giant balls of yarn. We look for burned-down orphanages and old asylums."

"And how much have you seen, exactly? Supernatural, I mean?"

Abby and JP look at each other and laugh. Again, completely in synch. "We're still kind of waiting on that part," JP says.

The weed is making my head swim. The tension of the past few days is leaving my body. I feel oddly comfortable in the back seat of their car, in the middle of nowhere, alien festivities going on around us.

"So you go all over the country *hoping* something supernatural will happen?"

"Look," says Abby. "Everyone has to believe in something."

Don't I know it.

I think of Norie. I wonder what she and Merrill are doing right now. I wonder if Juniper and Calvin are hooking up, having a little after-prom party of their own.

"We came out this way to see a famous hotel," Abby says. "It's haunted by the ghost of a prostitute who was killed there."

I know the hotel. It's in the town next to Tonopah. Thinking of Tonopah makes me think of the Clash. Which isn't the *last* thing I want to dwell on, but pretty close.

"That story's fake," I say.

Sweet Pete nods. "Most of them are."

"We didn't get in anyway," JP says. "The sheriff caught us trying to jimmy a window. Luckily, we were let off with a warning."

"We were going to head to California," Abby chimes in. "But then we heard about the UFO Festival and decided to stop here first."

JP's turn. "Imagine our surprise when we stopped in this little bar in some nowhere town—what was it?"

"Alamo," Sweet Pete says.

"Right, Alamo. And there's some drunk guy babbling about how aliens are real and they gave Madison a magic wishing well."

A wishing well. I guess it's close enough to the truth.

"Clearly, we had to check it out," Abby finishes.

They have nothing. I know right then that I can make up a story. I can smile and lie, lie, lie. I can say *their* story is complete crap, and they'll buy it, because they didn't really believe it in the first place. This is all fun and games for them, and with a few words, I can send them on their way.

I stare at them.

They look back expectantly.

I need to say something. I need to keep them out of Madison.

Instead, I think of my sister dying in a hospital bed. I think of Fletcher *not* dying. I think of my parents and how their lives could have been but aren't. A slideshow of wishes, of *wishers*, runs through my mind. All the tears and anger and loss.

The rage that's consumed me lately comes rushing back, but this time, it's not directed at a single person. It's not even directed at myself. I'm angry at Madison. I'm angry at *wishing*.

I hate it. I hate everything about it. I've seen firsthand how many lives it can ruin. It's ruined *my own* life.

And I'm supposed to *protect* it? I'm supposed to keep the town's secret, keep these legend trippers moving, make sure wishing stays hidden for upcoming generations so it can ruin more lives?

Why should I guard wishing?

Why?

What the hell has that *ever* gotten me?

I don't do Mr. Wakefield's count-to-ten thing. Because this anger? It feels good. It feels *right*.

And that's why I don't send the legend trippers packing.

That's why I say, "I wouldn't exactly call it a *wishing well*."

*   *   *

Talk can be therapeutic, yeah? It feels good to tell someone the secret I've been forced to keep my entire life. No, it feels *great*. As the story pours out, it's as if I'm destroying the pain and anger within me.

Abby and JP listen raptly. Even Sweet Pete puts aside his bag of chips. The jokey vibe in the car is gone. They hadn't expected this. It had been a game to them, and I made it real.

"Are you messing with us?" JP asks.

"No."

Abby and JP look at each other. There's a long silence. They don't believe me. They want to believe me, but they don't. They think I'm either lying or delusional. Newsflash: I'm neither.

"I can take you there," I offer.

"Could we go in?" Abby asks.

"We'd have to cut through the bars."

They still look skeptical.

"It's been done before," I say, thinking of Silas Creed, the man found with a bullet in his head. If you believe old stories anyway.

"What would happen if we got caught?" Abby asks.

"I have no freaking clue."

I don't. And the truth is, I don't really care one way or another.

"There are all these conspiracies," I say. "Some people think the rules are lies. Let's find out what happens if one of you tries to wish."

They aren't from Madison. They aren't about to celebrate their eighteenth birthdays. According to everything I've been raised to believe, it should be impossible for their wishes to come true. But I want to know for sure. I *need* to know. I need to know just how much I've been lied to my entire life.

Abby and JP are still cautious. Who can blame them? Until I described it to outsiders, I hadn't realized how ridiculous wishing sounded.

"Here's the deal. If there's no cave, and I turn out to be some creep, it's not like you're in danger. Have the Hulk over here kick my ass, and be on your way," I say, nodding at Sweet Pete. "On the other hand, maybe you'll get to make a wish, and all your dreams will come true."

"When would we do this?" Abby asks. "Tonight?"

"No, tomorrow evening. There's a big football game. The entire town will be there."

No one will be paying attention to the wish cave, that's for sure.

Abby and JP share another long look. I have the feeling they know what the other is thinking. They're that in tune with each other. It makes me miss Merrill. I wonder what he'd think about all this.

Then I get annoyed at myself for considering it. Who cares what Merrill thinks? I imagine the look on his face when he finds out I broke into the wish cave without him. I hope it will be a punch to the gut. I hope it makes him feel like he's been left behind.

"So?" I ask.

Abby nods. "OK. I'm in."

"Same," says JP.

They both look at Pete, who shrugs his massive shoulders. "Sure. Why not?"

There's no more smoking after that. We need to be sharp. There are plans to be made. We're going to make wish history. It's at that moment that I finally feel like I'm on the right path.

* * *

Abby walks me back to the minivan. We wander through the remnants of the UFO festival, passing alien fanatics who are holding out to the bitter end. I look for Robert Nash, but the stage is empty.

"Why are you doing this?" Abby asks.

"What?"

"Blowing your town's cover."

I shrug. "It was going to happen eventually. I might as well get some answers first. My friend Merrill, he thinks wishing is a conspiracy."

"What kind of name is Merrill?" Abby asks, making a face.

"I'd say JP and Sweet Pete aren't much better."

Abby laughs, tilting her face up to the sky. She says, "JP stands for John Paul. He was named after a pope. Hardly anyone knows that about him."

I don't know anything about the pope either, so I don't comment. Instead, I ask, "How long have you guys been dating?"

"Me and JP?" Abby seems surprised. "We're not dating."

I raise my eyebrows at her.

"Dating would ruin what we have," she says. "It makes things messy. Too many rules and feelings. And most likely, it'll end with a breakup."

"Friends can break up too."

My mood turns dark again. Even if Abby and JP aren't dating, they have a bond. This trip they're on, it's all about the two of them. Sweet Pete is simply along for the ride. The dumb football player, stuck in the back of the car. That's all I'll ever be to Merrill and Norie. As long as they're together, I'll always be the third wheel.

We reach my parents' minivan and stop.

"Are you really sure you want to go through with this?" Abby asks.

"Positive."

"OK then." She smiles. "I'll see you tomorrow."

It's not until I'm halfway back to Madison that I'm hit with the enormity of what I'm about to do. I pull over to the side of the road and sit there in the darkness, the empty highway on one side of me and the desert on the other.

I'm going to break into the wish cave. I'm going to blow the lid off wishing. I'm going to do something that no one has ever dared to do before.

Have I made a terrible mistake? Should I call it off? There's still time.

No.

I push aside my worries. I turn the car back on and head toward home. Nothing is going to stop me.

Wishing is cloaked in secrecy. And tomorrow, I'm going to bring those secrets to light.

CHAPTER 28

COUNTDOWN: 3 DAYS

You grow up in Madison, you know what it feels like to wait. Your life is one big countdown. I hear that on your actual wish day, each hour feels like a week. An endless stretch of checking watches and clocks and cell phones, making sure time hasn't stopped, reassuring yourself that your wish hour is getting closer.

That's how it is for me the day of the Drosophila-Mucker Clash.

I pace my room. Don't bother turning on the radio. All I can think about is getting through the next minute and the next and the next. Stay calm. Don't think too much about what I'm on the verge of doing, because thinking too much, well, that can make you lose your nerve.

Merrill blows up my phone with text messages about how we need to talk. I've never wanted to talk to him more in my life. I'm about to become one of the rogue wishers Merrill's spent his life preaching about, and I want to let him in on the scheme.

I push aside that feeling by thinking about him and Norie at prom together. Thinking about him and Norie *after* prom. Doing God knows what. Without me. Because what place do I have in their lives now?

Merrill doesn't deserve to know my secrets. I don't respond to his messages.

While my parents eat lunch and talk about the upcoming game, I dig around in my closet for an old backpack I haven't used for years. Then I go into the garage to gather my dad's tools. I put the TV on as cover. There's a recap of the UFO festival on the news. For a moment, I watch the footage of people wandering around Rachel, looking for something spectacular. I try to spot myself in the crowd. Would I look like another UFO hunter or could you see that I'm about to betray the town I call home? The news cuts back to the studio, and the anchor moves on to the next story.

I get back to business. I pick up my dad's reciprocating saw, grab the battery off the charger, and push it into place. I unzip my backpack to shove the saw inside when something catches my eye. There's a crumpled piece of paper at the bottom of the bag. I pull it out, smooth the paper on my dad's workbench.

Tag, loser!!! You're it!

Ebba.

My insides crumple. I wilt. I stagger over to the couch, note still in my hand, and sit down heavily.

I miss my sister. I want her here right now. I want to tell her what I'm about to do and watch her roll her eyes. I want to hear her voice as she tells me it's the worst idea ever. I want this to be one of a million secret notes she'll leave me.

I gasp for breath and press my fists into my eyes, like that's all it will take to stop the tears.

It isn't. They come anyway.

Ebba won't leave me notes anymore. I found the last one, and by finding it, she'll disappear a bit more. This is the end. There's no more hope.

I carefully fold Ebba's note and put it in my pocket. It'll be my good luck charm tonight.

I go back to loading tools into my backpack but with less enthusiasm than before. I know I'm taking more than I need—pliers or a hammer aren't likely to get me into the wish cave, yeah? But I want to be prepared just in case.

I'm zipping my bag when the garage door opens. I nudge my backpack aside and throw myself down onto the couch, try to look casual. Like I'm watching TV. Totally chill. Not at all on the verge of committing a major crime.

My dad steps into the garage. He frowns at me like there are a million things he wants to say but doesn't know where to begin.

"I'm heading to the game."

"OK."

We look at each other for a long moment. I melt into a pile of shame.

"Are you coming?" he asks.

"What, I'm not banned from the stadium too?" I wince as soon as the words are out of my mouth. Why can't I stop being such a dick?

"I'll see you later tonight," my dad replies quietly. He turns to leave.

"Dad, wait."

Once his eyes are back on me, I have no idea what to say.

"I hope you win," I say finally.

"Thanks, buddy."

He turns again.

"And I'm sorry," I blurt out. We both have places to be, and I don't know why I'm suddenly so desperate to keep him here. "I know how much you wanted me to play."

"Didn't *you* want to play, Eldon?" he asks.

"Honestly, I don't think I love football that much."

He looks surprised. "Why didn't you ever say so?"

"I don't think I realized it."

"Well, you could have found a better way to get out of the game."

I snort with laughter. My dad smiles.

He looks like he wants to say more. I *want* him to say more. And I want to tell him everything I've been feeling for the past few months.

But instead of sharing wise, meaningful thoughts, my dad says, "Hey, check it out." He walks over to the side of the garage where the sink is all set up. He turns the faucet, and a stream of water shoots out.

"That's really great, Dad."

"I think so too," he says.

I'm glad he has something to be proud of. Even if it isn't me.

Then he leaves for the football field, the place he loves most. Concerned with nothing but putting the Tonopah Muckers in their place. For him, winning the game is the same at winning at life.

For me, well, I'm playing a totally different sport.

* * *

The sun is setting as I walk to the edge of town.

My parents took the van, and I don't want to risk Abby picking me up at my house. There'd be too many questions if anyone saw.

The town is dead. Everyone's at the game or on the way there. It feels like I'm the only person left in Madison. It should be creepy, but instead, it's liberating. Like being the lone survivor after the apocalypse. Maybe that's the way it should be. There are some things you have to do alone.

Abby's car is waiting where we planned. I hop in the back seat.

"You sure you want to do this?" she asks.

I nod and direct her down the dusty road, through the hills that lead to the wish cave.

"Here," I say when we reach the flat, cleared-out space that's used as a parking lot. "We have to walk the rest of the way."

I go first, and Sweet Pete brings up the rear. Light fades from the sky rapidly.

We twist up the path, hugging close to the mountain. It's steep and rocky, but my frequent trips to the hot springs have given me plenty of practice with the terrain.

"Are there rattlesnakes out here?" Pete asks.

"Not in Madison. Someone wished for the rattlesnakes to disappear a long time ago."

"Like some twisted St. Patrick," Abby says.

I don't know anything about St. Patrick. I thought he had a holiday when people got drunk.

"Hey," I say, "do people ask you guys what you want to be when you grow up?"

Abby gives me a weird look.

"I see it on TV a lot," I say. "Adults asking little kids what they want to be. I wondered if that was real or not."

"Yeah, man," says JP. "Of course they ask."

I'm struck by the strangeness of that. How different a person's life might be because of where they were born. "No one does that here," I say. "They ask what you're going to wish for."

We're all sweating and gasping for breath by the time we reach the summit. There, in a cleft of rock, is the cave. The last rays of sunlight glint on the metal bars.

"Jesus," says JP. "It's real."

I toss my backpack to the ground and pull out the reciprocating saw.

"Is that going to work?" Abby asks skeptically.

"According to my dad, it'll cut through anything." I take a deep breath. "Ready?"

Everyone nods.

I press the button, and the saw comes to life. It screeches when I hold it to the first metal bar. It's so freaking loud, I'm half convinced the noise will travel all the way to Vegas.

But I don't let that stop me.

* * *

It turns out cutting through metal bars isn't exactly a breeze. The saw works, but it's slow going. The sun is fully set by the time I make real progress.

JP taps me on the shoulder to get my attention. When I turn off the saw, he says, "That's enough."

I examine the hole I've made.

"What about him?" I nod at Pete. "He won't fit through."

"I'll be the lookout," Pete says.

"OK then. I guess we're ready."

I stare into the darkness of the wish cave, still not entirely believing what I'm about to do. It seems monumental. I reach into my pocket and close my hand around Ebba's note.

"You have a flashlight?" Abby asks.

I rummage in my backpack and pull out three candles.

"You're joking."

I shrug. "They say it has to be this way."

JP lights the candles, and I hand Sweet Pete the hammer, tell him to bang it against the bars if there's any trouble.

It seems like we should mark the moment. Say or do something ceremonial. But JP and Abby slip quietly into the cave, twisting their bodies to pass between the rough edges of the bars. I follow them.

Inside, the temperature drops. All noise stops. It's like being underwater.

"Go straight," I say. "Stay on the main path until you hit a big cavern."

We walk.

The cave is everything I'd been told. Smooth walls. Hard-packed ground. No light except for the flickering candles. It makes me think of crypts. Of passages inside the pyramids. It's otherworldly, and I suddenly understand how people can believe in aliens or God. The wish cave doesn't feel like a place for humans.

A few passages shoot off the main tunnel. I peer down them but can't see far. I don't linger. The last thing I want is to lose Abby and JP.

None of us speak while we walk, as if making noise might wake up some ancient creature inside these stone corridors.

But at one of the branching passages, I have to pause.

"Wait," I whisper.

Abby and JP shuffle to a stop.

I feel a breeze from the end of the passage. I look down at my candle. Sure enough, it's flickering.

"Is that the way?" Abby asks.

"No, but—"

"Come on then."

We go on.

I figure we must be near the cavern now. But before we find out for sure, there's a noise behind us. A hammer clashing against metal.

We halt again. I meet Abby's gaze in the flickering candlelight. She doesn't look afraid. I wish I could say the same for myself.

Sweet Pete's voice echoes down the long corridor.

"Shit," JP says.

We can't make out what Pete's shouting. Another indistinct voice joins his.

"I think we've been caught," Abby says.

My heart speeds. I've got so much adrenaline that it's as if I'm in the final, critical moments of a football game. I have the urge to run, but running deeper into a labyrinth cave system doesn't seem like a brilliant idea, yeah?

The squeal of metal hinges echoes down the corridor. The door is opening.

And like that, all my hopes are dashed. We've been discovered. The mayor may have cameras set up somewhere for all I know.

"If we keep going, we can make it to the cavern," I say. "You can wish before they get here."

But I can already hear shoes pounding on the ground, rushing down the passageway. It turns out sound carries really well in a cave.

Abby calmly shakes her head. "It's too late."

JP grins and leans against the wall, totally casual. I don't get why I'm the only one freaking out.

"What are you doing?" I ask.

"Nothing to do but wait. This isn't exactly our first run-in with the law."

"It's all part of the fun," Abby says. She leans over and kisses me on the cheek. "Thanks for the adventure, kid."

Then from around a bend in the cave, the mayor's goons appear, looking ready for a fight. Sheriff Crawford is behind them. His face is painted in the Madison High School colors, and he's wearing a Drosophila jersey. I'm certain he's not thrilled about leaving the game.

Pulling up the rear is Mayor Fontaine himself. He's wheezing and struggling to keep up. And let me tell you, he does *not* look happy.

CHAPTER 29

COUNTDOWN:
2 DAYS

I've wasted countless hours thinking up clever ways to get out of school on Monday mornings. But spending the night in jail had never occurred to me.

I'm alone in a holding cell at the police station. I have no idea what happened to Abby and JP and Pete. I haven't seen them since the confusion last night. Madison doesn't exactly have a huge prison network. Them not being here with me is cause for concern.

"So how long am I going to be locked up?" I ask Leo Treadway, the guard who's sitting with his feet propped up on a desk at the end of the hall. It's about the fiftieth time I've asked, and he has yet to respond.

I glance at the wall clock hanging above Leo's head. Despite feeling like time has stopped, the seconds continue to tick away. I sigh and lie back down on my cot. I haven't been able to sleep. I'm too anxious about whatever punishment is coming.

The mayor hardly spoke to me last night. Mostly, he glared

and shook his head in disgust. For that, I'm grateful. I'm really not up to a huge lecture.

I wait and wait. I gaze at the bars of my cell and think about how handy my dad's saw would be right now. I wonder where the others have been taken and if I'll be stuck in here forever. I wonder if it's possible to die of boredom.

It's around ten in the morning when the outer door swings open and one of the other guards pokes his head in the room.

"Fontaine wants to see him," he tells Leo.

Leo shuffles over and unlocks my cell. I follow him into Sheriff Crawford's office where I'm greeted by a very unwelcome sight.

The mayor is sitting behind the desk like it's his own, while the sheriff has been relegated to a small chair in the corner. Sitting across from Mayor Fontaine, looking extremely furious, is my mom.

"Hi, Ma," I say.

"Sit down," she replies with an icy tone.

I sit in the chair next to her.

This office is too small for all four of us. I shift uncomfortably while they stare at me. Maybe they're waiting for me to talk first.

"What happened to Abby and them?" I ask finally.

Sheriff Crawford opens his mouth, but the mayor beats him to speaking.

"They've been taken care of."

A chill trickles down my spine.

"We've been discussing what to do with you," my mom says.

"What did you come up with?" I ask nonchalantly.

"Do you think this is a game?" Ma snaps. "You could be charged with criminal trespassing. Do you understand that?"

I consider pointing out that I'm still a minor for another few days. I had plenty of time to think about that overnight. Nothing they charge me with will have devastating consequences. Still, I don't like the glint in the mayor's eye. It makes me very uncomfortable.

"In Madison, we believe in our own brand of justice," Mayor Fontaine says.

The sheriff leans forward. "Well, that's not exactly—"

Mayor Fontaine silences him with his hand.

When no one continues, I say, "What, are you going to take me out back and shoot me?"

"Now, let's not get worked up," Sheriff Crawford says. "No one's getting shot."

But the mayor's face tells me that's *exactly* what he'd do if he could.

"Crawford, please. I've got this under control."

The sheriff dutifully sits back in his seat, but he doesn't look happy about it.

"I can't believe you, Eldon." My mom actually starts crying. "How could you do something like this? How *could* you?"

My face heats, and I look away.

"Perhaps it's best if Eldon and I discuss this privately," the mayor says.

Ma starts to argue, but Mayor Fontaine's expression must change her mind.

"I'll wait in the car," she says.

Mayor Fontaine gives the sheriff another pointed look.

"Me? This is my office," Sheriff Crawford sputters.

"We'll just be a moment."

I think—I *hope*—the sheriff is going to challenge him. He doesn't. He gets to his feet and follows my mom out of the room.

Once we're alone, the mayor looks at me for a long time. His fingers tap on the desk. I wonder if he feels inadequate there, in the small room, behind a desk made of particle board.

"What are we going to do with you, son?"

"It sounds like you already know. Sir."

His beady eyes bore into me. I wish my mom was still here.

"It's clear that you don't have any appreciation for the incredible gift you've been given."

"I guess I don't see wishing as a gift."

A misshapen vein runs the length of his temple, and I imagine it's throbbing.

"When I was your age, we were taught respect. Respect for ourselves and our elders and, above all else, respect for wishing."

I don't respond.

"Clearly, that's lost on you."

I still have nothing to say.

"Do you know what I wished for?"

"You wished to be mayor."

"I did. Though I did it very carefully," he replies.

I zone out while he tells me how clever he was constructing his wish. I look around for a clock but can't find one.

"And do you know why I did it?" he finishes.

"Because you like to be in charge?"

His eyes narrow. Again, I wish my mom were here.

"I did it because I love Madison. And I will do anything I can to protect it. *Anything*."

Yeah, right. He doesn't love the town. He loves power. He loves wishing, because it gives him *more* power. I want to know what he's done to Abby and JP and Pete.

"Usually when we talk about protecting wishing," Mayor Fontaine says, "we mean from outsiders. But sometimes, threats can come from within as well."

He looks at me pointedly.

"So what's my punishment?" I sigh, letting him know how bored I am with the whole conversation.

I figure I won't get jail time. Community service is more likely. I'll probably end up doing volunteer work with Penelope, but there are worse things in life than that.

"I've decided you will forfeit your wish," Mayor Fontaine says.

Now he has my attention.

I try to process his words. "I'm not allowed to wish?"

"You are not. This is the first time in the history of Madison that a wish has been revoked. I hope it was worth it."

I'm stunned. *That's it?* I'm not even sure I *wanted* to wish. I'd more or less known I was giving up my chance when I told outsiders about the cave.

The mayor clearly expects me to put on a big show. Cry or rant or whatever. But I don't see the point of pretending.

"Well, that's a shame," I say calmly. "Can I go now?"

✳ ✳ ✳

I figure there's going to be a big lecture from my mom. Probably about how she never thought she'd have a kid who let her down this badly.

Instead, she's silent, which may be worse.

When we get home, Dad looks at me and shakes his head.

"How'd the game go?" I ask.

"We lost."

"Can't win them all."

He and my mom stare at me like I'm a monster. Like the aliens in Rachel have scrambled my brain. But let's be honest here—they've been looking at me that way for months.

I spend most of the day in bed, tossing and turning, waking up confused and disoriented. When dusk falls, I get up and go to the kitchen for food.

My mom is at the table, surrounded by coupons for spa days and patio furniture. I'm peering into the refrigerator when she speaks.

"You killed your sister."

Suddenly, I'm not hungry.

"No, Ma," I say, turning around. "Ebba died months ago."

Tears stream down her face, though she doesn't make any sound.

"You could have fixed her. You could have healed her with your wish, and you threw it away."

"She's already gone." I try to keep my tone even, but my voice starts to rise. "She was gone the day Fletcher hit her. There's nothing anyone could've done. Don't you get that? It's just her body lying there at the nursing home. Ebba is gone. She's *dead*."

With a cry, my mom sweeps her hand across the table. Coupons fly in the air. She stands so forcefully, her chair tips to the floor. She sobs. It's like all the emotion she's tried to keep inside since the accident is flooding out at once.

"Ma, I'm sorry. If there was anything I could have done—"

"Get out," she says. "I can't be around you right now."

"Ma." I take a step closer to her.

"Go!"

So I go.

*   *   *

I end up at the skeleton house. I sit in the driveway, my back against the framing for the garage. My head pounds. I feel sick and lost.

I close my eyes and don't open them again until I hear footsteps crunching through the rocks and tumbleweeds.

"Thought I'd find you here," Merrill says.

"Here I am."

He sits down next to me. For a while, neither of us speak, just stare out at the ghostly neighborhood, one more thing in Madison that never had a chance.

"Is it true?" he asks at last.

"Depends on what you heard."

"That you and some random out-of-towners broke into the wish cave."

"It's true."

"Personally, I think it's pretty messed up."

"Not you too," I say with a groan.

"I mean, it's pretty messed up you decided to have your revolutionary moment when I wasn't around."

I look at Merrill. He grins at me.

"Yeah, right," I say. "You would've been too much of a wuss to come with me anyway."

"Me? I'll have you know that despite outward appearances, I'm probably the most courageous motherfucker in this town."

We both burst out laughing.

And just like that, one piece of my life is restored.

"Tell me everything," Merrill says.

I do, starting with meeting the legend trippers at the gas station. Merrill shakes his head and laughs all the way through.

"I can't believe it," he says when I finish. "I didn't think you had it in you."

"I only wish we would have made it to the end of the cave."

"You're a legend either way. The whole town's gossiping about what you did."

"What are they saying?"

"Honestly, mostly people are talking about what happened to those other kids. They disappeared, dude. People are saying the mayor had them killed."

I think of Abby with her wild smile. Sweet Pete, who seems pretty freaking deserving of his nickname. Another trickle of fear runs through me.

"You don't think that's true, do you?"

"Let me tell you something, Eldo. Norie's right about wishing being a religion. People here will go to extreme lengths to protect it, and the mayor is the worst of them. Have you heard the story of Silas Creed?"

I roll my eyes. "Only about a million times, Merrill."

"OK, OK. So you know what I'm saying."

"Speaking of Norie—"

"We don't need to talk about it, Eldo."

"I'm happy for you guys. Really." And I really am. "I just... I don't want to become irrelevant to you."

Merrill looks at me like I'm speaking gibberish. Like breaking into the wish cave made perfect sense, but *now* he doesn't understand me.

"Dude. You're my best friend. You'll *always* be my best friend."

"Thanks," I say softly.

We lapse into a comfortable silence. There are a million things to say to each other, but it feels like we're able to say them without speaking. It makes me think of the way Abby and JP were together. And I feel lucky. Some people go their whole lives without finding a friend like this.

"You really think the mayor killed them?" I try not to ruin the moment with the guilt that's creeping in.

"Eldo, I have no idea what he did. That guy is straight-up *evil*."

He is. Mayor Fontaine is awful and terrifying. But like the rest of us, he's human too.

CHAPTER 30

THE WISH HISTORY: CLANCY FONTAINE

Open the history book to the mideighties, and you'll find Clancy Fontaine, the boy who'll grow up to be mayor. The seventeen-year-old who still isn't over the day the he peed his pants.

No matter that he was five years old when it happened.

Some events, well, they linger.

Watch little Clancy in class.

The other kids are finger-painting, but he's frowning at the paper and paints in front of him. So very serious. So afraid to get messy. Even in kindergarten.

He eyes his paint-splattered classmates warily. Then a change comes over his face. Sudden surprise and fear. The realization that he has to pee and he has to do it now.

Little Clancy leaps to his feet. One hand is clasped to his crotch, the other waves wildly in the air.

He's so overwhelmed, so horrified by what's happening, he can't form a complete sentence. Instead, he simply shouts, "Pee! Pee!"

The teacher turns and tells him he may go to the bathroom.

But it's too late. A waterfall of urine gushes down his leg.

The classroom erupts with laughter.

And for the first time, Clancy Fontaine feels shame

Watch Clancy Fontaine grow up. Flip through the pages, and see how he never gets over that moment. How the other kids won't let him get over it.

Linger on middle school. Clancy walks down the hall followed by a chorus of "Pee! Peeeeee!*" He leaves a trail of wild, mocking pee dances in his wake.*

The kids, they call him Dancy Clancy.

Clancy Fontaine glares at his classmates. He clenches his fists. He grinds his teeth.

And at night, Clancy Fontaine goes home and cries.

Clancy learns to wear two faces.

At school, he's haughty. He sneers at his classmates, acting as if he's better than them in every way.

At home, Clancy lies in bed and relives every mocking word. His face shows the hurt he feels. The embarrassment.

Let's be real for a second. Clancy isn't the only kid who's peed his pants in school. It happens, yeah? It's probably safe to say his classmates aren't really making fun of Clancy because of his mishap. No, they mock him because they can. *Because they see how much it gets to him.*

And because he acts so superior to them. He makes them feel tiny.

All they have to do to tip the scales is call him Dancy Clancy.

Skip ahead a few pages. Now it's Clancy's freshman year. He scorns high school activities. Ridicules his classmates because they care about dances and sports and dating. Clancy tells himself he's above those social interactions. That he doesn't participate because he doesn't want to. He tells himself this so often, he starts to believe it.

He walks through the halls of Madison High School, head held high. He ignores the whispers.

Dancy Clancy. Dancy Clancy.

Those whispers follow him everywhere.

Especially from Gabriel Johnson. His whispers are louder and meaner than the rest.

Gabe Johnson loathes Clancy Fontaine.

But not as much as Clancy loathes him.

Clancy watches Gabe. Gabe, who's so popular, so handsome. So quick to make a joke at another person's expense.

Turn page after page after page and see how Clancy's hatred—and his secret pain—grows. How he lies awake at night thinking of Gabe.

Thinking of how to shut him up.

Thinking of how to destroy him.

Until finally, at the end of their freshman year, Gabe gets caught with a cheat sheet during the biology final. How did Gabe steal the answers? How did the principal know to look in Gabe's backpack? No one knows.

Gabe says he didn't do it. He's never cheated. Even after he's expelled, he insists he's innocent. For the rest of his life, Gabe will tell anyone who listens that someone set him up. When he's working low-paying jobs, when he's struggling with alcohol abuse, when he's hating every second of his miserable life, Gabe insists he was never a cheater.

Rumors fly around Madison High School. Kids whisper that Gabe really was innocent. They whisper that Clancy Fontaine set him up.

They don't realize Clancy started those rumors himself. He had planted the cheat sheet. And he wants everyone to know it. It's his message to the school, to anyone calling him Dancy Clancy.

Clancy Fontaine took matters into his own hands, and his revenge was a success. After a long, lonely summer, he returns to high school, and he's not mocked anymore. No one does a pee dance when they see him. He's not a source of amusement.

No, now he's detested.

Turn the page.

See how pleased Clancy is with the turn of events... Or is he?

He didn't want to be the butt of jokes, but is being hated any better?

Clancy tells himself he doesn't care if the other kids hate him. After all, he lost respect for his peers a long time ago.

It's not even right to call them peers, Clancy decides. He tells himself, those kids, they're no better than animals in a zoo. Pampered and brainless, going about their lives without seeing the cage they're in.

Every day, he tells himself his classmates are beneath him.

Clancy's armor is superiority.

And he wears it well.

That year, Clancy decides there are two types of people. There are leaders, and there's everyone else.

Clancy Fontaine knows he was meant to be a leader.

Just as he knows his father wasn't.

Yes, the town loves old Mayor Fontaine. They adore him. But love doesn't breed respect. Fear does. Kind words don't keep the world on course. Discipline does.

Clancy Fontaine has no intention of following in his father's footsteps.

And just like that, the animosity Clancy once felt for Gabe Johnson becomes directed at old Mayor Fontaine.

Clancy watches his dad putter around the house and is hit with waves of revulsion so strong, he might puke. Whenever he thinks about how his father's weak blood runs through his own veins, Clancy wants to cut himself open and bleed out.

One night, old Mayor Fontaine looks at his son and says, "I've tried so hard to love you. But I look at you and don't know who you are."

Clancy puts on his armor to protect himself from those words. Otherwise, he might revert to old Clancy, the one he despises. The one who lies in bed at night and cries.

Flip through the pages to Clancy Fontaine's eighteenth birthday, the day he'll make his wish.

There's no question that Clancy will be mayor when his father retires. He's understood that for years. But as his wish day approaches, Clancy realizes he may not have to wait.

Clancy takes notes when his class studies medieval history in school, basking in stories of sons deposing their fathers—and they didn't even have a wish cave to help them. He pays special attention in government class, does extra research, constructs his wish as if it's a bill to be passed. The finished product takes up a full sheet of paper, carefully outlining his demands in no uncertain terms. It'll be the longest wish ever spoken in the wish cave.

Seventeen-year-old Clancy Fontaine is ready to take over the town. But he doesn't wish to be mayor. Oh no, that could be overturned easily enough. Instead, boiled down to the simplest terms, Clancy Fontaine wishes to always have the two-thirds majority vote in any election.

This kid, he's so proud of his well-researched wish, he laminates the sheet of paper and keeps it in the drawer of his nightstand. He takes it out and reads it when he needs the confidence to help him get through another long, teeth-grinding night.

Let's watch how this wish turns out.

Watch Clancy Fontaine become Madison's youngest mayor.

Watch the town grow leery of him as the years pass.

Watch how, despite how far he's come, you'll occasionally hear whispers of Dancy Clancy.

But never to his face.

Never ever to his face.

These days, Old Mayor Fontaine is in a rest home. He and Clancy don't speak. Sometimes, Clancy sends him newspaper clippings about his leadership. What his father does with these clippings, Clancy doesn't know.

Look at Clancy Fontaine. All these years later and still so sure of himself.

Most people think he worships wishing, but they're wrong.

Clancy worships order.

Knowing that he, and he alone, has full control over a situation.

Wishing helps him keep that power, so he'll do everything he can to protect it.

And in doing so, he'll protect the people of Madison. All those poor, lost souls, unable to help themselves. They'd be adrift without his guidance. They would be ruled by their impulses, and the town would revert to its Wild West days. Without him as mayor, it would be like the fall of Rome—Madison would dissolve into chaos.

Clancy Fontaine won't let that happen. Not to his town.

Look at Clancy Fontaine today.

He's grown into his armor so well that it's become a part of him.

He couldn't take it off if he wanted to.

CHAPTER 31

COUNTDOWN: 1 DAY

At school, the halls are filled with gossip, but from the bits I overhear, it isn't much about me. Merrill's right. Everyone's talking about Mayor Fontaine and how he'd freaked out and killed some kids.

I guess I should have spoken up to correct the rumor. I got a text early this morning from Abby.

Hey, kid, we hightailed it to San Fran. Chill people, chill weather. Can't believe we got off with a warning. Ever want to get out of Strangeville, give me a call.

I was so relieved, I closed my eyes and thanked Norie's god. They aren't dead. The mayor has some shred of humanity. He let them go.

I'm not ready to let Mayor Fontaine off the hook though. So I let the other kids run wild with their theories.

I run into Norie on my way to first period.

"You're unbelievable," she says, shaking her head. But she's smiling. "I want to hear every detail later, OK?"

"Merrill didn't tell you about it already?"

"Jeez, Eldon," she says, rolling her eyes. "We're our own people. Is it true though? Did you lose your wish?"

"It's true."

"Are you OK?"

"Never been better," I say.

That's what I can't understand. No one asks me how I broke into the cave or what happened once I was inside. They want to know if I actually had my wish taken away.

"Eldon, how are you coping? Do you need anything? Do you want to talk?" Penelope asks.

"You're an idiot," Archie says.

"You have to admit, you kind of deserved it," Juniper tells me.

"Consider yourself lucky," Fletcher says in first period. He still looks like he crawled out of a grave, but his eyes aren't quite as haunted as they had been. I remember what Norie said, how she thought he was doing better. I think she's right.

"How are you?" I ask Fletcher.

He looks at me cautiously. "Do you really care?"

"Yeah, actually. I do."

"I'm OK," he says. His lips twitch into the first smile I've seen on his face for ages. "OK for a corpse."

I snort.

Fletcher flips through some papers on his desk. "So you want to do this project or what?"

"I thought you didn't care about grades anymore."

"Old habits die hard, I guess."

"I don't even remember what we're supposed to be doing."

"Creating art that's representative of how we changed since we started high school," he explains.

"Sounds depressing."

Fletcher laughs.

"Wanna take some pictures tonight?" I ask.

"Of what, exactly?"

"I don't know. Stuff around town. We'll think up meaning for them afterward."

Fletcher looks skeptical.

"Dude," I say. "I'll teach you how to half-ass assignments. High school could have been so much easier for you."

* * *

Getting called down to Mr. Wakefield's office isn't a big shock.

"Mr. Wilkes," he says, gesturing for me to sit. "I thought you might be in need of some conversation."

"I'm doing all right."

I sit anyway.

"On the surface, yes. But the loss of your wish must feel like a tragic blow."

"Actually, I feel kind of free."

Mr. Wakefield considers this for a moment. "Did you

intentionally sabotage your wish so you wouldn't have to go through with it?"

I shrug. "Perhaps."

"Sometimes, Mr. Wilkes, our fears get the better of us. Sometimes, inaction seems like the only path. But in the end, how can you feel peace when you've relinquished your power to choose?"

"It feels pretty OK to me."

He looks at me sympathetically, which I don't like.

"Mr. Wilkes…Eldon. You're on the path to becoming an adult now. And part of that is accepting responsibility."

I'm silent.

"Running from what you're afraid of only causes more harm in the long run."

"I guess I consider knowing when to run and when to fight part of being an adult."

"Hmm. Yes. That's valid."

I can see he doesn't mean it though.

The weirdest sensation comes over me. Regret. I'm upset I disappointed him.

For all his strangeness, Mr. Wakefield isn't a bad guy. I don't like him thinking that I took the easy way out. I don't want him to see me as a coward.

✶ ✶ ✶

Merrill can't believe I'm spending the afternoon with Fletcher Hale. He asks about fifty times if I want him to come with me.

"We don't need a chaperone, Merrill."

"You're the boss," he says, holding up his hands.

I meet Fletcher at the gas station. We both walked here.

"I don't drive anymore," Fletcher says.

We wander through town, through the crappy park, past the bars. We take pictures of buildings and street signs. Whatever.

"It's art class. We can say it means whatever we want it to," I tell him.

"That feels like cheating."

"It's being creative."

It's a nice evening. Nice for Madison anyway. It's hot but not hellish, and the wind is more of a breeze. Lots of people are outside, and I know they're watching us. Fletcher and I aren't usually seen together. Well, not unless I'm putting my fist in his face.

Which reminds me.

"Hey, sorry about that time I kicked your ass," I say.

Fletcher looks at me suspiciously.

"No, seriously. I mean…I think I had a right to be pissed. But I should have handled it better."

"You don't need to apologize to me," he says. "For anything."

Madison isn't that big of a place. We eventually end up on the corner we've both been trying to avoid. There's a wooden post stuck in the dirt, with a flowered wreath hanging on it. I didn't put it there. I don't know who did. One of Ebba's friends, probably. She had a ton of them.

"In other places, they do roadside crosses," Fletcher says. "I guess that wouldn't make sense here."

After a moment, I say, "I never hated you because you hit her, you know. I hated that you didn't wish her back."

"You should hate me for all of it."

We look at the post in the ground instead of each other.

"Tell me what happened that day."

"Exactly what you think. I was late. I was always late to everything then. I thought I might miss my wish, and I was speeding and not paying attention."

"She shouldn't have been crossing. People said the 'don't walk' sign was up."

"I still should have been watching."

"Then what?"

"I got out of the car to see if she was OK. I was so freaked out. My wish was the last thing on my mind. But suddenly, the mayor was there, telling me to get to the wish cave. The sheriff showed up, and he and Fontaine got in a fight. Crawford kept saying I had to stay, answer questions, and fill out paperwork. Maybe he wanted to arrest me, I don't know.

"The whole time, I kept trying to get to Ebba. They held me back, told me not to touch her, I could accidently hurt her more. The sheriff said an ambulance was coming and Ebba was being taken care of. Next thing I knew, Fontaine was driving me to the wish cave."

"And you made your wish."

"I was so screwed up, Eldon. I wasn't thinking. I wished like I'd planned, and it didn't occur to me until the next morning that I could've wished to save her."

Fletcher has tears on his face. I do everything I can to keep from crying too. The town would have a field day with gossip if they saw me and Fletcher standing here sobbing together.

After a little while, I say, "The accident was my fault too. And Ebba's. We were all at fault."

I start walking again, and Fletcher falls into step next to me.

"Want to know what sucks?" he asks. "My wish turned out to be pointless."

"Why?"

"I couldn't wish my way into Harvard. So I asked for a perfect transcript. The thing is, I'd already spent years working hard. I got great grades, joined clubs, did community service. After my wish, when I looked through my paperwork, hardly anything changed. I'd already done it on my own."

"Wishing made it a sure thing though."

"But who wants a sure thing? Life is about gambles. What's the point of all my effort if, in the end, I cheated my way into school? How could I ever feel like it was really my accomplishment?"

More evidence that wishing never does any good for anyone.

I should feel lucky to not have a wish anymore. But something nags at me. Fletcher is right; I agree with everything he said. But there's a voice in the back of my mind whispering that maybe throwing away my wish isn't the right path either.

We take a few more pictures. We work out how the presentation will go and what we'll tell Ms. Dove the pictures mean. I took a photo of the post with the wreath of flowers and figure we'll get a passing grade for that alone. The two of us together, overcoming adversity and blah, blah, blah.

"What are you going to do now? After graduation, I mean?" I ask.

"I haven't decided. There's still Harvard. But I'm such a mess now."

"Tell them you were in a bad car accident and defer for a year. It's not untrue."

"I don't deserve Harvard."

I stop and turn to Fletcher. "Listen, dude. You may not be happy about Penelope's wish, but it's done. Whether you like it or not, you're getting a second chance. Don't waste it. Ebba wouldn't want that."

She wouldn't. I know that for sure. My sister was the most forgiving person on the planet.

"What are *you* going to do after graduation?" Fletcher asks.

I pause.

I have no freaking clue. I've spent so much time thinking about my wish that I hardly considered what will come after.

"I don't actually know."

"Yeah, well, you shouldn't let yourself get stuck in Madison either. This place destroys lives."

Maybe it isn't the place though.

Maybe we destroy our own lives.

*　*　*

That night, after my parents fall asleep, I go into Ebba's room.

It isn't a conscious decision. I'm on my way back from the bathroom, and instead of opening my door, I open hers.

Nothing's changed since the accident. The walls are covered in posters and pictures. Her hot-pink comforter is balled up in the center of her bed. Her dresser is lined with glitter nail polish and lip gloss and plastic bracelets and all kinds of other crap I used to tease her about.

I lie down on her bed and stare at the ceiling.

What would Ebba think about all that's been going on? She'd have an opinion, that's for sure. She'd probably have plenty of snarky stuff to say about my little escapade in the wish cave.

I would give anything to hear her laugh again. To have one more conversation with her. There are so many things we never talked about. I thought we had forever.

If Ebba were here, life would be easier.

If she'd made it to her wish day, she would've had the perfect wish. She'd wish the world into being a better place. Ebba wouldn't get it wrong.

That's when it happens.

My mind clears, and the puzzle pieces click into place.

That nagging feeling I had when talking to Fletcher becomes a concrete idea. An idea that's, quite possibly, been waiting dormant in my mind for months.

After everything that's happened, I finally have the perfect wish.

CHAPTER 32

WISH DAY

I ask Merrill and Norie to meet me at the skeleton house an hour before school. Merrill shows up looking like he just rolled out of bed.

"Please tell me you have a good reason for waking me up at this godforsaken time," he says. "And happy birthday, by the way."

There is no time to waste, so I jump right in. "This is probably going to sound ridiculous…"

They look at me expectantly.

"I want to make my wish after all."

Sure enough, Merrill and Norie stare at me like I've grown a second head.

"Well," says Merrill, "this is an unexpected turn of events."

"Isn't it too late for you to make your wish?" Norie asks gently.

"Hey, you're supposed to be the one who has faith," I say. "It's never too late for anything."

"Eldon, you're banned from wishing."

"Yes, Norie, that's a great point. But *the mayor* banned me. Not the wish cave."

Neither of them look sleepy anymore.

"Are you saying what I think you're saying?" Merrill asks.

"What do you think I'm saying?"

"That you want to go rogue and break into the wish cave and make an illegal wish."

I nod. "Yes. That's exactly what I'm saying."

Merrill and Norie look at each other. They look at me.

"Well, shit," Merrill says. "This is going to be the greatest coup in Madison history."

"So you're in?"

"Wouldn't miss it for the world."

"Let's be practical for a second," Norie says. "I'm good with you wishing. But how are you going to get into the cave? You can't exactly waltz through bars."

"It's like what happened after Silas Creed's illegal wish," Merrill says. "They reinstalled the bars, and they're a million times stronger than before. Mayor Douchebag went all out from what I hear."

"That's just it. I don't think I need to use the entrance."

"Have you mastered teleportation?"

"I think there was a cave-in," I explain. "When we broke into the cave, I noticed a draft. Like, a big draft."

For the first time, I'm grateful Madison is in the middle of a constant windstorm.

"No way," says Norie. "Someone would have noticed."

"Not if it happened recently. Like, in the last earthquake. Who goes to that part of the mountain anyway? The only people who go in the cave are wishers, and they're too distracted to notice something like that."

"I'm sure the mayor does some sort of regular maintenance," Norie says.

"Then we have to hope he hasn't thought about that in the past few days."

I'm willing to bet he hasn't. Not with the flack he's been getting for "murdering" the legend trippers, plus the hubbub surrounding Penelope's wish. If I'm lucky, Madison has been so chaotic lately that cave maintenance has been pushed down on Mayor Fontaine's priority list.

"This might actually work," Norie says with awe.

"There are a few details we'll need to iron out."

Merrill glances at the time on his phone. "Then we better get to it."

* * *

Most kids are celebrities on their wish days. I only get a few mumbled happy birthdays and sympathetic looks.

But all day, it feels like Merrill, Norie, and I have the most amazing secret in the world.

We hung out at the skeleton house, planning, until it was time for school. We considered ditching but didn't want to raise suspicions. We probably could've gone to the wish cave straight away to carry out our plan, but wishes are always scheduled within an hour of the time a person was born. I don't know if that's a hard rule for wishes coming true, but I wasn't going to chance it.

I was born around two thirty in the afternoon. So right after the school day ends, it'll be wish o'clock.

"Hey," Merrill said as we walked into school. "What are you going to wish for anyway?"

Norie nudged him. "If he wanted to tell us, he would have."

She was right. They'd find out soon enough.

The school looks different today. Like the fog I've been in has lifted. Like I'm finally on the right path.

✶ ✶ ✶

I should have guessed that if someone was going to interfere with my plans, it'd be Mr. Wakefield.

"Mr. Wilkes," he says, stopping me in the hall. "I want to invite you to my office after school today."

"Um. No thanks?"

"I really feel you should be with someone on this day of all days. When the time of your wish comes and goes, you're likely to experience deep emotions, and you'll want someone to converse with."

"I don't think I will," I say. "Really, I'm OK."

I start to walk away.

Mr. Wakefield puts his hand on my shoulder. "Actually, it's not a request."

"What?"

"Mayor Fontaine insists that someone keep you company."

"You mean keep an eye on me."

"We have different thoughts on the purpose, perhaps, but it amounts to the same."

"That's bullshit," I say.

"The mayor wanted to meet with you himself. I convinced him your time was better spent with me. Either way, someone will be with you this afternoon. You choose who."

Like there's any question.

"I guess I'll see you after school then," I say.

I text Merrill and Norie that we have a minor snag. We skip fourth period to work it out.

*　*　*

The day flies by. I don't know what happens in any of my classes. I can hardly keep still.

I watch the clock hands whirl. Hours pass like minutes. Suddenly, the day is over, and I'm on a tight time line. I need to get to the wish cave ASAP. There are no do-overs with wishing.

Mr. Wakefield is waiting for me in his office. I slide into the seat across from him.

"How are you feeling?" he asks.

"I'm OK."

He frowns.

"Actually," I say, "I'm a little conflicted. You were right when you said I sabotaged my own wish. And I guess I'm not really sure what that means."

He leans forward. "We can certainly discuss that. Together, we'll arrive at a conclusion."

"That sounds great," I say.

He babbles. I keep my eyes on the clock. *Any time now, Merrill,* I think.

After what feels like an eternity, there's a knock on the door.

"Pardon the interruption, Mr. Wilkes," Mr. Wakefield says before calling, "Come in."

Merrill peeks his head into the office.

"Why, Mr. Delacruz. Here to keep your friend company?"

Merrill gives me a suspicious look. "What are *you* doing here?"

"Talking," I say.

"You told him, didn't you?" Merrill accuses.

Mr. Wakefield's gaze ping-pongs back and forth between us.

"No. I didn't tell him," I say. "I mean, I might have mentioned something. But only in passing. I didn't say *names.*"

"Well, *now* you did," Merrill snaps.

"Look, I was worried, OK?" And I *sound* worried. I'm pretty sure the drama club couldn't put on a performance as good as the one we're giving right now.

Mr. Wakefield stands. "I think you boys need to tell me what's going on."

"That time in the hall," Merrill says to him, wiping at nonexistent tears, "you asked if it was me. And I was so ashamed that I said no even though, even though…"

Mr. Wakefield's eyes widen. I think he knows where this is going. He passes Merrill a box of tissues and soothingly says, "All that matters is that you're safe now."

I glance at the clock. There's time, but not a lot.

"Tell me what happened, Mr. Delacruz," Mr. Wakefield coaxes. "Nothing you say here will be repeated."

"Mr. Wakefield. It's all true." Merrill blows his nose. "I've been…taken advantage of."

Mr. Wakefield hesitates, as if deep down he's still questioning if this story is legit. But he's not the kind of guy who will turn away a student in need. "Please. Sit down. We can work through your feelings together."

Merrill glances as me. "Not in front of Eldon. Our friendship would never be the same."

I have to turn from Mr. Wakefield, because the truth is surely written all over my face.

"Well…I can't send him away right now."

"It's fine. I understand." Merrill starts to leave.

"Wait!" Mr. Wakefield says. "I don't want you wandering around in this state."

"Maybe we could step outside your office?" Merrill suggests. "Everyone's gone, and you'd know exactly where Eldon is."

"Well…"

"It's OK, Mr. Wakefield," I say. "We can explore my feelings about my wish later. This is so much more urgent."

After another minute of hemming and hawing, Mr. Wakefield gives in. As soon as the door shuts, I'm at the window, tugging it open. It's the same window Mr. Wakefield pointed out weeks before. A world of possibilities and all that.

It turns out he was right.

A moment later, I'm climbing into Norie's car, and we're speeding toward the wish cave.

* * *

Getting to the cave is a nightmare. The hike was tiring enough when I took the path. Trying to climb up the mountain *off* the path is nearly impossible.

"We should have risked it," I pant. "The mayor can't have the *whole* trail guarded."

"Not worth it," Norie replies.

We stumble up, half crawling at times. I keep expecting to run into a boulder or ravine that blocks us entirely. I check the time constantly.

"You're making it worse," Norie says.

"Can't help it."

I wonder if Mr. Wakefield realizes he's been scammed yet.

Finally, we near the top. We're on the opposite side of the peak from the barred entrance to the cave. At least, I think we are. All the crags have started to look the same. I know the cave is somewhere below us, but other than that, I'm completely disoriented. The mountain didn't seem so big when I came at it from the front.

"This way, I think," I say.

I peer behind every rocky outcrop hoping to find the hole. The hole I'm not entirely sure exists. The clock ticks. I go further around the mountain. I go up and down.

In the end, I almost step right into it.

"Norie!"

She runs over from where she's doing her own exploration.

We look at the hole in the ground.

"Well, shit," I say.

I expected I'd be able to crawl through. But the hole is in the cave's ceiling. I'll have to drop down into it.

"I don't even know if you can fit through there," Norie says.

"Let's hope so. It would really suck to have to call the fire department because I'm stuck."

Norie takes out a flashlight and shines it down.

"The good news is you're not going to die from the drop."

"I'd call that *great* news."

"The bad news is that once you're in, you won't be able to get out."

"Definitely less than great, but I can work with it."

Norie straightens. "Are you sure you want to do this?"

"Yes."

She hugs me. Then I sit down and lower myself into the wish cave.

I get stuck around the shoulders. For a second, I think I'm actually not going to fit. But after wiggling around, I manage to squeeze through. I drop down hard on my feet.

"You OK?" Norie asks, shining the light into the cave.

"Yep."

She tosses me the flashlight. I'm not going to mess with candles. Not until I get to the cavern anyway. I'm not taking any risks on this trip.

Norie checks the time. "You need to hurry."

"I'll see you on the other side."

She nods, then moves out of my line of sight. She'll hike back to the cave entrance, where she'll try to hold off the mayor if he shows. Not that she'll be able to for long. We both know that.

"Norie," I call. She peers back through the hole. "Thanks."

She smiles, and then she's gone. I'm alone.

I start down the narrow corridor.

I try to focus on the beam of my flashlight, concentrate on getting to the main tunnel.

But in a place like this, your mind can't help but run wild, yeah? I have no way of knowing where I am. This tunnel may not even connect to the main cave. And if it *does*, there could be other turnoffs. No one knows how elaborate this cave system is. It's never been fully explored. It's because of superstition, I think. Exploring too much of the cave could ruin its power.

Which basically means I could get lost in the mountain forever. Even if someone tried to find me, who knows if they'd be able to. People get lost in caves and old mines all the time.

I walk and walk, way longer than I expected to. My heart pounds. I feel like the walls are closing in on me. Then I realize the walls *are* closing in. The passage is narrowing. My adrenaline wears off, and the severity of what I'm doing finally hits me.

There's no going back, even if I wanted to.

Which I don't.

At one point, the cave gets so tight, I have to turn sideways and squeeze through. I never considered myself claustrophobic before now. You learn all kinds of new character traits when you're wedged into a narrow fissure.

But when I come out on the other side, I see, to my relief, that I'm only a few steps off the main path. I made it!

I break into a run. I don't know what time it is, but I'm sure I don't have much longer. My birth hour is passing. By now, Mr. Wakefield has certainly checked on me and discovered I left. And he'll certainly know where I've gone. Climbing in through the secret entrance bought me some time, but who knows what other safeguards the mayor has in place to keep renegade wishers out.

I don't stop to listen for sounds drifting from the entrance. There's no time for that. I run.

Then the cave widens. I shine my light across the way. There's the pool of water. I'm in the cavern.

I drop the flashlight and fumble a candle and lighter from my pocket. My hands are shaking so hard that it takes a couple of tries to get it lit.

Once it is, I wade into the water up to my knees. I don't bother taking off my shoes.

With the candle clenched in one hand, I take a deep breath and hold it. I close my eyes. I tell myself that there's still a chance to turn back. Wish for money. Wish for happiness. Wish for the sake of wishing.

I let out my breath, open my eyes, and say, "I wish for this cave to stop granting wishes."

☆ ☆ ☆

There's no outward sign of change. There's the same dark rock and cold water and big empty cavern. I have no idea if my wish worked. Time will tell, I guess.

I leave the water and make my way toward the cave's entrance. My feet are freezing, and my shoes slosh when I walk. I'm about halfway there when I hear noises. Norie and the mayor are arguing. There's a shout.

I emerge from the shadows as Mayor Fontaine swings open the metal gate.

"How dare you?" he demands.

I walk past him into the hot afternoon sun. He makes a move to grab me, but I sidestep him.

"It's already done," I say.

There's quite a group gathering around the cave's entrance. Norie stands to one side, biting her lip and rapidly twirling her ring. Sheriff Crawford is here, and a few of the mayor's goons. I hear another shout. Merrill runs up the path toward us, Mr. Wakefield in pursuit.

Mayor Fontaine shakes with anger.

"What have you done?" he asks.

"I made my wish."

Merrill arrives, panting. He stops and stares at me, expectantly. They're all staring at me.

I feel like I just played in the hardest football game of my life. I'm exhausted. I might fall over at any moment, because my legs are too rubbery to support me.

"What have you *done*?" the mayor repeats, taking a step closer to me.

I step back, but he grabs me by the shoulders and shakes me, screaming into my face. "What have you done?"

"Clancy," Sheriff Crawford says, pulling at the mayor's arm.

I take the opening to jerk away from the mayor's grip. Except now I'm backed against the wall of the cave. I blurt out, "I wished to end wishing."

Silence. Mouths drop open. Eyes get big. It's all very dramatic, yeah?

"You didn't," Mayor Fontaine says quietly.

"This cave won't ruin any more lives."

The mayor lets out an animallike howl, and before I have a chance to so much as blink, he pulls out a gun and levels it at me.

"You didn't!" he screams.

I freeze. My heart rate soars.

No one moves. I glance at Sheriff Crawford from the corner of my eye. All the years of letting the mayor walk all over him have led to this moment. What's he doing to do?

Come on, Sheriff, I plead silently. *Fontaine isn't the law. For once, take charge.*

But it's Mr. Wakefield who breaks the quiet, speaking in a trembling voice.

"There's surely a nonviolent way to handle this predicament."

The mayor steps closer. His arm shakes. There's no sign of the cordial mask he always wears. And it's not only rage I see on his face. There's also terror. "Who the hell do you think you are?" he roars.

His shout seems to wake Sheriff Crawford from his daze. The sheriff steps forward, drawing his own gun on the mayor.

He speaks with more authority than I've ever heard in his voice. "Drop your weapon."

The mayor falters. His eyes flit between me and the sheriff in disbelief. "You must be—"

"That wasn't a request." Sheriff Crawford seems to grow taller in front of my eyes.

"He destroyed my town," Mayor Fontaine protests.

"Drop your weapon *now*," the sheriff commands.

And the mayor does. His arm falls to his side.

"Give it here," Sheriff Crawford says, and I sigh in relief when, once again, the mayor complies.

Mayor Fontaine's breathing is ragged. He looks so lost that I'd almost feel bad for the guy. If, you know, he wasn't a complete prick.

"Eldon," Sheriff Crawford says, "I'll deal with you later. Clancy, you're coming with me."

"Where—" the mayor begins.

"Walk," Sheriff Crawford orders.

Shoulders slumped, Fontaine turns and begins down the path to the parking lot. Sheriff Crawford gestures for the goons—who have backed away from the mayor, removing themselves from the situation—to follow. He takes up the rear, carefully monitoring their descent.

Mr. Wakefield gives me a long look, one I can't interpret, before making his way down the path too.

Merrill, Norie, and I watch their retreat. The group reaches the parking lot before any of us speak.

"You're not screwing around, are you?" Merrill asks.

I shake my head, hold my breath, and wait for whatever will come next.

Merrill lets out a whoop.

"Attaboy, Eldo! You broke the system!"

"We have to get out of Madison," says Norie. "You'll have a price on your head after what you did."

Merrill laughs and practically dances around. It's the revolution he's been waiting for. But I only feel empty.

"Are you mad at me?" I ask Norie.

"Why would I be mad?"

"I thought you'd say I was playing God. That no one has a right to do that."

Norie considers. "God made the wish cave, but He also made you. And gave you the ability to make choices. This was a choice." She pauses. "It's not for me to judge whether it was right or wrong."

She slips her hand into mine and squeezes it. Merrill wraps his arm around my neck, still laughing and celebrating. Together, we stand at the entrance to the wish cave and look out over the parking lot, and past that, to Madison.

And beyond that, to a world of possibilities.

CHAPTER 33

1 DAY POSTWISH

News doesn't spread as quickly as I imagined. I figured the whole town would be in an uproar by the time we make it back. But everyone is going about business like normal. I go home, wave to my parents as I head to my room, and collapse into bed. I fall asleep instantly, even though the sun is still out.

The next morning, I wake up to my mom shaking me. I groggily sit up and glance at my alarm clock. I slept for thirteen hours.

"Eldon," Ma says, "I got a phone call."

She's perched on the edge of my bed.

"Is it true?" she asks.

"Yes."

She crumbles a little. I brace myself for her rage, but it doesn't come.

Instead, she sweeps me into her arms.

"Oh, Eldon."

She holds me for a long time, her shoulders shaking. I don't know what to do or what she's thinking.

She pulls back, her face wet with tears. "Honey, you won't be able to stay here. We need to leave."

"I know."

For the first time, I feel afraid.

"Do you hate me?" I ask.

"Hate you? You're my son. I could never hate you." She wraps me in a hug again. "I'm scared for you. I don't know what would make you do something like this."

Then, before I know it's going to happen, I'm crying too. I hold onto my mom and sob. She comforts me the way she used to when I was a kid. The way I've needed her to for months.

"Wishing ruined everyone's lives. Yours and mine and the whole town's. If it weren't for wishing, Ebba would still be…"

I'm crying too hard to go on. My mom strokes my hair and tells me everything is going to be OK.

"I'm sorry I couldn't save her," I say once I've calmed down.

"What you said the other day is true. No one could've saved her," my mom says sadly. "I just didn't want to hear it."

And then we both cry again.

After a little while, I ask if Dad is mad at me. Ma says he's in the garage and I should talk to him myself.

So I do.

I find him standing at his workbench, a crutch under one arm. He flips through a book of woodworking projects.

"Hey," I say uncertainly.

He turns and stares at me for a moment. Then he holds out his free arm for a hug. "Come here."

I don't move though. Not yet.

"I'm sorry," I say. "I know you must be ashamed of me. For ending wishing, and for my behavior in general these past few months."

My dad shakes his head. "Shame is a strong word, buddy. I'm not *ashamed* of you. Though I do think you've made some poor judgment calls."

"I won't argue that."

"So what are you going to do about it?"

"I don't know yet," I reply, because I don't. I can't see further into the future than this moment. "But I'll figure it out."

Dad smiles. "I know you will."

He holds out his arm again, and this time, I go to him. The hug throws him off balance. His crutch wobbles, and he leans into me for support. But that's OK. I'm leaning on him too.

✶ ✶ ✶

My mom thinks we should leave town right away, all three of us. Pack up what we can and drive to Vegas. I'm the one who says no.

"Not yet," I say. "I want to find out if my wish worked."

"It's not safe for you here," she argues.

But I insist. I don't tell her I've been dreaming of leaving for weeks, but not with her and Dad. There's no reason for them to uproot their lives when I can go with my friends. Other kids go away to college after high school. It won't be any different from that.

My mom also wants me to stay home from the town meeting at noon. I refuse to do that too.

School is closed for the day. So are all the businesses. The entire town gathers at the community center, the same as we do for any tragedy.

I see Merrill and Norie in the crowd but don't go over to them. My parents aren't exactly eager to let me out of their sight.

I sort of expected a lynch mob. And the truth is, even though I'm acting casual, I'm scared shitless. But it's like walking into a funeral. Everyone's pale and looks shell-shocked and speaks in whispers. People give me cold stares, but it's only the young people, the kids who haven't made their wishes yet, who glare at me like they've got murder on their minds.

Everyone is here. Gil Badgley in his worn-down cowboy boots. The Samson sisters, both with notebooks, documenting the occasion. Even Othello Dewitt is lurking in the back of the room.

Well, *almost* everyone is here. I don't see the mayor.

Sheriff Crawford runs the meeting. He mumbles a bit in the beginning—this is the first time he's running the show, and he's obviously nervous. But as he speaks, his confidence grows. He tells the town exactly what happened. People murmur and turn to each other, as if to offer condolences or shoulders to cry on.

The sheriff says there's no telling how to proceed, not yet.

They have to find out if my wish was successful, and that won't happen for a few days yet, not until Archie Kildare's birthday. Until then, we all have to wait.

After that, Mr. Wakefield goes to the front of the room.

"This is a curious time in the history of our little town," he says. "There are a lot of strong emotions right now, and sorting them out may prove challenging. I'll be offering around-the-clock counseling for anyone who desires it. In addition, I've put together packets on dealing with grief."

As he drones on, Penelope gets up and passes out the packets. She's the only person in Madison who's still smiling. She's probably in her glory, surrounded by so many people who need help at once.

Afterward, folks mill around and talk in hushed voices, but my parents want to go home right away. We walk quickly to the minivan. Barnabas Fairley is waiting there for us.

Tears streak his grimy face. He moves toward me, and my dad tenses, ready for trouble. Not that he could do much. He's having an especially bad day—even with his crutches, he seems unstable.

But Barnabas doesn't try to hurt me. He wraps me in a hug. I don't pull away from him—in fact, I hug him back. When he lets go, my family solemnly watches him climb on his bike and pedal down the deserted Madison street.

* * *

I have to sneak out to meet Merrill and Norie at the skeleton house. We have more planning to do.

"The whole town's in chaos," Merrill says. "No one knows what to do with themselves."

"There seems to be a split," Norie says. "About half the town is enraged and wants to, I don't know, throw you in jail or kill you or something. The rest of them are wandering around like zombies."

"No one's, like, secretly celebrating?" I ask.

Merrill gives me a pointed look. "What do *you* think?"

I brush off his question. "What will it be like around here without wishing? What will everyone do?"

Merrill shrugs. "Probably start wishing on stars."

Maybe he's right. Maybe wishing is a way of life, wish cave or not.

"The really interesting news is about the mayor," Norie says.

"I noticed he was absent today."

"Yep. In hiding," Merrill replies. "Lots of speculation going on about that. Sheriff Crawford telling everyone Fontaine pointed his gun at you, combined with the rumors about him killing those kids…well, it doesn't look good for him."

Again, I feel almost sorry for the mayor. He *didn't* kill the legend trippers. And though he pulled a gun on me, I'm not sure he actually would have shot. Fontaine spent his entire life trying to look tough, but the second his authority was challenged, he crumbled.

But still, the dude pulled a *gun* on me. So I'm not exactly jumping to defend him.

"The whole town disliked him and his power trip anyway," Norie continues. "This gives them a concrete reason to get him out of office. I don't think he'll be mayor for much longer."

I never thought I'd see an uprising against Mayor Fontaine. In a few months, I wonder if I'll recognize Madison. It won't be my town anymore, the place where I grew up. The old way of life will be a memory. One day, people will look back and talk about the time when there had been wishing.

"So what's our plan?" I ask.

"Not much to it," Norie says. "Graduation is Saturday. I say we take off that night. Sunday morning at the latest."

"No," I say.

They look at me.

"I want to wait until after Archie's wish. It's only a couple more days."

"Do you really think that's a good idea, Eldo? We can guess the outcome."

"I need to know for sure."

Merrill and Norie agree to wait.

"Where will we go?" I ask.

"Anywhere," Norie says. "It doesn't matter. If we go somewhere and don't like it, we'll go somewhere new. It's not like wishing. You can change your mind. There's more than one chance."

"What about money?" I ask.

Because that's really the biggest concern. I have enough from the gas station to get by for a little while, but not long. Not long at all.

Merrill and Norie glance at each other.

"Actually, Eldo," Merrill says. "I've been meaning to talk to you about that..."

CHAPTER 34

THE WISH HISTORY: MERRILL DELACRUZ

M *aybe you're thinking you've heard this story before.*

Think again.

Skip past the beginning—after all, you know how it starts.

It's not like Merrill Delacruz hasn't questioned his decision. He's had people left and right telling him he's a dumbass.

Saying, "Wish for money, and you can pay to have your eyes fixed."

But Merrill knows surgery can go wrong. Knowing his luck, he'd probably end up blind.

Merrill Delacruz, all he's ever wanted is to be a pilot. To be up in the air, soaring, free. And with his eyesight, it'll never happen.

There's no question about it—when Merrill's wish day rolls around, he's going to walk out of that cave with perfect vision.

But you already know all this.

Flip to the next page. Take a peek at a scene in Merrill's life you haven't come across yet.

It's a few months before his wish day, and his dad is laying into him again.

Look at how drunk Benny Delacruz is. See how he can barely stand. Yet despite that, he's still able to cut deep.

"You and your flying. Think that's a noble cause? No. Noble is taking care of your family."

"Like you do?" Merrill asks.

His father slaps him across the face, openhanded, but it stings.

"I'm glad your mother didn't live to see how you turned out," Benny Delacruz spits.

That stings even worse.

It's also bullshit. Merrill knows as well as we do that his mother supported his dream. Always buying him toy planes, bringing home movies about flying, talking to him about all the places he'd go.

But knowing this isn't enough to erase his father's words.

"Say whatever you want." Notice how sure Merrill sounds, even though he's shaking inside. "It doesn't change my wish."

"You'll regret this."

"It's mine to regret. You already got the chance to screw up your life."

Merrill's certain his father's going to hit him again and that this time, it'll be a fist. He doesn't though. Instead, Merrill's father laughs. This is when Benny Delacruz drops the bomb. He says the very thing Merrill knows but has always managed to put out of his mind.

"How the hell you gonna be a pilot in Madison? Huh? You see any fucking planes around here? Go on, boy. Go fix your eyes. Then spend the rest of your life sitting here with your dreams."

Merrill's father is cruel. He's a drunk. He's not the smartest man in Madison. But on this one point, Benny Delacruz is one hundred percent correct.

Merrill needs to escape Madison.

He can't let this town suck him in.

And getting out of town while you're broke, well, Merrill understands that's easier said than done.

It's possible that in this moment, on this page of history, Merrill Delacruz understands the true value of money for the first time. Money doesn't only make life comfortable. Wishing for money doesn't only let you buy nice things and live in luxury. Money helps you get the hell out.

Watch as Merrill continues to tell people he's wishing for perfect eyesight. As he acts like there's no internal struggle, like his plan is A-OK.

Take a look at Merrill, hanging out in his brother's bedroom. The two siblings—one who's already given up on life and the other struggling to make a future for himself—pass a joint back and forth. One of them is about to realize not everyone buys his charade.

Royce Delacruz, in a rare moment of clarity, blows out a plume of smoke and starts laughing.

"What?" *Merrill asks.*

"You're gonna do it. You're gonna wish for money."

"No, I'm not," *Merrill insists.*

Merrill lies.

Royce shakes his head. "Man, he broke you. I didn't think the old man had it in him."

"My wish has nothing to do with him."

Royce sobers up a bit. He looks at Merrill sadly. "You do what you have to do, baby brother."

Flip ahead a few pages, and there it is.

Merrill Delacruz wishing for money.

Wishing for money, but keeping it secret. Repeating his ridiculous lie about wearing his glasses even though he doesn't need them.

Merrill knows no one in town believes that story. Except, of course, for the person who matters most. Benny Delacruz is too inebriated to see through his son's little fiction.

Which is the whole point of the lie.

Merrill isn't going to let his dad touch a penny of his money.

Except, if you skim through this wish history, you'll notice there is one other person who Merrill's fooled.

And you've gotta wonder, what kind of person has his head stuck so far up his ass that he can't see what's going on with his best friend?

Maybe, hopefully, Merrill's oblivious friend would've caught on if he'd been in his right mind. But Merrill's wish day was only a few weeks after that terrible accident. So maybe we should cut this oblivious friend some slack. The kid's hardly functioning. Maybe he misses the clues about Merrill's wish because his head is screwed up and not because he's a self-absorbed asshole. Maybe.

Why doesn't Merrill tell his friend the truth?

Why is he still acting like his glasses aren't prescription, discreetly withdrawing money from the ATM, secretly making plans for after graduation?

It's simple, really.

All those plans Merrill's making, they involve his friend. Oblivious or not, self-absorbed or not, Merrill has no intention of leaving his friend behind when he books it out of Madison. He's bringing his buddy with him.

And yeah, Merrill plans to share this with his friend. Eventually. When the moment is right. When he can be sure his pathetic, screwed-up pal can handle having another bomb dropped on him. When he's sure his friend has figured out his life enough to nod and say, "Let's do it. I'm ready to go."

So Merrill's stockpiling money. He's planning his escape. Graduation is approaching, and he's ready to get the hell out of Madison.

This doesn't mean he's given up on his dream though. He's still going to be a pilot. He can figure out the logistics later, once he's free. Once he's out of town, Merrill will have all the time in the world. He can do any-thing, be *anything.*

His whole life, Merrill's told people he didn't want cash. He wanted the fucking sky.

At eighteen years old, he's discovered there's more than one way to get there.

CHAPTER 35

2 DAYS POSTWISH

At school, I'm greeted by Archie, who slams me into a locker roughly thirty seconds after I walk in the door.

"You stupid motherfucker."

"Morning, Archie." I turn my face from his foul breath.

"You better *pray* my wish comes true. Because if it doesn't, I will *destroy* you. Got it?"

"Got it," I say, wincing.

He lets go of me. I rub my shoulder, which took the brunt of the blow.

"I'm not joking, Wilkes," he says, backing away slowly, his eyes locked on mine. "You screwed up *big*."

He stalks away. I'm slammed into the locker again, but this time, with the sheer force of Penelope.

"I can't *believe* you," she rages.

I'm surprised. I assumed Penelope would be disenchanted enough with wishing to cut me some slack.

"Come on, Penny," I say. "After what happened with your wish—"

"This has nothing to do with *wishing*," she snaps.

"Uh. It doesn't?"

She gets in my face, eyes flashing. "There are people in the world, *children*, who survive appalling situations. For you to make a mockery of that, turn it into a *joke*—"

"Penelope, I have no idea what you're talking about."

She gapes at my ignorance. "Using child sex workers to trick Mr. Wakefield. How *could* you?"

How has she even heard about that?

I open my mouth to tell her I wasn't thinking, that I didn't know how awful I was being. But that's a lie. I did know, and I did it anyway.

"I'm sorry," I say.

"There are bigger problems in the world than wishing, Eldon. And it's selfish and disgusting to use those problems to your benefit."

Penelope spins on her heel and storms away.

And yeah, OK. I'll admit it: I feel like a jerk.

That's hardly new though.

I make my way to first period, still reeling from Penelope's anger.

Fletcher's already in his seat. If nothing else, he's punctual now. When I sit down next to him, he holds out his hand to me. I pause, then reach out, and we shake.

"Well done," he says.

It's the most we speak about my wish. But it's enough.

* * *

The funny thing about school today is that I became popular again. Well, maybe not *popular*. But everyone wants to talk to me.

Granted, most people only want to talk to me long enough to tell me what an asshole I am and how I ruined their lives. Others want to know how I did it, why I did it, and what I think will happen next.

It's exhausting. I'm almost grateful when I get called to Mr. Wakefield's office.

"Mr. Wilkes. What a week you're having," he says.

"Look," I say, "I never said I was sorry. It was messed up to trick you like that."

"I accept your apology."

Rather than launching into some psychobabble, Mr. Wakefield gazes out the window. He may have accepted my apology, but he certainly hasn't forgiven me yet.

"Is everything OK?" I ask after an awkward silence.

"It's just…when I told you to face your problems head-on, I didn't expect this."

"It was better than doing nothing, right? Better than running?"

"You tell me," he says, looking me full in the face for the first time since we left the wish cave.

I don't have an answer for him.

He sighs. "Either way, it's done now. All you can do is live with the consequences, whatever they may be."

"That's a pretty scary prospect," I say.

Mr. Wakefield smiles sadly. "Welcome to adulthood."

I hesitate before leaving his office. "Hey, Mr. Wakefield? Thank you."

"For what?"

"For helping me through all this. I know you really were trying."

This time, his smile seems more genuine.

"That's what I'm here for. My office is always open to you. I suspect you'll need some therapy in the coming days."

In the coming days? Yeah, right. After all this, I'll need therapy for the rest of my life.

✶ ✶ ✶

I walk home from school alone. Merrill and Norie are going on a date, which I'm still not entirely used to. I'm lost in my thoughts when a car pulls up behind me.

A truck, actually. A big, loud, rumbling truck.

"Hop in," Gil Badgley says.

I climb into the passenger seat, scooting Tuco closer to Gil.

"Home or somewhere else?" Gil asks.

"Home."

"Smart boy. I wouldn't be caught wandering the streets if I was you."

"Do you hate me too?" I ask.

"You wouldn't be in my truck if I did."

He drives through my neighborhood slowly, one hand on the wheel, the other hand holding his tin can in his lap. Tuco curls up on the bench seat in between us.

"They're getting rid of Fontaine, you know," Gil says.

"Who is?"

"Everyone. The town."

"I thought he'd always win the election."

Gil laughs his deep, raspy laugh. "Nah. He messed up with that two-thirds wish. They're phrasing the ballot to read *Who wants to vote the mayor* out *of office?* And as you know, majority will win."

"Won't he just enter the next election?"

"I don't think he'll run again."

Gil pulls up to my house and lets the truck idle for a moment.

"Half this town is gonna hate you forever," he says. "And the other half is gonna call you a hero. What you need to do is not let either side get to you. You just worry about figuring yourself out and ignore the rest. You understand me?"

"I think so."

"Good. Now get on out of here. Tell your folks I say hello."

I don't know if this means Gil is on my side or not. I don't even know if there *are* sides. Maybe the world isn't as black and white as I thought. Maybe my wish was both right and wrong. Or maybe it's nothing at all. In the grand scheme of things, maybe none of this ever mattered.

CHAPTER 36

3 DAYS POSTWISH

I always assumed graduation day would be one big party. As it is, most people aren't speaking to me, and I have to spend an hour convincing my parents it'll be OK for me to even attend the ceremony.

Eventually, they say I can go, but I have to sit in the audience. I point out that being in the middle of the mob is probably more dangerous than walking across stage, and they finally relent.

Usually, the mayor runs the graduation ceremony, but he's nowhere to be found. Rumor has it he knew he was about to be voted out and he took off in the night. I keep expecting him to pop back up with some evil scheme—like in horror movies when you think the killer is dead, but they revive to make one last stab at it. That doesn't happen though. It's an anticlimactic ending. Maybe most endings are.

With Mayor Fontaine gone, Mr. Wakefield runs the event, which means the whole ceremony is sappy and long winded. He has to stop his address twice because he starts crying.

Fletcher limps across the stage to give the valedictorian speech, and everyone actually pays attention, but probably less because of what he's saying and more because he still looks kinda undead.

After that, it's finally time to get our diplomas.

I'm at the end of our graduating class. I watch everyone walk across stage. Norie, serious, hardly smiling, hating the attention. Penelope's at the other end of the spectrum, beaming and practically skipping across the stage. Juniper's the only person who manages to make a graduation gown look fashionable. And Merrill attached blinking lights to his cap.

I should be celebrating. Instead, it's like I'm watching ghosts. My whole past lines up in front of me. I'm on the outside, not a part of it anymore. When I ended wishing, I gave up a big piece of my life. Or maybe this is always how the end of high school feels, and wishing has nothing to do with it.

At the end of the ceremony, everyone cheers, and a few people throw their caps in the air, even though we'd been told we weren't allowed to do that. Then all of Madison goes to the park.

✷ ✷ ✷

Othello Dewitt has come out of hiding. Briefly anyway.

Apparently, he's been working on some big sculpture that he wants to dedicate to the town. As far as I know, no one's seen it yet.

There'd been a lot of discussion about where to put it. The first choice was the community center, but Othello insisted it be kept outside, the air and elements giving it life and blah, blah, blah. So a place has been made for it in Madison's only park, where no one really goes anyway. It's all dirt and a few pieces of metal playground equipment that kids can't play on because they get too hot in the summer sun.

According to rumor, the sculpture is a tribute to wishing. Seeing how wishing is dead and all, Sheriff Crawford asked Othello if he still wanted to go through with the reveal. Othello told him that wishing will always be part of this town, whether it's in the past, present, or future. Maybe he's right.

At the park, most of the town is milling around, and Othello paces back and forth excitedly in front of the sculpture. It's covered with a tarp. The wind is especially bad, and three men have to hold the fabric down to keep it from blowing off.

We gather in a big semicircle, then wait.

"Thank you for coming," Othello says. "I have always felt that art is a gift, and gifts are meant to be shared. I've been toiling over this piece for months. For me, it represents the heart and soul of Madison and everything that this town stands for. I can only hope that viewing it touches you as deeply as creating it did for me. I call this piece *A Menagerie of Wishes*."

Without further ceremony, the tarp is pulled off.

No one speaks. Because no one quite knows what to make

of it. It's like the sculptures Merrill, Norie, and I saw at Othello's Hideaway. Bits of scrap metal and random objects are welded or tied or glued together. The form is tall and shapeless. It's made of hubcaps, an old mirror, a car door covered in buttons, and other odds and ends.

A few people clap. Others look around like they're hoping someone will step forward and explain the sculpture to them.

Uncle Jasper, already drunk, lurches through the crowd. "What the hell is it supposed to be?" he asks loudly. No one answers.

I glance at my parents. My mom frowns.

"Harmon," she says to my dad. "Is that my cast-iron skillet in there?"

I cough to cover my surprised laugh. I wonder how many other people will notice their missing stuff twisted into the sculpture. For all I know, it might hold a piece of every family in Madison.

I catch Merrill's eye across the crowd. He's grinning.

"I think it's…lovely," Mr. Wakefield says. He starts clapping loudly, and other people join in. Othello beams.

Even without wishing, Madison is one strange place.

Merrill stops me as we we're all leaving and asks if I'm going to the hot springs tonight.

"Yeah, right. Someone would probably throw me off a cliff."

"I'll catch up with you later then," he says. "I want to go one last time."

Of course he does. It's graduation night. I'd always expected we'd spend tonight together. I watch him go sadly. Then I head home.

It turns out to be for the best. When we get home, my parents sit me down and tell me we need to talk.

CHAPTER 37

4 DAYS POSTWISH

We leave for Las Vegas early in the morning. It isn't like when I was a kid. Back then, Ebba and I would fight in the back seat, and my dad would sing along with the radio while my mom planned our activities for the day.

This car ride is silent.

We stop for breakfast in Alamo, which is pointless. None of us eat. We push food around our plates until it's time to go. Ma keeps dabbing at her eyes with tissues. Dad squeezes her hand.

At the nursing home, the staff is even nicer than usual. They're full of sympathetic smiles. I wish they'd go away.

Before they let us into Ebba's room, the doctor sits down with us and tells us what to expect. I want him to keep talking. I want him to talk forever so we can put off what happens next. Even though I'd said from the start that this was the only choice, now that the moment is here, I'm sick to my stomach.

We gather around my sister and cry and tell her how much we

love her. It's terrible, and I wish I could switch places with her. I try to tell myself it's OK. It's the right thing to do. Ebba deserves to be at peace.

When they turn off the machines, we move closer to her. I hold one of her hands, and my dad holds the other. My mom strokes her hair. This is the last time we will ever be a family.

Memories race through my mind. Holidays and birthdays and first days of school. All the secrets we kept from our parents. The way we'd fight but never stay mad, because Ebba couldn't stay mad at anyone. All of that, about to be gone forever.

I reach into my pocket and wrap my hands around the folded-up paper there. The last note I found from Ebba.

Tag. I'm it.

It's just me now. I have to live for both of us.

I don't think I can handle it anymore. I feel like I'm going to explode. So I slowly start counting. I get to six hundred and twenty-five. And then my sister is gone.

My mom wraps her arms around me. My dad wraps his arms around both of us. I don't know how long we stand there like that. Our family is so much smaller without Ebba. So much *sadder*. But we're still a family. Nothing can break that.

☀ ☀ ☀

We return to a Madison that feels changed. Has the town always been so empty? Have the buildings along Main Street always been wedged so tightly together? Have the surrounding mountain peaks always looked so jagged and hostile?

I feel claustrophobic. I feel empty. I feel destroyed.

My dad guides the minivan into our driveway. Our house seems to have shrunk. The stucco siding has more cracks. An ocean of weeds has sprouted in the yard. Everything is bleaker than when we left.

Another difference is, when we left, Uncle Jasper wasn't sitting on the front stoop.

Dad lightly touches Ma's arm. "I'll get rid of him."

She shakes her head. "No. It's OK."

We climb out of the van, and Jasper stands and makes his way over to us. He's not exactly steady, and his eyes aren't exactly clear, but at least he doesn't reek of booze.

"Lu," he says. "Did you... Is she..."

Ma nods.

And then something happens that I can't remember ever happening before. Uncle Jasper pulls my mom into a hug. She cries into her brother's shoulder. For the first time, he's the one taking care of her.

My own tears return. They're happy tears, in a way. The kind of tears you cry when you see that there is still good left in the world.

But they're bitter tears too.

No matter how screwed up Ma and Jasper's relationship is, at least they have each other. I don't have a sibling to comfort or to comfort me. I'm alone.

"Eldon," my dad says, putting his hand on my shoulder. "Why don't we go to the garage?"

Well, maybe not *completely* alone.

"You started a new project?" I ask.

"Not yet. You can help me decide on one. Or not. We could watch TV or talk. Whatever you want."

I nod. Dad slings his arm around my shoulder, and we make our way to our safe place together.

"Dad," I say, once we're in the sanctuary of the garage, "do you ever wish it was me instead?"

"What?" he replies, incredulous. "Of course I don't. Do *you*?"

I nod.

"Eldon, your mother and I love you very much. As much as we love Ebba."

"I'm such a screwup though," I say. Now I'm crying again. "I ruin *everything*."

Dad leads me to the couch and sits me down, like I'm a kid. He carefully kneels in front of me, wincing a little at the pain, and looks me straight in the eye. "Eldon, we *all* mess up. No one should measure their worth by how often they screw up. What matters most is how a person deals with the aftermath. How they grow and change."

"What if I don't grow?" I ask meekly.

My dad laughs. "Buddy, you already *have.*"

✴ ✴ ✴

I can't stay home tonight. My house is suffocating me. And my parents keep asking if I'm OK, which I'm not. Neither are they.

I have nowhere to go and nothing to do. I can't face Merrill. He'll want to know how it went, how I'm holding up. I'm not ready to talk about it yet.

So I wander aimlessly through Madison. It's a quiet night. Everyone high-school aged is at the hot springs. Everyone else is hiding from the heat.

I end up at the park, sitting on a bench across from Othello Dewitt's sculpture. His *Menagerie of Wishes.* In the moonlight, it looks menacing. An alien machine sent to destroy the town. People up the road in Rachel will probably get a kick out of it. Madison finally has its own roadside attraction.

I gaze at the sculpture and let my mind wander. Mostly, I think of Ebba.

In my mind, my sister had been dead for months. Ever since I realized there was no wish that could save her, really. I thought I'd already grieved. I thought her actual death would be manageable, because she'd already been gone.

I was wrong.

There's an empty place inside of me that'll never be filled

again. Part of me died with Ebba. The part of me that she loved, the part of me that was a big brother.

When someone dies, it doesn't just take them. It takes a piece of everyone who ever loved them and everyone they ever loved. I hadn't understood that before.

"Eldon?"

I look up.

Juniper Clarke is standing a few feet away from me.

"I thought that was you," she says.

I wipe the tears from my eyes.

"Are you OK?"

I nod. She sits down on the bench next to me.

"What's going on?" she asks.

To my horror and embarrassment, I burst into tears.

"Sorry," I say once I calm down, once I've managed to tell her about Ebba.

Juniper looks like she might cry too. "Don't apologize. She's your sister. It's OK to cry."

"The last time I needed you, you weren't so understanding," I say. I'm simply stating a fact. All the bitterness I used to feel seems irrelevant now.

Juniper startles. "What are you talking about?"

"After the accident. I was a mess. And you ditched me."

"Eldon, we'd just broken up. You hadn't been very nice about the whole situation, if you remember."

She's right. I'd been an asshole. Complete with name-calling and talking shit about her to anyone who would listen.

"Of course I wasn't nice," I mumble. "You dumped me for another guy."

Juniper sighs and rolls her eyes. "I've told you eight billion times. I didn't break up with you for Calvin. He and I didn't start dating until, like, a month later."

I'd always assumed that was a lie. As soon as he wished to take my position on the football field, she'd been done with me. Juniper had an idea of the kind of guy she wanted to be with, and it wasn't me.

"Why then?" I challenge.

"We've been through this," she says. "Because you were obnoxious. Because you were so completely full of yourself that it became unbearable to be around you."

"I've changed," I say.

"Have you?" Juniper asks, raising an eyebrow.

"What? You don't think so?"

"You wished away wishing for an entire town. So I'd say no, you haven't changed."

"I was trying to *help* people," I say. "Wishing ruined everyone's lives."

Juniper shakes her head, as if I'll forever be a person who just doesn't get it. "If people want to ruin their lives, that's *their* choice. You could have not wished if you hated wishing so much. You didn't need to take it away from everyone else. Who do you think you are that you get to decide other people's futures like that?"

A wave of shame rolls over me.

"You're no better than Clancy Fontaine," she goes on. "Acting like you know better than everyone in this town. As if we need you to swoop in and save us."

"But I talked to people about their wishes," I offer weakly. "Everyone was miserable."

"Yeah, who did you talk to? Barnabas Fairley? *Fletcher?*" Juniper asks. Her eyes are still beautiful, but it's hard to appreciate them when she's looking at me with so much disappointment. "You sought out people you *knew* were unhappy. You had your mind made up about wishing from the start, and this whole journey was your attempt to confirm how terrible wishing is."

My stomach churns. Is she right? Had I avoided people who were happy with their wishes? I thought I'd moved past all my confusion, but now I'm feeling more mixed up than ever.

We sit in silence, because I don't know how to respond. When Juniper speaks again, the anger seems to have drained out of her. "I don't think you're a bad guy, Eldon. You just need to grow up."

"I'm trying," I say.

She smiles. "I believe you."

Juniper leaves, continuing on to wherever she'd been going. I consider asking if she's going to hang out with Calvin but stop myself. It's none of my business.

I stay on the bench for a long time, staring at Othello Dewitt's sculpture. Maybe if I look long enough, it'll make sense. Maybe it has the answers I need.

CHAPTER 38

5 DAYS POSTWISH

There's probably more fanfare for Archie Kildare's wish than there has been for any other wisher.

Half the town is waiting anxiously at the community center for the results. The other half is following Archie up the trail to the wish cave.

"I drove by to see it," Merrill says when he finds me and Norie in a corner at the community center. "They're following him up the mountain like he's the freaking Pied Piper."

Norie chokes back a laugh. The people nearby shoot us nasty looks.

The town's making Archie wish for cash. They need something tangible to test if wishing works. I wonder if Archie's sad to see his dreams of becoming a pro wrestler go out the window—not that he could have wished for that anyway.

"What do you think's gonna happen?" I whisper.

"There's no doubt in my mind," Norie says. "The wish won't work."

I hope she's right. The recent drama in Madison has sucked. It'll suck much worse if it turns out it's all been for nothing. On the other hand, if Archie's wish *does* work, it'll give me a chance to redeem myself.

But that's the thing. Even though what Juniper said last night hit me pretty hard, even though I feel ashamed when I think about how I disappointed Mr. Wakefield or how much I pissed off a ton of people, there's still part of me that believes I did the right thing.

Maybe I'm an asshole. Maybe I took away people's choices. But sometimes, people get stuck in bad situations because they don't know how to stop them or don't know any other way of life. Like Uncle Jasper, who'll drink until the day it kills him. Or this whole town, letting themselves get pushed around by a mayor they hate simply because that's how it's always been. Yeah, they're free to get out of the situation. But that doesn't mean they *can*.

Sometimes, people don't know how to help themselves. They need a push. Penelope would understand.

I let my gaze wander around the community center while Merrill and Norie go over plans for the next day. We'll be leaving at dawn. By evening, we'll be farther from Madison than I've ever been in my life.

"I'm getting some water," I say. I need to do something. I wander to the drinking fountain and run into the Samson sisters on the way.

"Good evening, Mr. Wilkes," says Marla or Eulalie.

"Yes, good *evening*," says the other.

I nod to them.

"So you know, you will have a *very* special place in the wish museum."

"Oh yes, the *most* special, even."

"We're working on an entire display dedicated to your wish."

That's unexpected. "Aren't you angry at me?"

They both tilt their heads and look at me quizzically.

"I mean, without wishing, there can't be a museum, right?"

"Don't be silly!" says Marla-Eulalie.

"The museum will *always* be here," her sister agrees.

"Well, good," I say.

And it is, I guess. It's good to know our town history will survive this mess. At least for as long as the Samsons are alive.

I make my way back to Merrill and Norie, checking the time. Archie should be in the cave now. He might be making his wish at this very moment. Everyone else in the room seems to realize this as well, because conversations become hushed.

I look around at all the faces that, after tomorrow, I'll probably never see again. There are so many people I won't have a chance to say goodbye to. I'll miss my sister's funeral. I thought leaving would be easy, but nothing in life is as simple as you expect it to be.

A half an hour later, the door of the community center opens, and Sheriff Crawford enters. He doesn't say a word, just soberly shakes his head.

No one speaks. Some people bow their heads. Some people's shoulders hunch. A girl who I think is a freshman starts crying. But most people file silently out of the room.

They'll go home, I suppose. They'll go to bed as if it's any other night. And in the morning, they'll get up and start figuring out how to live in a world where they have to forge their own paths.

"I guess that's it," Merrill says.

"We should get some sleep," Norie says. "We have a big day tomorrow."

So we leave with the rest of the crowd. We wander home through our hot, windy town where there's no such thing as wishing.

CHAPTER 39

GOODBYE, MADISON

When the sun is high in the sky, Madison will be scorching hot. Later, the wind will kick up and drive people indoors, where they'll wonder why they chose to live in such a desolate place.

But right now, it's early, and the air is still, and the worst of the heat is hours away. Madison's residents haven't woken up yet, and there's an unreal feeling about the empty streets, as if I'm on a movie set instead of in an actual town.

I walk past the tiny movie theater. I walk past the bar where there's probably some drunk, maybe even Uncle Jasper, passed out in a booth. I walk past the high school football field where I've had some of my best and worst moments.

Even though it's the same town I grew up in, Madison is different this morning. Or maybe *I'm* different.

I barely slept last night. I watched TV in the garage. I paced in my room. I turned on the radio and heard, *"Tonight on Basin and Range Radio, we're exploring a mysterious town in Nevada where alien overlords have been known to grant wishes!"*

I laughed and laughed until, for some reason, I cried.

After that, I spent hours sitting in Ebba's bedroom, thinking of all that had happened and all that would happen next. Wondering if I'd saved Madison or destroyed it. Wondering, if I had to do it all over again, if I'd take the same path.

There are no do-overs though, not with wishing. There are only consequences. And I have to learn to live with mine.

Merrill and Norie are waiting at the gas station, where I texted I'd meet them. They're sitting on the hood of the Mustang that Merrill's liberating from his dad.

"The guy's so drunk, he probably won't even notice the car's gone," he told us last night. "Besides, he shouldn't be on the roads anyway."

"Morning, Eldo," Merrill says now. He's alert and bright-eyed. He's ready for adventure.

Norie hops off the hood and opens the passenger door, shifts some stuff around inside. Merrill doesn't move though. He frowns and stares at me. I stare back.

"Where's your bag?" he asks.

"I'm not going with you."

Norie stops what she's doing. "What?"

"I'm sorry."

There's a long silence.

"Dude," Merrill says. "You can't be serious. This is our moment. This is what we've been waiting for our *whole lives*."

"It's *your* moment," I tell Merrill. "Yours and Norie's."

"What about you?" Merrill asks, his voice rising. "You're going to stay here in this shithole? Get a job coaching football or something?"

I shrug. "I don't know yet."

I've been thinking about the future though. Last night, lying on Ebba's bed, I thought about it a lot.

The future, the very thing I've been trying to avoid.

It's easier to pretend the future doesn't exist, that there's only this moment. But that's a lie. I have years and years ahead of me, and I don't want them going to waste. I *can't* let them go to waste. My sister doesn't have a future anymore, and I owe it to her to make the most of my own.

Merrill looks horrified. It's as if his whole world is crashing down. I should know—that feeling has become pretty freaking familiar.

"I don't regret my wish," I tell Merrill. "But it made a mess. I need to stay until it's cleaned up."

"That's what they *want* you to think. Don't you get it, Eldon?" Merrill says, his face getting red. "You're going to be one more casualty of wishing. This is your chance to get out, and the town is sucking you back in, and it's going to destroy you, because that's what this place *does*."

"Hey, Merrill?" I say, smiling.

"Yeah?"

"What are you going to rant about when you're out of Madison?"

Merrill deflates. He smiles too. "Don't worry. I'll find something."
He glances at Norie. "Maybe I'll start a crusade against religion."

Norie rolls her eyes.

In this moment, I want to change my mind. I can't bear the thought of them driving away from me. I want to hop in the car, even though I haven't packed, haven't said goodbye to my parents, haven't made peace with Madison.

But I'm done running.

I've always thought Madison's the kind of place that traps you. The thing is, most people, well, they *want* to be trapped. Merrill's wrong. I'm not letting the town suck me back in. I'm going to leave someday, but I'll do it on my own terms. Not because I'm afraid or trying to avoid consequences. The old Eldon ran away when situations got tough. I'm sick of being a coward.

"I want to fix what I broke," I tell Merrill. "Help rebuild the town or whatever."

"How?" he asks, looking incredulous.

"I'm not sure."

I bet Penelope has a few ideas though.

Last night, I thought about the coming days. I can finish writing my wish history maybe. Work through some of my recent struggles with Mr. Wakefield. I can look for a new job. Save money. Figure out what I want long-term. I looked up community college classes, and there are a few I can take online. It's not Harvard, but it's an option. Suddenly, life seems full of options.

"I need to be here for my parents," I tell Merrill. They already lost one kid this week. Can I really ditch them now? "I need to be here for Ebba's funeral."

Not to mention I need to be here for the days that will follow, which will probably be even harder for my family. We need to grieve for Ebba together.

Merrill nods. He doesn't like it, but he understands.

"You won't reconsider, will you?" Norie asks.

"No." And as difficult as it is, I say it like I mean it.

Norie hugs me tightly. "Good luck then. Come find us when you're ready."

She climbs into the passenger seat, leaving me and Merrill to say our goodbyes alone.

"I don't know what to say." Merrill sighs.

I don't either. I've lived next door to Merrill my entire life. I see him nearly every day. I don't know who I am without him by my side. It never occurred to me that one day we'd have to say goodbye to each other. It's not as hard as saying goodbye to Ebba, but, well, it's up there.

"Thank you for everything," I say finally.

"Dude, nothing to thank me for. You're my best friend."

"Always," I agree.

Merrill pushes up his glasses and rubs at his eyes.

"Dust," he explains when he sees me looking at him.

"Yeah, sure," I say.

"I'm very sensitive to allergens, you know."

I laugh, but the truth is, I'm tearing up too.

"You need to get going," I say.

Merrill nods. "Take care of yourself, Eldo."

"You too."

He climbs into his car, starts the engine, prepares to drive away.

"Hey, Merrill," I shout. When he rolls the window down, I tell him, "Go get the sky."

Merrill grins. "You bet I will."

I watch the Mustang drive away from the gas station, the same way I've watched countless cars disappear down Madison's main street. When the Mustang is a dot on the horizon, I start walking.

The streets are still empty, but they won't be for long. People will come out of their houses, ready to face the day. Ready to face a wishless world. And I'll be there to figure it out with them.

For now anyway.

There's a whole world out there waiting for me. In time, I'll leave Madison and find out exactly what it has to offer. I'll meet up with Merrill and Norie. Or I'll get ahold of Abby, take her up on her offer. *If you ever want to get out of Strangeville…* I'm sure Madison isn't the end of the road for me. And when the time comes to say goodbye, I'll do it the right way. I won't sneak off at dawn, leaving my parents with a hastily scrawled farewell.

"Wilkes, you motherfucker," says a voice behind me.

I turn around.

Archie Kildare stands in the middle of the street. He looks like he slept in a gutter. I can smell the alcohol on him. Where did he come from? He seems ready to challenge me to a Wild West–style duel.

"Morning, Archie," I say.

He advances.

"I fucking told you what would happen," Archie says.

I sigh and accept my fate. This meeting was inevitable.

"All right, Archie," I say. "Let's get this over with."

Archie grins. "Good boy."

He closes the distance between us. Two seconds later, his fist slams into my face. I stagger backward, catch myself, wipe my mouth. My hand comes away bloody. Before I can recover, Archie sucker punches me in the gut, and I double over, gasping for breath.

This isn't exactly how I hoped to spend my morning. No one loves getting their ass kicked, yeah? But a lot worse can happen in life.

And let's face it, I probably deserve this.

"What are you doing?" Archie rages. "Fight back!"

I won't though.

I'm done using my fists to solve my problems. It never solved anything anyway.

Archie hits me in the face again, hard enough to make me dizzy. I sink down to my knees, lean forward, and brace myself against the pavement, trying to make the world stop spinning.

"Fight me, Wilkes!" Archie screams.

He kicks me.

I groan, struggle to breathe, spit blood.

Archie takes a step back. He's panting too, and even through the haze, I can read confusion all over his face. "What's your *problem?*"

"I'm not gonna fight you," I choke out.

Archie scowls and crosses his arms over his chest. "I could kill you, you know."

"It wouldn't change what happened," I say.

"Yeah, well…" Archie frowns, trying to puzzle through this turn of events.

I wait and attempt to keep my expression neutral, keep him from seeing how much pain I'm in.

"You're a pussy," he says finally.

And then something truly magical happens: he turns and starts to walk away.

"Does this mean we're cool then?" I call after him.

"Don't push your luck, Wilkes," he replies, shooting me one last glance over his shoulder.

I watch him, make sure he's really leaving. Then I roll over onto my back beside the road. The ground is already heating up, but the pain in my face is so bad I hardly notice. I stare at the sky for a while. It's another cloudless day, bright and sunny and beautiful.

I'm sure someone will come by soon. See me lying here and help me to my feet, drive me home. Barnabas on his bike or

Gil in his truck or Othello in whatever he drives. A spaceship, probably.

But no one comes.

Maybe that's for the best. Maybe it's time to help myself instead of waiting for someone else to do it.

Slowly, carefully, I get to my feet. My body screams in pain. I'm still light-headed. I run my tongue over my teeth to see if anything's been knocked loose.

My mouth seems intact. My nose is probably broken, but it's not the first time. I'll be sore for a few days, but I won't be in a body cast or anything. All in all, Archie could've done a lot worse.

I begin to stagger down Main Street, heading in the direction of my house. I pass Madison's dusty, worn-down buildings, the landmarks I've grown up with. Today, they don't make me feel trapped or suffocated.

For the first time in Madison's history, this place is exactly what it always pretended to be: ordinary. A nowhere, nothing town in the middle of the Mojave Desert.

That's cool with me though.

Being extraordinary is kind of overrated.

ACKNOWLEDGMENTS

If I could make a wish (that was guaranteed to come true), I'd wish all the best things for the people who were with me on this book-writing journey. In lieu of a magical wish, I hope everyone accepts my deep gratitude.

Thank you to my agent, Suzie Townsend. Her knowledge, passion, and overall awesomeness have helped me through every stage of the writing process—and often kept me from falling down the anxiety spiral. I'm so grateful to everyone at New Leaf Literary and the hard work they've done.

My wonderful editor, Annette Pollert-Morgan, helped me turn this into the book I hoped it would be. Her spot-on advice took the story and characters farther than I could have on my own. She also tirelessly points out my crutch words. (*How many will make it into this section?* I wonder.) The entire Sourcebooks team has overwhelmed me with their dedication and enthusiasm, and I'm thankful to have them by my side.

My earliest readers: Jo Farrow, Anna Priemaza, Katelyn Larson, and Josh Hlibichuk. They cheered on this book from the start and pointed out flaws in the nicest possible ways.

Thank you to Steve Conger, who helped me develop Norie's religious beliefs, and Tasha and Ben Christensen, who gave input that rounded those beliefs out. Thank you to Jess Flint who always motivates me on days when writing feels impossible.

The r/YAwriters crew: Greg, Katie, Kristine, Leann, Morgan, Phil, Rachel, plus the others already mentioned. Whether we're together in person or chatting from opposite sides of the country (or the *world*), they're the best writer family I could've asked for.

My local critique group, especially: Chris, Elizabeth, Gordon, Greg, Mandy, Paul, Rachel, Raz, Tonya, and Zeenat. My appreciation for them is as eternal as our Everlife Balloons.

My online critique group: Jilly Gagnon, Bridget Morrissey, and Lana Popović. I'm so grateful for their insights and awed at being among such talented writers.

Thank you to my mom for supporting my writing since I was a little kid, Uncle Dan for the UFO story, and Darrell "Shu" Davies, who once asked a "what if" question that sparked the idea for this book. Inspiration really can come from anywhere.

My wonderful husband, Steve Phillips, deserves a lifetime of thanks. He provides me with an endless amount of love and encouragement and makes amazing pizza that gets me through the bad writing days. (He also answered a lot of questions about football.)

And thank you to all the strange and wonderful desert towns that inspired the setting of this book. The Mojave might not have wishing, but believe me, there's still magic here.

ABOUT THE AUTHOR

Chelsea Sedoti fell in love with writing at a young age after discovering that making up stories was more fun than doing her schoolwork. (Her teachers didn't always appreciate this.) In an effort to avoid getting a "real" job, Chelsea explored careers as a balloon twister, filmmaker, and paranormal investigator. Eventually she realized that her true passion is writing about flawed teenagers who are also afraid of growing up, like in her debut, *The Hundred Lies of Lizzie Lovett*. When she's not at the computer, Chelsea spends her time exploring abandoned buildings, eating junk food at roadside diners, and trying to befriend every animal in the world. She lives in Las Vegas, Nevada, where she avoids casinos but loves roaming the Mojave Desert. Visit her at chelseasedoti.com.